INTO THE HILLS

An Inner Adventure Novel on the
Buddha's Noble Eightfold Path

Stephanie Noble

Both/And Books

For my children, grandchildren,
nieces, and nephews,
with love and gratitude for
the kindness and creativity
they share in the world.

Other books by Stephanie Noble

Tapping the Wisdom Within, A Guide to Joyous Living

Asking In, Six Empowering Questions Only You Can Answer

Invitation to Insight, Meditative Poems

Introduction

Dear Readers,
This novel arrived fully formed in a dream I had one night in May 2025. Yet, in its content, it was decades in the making, since the subject matter is what I have been exploring and then teaching: the ancient, honored wisdom of the Buddha.

A novel that teaches is unusual, but because we are a story-telling species, the knowledge can stay with us in ways it wouldn't if it were presented in a textbook. We remember characters, conversations, and stories, which, by their very nature, engage us.

My meditation students had asked me to turn my many Dharma talks on the Buddha's Noble Eightfold Path into a book, but I wasn't inspired to do so. Then I went on a meditation nature retreat, where my thoughts settled and the creative impulse spawned a solution.

On the third day of the retreat, it came to me: Aha! A workbook! Yes, that was the answer. The user reads, ponders, and writes down their thoughts, sparking their own inner wisdom, each day the workbook would become an increasingly personal guide.

But within days after returning home, it was clear my muse wasn't done. Yes, to a workbook, but only as a companion to a novel. A novel? I wasn't a stranger to the form. But one about the Eightfold Path?

In conversation with Jack Kornfield, I remember him telling me that when we share the Buddha's teachings, the Dharma has its way with us. And that's exactly how it was with this book. The storyline was clear to me from start to finish. All I had to do was get to the keyboard and let my fingers fly. It was like putting together a jigsaw puzzle where the outline and overall picture was clear, but it took many middles of the night awakenings to put all the pieces together. I had to quit teaching for a while because I couldn't guarantee that I would be sufficiently awake to teach after a middle-of-the-night writing session.

Using memorable characters who share their stories, helpful metaphors, and mnemonic devices, this book embraces the Buddha's essential teachings in an engaging guide for living in the world with Wise Intention, Wise Effort, Wise View, Wise Mindfulness, Wise Concentration, Wise Speech, Wise Action, and Wise Livelihood -- his prescription for the end of suffering.

There will be those who find this approach to sharing the Dharma unorthodox and even unacceptable. But many more who might not have understood the value of the Eightfold Path or had never heard of it, may find inspiration to explore more deeply in their own practice, which is exactly what the Buddha intended in all his teachings.

As you read a story filled with people you may come to care about, you'll see how these eight aspects work together, how they make a difference in the lives of the novel's characters, and potentially in your own. **Download the Workbook** pdf using the link on page 350 to document your practice and inner explorations of these most vital teachings.

— Stephanie Noble, 2026

PART ONE

Storm Brewing

1 When Lust Loses Its Luster

Okay, okay. Eva could no longer deny the cracks in Chad's polished persona. She'd discounted every clue and ignored every warning for all these weeks. But on Wednesday afternoon, when she stopped by to surprise him with a piece of Chelsea's leftover birthday cake, the cracks widened into post-earthquake fissures, verging on a sinkhole.

Why am I bringing him this piece of cake in the middle of the week? They had established Saturday nights as their thing. But she hadn't really thought it was a hard and fast rule. And how could they have so many rules so early in their relationship?

Was it a relationship? Wasn't it just a series of one-night stands? And did she really want to make it more than that? Did she even, at this point, want even that?

This impromptu drive-by delivery clearly had nothing to do with the cake. Yes, it was delicious, and Chelsea, fellow elementary school teacher and housemate, had been properly surprised in the teachers' lounge. Eva took the leftovers home, where she and her oldest friend and newest roommate Heather, watched as the birthday girl unwrapped a dark blue galaxy bedspread.

"Wow!" exclaimed Chelsea. "Thank you, both! It's just beautiful. And looking at it reminds me how much I need to go lie down. I'm exhausted and I still have work to do. The planetarium trip is fast approaching. Anyway, I feel sufficiently celebrated for a weekday! Thanks again."

"Will you be going to your folks on the weekend?" Eva asked. "I imagine you'll be celebrated there as well. You are very loved."

Chelsea nodded and sighed. "Yes, I do feel blessed. It's just hard to feel too celebratory when Daddy's so ill and we don't know, from day to day…Anyway, this gorgeous bedspread will keep me warm and give me sweet dreams, I just know it. Thanks so much again. Love you both. Goodnight!"

Heather and Eva threw her kisses. Then Heather got up from the table and stretched her willowy body. "I've got office work to catch up on back at the studio. I really had no clue that opening a business would be this much desk work. Ugh!"

"I thought you had hired someone to do all that."

"I told you that didn't work out. It's easier just to do it myself, so I know where stuff is. I have to go in to teach my evening yoga class, anyway."

"What about the cake?" Eva had asked.

"I'd say we're done, but it's not up to me."

"Chelsea?" Eva called out.

Chelsea peeked out of the bathroom door, her hair piled on top of her head, and her chocolate skin shiny with cleanser. "Huh?"

"What do you want me to do with the cake?"

"Delicious but done!" Chelsea said. "Thanks so much again!" Then she closed her door.

"Compost bin it is," Heather said, "Well, I'm off."

As Eva sat alone in front of the remains of the cake, Trusty looked up at her hopefully, but Eva told him, "Sorry, T, cake is not for dogs." She gave him a suitable dog treat, and he had to make do with that. He settled his large brindle-coated handsome self down on his haunches, chomped twice, and then looked up at her with his amber eyes, waiting to see if she would change her mind about the cake.

No way. But it did seem a shame to waste it. And that's when she thought, *why not bring it to Chad? Didn't he deserve a little treat? And wouldn't he be surprised?* So she sliced an attractive piece, wrapped it in wax paper, and put it in a small canvas shopping bag.

She drove over to his house deep into the outsized housing development with its radiating dead ends -- oh, excuse me, cul-de-sacs -- reaching up into the open space where she roamed when she and Heather were young intrepid adventurers.

She had decided to forego texting him to let him know she was coming, which would ruin the surprise. But Eva was the one who was surprised. The cul-de-sac was filled with cars, and Chad's house was the only one with lights on.

Was he having a party? Did he even have friends in town? None that she'd met.

She didn't recognize any of the cars. She didn't hear any music coming from the house. She tried to imagine him involved in any group activities. Maybe a poker night? Or maybe this was business. She still knew so little about him, since he deflected all her inquiries into his interests, saying, "I'm not much for chitchat."

She pulled over and parked her beloved, older electric car, a Nissan Leaf, which she had named Zippy for its ability to zoom up the hills surrounding their valley town. Heather, Chelsea and she lived in the flats in a tree-lined older neighborhood close to downtown, where they could walk everywhere. The newer constructions, called 'Italianate villas' were to her an abomination, and before meeting Chad, she had avoided coming up this way. Which meant she had been cut off from the hills behind the development, where she had always loved to roam.

The past weeks she'd been here every weekend, lounging around in a house far too large for the single man who bought it. Were gatherings like this the reason he felt he needed such a big place? How would she know? She would just pack her overnight bag on Saturday afternoon and stay through Sunday morning.

Heather watched her packing one time, and asked, "What do you really know about this guy? What do you two even talk about?"

Talk? Hah! Chad constantly thwarted Eva's efforts to engage in conversation.

He'd say, "It's hard to plant a kiss when your mouth's a moving target."

But she couldn't tell Heather that, could she? So, instead, she'd made up things. She'd lied to her best friend! And they had always told each other everything. Everything! But she had to lie. She couldn't tell the truth. Because the truth was, she knew absolutely nothing about him, except the texture of his skin, the smooth shoulders, the stubbled chin, the…oh stop!!!

Whatever was going on in Chad's house now, she didn't want to intrude, and she should just turn around and go home. Yes, that's precisely what she would do.

But it seemed a shame to waste the cake, and what would be the harm in dropping off a piece of cake? She was just being thoughtful, wasn't she? What's the worst thing that could happen? That he'd tell her thanks, but he was busy right now?

As she grabbed the bag, she saw that it had been squished by the weight of the water bottle in her day pack as she drove up the hill. Now it was a pathetic offering and an even more obvious ruse. She should just go home.

Trusty huddled in the back seat. Eva knew he didn't like Chad, and despite her best efforts, she had to admit that for Chad, the feeling was mutual.

But Eva was so curious to know who all these people were. Friends from out of town? From wherever he used to live? She hoped that was true. She wanted that for him. And wouldn't it be an opportunity to introduce his new girlfriend to them? How could she pass up this clue into his life? But if he had wanted to introduce her, he would have invited her over.

And with no cake to offer, she had no excuse to knock on his door.

She was about to start the car, but then she thought of the trail that wound behind the house. His property had a high stone wall, but the trail would place her higher up. It was turning dark enough that she probably could see what was going on through the sliding glass doors that opened to his lavish swimming pool area. Before she could talk herself out of it, she grabbed Trusty's leash and whispered, "C'mon, boy." Trusty knew the leash meant a walk, so he hopped out.

Over the past weeks, she and Trusty had walked this trail many times. But if it were dark out, she'd always turn on her phone's flashlight. She didn't want to do that now. So she really had to lift her feet and carefully watch her step. When they got behind the house, she paused as if to let Trusty do his business. She pulled a poop bag out of her daypack and had it ready, just in case.

Meanwhile, she peered over the wall into the living room. But what she saw she couldn't understand. It was a bunch of men. But it wasn't a party. Or a poker game. It seemed more like some kind of business meeting around his dining room table. Others sat on the L-shaped couch. Everyone had laptops and earphones. Was it a phone bank? What was going on?

She looked for clues as to what kind of business it might be. In their time together, if it weren't for the frequent annoying dinging of his phone, that always took priority over whatever they were doing, she would assume he didn't have a job, that he was a trust fund baby, or that some start-up he'd been part of had gone public and he'd struck it rich. Of course, displays of wealth sometimes just meant good credit scores to purchase fancy houses and cars. For all she knew, he could have been completely out of money or even heavily in debt.

Whatever his financial state, he wasn't telling. And maybe he felt it wasn't any of her business. Work is essential to life and shapes our identity. He probably knew more than he wanted to know about what she did for a living, as she filled in the gaps in their silences with news of her week at school, funny little anecdotes about students, or frustrations about the administration or parents. She was trying to prime the pump of a real conversation, so he'd feel he didn't need to hold back if he had some work issues he wanted to talk through. It seemed so lopsided and only fair for her to know something about his work. And if he wasn't going to tell her, she could maybe convince herself that she was perfectly justified to peek. Over a wall. In the dark. Hmm.

She tried to override how uncomfortable that made her feel. She wasn't a spy. But now that she was seeing this…whatever it was, she couldn't unsee it. It might have a perfectly reasonable explanation, but something felt very off.

Or at least off-putting. Were they selling something? She hated sales calls. She didn't know anyone who liked them. Were they selling or scamming? She had a sinking dread that Chad might be involved in something illegal.

Now she could see him standing in front of a whiteboard and talking to the group. What was on that whiteboard? She couldn't quite read it, though the writing looked big. Well, if she was going to spy, she might as well use her phone's camera to get a close-up of the only clue available. So she quickly held it up, adjusted the distance, and snapped the photo. Then she stuck it back in her bag, checking to see if Trusty had done anything. He hadn't. Suddenly, she wanted to get out of here. It felt dangerous. All those men. Who were they?

Something about this whole thing gave her the creeps. So she and Trusty headed back down the trail toward her car.

In the cul-de-sac, she thought the license plates on all these cars would give her a clue as to who those men were. She got close enough to see that the plate holders were from dealerships within fifty miles of town, so they could be local. Or not.

Then she noticed a few bumper stickers: "Dean Delivers!" and "Dean Defends!" with a gun image. "Dean Deports!"

Her heart sank. This was bad. Really bad. Gregory Allen Dean was an odious man who stirred up hatred wherever he went, scapegoating any minority group he could, while making sure that his wealthy cronies knew that they would be rewarded for their unwavering support. She didn't know him personally, but she'd gone to school with his son,

Rusty, who was a real piece of work, picking on anyone weaker. Like her. She bristled at the memory.

What did Chad have to do with this? On their weekends together, they didn't talk about politics. She tried to start conversations by sharing her experiences and views, hoping he would reciprocate. But, so far, he'd found that being a 'wordless wonder' was working wonders on her. And he hadn't been wrong. Just the touch of his smooth skin on perfectly formed shoulders, and the scent of sandalwood made her swoon like a heroine from a gothic romance.

Stop it! she told herself. There was no time for this. Shaken and wanting to get out of there fast, she opened the back door of her car, and Trusty jumped in. She was glad to have her quiet electric car, so she could exit the cul-de-sac without drawing any attention.

Rattled and still trying to make sense of what she'd seen, as she drove home, she continued to ponder the meaning of her discovery. She was so distracted that she almost hit a pedestrian at a crosswalk.

"I'm so sorry!" she called out.

"Turn on your damn lights!" he yelled.

"Oh my God, I'm so, so sorry." She turned on the headlights, ashamed of herself.

She took a breath and focused on her driving.

When she got home, she was relieved that Heather was at the yoga studio and Chelsea was holed up in her room. She could barely hear her voice talking on the phone, probably with one of her sisters.

So Eva fed Trusty, tidied up the kitchen, and headed for her own cozy bedroom, still struggling to make sense of what she had seen at Chad's. She changed into her sweatpants and baggy T-shirt and climbed under the cozy quilt her mother had made for her one Christmas. She tried to imagine all her mother's warmth in that quilt from the many hours her hands had worked on it. *Oh, mommy, I miss you so,* she sighed.

But thinking about her mother made things worse. She took another breath -- Heather's answer to everything! But it did help -- and tried to cleanse her mind of anything but being here in this home with her two dear friends.

She remembered how, almost a year ago, she and Chelsea, both happily single, had been delighted to find a place to rent that was close enough to the school for them to walk or ride their bikes if they wanted. They had each been dealing with long commutes that drained them, wasted time and money, and polluted the atmosphere.

They had bonded over their deep concern for environmental issues. Together, they initiated a program at school to provide students with an experiential understanding of the interconnectedness of all life. Microcosms and macrocosms. Even quantum entanglement! Chelsea knew more about it than she did, but Eva was enthusiastic. They applied for a grant to improve the science equipment and other supplies, and the students loved the program. The principal was pleased and gave the go-ahead for the following year.

But, when Eva's mother became so ill, she had to reduce her time on the project. She felt bad about leaving Chelsea to handle it alone, but she understood the situation. Then, when the first-grade teacher went on maternity leave, Eva accepted the offer to fill in. A substitute took over for the fifth grade. He was a good teacher, but more focused on history than science, and not ready to take on extracurricular activities. Again, Chelsea understood and picked up the slack. But when the first-grade teacher said she wasn't coming back and Eva's position became permanent, Chelsea couldn't help but express her disappointment.

"You're in a temporary situation with your mom, Eva. Why are you applying a permanent solution that I don't think will make you happy, and it undermines everything we've worked on together? This program is our baby! I can't do it all alone."

Eva had apologized profusely, but it felt like the only thing she could do. And, as it turned out, Chelsea had been wrong about it being a temporary situation. Eva's mother was dead. That was Eva's very permanent and very painful situation.

So she was grateful that the teacher who quit had left her with a tried-and-true lesson plan and was happy to offer support. It was a turnkey operation that made life much easier.

She'd imagined it would be boring, but she hadn't quite realized what a great gift it was to see the remarkable transition from children looking at words as just lines in funny shapes on a page, to them discovering the stories and information within the pages of books. It was magical!

And, admittedly, these little people were a balm rather than a challenge. Rightly or wrongly, they held their teacher in high regard. And, as she explained to Chelsea, it was what she needed now. Chelsea hugged her. All was forgiven.

Which was a huge relief, as it wouldn't do to have discord in their relationship as friends, coworkers, and housemates. She remembered how, when they found this house, they figured the rent was just barely manageable. But they hadn't counted how much more it costs to heat an older home with winter drafts in a valley that often had frost at night. The windows were single-pane, and if there was any insulation, it was insufficient. When they rented it they were only thinking about the perfect location and the great backyard with a little potting shed and greenhouse where they could grow vegetables year-round. Theoretically. The third bedroom sparked their imagination, too. It would be a dedicated project room for making science displays and anything else they wanted. But as they struggled to pay the bills, that room quickly began to seem like a luxury they couldn't afford.

So when Heather arrived in tears, collapsing in Eva's arms, explaining between painful gulps that her marriage was over and she had no place to go, it only took one glance between Chelsea and Eva to recognize the solution to their financial challenge. Chelsea didn't know Heather that well, but she liked her, and trusted Eva's judgment about her best friend since childhood.

The rental arrangement had worked out well. The three of them shared values, expenses, and chores. And, most importantly, they truly enjoyed each other's company.

Not that they saw that much of each other. Heather's new venture kept her quite busy. And on weekends, Chelsea usually spent Saturday nights at her family home so she could attend her beloved Black Baptist church the following day and enjoy her mother's gumbo, red beans and rice, potato salad, and other dishes that she was embarrassed to admit she couldn't create herself but had no problem enjoying.

Her mother made sure Chelsea returned home on Sunday evenings with something for her housemates. Eva especially loved the lemon meringue pie, made from fresh lemons from their garden. And more recently, sweet potato pie. It was so different from pumpkin, which, in her estimation, was only good one day a year.

Ugh. She dreaded thinking about Thanksgiving coming up. It would be her first without her mother. Being only the two of them, they always treated themselves to a fancy restaurant meal. But now what? Whatever she did, it wouldn't be a tradition. And Thanksgiving was all about tradition.

She'd think about that later. For now, she was determined to think only of happy thoughts, as she resettled her pillow, and hoped soon she'd be asleep. One happy thought was the memory of Chelsea's mother inviting Heather and her to visit that felt more like a command to inspect Chelsea's roommates. They were glad they went. Eva loved seeing Chelsea with her family, and she could picture her on Sunday mornings, singing in the choir.

More invitations followed, but they hadn't found the time to visit again. Heather's studio was at its busiest on the weekends. And recently Eva had been with Chad. And, of course, now that Chelsea's father was ill…Whenever she asked Chelsea how he was doing, she'd say, "Oh, he's bad. Really bad. And I'm trying to help as much as I can, but there's only so much I can do from here.

"I feel guilty about being so far away. My sisters are taking the brunt of it, stopping by after work every evening, and dividing up chores so Momma can just sit with him. He's stubborn, and he refuses to go to the hospital, saying *that's where people go to die.*

"On weekends, when people are off from work, the living room is filled with relatives, friends, and neighbors who bring food. We have more food than we can fit in the fridge, and we make sure it gets repackaged and distributed, especially to the younger cousins living on their own. Otherwise, it just goes to waste. And though they're coming to console or lend support, it's a bit much, you know?"

Eva couldn't imagine. Her recent experience of caring for her mother had been so very different. As always, it had been just the two of them. And a whole lot of nurses. In the last few days of her mother's hospice, Aunt Evelyn had come across the country, but that was it.

Happy thoughts. Happy thoughts.

Okay, well, those nurses at the hospital. Thank goodness for them. One, a stocky Irish woman in her fifties, really went the extra mile to help Eva cope. It clearly was much more than just a job for her.

She wished that the nurse was here right now to comfort her.

Before she could stop herself, Eva's thoughts drifted down the rabbit hole of self-pity, wondering why life was always about losing the ones we love? As an only child and now an orphan, Eva had envied Chelsea's close ties with her large family. She envied how they all came together and looked out for each other. She knew they had disagreements and lots of opinions about each other's choices, but underneath it all, there was an unbreakable bond of love.

Her mother's words reminded her: *Envy is an ugly thing. Count your blessings.*

But it's not envy. All she was thinking was that even all that love didn't protect Chelsea from the pain of losing her loved ones, too. *Death, death, death. It sucked!* She hated it! It was unfair. Especially since her mother had been so young.

Happy thoughts. Happy thoughts. Okay, how about this home the three of them had filled with things that had meaning: Heather's favorite painting from her artsy period, Chelsea's seashell collection from the family's beach vacations, and Eva's grandmother's blue and white porcelain plates that had, until just recently, been her mother's pride and joy. Their mix-and-match assortment of furniture from garage sales was clean and comfortable. They'd found enough posters and student art that delighted them to fill the walls. How much fun they'd had outfitting their home!

Ah, that was better. But that sweet memory only reminded her of how, when she asked about pieces of art in Chad's house, he said offhandedly that he didn't know anything about them. She couldn't understand how that was possible. But Elliot, her old friend and Chad's realtor, told her that he had just purchased all the staged furnishings. There was nothing personal about him there. It was all for show.

Elliot! Chad was all Elliot's fault. That wasn't fair, but really! If only he hadn't invited Chad to that party…

The annual *So Long to Summer* pool party at Elliot's house just hadn't been the same this year. Heather was leading a yoga daylong, and Chelsea was at her parents'. So Eva was on her own, or as on her own as one could be with a bunch of people she'd known forever. But she wasn't much up for a party, tradition or no. It felt too soon after her mother's funeral, and most of them understood that and gave her sad looks and hugs, before returning to tossing salads or flipping burgers on the barbecue.

She had thought she was ready for this when she got dressed for the party. It was her chance to say goodbye to her season of sorrow with Mom's slow, painful hospice. She sat by her mother's hospital bed in the care unit for hours on end, until her mother would send her home to bed.

After her mother was gone, Eva thought she'd have time to take care of herself. But there was too much to do to take time to grieve. The funeral arrangements, the death certificates, the notifications to Social Security, the banks, and so on. It just went on and on. She was glad, at least, that it had happened in the summer, so she wasn't trying to juggle teaching as well as all these sad and challenging chores. And the grieving. She kept putting that part on the back burner. Way back.

She just couldn't imagine life without her mother. For so long, it had just been the two of them. When she was growing up, they shared a bedroom, as if they were sisters in their matching twin beds. Her friends thought that was weird, but it worked for them. And if she had friends over for the night, they'd sleep on the foldout couch in the living room, where they could watch TV and raid the fridge without disturbing her mom. It was fine! Really!

Well, it was fine for her. Now she realized how much of her own life her mother had put on hold just to be there for Eva 100%. And then, just when other women her age were looking forward to retirement and finding some fun in life, she got ovarian cancer that was too far gone to treat. It all happened so fast and felt so unfair.

Ever since that diagnosis, Eva's life had been a nightmare that continued, even after losing her mother. At her annual pap smear, the doctor "strongly advised" that she get tested because of her mother's ovarian cancer. Eva agreed in a panic, and when she tested BRCA positive, a hysterectomy felt like the only choice she could make. It all happened in a blur of grief and worry. And now she was scheduled for surgery in late December so she could recover over the holidays.

Oh, joy.

So, who could blame her if, at that pool party, having had a margarita or two, she felt like she just wanted some pleasant distraction while she could enjoy it. She wanted to seize the day! Go for the gusto!

She wanted to experience a lust for life! Right now! Who knows what would happen to her body, her hormones, her sense of herself as a woman once she had the operation. Her mother's life had been erased, and now an essential part of hers would be as well.

What she had wanted was a wonderful wild fling. And what better place to begin than a pool party? But as she looked around, she realized that the annual pool party, where they used to dance and go a little wild, had morphed into a family fun time. So many of her friends had married and had children, and here they were bouncing, screaming, and swimming.

This was no place for a fling. Ah well, she probably wasn't up for it, anyway. She wasn't a fling kind of woman.

So she sat in her lounge chair and made small talk with anyone who passed by. She was sitting next to Elliot's latest girlfriend. She was blanking on her name, but it didn't matter because she had her eyes closed. On the other chair was a pile of towels, kids' discarded clothing, and a diaper bag. So she was on her own.

She watched everyone in the pool bouncing around, tossing a ball, laughing, and chasing each other. She nodded to the music, Green Day's 'Boulevard of Broken Dreams.' The afternoon heat and her drink made her lightheaded. She set the glass down. She realized she wasn't ready for this. Probably she should leave.

But just then, she noticed an unknown man rising from the pool like Adonis, the water dripping and glistening on his tanned skin. If Heather had been there, they would joke about how he looked like some ridiculous commercial shot at Slow-Mo to capture every water droplet flinging from his wet, dark curls as he shook his head.

They would have had a good laugh. But Heather wasn't here, so Eva just watched him from under her wide-brimmed hat, glad for her sunglasses to hide her gaze. He pulled on a loose shirt, leaving the front open. Then he straddled a lounge chair and sat down, raised his face to the sun, and closed his eyes.

Who was he? Why had she never seen him before? She knew everyone else at this party, or at least who they were with. But which of her friends had brought him?

In the next ten minutes, no one approached him. He was like an island to himself. He was just sitting there, sipping his drink, watching the activity in the pool without any expression.

But then Matthew arrived at her side. "Girl, are you sinking into a stupor?"

He set down his drink, tossed the assorted towels off the chair, and plopped down beside her.

"Oh, it's so good to see you. Where's Gabe?"

"We're not joined at the hip, just married. Anyway, he is on a daylong acting retreat where each one plays a different emotion or something. Not that he needs help in that department—such a drama queen.

"And you're not!" she laughed. Matthew had been a friend since high school, when they were both intensely interested in boys, whom they checked out from afar. She had no gaydar and would start crushing on someone whom, she was mortified to discover, had no interest but was sometimes happy to play along, and then say, "Oh, wait until I tell my boyfriend! It'll make him so jealous." So Matthew took pity on her, and they developed a game where she'd ask, "Your team or my team?"

So now she said, "Hey, see that guy over there all by himself? Do you know him?"

"Never seen him before. Quite hunky, isn't he?"

"Your team or my team?"

Matthew studied him for a bit. "Definitely your team. You should go for it. You deserve a bit of fun after the summer you've had. Meanwhile, I'll keep an eye out for any girlfriend approaching and give you a whistle."

"Oh, I don't know. I couldn't…"

"If he were on my team, I would!"

"You wouldn't! You're a married man. Otherwise, what were those vows for?"

"No, I guess I wouldn't. But you know that the whole being faithful business is just to be sure the baby is the husband's, right? It doesn't really apply to us. But before you get all preachy, we're keeping it between us. We're more than just legal, we're in loooove." He wrapped his arms around himself, puckered his lips, and closed his eyes. "But, just to keep it fresh and fun, we agreed to tell each other who our current celebrity crush is. And we have full permission to gush and go on about it, knowing nothing's going to happen. And then of course we tease each other about it. It's innocent."

"So who's your current celebrity crush?"

"I'm not telling you!"

"Oh, come on!"

"Okay, how about this: I'll tell you my celebrity crush after you go over and say hello to that beautiful man."

Eva's curiosity finally got the better of her. And not just about Matthew's celebrity crush.

"Okay, but don't watch me! Look away."

So, even though she wasn't hungry, she got up and wandered over to the table full of appetizers and put a few olives and cheese slices on a small plate. And there just happened to be an empty chair next to him. "Is this seat taken?"

He shook his head and opened his big hand to invite her to sit. She moved the chair a bit so that her back was to the sun. It angled it away from the pool, and as she sat down, she realized she was now facing him. Oh well, it would be awkward to readjust, so she stayed put and busied herself with the food on her plate. But when she looked up, he was looking straight at her, a glint in his eye and a slight smile on his lips as if he was aware of her discomfort. "I'm Chad, by the way."

She introduced herself. "I've never seen you at these parties. Are you here with someone?" Of course, he could easily be with any of the other singles, male or female, but why weren't they claiming him? Had they fought? Were they stuck in the bathroom? Were they making a dessert dish in the kitchen that required so much time, leaving this amazing man alone? There had to be some explanation. He wouldn't have just crashed the party.

"No, Elliot's my realtor. I just bought a house in town. And he was nice enough to invite me over."

"Very neighborly. Well then, welcome to the neighborhood."

She wondered when Elliot started inviting his clients to their gang parties. Oh well, it was his house, obviously, he could invite whomever he wanted. Still…

"Thanks," Chad said.

"So what brings you to our little neck of the woods?" she said in a way that felt like a revoltingly folksy way to ask a simple question. Most guys she knew would leap at the chance to share their whole work story, but this Chad just shrugged. "Oh, you know…"

Well, no, she didn't know. Maybe he needed a little prompting. "I'm a teacher at the local elementary school. It's six blocks from here. So convenient! Do you have school-age children?"

"Nope. None that I know of."

Well, that answer was not as charming as he might think, but she'd cut him some slack. "No? I don't either. I just never got around to it, I guess. And now…Anyway, I've got my students. And with the human population at over eight billion, I figure I'm helping…"

She noticed he wasn't exactly entranced with her line of conversation.

His eyes were an interesting color, like the olive in a martini. And she could drink him all up! Oh my, she realized she must be tipsy! Maybe it was just as well they didn't talk. She didn't want to ramble as she was prone to do, seeing 'awkward silence' where other people just felt comfortable in quiet moments.

Maybe he picked up on her nervousness, because after a few minutes, he pulled out his phone and said, "Oh, man, sorry to say, I've got to go."

Yup, she'd blown it. She'd driven him away from the party. He was checking for escape routes. How had she become so bad at this?

But then he said, "Let me give you my number." He reached out, and she pulled her phone out of her bag, handing it to him, a total stranger.

Then he gave it back, lightly touching her hand, and said, "Call me."

As he walked away, she heard Matthew making a little triumphant *whoop!* Embarrassed, she shot him a dirty look. But then they grinned.

*   *   *

After the pool party, Eva thought about calling this Chad. Over the next few weeks, she thought about it a lot. Whenever she was feeling so down, she didn't know what to do; she'd think, I could contact Chad. She hadn't told her housemates about him. He was her secret. Maybe it was best just to have that little memory and the fantasy of seeing him again.

*   *   *

Weeks later Eva's phone dinged with a text from an unknown number. "Chad here."

Had Elliot honestly given her phone number? Or did Chad get it from her phone himself when he put his in. Either way, it bothered her.

And yet. The thought of seeing Chad again sent a thrill up her spine that she couldn't deny. And why should she?

But inside that little 'and yet' it was like a sticky web, and she had fallen in like a helpless fly. Oh my.

*   *   *

Their first outing was a meeting at her favorite coffee shop, then a stroll in the park. On a bench, he reached for her hand. His touch was like lightning, sending an electric jolt through her whole body. She let him walk her home. She pointed out the fading green of the foliage on the tree-lined street and how soon the leaves would turn colors. He looked up and nodded.

"Do you get much fall color where you're from?"

"Some."

Maybe sensing her discomfort with his clipped answer, he expanded. "I grew up further south, so less than here. A little town you would never have heard of."

Well, she would have loved to hear more, but they'd arrived at her house. She hoped maybe someday soon he'd tell her about his childhood. She looked forward to getting to know him.

She knew her housemates would kill her if she invited him in without warning, so she turned to him and thanked him for the coffee. He leaned down and kissed her. OMG, his sandalwood scent was enough to make her swoon.

She noticed Chelsea and Heather at the window. "Would you like to meet my housemates?"

He shrugged. She waved and gestured for them to come out and meet him. They were cordial enough, but she could see them trying to get a read on him.

When he walked back up the street, they all watched him. "Well, he's something," they agreed. Inside, they asked for details.

"Tell us everything," Chelsea said. "What exactly do you see in him, other than the obvious?"

"The obvious is enough for now," she answered, smiling. "I'm sure I'll find out more in time. Anyway, it's not like I'm interviewing for the perfect future life partner. Just a diversion! Why does everything have to be so serious? Girls just want to have fun."

They laughed, half-heartedly. They knew her better than that.

"No, really," she said. "I need this. Don't rain on my parade. Okay?"

They nodded but were clearly not convinced. A fling had never been Eva's thing. Not the Eva they knew.

But maybe she wasn't the Eva they knew at that moment. Not the one that dreamed of a meaningful relationship, a life partner, something her mother had never had but had clearly longed for.

Eva knew her friends didn't think this was who she was. But just for now she wanted to forget her pain, her mourning, and her worries about what surgery would bring. She was looking for a way to live all the wild lustiness of her being in the time she had left before her body changed forever. But even as close as they were, she just couldn't bring herself to tell them that.

*   *   *

After two more dates with Chad, both ending up in his luxurious upstairs bedroom, Heather and Chelsea stopped asking for details and started offering warnings. Then even Matthew began to text her:

— Girl, you're taking my pool party dare way too far.

Yes, it was true. She was too far gone. Like the whole world fell away, and she was consumed by a passion that blissfully, albeit temporarily, burned away all other thoughts and emotions.

But she discovered that the heat burned both ways. Chad was volatile. Moody. Voracious one minute, distracted the next. He expected her to read his mind, to know what she had done to turn him cold and gruff. What had she said? She kept second-guessing herself. She started keeping notes in the journal she carried in her daypack. She'd check back to verify past conversations. But what good were her notes? Was she going to show them to him? Say, "See there, on October 2nd at 2:35 you said…" No that was ridiculous. But the notes helped her keep her sanity. Though how sane could she be to keep returning to him? Subjecting herself to his gaslighting, his moods, his temper that simmered long and slow, then boiled up in a venomous harangue, twisting everything she said. None of this would she have guessed from their first innocent date.

Every weekend when he'd text her, summoning her to spend the night in that cavernous, outsized house, she willed herself to say no. But instead, would find herself like a zombie, tossing her overnight bag in the car, opening the back door for Trusty—who climbed in with reluctance, as if sense what was coming—and heading off across town.

Then Chad bought a Lamborghini. Something in Eva snapped at that. She looked the car up online and found that it was one of the most gas-guzzling vehicles he could have chosen! Ugh! He shared so little of himself, but this was a big clue. They were so ill-matched! What did this gorgeous man with money see in her? Especially since he had zero interest in what she thought, read, or hoped for. Did she have no self-respect? Apparently not. She was too busy trying to dodge the past and the future. She was sinking into an oblivion that she'd thought would feel better than this. She thought it would be blissful. Ha!

It was increasingly obvious that he thought she was lucky to be with him. He'd made it clear that he thought that teaching was a loser job, something you did if you couldn't "make it" in the world. When he said it, she laughed, like he was kidding. But when she saw he was serious, she pulled herself together and pronounced that teaching was the highest, most noble calling. "And the younger the grade, the greater the impact."

Silently, she thought, *whereas your work is obviously superficial, money-grubbing, and maybe even evil for all I know. What is it that you even do???*

She would never say that out loud. *But if I'm thinking that, why am I still with him? And what kind of relationship is this? I should stop it. Definitely.*

But then what? She still felt she needed to keep herself busy to forget. What could she do? How could she distract herself? A night class? Knitting? Tai chi? With all that was going on in her life, Heather still found time for the group she attended every Tuesday night and found it helpful. Maybe Eva could join her?

Yet the thought exhausted her. It made her want to pull the covers over her head and stay in bed forever. She rolled over on her side, hoping to sleep, but memories of the touch, smell, and taste of Chad seduced her thoughts. It reminded her of how tendrils, seductively attractive and seemingly harmless, can weave in and ultimately choke a plant. Whenever Chad texted, summoning her, she felt helpless not to succumb to his bidding, and off she went.

Worst of all was how she dragged her poor, reluctant dog along with her. She had been so sure that in time, Trusty would adjust, that he and Chad would get over their alpha male antagonism and be great friends.

When and how had she thought that would happen?

Their pattern was set: The minute she walked in Chad's front door, he whisked her up into the bedroom and shut the door against Trusty, who sat outside whimpering and occasionally barking when he heard anything concerning.

Her housemates' warnings went unheeded, and over the weeks, they seemed to accept that this was how it would be for now. They'd just have to wait it out. Surely, eventually, Eva would come to her senses. Hadn't she always been the sensible one, after all?

Not now, obviously. She was delusional! She could see that now. Her lust had been a way to avoid dealing with what she was feeling. Chad was just a handsome man who had turned her into a puddle of hormonal confusion. If she had wanted a real relationship, this would not be it!

And now, of course, Eva knew her friends had been right, and that they'd had her best interests at heart.

She felt like such a fool.

It takes one to know one, her mother's voice came to her now.

That reminded her of the time her mother had shared how foolish she'd felt when she had fallen for a phone scam. It had been in one of their 'true confessions' moments, when they promised each other to listen and forget, so they could wipe the slate clean.

"Oh, it was the craziest thing!" her mom told her. "But his voice was so, I don't know, authoritarian and urgent. And I just felt like I had my marching orders. I grabbed my purse, got in the car, and headed straight for the ATM, like an automaton. I put in my debit card and was about to push the buttons for the maximum amount, when I remembered how he had said I had to pay *in cash today* for some overdue fine I had never even heard of, but just assumed it must be correct. Sometimes I am forgetful, but could I have forgotten something like that? Don't they send plenty of notices through the mail even if I had? Who in the government ever calls and says, 'In cash today'. And then I wondered what would happen if I didn't pay? Did I think the county sheriff would show up at my door, even if there was an overdue fine? Which, of course, there wasn't. You know me. I pay my bills promptly. I never incur interest. There was no way…Anyway, fortunately, I came to my senses before following through.

"So that's my true confession. Absolution, please!"

But although Eva had granted her mother's request for absolution many times over the years, and her mother had granted just as many to Eva in turn, that time, for some reason, Eva couldn't say, "You're forgiven. Go forth and do well in the world." Or any of their fanciful variations of their cherished tradition.

No, that time Eva had been just so horrified, she said, "Oh my God, Mom, how could you have been so stupid?"

Now those words came back to her, making her feel ashamed. How could she have been so cruel to her mother, who was diagnosed soon after and died within six months?

With all the sweet memories they shared, even in those last months -- the tender whispered moments at her mother's bedside -- it was *those* horrible words that haunted her: "How could you have been so stupid?"

How could Eva have been so cruel? And anyway, who was the 'stupid' one now? After all, her mom had stopped before handing over the money. And it was only money. While Eva had spent the past many weekends handing over her life to a man she didn't respect, let alone love.

Now she tossed the covers off her, feeling overheated.

What would her mother have said about Chad? Oh, Eva could just picture it. She would have turned very icy in the nicest possible way. She would have been ultra-polite and even complimentary. She would have told her daughter he seemed like a very nice man. She would praise him to the skies until Eva rose to the bait and set the record straight.

She had done that once with someone Eva dated when she was twenty. She had such complimentary things to say about him that Eva finally broke down and said, "Well, he's not *that* nice, believe me." And then she elaborated with unsavory details that her mother took in, nodding knowingly. Now she wondered if she chose Chad because her mother wasn't around anymore to judge her choices.

Eva began to weep. "I'm so sorry, Mommy. So very sorry," she cried. Trusty hopped up on the bed and licked her tears, then nestled in to comfort her. And she fell asleep.

2 Intrigue

The weekend was coming up quickly, and she hadn't had a moment to think about what she'd seen through Chad's back window on Wednesday evening. Well, she didn't want to think about it. Because it led to all kinds of horrible speculation and dread, but she was going to have to do something.

But what? Go ahead with their standing Saturday night arrangement? Pretend she hadn't seen all those men in his living room collaborating in some way? The bumper stickers for that odious man, Gregory Allen Dean.

She couldn't tell him what she'd done and what she'd seen. Obviously. And would he feel he owed her an explanation? Anyway, how could anything he said change how she felt about the company he was keeping when she wasn't around?

Her brain was in such a whirl that she decided she should just text him to say she couldn't make it, delaying any confrontation. But that felt worse. She would go. She had to go. And then she would have a sensible adult goodbye, a no-fault parting of the ways. Very civilized.

So when Saturday came, she deliberated packing her overnight bag. It would be weird to walk into the house without it. It was unlikely he would notice, but if he did, it would force her to start right in on a conversation that was going to take some delicacy to handle well. But to be sure she didn't spend the night, she didn't wear or pack anything he would want to see her in, that ridiculous lingerie he'd chosen that, admittedly, did make her feel...No, just a few ordinary things to give it a little weight. Anyway, she had the bare necessities -- toothbrush, pills, emergency underwear, etc. -- in her daypack.

On the drive over, she tried to think of how to start a conversation with Chad that wouldn't provoke him. She just felt like she needed to know what he was up to. She heard her mother's voice saying, *Curiosity killed the cat.*

But was it just curiosity? Didn't she really want an explanation that would completely exonerate him? Hmm. Was that even possible? Yet she felt herself hoping against hope that he would reveal new facets of himself, ones that he'd erroneously kept hidden, but now allowed him to be the wonderful, loving expression of the man who was so beautiful on the outside? What was the key to unlocking his true nature?

Listen to yourself! You are delusional! Stop it!

But it wasn't easy. She always wanted to see the good in people. Because she spent so much of her time with children, she thought of their behavior as conditioned and their beings as malleable. A bully was a child who'd been bullied or abused, needing love and clear guidance. There may be exceptions, but she'd seen amazing transformations in behavior, enough to make her believe anything was possible. She believed in the goodness of people, that anything else was just reactions to bad things that happened to them. But maybe she was kidding herself. Or maybe it was different with adults. Were children like clay and adults fired in the kiln of life, taking a solid shape that can't be reshaped, only broken into shards that hurt everyone who touched them?

Every encounter with Chad, every imagined delight had ended up cutting her. She had wanted to get away from the pain of her grief, to be transported into a romantic fantasy, to numb the pain, to postpone any processing she knew logically would have to be done. She knew it was childish. She felt like a child. A motherless child. Tears sprang up. She pulled off to the side of the road and let herself have a good cry. This was so hard. Trusty stuck his head between the seats and nuzzled her, whimpering in sympathy.

Her mother's voice whispered, *Count your blessings.* Well, Trusty was a big blessing, for sure. And if she couldn't see her way to ending this relationship with Chad for herself, she would do it for Trusty. She would stop deluding herself that underneath it all, there was a kinder, gentler Chad.

In fact, maybe she shouldn't go over there at all. She could text him and say she wasn't coming. Why not? Would he even really care?

Could she just let the relationship fade away? Wouldn't that be ghosting him? She wasn't that kind of person. Whether he deserved it or not, she needed to feel okay about the way she ended this relationship.

She eased back into traffic and, in a few blocks, turned left onto the street that led toward the hills.

*   *   *

She rang the bell, and when there was no answer, she tried the door. It was unlocked, so she opened it and called out, "Chad?" She set her daypack on the table by the door, as she took it whenever she walked Trusty. She left Trusty's water bowl in it because they wouldn't be here long enough for him to need it, and Chad wouldn't notice that difference. She thought about leaving her overnight bag there as well, but that might tip her hand, so she brought it in, holding it in front of her like armor.

"I'll be down in a minute," he replied from upstairs. Eva looked around the room, noticing that everything was in perfect order, not a hint of the other evening's gathering. She was glad this was the last time she would be in this sterile room.

"Oh, hey," he said casually, coming down the stairs from the master bedroom, as if he hadn't been expecting her, a bath towel wrapped around his waist, his arms raised, using a hand towel to dry his hair. He descended the staircase like a grand entrance. A hint of a knowing smile on his face, as if reading her thoughts. He knew precisely what impression he made.

She noticed how her pulse rate increased on cue at the sight of him. She was like Pavlov's dog.

She felt ashamed of herself. But then it dawned on her that Chad had been training her, hadn't he? And he knew her patterns. He would have known exactly when she would arrive, because she was so punctual -- as a schoolteacher, she had to be. And he staged this towel exposure of his damp hair and chest, so reminiscent of the first time she'd seen him coming out of the pool.

He totally staged it. Just like his house was staged, every move he made, everything he did was for a particular purpose.

How had she not seen that he planned this like a predator waiting for its prey, knowing just the right lure at just the right moment?

She was probably one in a stream of women who had succumbed to his ploys. But for what purpose? He didn't need to go to all this effort to get laid.

She had so many questions! *Curiosity killed the cat. Curiosity killed the cat.* Yeah, yeah! But she felt she just had to discover the truth about Chad. What was his deal? And why was she his chosen prey?

She would just act normally for now. And she'd get him into his clothes before any conversation.

Easier said than done. Chad tossed the hand towel on the back of the couch and took her in his arms. She pulled back. "Let me just set my bag down," she said, purposely getting to the other side of the couch.

But he followed her, and once she'd set down her bag, he took hold of her and walked her backward up the stairs toward his bedroom, letting the bath towel fall from his waist as he did so.

"Whoa, slow down there," she said, laughing. "What's the hurry? I just got here. Give me a bit."

He backed off, hands in the air. She went past him, back down into the living room, assured Trusty she was fine, while Chad headed upstairs to get dressed.

She looked around, hoping there would be something she could casually pick up and say, *Oh, what's this?* And he would say, *Oh, that's from the other night when…*

And it would be all so innocent. But Eva didn't see anything. So she headed down the dark hall she'd never bothered to explore, to all those other rooms a single man didn't need. Or did he?

"Eva?" he called out from the stairs.

"I'll be right back, just need to use the bathroom."

"There's one right by the kitchen."

"Yeah, sorry, I need a little more, um, privacy. Sorry, something I ate."

That would buy her some time, she figured.

The hall was dark, and she had no idea which door led to the main bathroom, which was good because it gave her an excuse to open each one until she found it. As she peeked inside the medium-sized rooms, she noted that they still featured the staged twin beds, dressers, and desks typically found in some imagined kids' rooms. There was even a nursery with a crib and a mobile of little stars and moons dangling over it. That made her pause for a beat, but no time for her thoughts to go there. She was a woman with a purpose.

At the end of the hall, she found a study lined with floor-to-ceiling oak bookshelves. Curtains were drawn and the room was dark. But she could see cardboard boxes piled up, at least four or five stacks of them. They could be books waiting for Chad to shelve them. But she seriously doubted it. She looked at the labels and saw that they were from a copy shop a few towns away. A sample was plastered to one side, but she didn't dare turn on the light to try to read it. She could guess what it might be, so moved instead to the desk and the computer there.

What am I doing? she asked herself. She was no secret agent and had no way to access what was on there, but she still wanted to see at least what might be on the screen. And bingo! It wasn't even passcode-protected.

The file titles made no sense to her. It could be as innocent as…No, it couldn't be. Not with what she imagined was in those boxes.

As she looked over at them, she saw something else. Leaning against the wall were what looked like a bunch of military-style weapons. She knew nothing about guns, but these were nothing like her Uncle Harry's hunting rifles, which Aunt Evelyn had told her to steer clear of when she visited on some summer vacations.

At the sight of them, Eva's nerves gave out, and she scurried out of the room, back to the bathroom, where she hurriedly flushed the toilet, washed her hands, and stared at herself in the mirror. She was white as a sheet. What was she doing here?

She thought she might pass out, so she sat on the toilet seat and put her head between her legs, as she'd had students do from time to time. She wished some kind protector was standing beside her, patting her back, assuring her it would be okay.

Then she heard Chad coming down the hall, knocking on the bathroom door. "All good?"

"I don't know. I'm feeling kind of woozy. I'll be out in a minute. Maybe a glass of water?"

"Okay, sure." And off he went to the kitchen. Phew. Meanwhile, Trusty stealthily made his way down the hall and whimpered at the bathroom door.

She came out and ruffled his fur, assuring him she was okay.

Back in the kitchen, a plastic water bottle was on the counter. Ugh. Her town had the best drinking water in the state! Why in the world? But she just thanked him, twisted the bottle cap, and took a sip. She sat down at the dining table. Chad leaned against the counter that divided the kitchen and dining area.

Sufficiently recovered, she tried another tack. "Your house is always so clean," she said, looking around the room again for clues.

"Huh?" he said, looking up. "Oh, yeah, the maid comes on Thursdays and Mondays."

"Nice. Twice a week though? Do you really make that much mess living alone?" She felt like she was giving him the perfect opportunity to say that he hadn't been alone on Wednesday night, and there had been a lot to clean up.

But instead, he said, "Yeah, I had to add Mondays because of your damn dog. He leaves so much of his hair all over the place."

"Oh, I didn't realize. Of course, he does. I'm so sorry. Listen, just tell me where you keep the vacuum cleaner and I'll run it around before I leave. No need to hire a cleaner for an extra day."

"I don't have a vacuum cleaner. But the cleaner did complain that the dog hair was clogging up hers."

"Well, I'm sorry, I didn't think of it. Trusty has a lot of German Shepherd in him, and apparently, that fur is particularly tricky to vacuum. But could you please stop calling him 'that damn dog'? You're giving him a complex. His name is Trusty."

He shrugged. Then, as if he couldn't leave it alone, he mumbled, "Trusty. What a stupid name."

Okay, here we go, she thought. But by now, she knew better than to rise to his bait, so she just explained how it came about. "When I adopted him, he already had the name Rusty, I guess because he had that rust color in his coat, which made sense. But it was the name of a horrible boy in my class growing up, Rusty Dean, and I just couldn't get past it. So I changed it to Trusty, and he's been true to his name," she said, reaching over and petting Trusty, who looked up at her with deep affection. He had grown into a massive, handsome fellow with a beautiful brindle coat.

She hoped that mentioning Rusty might spark a conversation. If Chad knew anything about Gregory Allen Dean, he'd know his son's name. But he only said, "You and that damn…Trusty should get a room."

She didn't reply, just took another sip of water.

Was she imagining things, or was he becoming increasingly cruel? In any case, she was not going to let this conversation go off the rails. She hadn't realized how much effort it took to contain herself against his jibes. Was this just because she hadn't hopped into his bed when she came in the door? No wonder she always got home exhausted on Sundays. It wasn't just the sex; it was this battle. He was like a little boy tormenting some helpless creature just to see what would happen.

But Chad wasn't a child. And there was no excuse for his behavior. How many women had he put through this kind of ongoing torture? And why was she just now seeing it for what it was?

She said, "Okay, I'll bring vacuum cleaner next time." Though there would be no next time. She knew that now, no matter what was going on with his visitors the other night. Even so, she felt like she had to know.

"So, why didn't you just switch days?"

He was scrolling through his phone, his default mode, and looked up, "Huh?"

"From Thursday to Monday. Why not just have the housecleaner come on Monday instead? Surely you don't need…"

"What do you care?" he asked, irritated.

"Oh, I don't, I mean…sorry, sorry…" she said, getting up to look out the window, sipping her water. Trusty saw her looking and stood up, hopeful. She shook her head, and he lay down again with a quiet sigh. Poor dog. This whole thing was so unfair to him.

After the visceral discomfort faded and Chad seemed to be finished scrolling, she tried to sound as casual as possible.

"You know you never talk about your work. I mean, clearly, it's very demanding. You're always on your phone."

"Yeah, I keep busy. Always something, you know?"

"But what exactly do you do?"

"You know, I hate to mix business with pleasure, and you're my pleasure. If you're feeling better, how about we…"

Ack! She needed some diversion.

"Hey, by the way," she said.

"Hmm…?"

Before she could chicken out, she said, "Well, Wednesday was Chelsea's birthday, and the teachers all went in on a fancy cake for her. She had some leftover, and I thought you might like a piece, so I came by but could see that you had company, so I didn't want to intrude."

He looked startled, then a little nervous, perhaps even guilty.

But he composed himself and just said, "Huh. So what kind of cake was it?"

"Red velvet."

"Well, then, no problem. I'm not a fan."

He clearly wasn't going to tell her outright what was going on. She was going to have to ask.

"So, who…"

"Look, Eva. What we have is great. But it's a weekend thing. We agreed in the beginning, right? I have my life, you have yours."

Had they? Had she missed that discussion? It didn't matter, but still…

"Right, but even so, it can't be all about bed, can it? I mean…"

"Works for me," he said, reaching for her. He was like a little boy trying to change the subject and get on her good side.

"Well, it doesn't work for me. I just want to know you a little better. I'm glad you have friends…"

"They're not friends."

"Oh! Oh, good! Well…"

"Why good?"

"Well, I couldn't help noticing they had...um...bumper stickers for that awful Gregory Allen Dean, who...well. Anyway, I'm glad they're not your friends. Business meeting, then?"

"Honestly, Eva, it's none of your business who I have over here, or who I consort with, or even what I think, or who I vote for. It's a free country! But, yes, if you must know, it's business. I can't tell you much, but I'm hired to do this work, and it's nothing illegal."

"Well, that's good to hear. However, many things are legal but not ethical. I hope you're not selling some product that..."

"Eva, please, stop. I don't know how to make it any clearer that I'm not at liberty to tell you exactly what I do."

"Okay, well, if you've signed some NDA or something, obviously I won't grill you about it. But I'm talking to you, Chad, as a person. Are you feeling okay about what you do? Is it fulfilling?"

"Fulfilling? What world are you living in? It helps me pay student loans while living in a company-owned fancy house and driving around in a company-owned sports car. Do you think I could do any of this if I did whatever I thought I wanted to be when I was ten years old?"

"What did you want to be when you were ten?"

"Oh, God, Eva, I don't remember. The same stupid things little boys want to be. Superhero, fireman, detective, basketball star. Who remembers? And it doesn't matter because the world doesn't work that way."

"Well, as a teacher, I want my students to..."

"Yes, yes, I know. But do you follow up on them? How long have you been teaching now? How many of your students are adults? And what are they up to? I'll tell you! They're struggling. They're accepting jobs that don't save the planet, I'm sorry to tell you. I know that's what you want, but it's not going to happen. The world's going to hell, and I just want to enjoy it while I can. So can we please, please, please just go upstairs?"

"Uh, no."

"No? Here I'm being honest with you, spilling my guts, just like you've been wanting me to, and you turn me down? Seems like you're proving me right. I should have stayed the 'strong, silent type'. You're no longer attracted to me."

"Oh, Chad, I wasn't going to sleep with you today anyway. I came to break it off. But I just needed to know about all those cars, all those men on their computers and headphones, and why all men, anyway?"

OMG, had she really blurted that out? Oh no!

"And how would you know that?"

She looked down, ashamed, but her hand pointed at the floor-to-ceiling window that turned this house into a stage set for any passerby who cared to peek. Like her.

"You snuck behind the house and looked over the wall? You…"

"No, not *snuck* exactly! I mean, uh, Trusty hopped out and headed up the trail, and so, uh, of course, I chased after him, and…" She was a terrible liar, which she was usually proud of, but it would have come in handy here because she could see that he was furious.

"You invaded my space! You violated my privacy! What exactly did you see?"

Trusty leaped up at the raised volume of Chad's voice. So Eva tried to speak in a normal tone to calm him down. The last thing she needed was for her dog to attack Chad.

"Nothing. I mean, just a bunch of men on computers and you at a whiteboard. Nothing specific. Just…what is it? What were you all doing?"

"NONE OF YOUR DAMN BUSINESS!!! I told you! And if you tell anyone…"

"I wouldn't! I mean, what would I even say? It's just I'm supposed to keep a low profile, and if you could see…I didn't think about anyone hiking trails at night, sneaking peaks over the wall. Why would I even think that? It's crazy, right? It's crazy that you did that, you know that, Eva? It's a little psycho."

"I'm just curious. And who wouldn't be? But why would this incredibly ostentatious house be low profile?"

"Have you ever even seen any neighbors here?"

She shook her head. It was true. It was so different from her neighborhood, where there was always someone out gardening, walking the dog, carrying on conversations with neighbors, or the postal worker delivering the mail on foot. Up in these hills, it was so quiet you'd think that all the houses were empty. And maybe they were. There was certainly no sense of community. And because she only came on weekends, she didn't see any of the workers that might come and go -- the housecleaners, maintenance workers, gardeners, delivery vans. It was like a ghost land.

"So, it's perfect, right? Since I've been here, not one person has shown up at my door to welcome me. If I had personally bought this house and had a family, I might have felt offended. However, the company knew exactly what it was buying. And this isn't the only one, or the only town…"

He stopped and took a breath. He realized he may have said too much.

"Chad, I'm worried about you."

"Well, you don't need to. Worry about yourself!"

"What does that mean?"

"Exactly that. I can't say anything about my job, but I can say that the world is turning away from your vision of the way things should be. People are afraid, and when people are afraid, they do crazy things, believe crazy things, and people in power see that as money in the bank."

"And that's okay with you? Being part of that?"

"I didn't say I was a part of it." But his eyes told a different story.

"You know, I would have much rather come upon you having an orgy than this."

"Oh, me too!" he smiled. "But, Eva, this is the way it is. And if you're saying goodbye, well, so be it. But maybe one last…"

"You are persistent, I'll give you that. I can see why they hired you. But I'm shaken by all this. So…"

"Okay, well, listen, I think I said too much. I'm worried about what you're going to say and do. You're such a do-gooder. So, I'm going to ask you to stay a little -- we don't have to do anything -- but I need to text my boss and see if…"

Suddenly Eva felt a terrible sense of foreboding, a chill running down her back. She'd never felt anything like it. She remembered the guns in the study, the bumper stickers on the vehicles, the murky business he seemed to be in, and she realized she could be in danger. *Shit, shit, shit!*

Chad had turned his back to tend to his phone, so she signaled to Trusty that they were leaving, grabbed her daypack, and raced out the door.

If she got in her car, he'd have to chase her down. He'd overtake her in a minute and put other people in danger. So she turned up the trail, running as fast as she dared, not wanting to trip, but wanting to go beyond the open space and into the trees.

3 Fright and Flight

As fast as she was hiking, Trusty raced ahead up the path. He followed his nose and was happy to roam, unaware of any potential danger. And at a certain point, Eva felt safe to slow down. Chad didn't want to hurt her. She was just imagining things. Right?

Trusty loved to investigate, but he wasn't a hunter, so local wildlife was safe. And he always circled back to check on her. But she was fine. Really. She had made some serious mistakes, but here she was. No one was chasing her down. Though she'd have to stay out until she was sure she could go back for her car without him seeing her. Fortunately, it was late autumn and the sun set early. Still, she didn't want to be on the trail in the dark. The last thing she needed to do was stumble and fall. No one would know she was here.

As she hiked, she reviewed Chad's words. She had always wondered what he'd seen in her, instead of the more glamorous single women at Elliot's party. It seemed obvious that he could have any woman he wanted. He was, on the surface, the whole package so many women claimed to be looking for.

Now she wondered if maybe he had chosen her instead of a more glamorous, younger woman precisely because of her schoolmarmish do-gooder nature, and especially her championing of the environment. Perhaps he had been encouraged to study the 'opposition' and even distract and undermine her! Wouldn't that be something? She wasn't shy in her support for candidates who recognized the urgency of saving the planet, endangered species, and the future for the children of the world, including her students, many of whom, especially the older ones, were traumatized with fear. What if he had purposely sought her out?

And what were his beliefs? He seemed to have none. Or he felt that collaborative ethical behavior was naive. If it were just for the money, she was sure he could find something less insidious than whatever this was. Now she felt like it must be a political pact that was following the dictator playbook she'd been hearing so much about. Could he possibly believe that living in a fancy house, driving a sports car, and making whatever salary or commission he was making was worth putting his country in danger? Or could he believe that what his employers were up to was right? And then, did he think that in some sick way--by distracting her, seducing her, and persistently subduing her-- he was winning a fight against liberal thinking?

Then she remembered the photo she had taken of the whiteboard the other night. She stopped walking, pulled her daypack off, and dug around for her phone. When she opened it and clicked on the camera, the most recent photo appeared. She used her two fingers to get closer in order to see the writing on the whiteboard, and there it was:

REMEMBER:

FEAR IS A FRIEND WHEN USED FOR OUR BENEFIT.
FEAR IS CONTAGIOUS -- JUST LIGHT THE FIRE!
FUEL FEAR INTO FOCUSED ACTION!
GET THEM TO VOTE FOR GREGORY ALLEN DEAN + DONATE TODAY!

Eva gasped. *Oh my God, how could I have been so blind????*

She felt ashamed of herself. Angry at herself. No, furious with herself. Hadn't she had about a million clues that this was who he was?

She paused to calm herself down. *It's okay. It's over now.* She wasn't so sure that was true, but she didn't want to have a panic attack.

She took a deep breath and exhaled slowly. She looked around the hills, and back down at the valley, looking into the past, before all these mini mansions were built. There had been something magical about the pastures, the weathered red barn, the farmhouse, and the old couple who lived there. They kept to themselves but never had any problem with kids from the area climbing the massive tree on the property and sitting on what generations of young adventurers had called Swinging Limb. She remembered how it swayed under their weight but never broke.

When the couple passed away, their heirs sold the farm to a developer. They hadn't even cared if Swinging Limb survived. And then the town was stuck with this development that didn't seem intended for housing people, but to create showpieces for exalting already puffed-up egos. So she gave up hiking here and got into the habit of walking the creek path between their home, the downtown area, and the elementary school where she and Chelsea taught.

As she breathed in the fresh autumn air, the afternoon sunshine brightened her spirit, and the earth beneath her feet supported her. She felt her body relax a bit. At least these now she'd rediscovered these hills, her refuge.

Then she realized this would be the last time she would enjoy them. She couldn't return after this with Chad living right there by the trailhead.

Well, in that case, she would really explore. What was her hurry? She had all afternoon.

But, as she hiked, wanting just to appreciate the grassy hills and the woodlands she traversed, she couldn't help thinking. Now that she had left Chad, the floodgates had opened to all the things Heather had said, the words she had blocked out so she could keep returning into his snare.

"How could you, of all people, succumb to someone so…so…awful. He's gorgeous, okay, but c'mon! Can't you see through his veneer?"

No, apparently not. Yet it was so clear to her now that her friends had been right. As much as she hadn't wanted their concerns to be valid, and as ashamed as she now felt that she had been so blind, another feeling came up. A kind of liberation. She could drop her defenses and let her friends in again.

A mix of shame and affection rose up as she thought about them.

Chelsea was so wise and clear seeing. She could cut through the nonsense at a school meeting and point out the obvious conclusion that it would take everyone else hours, days, or maybe even years to reach. She was also fun, creative, and easy to be with at work, and at home.

As for Heather, where to begin? Heather had always had her back, ever since first grade when that awful boy, Rusty Dean, grabbed Eva's snack and ran across the schoolyard with it. Heather had chased him down and brought back the remains of the fruit bar, triumphant. Eva hadn't wanted to eat it because it probably had his cooties, but she did because this amazing girl had done this for her.

So why hadn't she heeded Heather's warning when she said, "Wake up, Eva! You don't have to live this nightmare! This is not who you are! You're kind, considerate, and caring. I know you're overwhelmed with grief and worry, but this is not the way to deal with it. Please, please, you know how much I love you and want the best for you."

Yes, she should have listened, but at the time, she had bristled at being told what to do, and they hadn't spoken for a good part of that day.

Well, now, all these weeks later, she had 'woken up'. She was so done with this nightmare! How could she have been so foolish? How in the world had she ended up in this volatile, mismatched mess? Hormones? Grief? Fear? Yes. But there was still no excuse for her behavior.

Okay, stop! She didn't have to keep rehashing it. It was done. D.O.N.E. Done!

She returned to noticing the glorious fall colors displayed on the hills beyond. She laughed in delight at Trusty's antics, chasing down every amazing smell he could find.

But her laughter brought up other emotions, and she found herself sobbing. She had made such a mess of things. And she felt contaminated. Oh, how she wanted absolution! The kind only her mother knew how to give. She bent over, put her hands on her knees, and sobbed.

She hadn't cried this much since her mother died. There had been too much to do. And then, she got into the habit of shunting those feelings aside. But here she was awash in tears.

She thought of how many children she had comforted on the playground who looked to be in the same state she was in now. She was kind but always assured them that this, too, would pass. As if she knew!

She knew nothing! Nothing about Chad. Nothing about how to mourn. Nothing about how to face her coming surgery and its possible repercussions going forward. She knew nothing about the future of her community, her country, the world, and the planet. And that was scary!!!

Still, she tried to comfort herself; she was healthy, well-employed, and had no reason to feel sorry for herself. Wasn't it just human nature to make mistakes? Especially in intense emotional states?

With her mother's death, Eva felt like the foundation of her life had crumbled beneath her. And in her tumbling freefall, she'd made bad choices and thoughtless decisions at every turn. *But I can recover from this,* she told herself.

Once Chad was history, her transgressions would be absolved. But how, without her mother to be her confessor? How could she forget what a fool she'd been? How would she heal from her grief? How could she face what was coming?

Step by step, day by day. Seeing the good in her life and building on that.

What she, Heather, and Chelsea had created together was life-affirming, collaborative, supportive, wholesome, and fun. That's what she had to remember. That's what she had to build on.

And, what about Trusty? Could she recognize his intuitive wisdom? He never took to Chad. Why had she?

Don't cry over spilt milk, her mother's voice reminded her. Right. Done. So done! For now, she'd just go wherever Trusty led her. At this point, his instincts were better than hers.

As they walked along, she gazed up at the calm, clear autumn sky. She breathed in the fresh air and felt cleansed. She raised her arms as if to embrace it all. She felt free! She felt like Julie Andrews in the panoramic opening scene in *The Sound of Music*, twirling about in joy and release. But Eva wasn't standing in an Austrian meadow but on a narrow rocky trail, and the next thing she knew, she was flat on the hard ground.

*   *   *

What just happened? Excruciating pain gripped her as she lifted her head to look around. She could see she had tripped on a root hidden in the shadow of a rock. *Damn.*

Her forehead hurt, and when she touched it, her hand came away bloody. She reached into her daypack for something to soak up the blood and found her cotton bandana. Pressing it to her forehead, she turned her attention to Trusty who was frantic, whimpering, barking, nudging and licking her.

She tried to assure him she was okay. But was she? Her ankle looked and felt weird. Could she walk? How would she get back down the hill? How had she been so foolish as to hike way up without anyone knowing where she was? *Stupid, stupid, stupid…*

Then everything went dark as she felt herself sink into the ground.

PART TWO

Over the Rainbow

4 Our Little Family

Eva woke to the vision of faces backlit by the radiant spokes of a brilliant, peach-colored paper umbrella decorated with white cranes. The effect was surreal. So many faces, smiling down at her. She couldn't see them clearly, but sensed a variety of shapes and shades, as if the poster in her classroom had come to life, with all the faces from continents around the world, and the title *"Our Little Family."* A student had created the original, and she loved the little drawing so much, she made it a class project to research and collage photos of faces from around the world. It's the one thing she would grab going out the door if she had to leave.

She blinked, thinking this collage of faces must be an apparition, but they didn't disappear.

"Looks like you tripped! Do you feel okay?" a stocky woman said warmly, reaching out her hand to gently help her sit up.

Okay? How could she feel okay? Didn't they see the blood gushing from her head? But when Eva touched her forehead, it was smooth and there was no blood. She looked around for her bandana and spilt water bottle, but they were both tucked away in her pack. Amazingly, there was no pain anywhere in her body. She felt just fine. Had she just imagined her injuries?

Trusty seemed totally refreshed and not a bit concerned about her having fallen, or about any of these people. His protective nature, sometimes bordering on suspicion, was gone. He seemed more lighthearted, like when he was a puppy. She got up and dusted herself off. She looked around, and the familiar hills seemed more majestic, and the autumn colors were more intense. She must have hiked further than she thought. Or maybe her fall had brought her to her senses.

"I'm Minna," the woman told her. "You're welcome to walk with us." She looked around at the rest of the group, and they all nodded. Who were they? It was a multi-generational group, but it didn't include any children. Some of them looked like typical hikers, but the oldest two were not. The woman, the shortest of the group, was dressed in loose linen pants and an overshirt, and carried a Japanese paper umbrella. Her white hair was piled on her head in a neat topknot. Her pale face had no make-up and many wrinkles, but the kind that suggests a life of laughter rather than frowns. She carried a canvas satchel, as if she were going to the farmers' market rather than for a hike. She introduced herself as Lily, and her pale blue eyes twinkled, as if she knew something about Eva that Eva didn't know herself.

The gentleman was tall, slender, and elegant. His thinning hair was grey at the temples. He was in khakis and a loose-fitting dress shirt with the sleeves rolled up. Eva felt as if he were from a different century. He carried a timeworn, slender briefcase. He introduced himself, "My name is Vicente. And yours?"

"I'm Eva, and this is my dog Trusty."

"Trusty, what an excellent name."

"He's lived up to it, believe me. If only I believed more in him."

"Ah, sometimes it's hard to listen to the ones who love us most. True?"

"Oh, ouch! So very true!" How in the world did this dapper man know that she had been disregarding the wisdom and instincts of those who loved her best?

"It's just human nature. But once we recognize it, then we can do something about it, right?"

She nodded. The rest of the group nodded and smiled. "Well, Lily and I have used this excuse to pause in our hiking long enough. As Minna suggested, unless you have other plans, you're welcome to join us. I sense the rest of the group is restless to get back to camp to show us what we're in for."

"Oh yes," Lily added. "The big reveal! I can feel their excitement and urgency. Please do join us. The more the merrier."

Eva didn't mean to seem ungracious, but she had wanted to be alone. Now, considering everything, she figured she would be better off being with others. "Um, okay. Thank you."

"Excellent! Alright, Connor, Allie, Eddie, and Sara, lead the way!"

The group laughed, and they turned and headed up the trail, clearly excited to reveal something. Three of them were young, possibly in their early twenties, and represented various continents in their facial features and coloring. So was this a college outing? Maybe. The dapper man, Vicente, seemed very professorial.

Minna, who had helped her up, was probably in her fifties, with a no-nonsense blonde haircut under a sunhat. She wore a flannel shirt, jeans tucked into thick socks, and sturdy hiking boots. She carried a daypack much like Eva's.

Lily and Vicente stepped aside so Eva could go ahead. "We'll be right behind you." As Eva took her first steps, testing her ankle, she realized she felt no pain. In fact, she felt light as air and full of energy, not like someone who had been hiking up into the hills for an hour or more. She wasn't thirsty or hungry. She was at ease.

As they walked, she was grateful that there wasn't any conversation. When she and her friends took walks, it was just a way to get exercise while catching up with each other's news. Of course, they hadn't been doing anything so dedicated as hiking together over the weeks she'd been with Chad. Visions of Heather and Chelsea's smiling faces danced before her, filled with love and concern. How had she been so thoughtless to…ah, well. She came back to this moment, not wanting to take another tumble.

The hikers were clearly just happy to be present in all this beauty and friendship. Their enjoyment was palpable. They belonged here, an accepted part of nature. She let go of thoughts of what she'd left behind in the valley and fell into step.

Then she started to see things that she hadn't noticed when she was on her own. All her senses seemed heightened, like the sudden Technicolor of Dorothy landing in Munchkin land. But these weren't Munchkins, and she hadn't killed a witch when she fell. Or herself, thank goodness.

Still, it felt somehow more magical. She could see the interesting patterns on the trees, the bark, the lichen, the shapes of the leaves, and the way the light wind rustled through them. She could hear the symphony of birdsong, and when she stepped onto stones as they crossed a stream, the babbling of the water was like a symphony. She delighted in the warmth of the sunshine and the soft breeze on her skin. Her nostrils filled with the scent of clean air. She felt transformed!

5 Beyond the Beyond

After a while, they arrived at an opening, a sheltered grove, with a circle of seats — round cushions and canvas back jacks — around a firepit.

Connor, Eddie, Allie, and Sara stood aside as if opening the curtains to the camp for the rest to walk in. Minna, Vicente, and Lily oohed and ahh-ed over everything. "This is perfect! Incredible. Congratulations. Job well done."

Vicente turned to Eva and said, "They were determined to create a nature retreat, and I think they've outdone themselves, don't you?"

"It's amazing," Eva replied, looking around. The towering trees created sheltered 'rooms' of a sort: this central area was a perfect circle of eight seats around a firepit in the center. To the left she could make out through the 'wall' of trees a camp kitchen that was impressive, to say the least. It was equipped with a long metal counter with a sink, a chopping block island, a stove and oven, a refrigerator, and a walk-in storage unit. How in the world was this even possible? It was like a kitchen from a cooking show, not a camp. Yet here it was.

On both sides of the camp there were open meadows. It was a beautiful setting; far more elaborate than any camp she'd ever been to. She was envious of them having each other and this experience.

But she realized that if she were going to make it safely back down the hill, she'd better get going. So she added, "I hope you'll have a wonderful retreat. Trusty and I had better get going."

Lily looked at her then. "You know, dear, you're welcome to stay. The retreat was meant for eight people, and we're only seven. So…"

"Oh, that's so kind, but I couldn't…"

"Well, let's take a little tour, why don't we? And then you can decide."

Eva agreed. She was very curious. Lily led the way, peeking into the kitchen area where, with the industry of beavers, the three youngest were already chopping vegetables. Minna motioned to Lily to follow her, and Eva went along. A narrow path between trees led to a group of pup tents, then beyond them were a few larger ones, and then a canvas tent fit for a queen. "Connor told me this one's for you, Lily." The three women entered and gasped.

Then Lily laughed. She sat down on the plush double bed, surrounded by elegant, patterned curtains. Persian carpets covered the floor. The walls were high and covered with brocade. There was a seating area with comfortable upholstered chairs and cushions. "This is beyond belief! Goodness! Did they really think I needed all this? I said I wasn't a camper, but…"

Eva thought it looked exactly like the tent in the *Sheik of Arabi*, the silent movie with Rudolph Valentino. Chelsea and Heather had conspired to find a clip of the almost-rape scene to show Eva, as if to warn her off Chad. As if she was some helpless fainting maiden. But how strange that it would show up here!

Minna told Lily, "It is a bit much! Especially when I know what a simple life you lead. But you know they love you and are so grateful for your teachings. I guess this is just an expression of their gratitude. And Connor did mention that it was important that you have a seating area for one-on-ones and such."

Okay, Eva thought, *so Lily was a teacher. But what did she teach?*

Beyond the seating area was a canvas flap that opened to reveal another small but perfectly satisfactory bedroom with a single bed and a dresser.

"I wonder who that is for?" Minna said.

"Is it for you?" Lily asked her. "Will we be tentmates?"

"No, Connor pointed mine out to me. It's one of the family-size tents, so I don't have to crawl around. We passed it on the way up. I'll check it out. I'm sure it's fine. He wouldn't put his old mom in anything too rough. At least if he knows what's good for him." She laughed.

Ah, so Connor was Minna's son. Okay, Eva thought. *So there was some family situation going on here.*

"And Isaac was supposed to bunk with Connor, but he's pleased to have a whole tent to himself."

"A shame about Isaac," Lily said. "But not all that surprising, really."

Who was this Isaac, and what happened to him? Eva wondered. But there was no time to wonder about anything. She really needed to get back down into town. The light was fading fast.

"I should go. I've got quite a trek to get back..."

Lily looked concerned. "Eva, as it turns out, we have this extra room right here. Please, at least stay the night. You've already fallen once!"

"Oh, that's so kind, but..."

But what? Lily was right. She'd be foolish to try to get down the hill now. And her housemates weren't expecting her back. So, why not? She still had many questions about who this group was and what they were doing here, but what was the harm in spending the night?

Unless they were a cult, and they were being so nice to draw her in. *Out of the frying pan into the fire,* her mother would say. And hadn't she proven she was gullible? Well, she'd just have to be on her guard.

"Okay, thank you. Just for the night. Oh, but what about Trusty? Can he stay in the tent?"

"Of course, we're not going to let a bear gobble him up!" said Lily.

"No bears in this neck of the woods, Lily. I checked before agreeing to this adventure," said Minna.

"No, no bears," agreed Eva, "and I've lived near here my whole life. But thanks for letting me keep Trusty in the tent."

"Good, it's settled then," pronounced Lily, brooking no argument. "Alright, now I'm going to unpack and take a little nap before we gather."

"Okay, see you in a bit," said Minna. And then, turning to Eva, gave her hand a friendly squeeze and said, "I'm glad you'll be staying. I would worry about you trying to hike down the hill in the dark."

"Thanks, I appreciate that." For having taken such a 'tumble', Eva felt, despite her misgivings, that she had certainly landed on her feet.

Since she didn't have anything to unpack, she walked back into the central part of the camp with Trusty at her side. She still felt a little dazed. Amidst the quiet bustle of the campers, she looked around in wonder. How had they ever gotten all this up here? Was it legal?

Again, doubt rose. *Look what had happened when I started seeing Chad without understanding what he was up to.* Was this her pattern? She had so many questions. But they were so lovely and welcoming; how could she ask them the rude questions that were now popping into her mind? She couldn't ask them 'Do you have a permit for all this? Is this some team-building trip? Do you all work for some huge conglomerate that's sucking the earth dry and causing massive destruction and an imminent end to life as we know it? And did that conglomerate airlift all this in so your little team could have a nice little time? What a perk! What a travesty!'

This imaginary line of inquiry was making her feel woozy. So she relaxed. She took a breath. *Don't look a gift horse in the mouth*, she heard her mother say. So she decided that, at least for now, she would accept this lovely gift of experience. It was just for the night, and she'd be much safer here than walking down the hill. And what if Chad was lying in wait? With his guns. Now that was something to be afraid of.

She looked around and felt that these were good people doing a good thing together. She felt safe, welcome, and more at ease than she had in a long time.

Note to Readers
In the coming chapters there will be rich discussion and exploration of vital concepts that are worthy of pausing to consider for yourself. So I created a downloadable PDF workbook with space for you to explore on your own. You'll find the link in the back of the book.

Or just read on and enjoy, taking in what is meaningful for you and letting go of the rest. - SN

6 Something stirring

The sun had set behind the mountain, and the rays glowed against the clouds in the most magnificent sunset Eva had ever seen, almost as if painted by an artist for a 1930s movie set.

The camp, sheltered by the trees, was getting dark. She began to doubt her decision to stay in a camp with strangers in the dark. Why had she agreed to watch *The Blair Witch Project* at Heather's 12th birthday slumber party? It was coming back to haunt her now.

But just then, the camp trails lit up with fairy lights! Magical!

When she arrived at the central circle, Eddie, who looked to be in his forties, with a bit of a dad bod, a kind face, and thick dark hair held back in a ponytail, was gathering kindling and then laying the logs for a fire.

She said, "The lights are amazing. But a lot of work! Who did that?" He shrugged humbly. "You? Wow. Thank you. I was starting to get a little creeped out."

He smiled. "I was against the idea. We have enough lights in the city. I wanted to be in the dark of night. But I was overruled."

"Then why did you volunteer to do it?"

"I'm in charge of the structural stuff in the camp. If you experience any issues with your tent or any other item, please notify me. I'm in the last tent up the hill, a little way beyond the lights."

"Ah, that makes sense. Okay, thanks."

Just then, Connor arrived from the kitchen area, carrying a large pot. Now that she knew he was Minna's son, she could see that he'd inherited her coloring, a swatch of reddish hair, and a sprinkling of freckles. He grunted as he set the pot on the sturdy wrought iron trivet over Eddie's handy work.

Eddie had made fire-building look easy! She remembered when she was twelve and begged to go to summer camp instead of to Aunt Evelyn's. Everyone else at the camp had been coming for years and knew how to swim to the island, paddle a canoe, weave friendship bracelets, and, it seemed, build a fire. They were nice enough, mostly, but she felt self-conscious when the counselor taught her, in front of everyone, the fine art of campfire building, emphasizing all the ways it could go wrong. Eva remembered trembling. But she had paid close attention and tentatively recreated a semblance of a balanced fire. She imagined all the other girls had fathers to teach them such things, and they could tell she didn't.

She would remind herself that although most of the kids she knew had fathers, not all of them were fathers she would want to have. And she couldn't quite imagine how a father would fit into their cozy life. She and her mother were happy. They would even say that to themselves. "We're as happy as two peas in a pod!" And then they'd laugh, delighted with themselves. Later, she realized that most families didn't tell themselves they were happy; perhaps her mother needed reassurance that they were fine.

Shaking off these thoughts, she asked Eddie, "What can I do to help?"

"Hmm, well, uh, here," he said, handing her a large matchbox. "You can light the fire."

She studied the box as if it were a foreign object, a relic from a bygone era. At home, the only use they had for fire was to light the gas grill on the back patio. All she had to do was push a button to create a spark or a flame. To strike a match along the rough sandpaper strip on the side of the box took her back to her childhood, yet again.

This time, she remembered the fireplace in the dollhouse that she and Heather built when Eva spent the night at her house. So thoroughly entranced by the little world they created, they naturally wanted a real fire. The moment the flame flared, they snapped out of their imaginary world. But they had no clue what to do. The matchstick logs blazed, and the cardboard fireplace began to burn. They panicked and started screaming. No one came. Young girls screaming together was normal.

Then the flame had died. The two of them stared at each other, eyes wide with shock. And then they laughed with relief. It was years later that Eva thought about how they might have burned down the dollhouse or the whole house. That realization had stayed with Eva. Fire was so powerful and scary. She found herself trembling.

If Chad had been here, he would have laughed at her, standing there staring at the matchbox. He would have grabbed the matches, pushed her aside impatiently, and said, 'Here, let me.'

Eddie let her have her moment. Aware of the trees around them, she couldn't help thinking about forest fires, whole towns burned to the ground, lives lost.

But she also had wonderful memories: cozy winter evenings in front of the fireplace, and the mesmerizing beauty of a candle flame. She thought about the floor heater warming the cold morning air, billowing her flannel nightgown. The gas flame under the saucepan of milk heating her hot chocolate.

Why stop there? She thought about how fire was also the warmth of the sun on her skin, the source of energy for plants that turned toward it as if in worship. She became aware of the fire within her body, the burning of calories for energy, and the synaptic electrical synapses of the brain. Fire! What a miraculous element!

And with that, she struck the match and reached out to light the wadded newspaper under the twigs nestled under the logs: a simple stroke, a lovely flare. A whole series of amazing events was set into motion. It felt somehow sacred, this privilege of lighting the fire. She handed the matchbox back to Eddie and smiled.

She noticed that there were eight seats around the fire. She guessed that one was meant for the missing Isaac. *His loss is your gain*, she heard her mother say. But which seat was hers? A few had personal items, such as an extra cushion, a water bottle, or a shawl. So she sat down on an empty back jack but stayed alert in case anyone claimed it.

Trusty settled by her and stared at the fire contentedly. His sense of ease assured her. But she wondered, *Why am I taking so many cues from my dog suddenly?*

Why not? After all, he had always been right about who to trust and who to steer clear of. If only I had trusted him more!

Now she took a cleansing breath, releasing lingering thoughts of Chad into the evening breeze, into the fire, into the night, into the earth. She never had to talk to him again. Ever. At this thought, it felt as if all the cells in her body just received some extra space. She let go of the need to chastise herself about her choices or to ruminate endlessly about all the ways she failed. She was here now. *Ahh.* She closed her eyes.

When she opened them a few minutes later, she saw that Minna was stirring the pot with a long-handled spoon. *What was there that needed such steady stirring? Perhaps it was simply that the contents were on a big open flame and might settle to the bottom, burning or bubbling up and boiling over.*

The few times Eva had made risotto or tapioca pudding that required constant stirring, her hand and arm ached, and she swore she wouldn't do anything so labor-intensive again. But Minna didn't seem to mind. She was totally into it. How beautiful she was with her round face glowing in the firelight.

Steam started to rise from the pot. The smell was delicious—oniony, with seasoning she didn't have the skill to decipher to flavor the carrots, celery, potatoes, and beans. She realized she was hungry.

She noticed Minna nodding to Connor, and he rang a bell. Then everyone who wasn't seated entered the area. Allie brought in a tray of bowls, napkins, and spoons. Sara brought a basket of bread. It wasn't a procession, exactly, but it did have a formality about it that felt like the food was being honored. Allie handed Minna each bowl. Minna ladled in the soup, then gave the bowl to Connor, who offered it to Lily, then to Vicente, then to Eddie, and finally to Eva. Then they each took a bowl of soup for themselves and carefully settled in their seats. Sara passed the breadbasket around, and Eva took a piece, feeling its warmth with appreciation.

As Eva breathed in the delicious aroma from her bowl, she let the steam bathe her face and soothe her eyes. She looked through the steam at this circle of lovely people. She noticed each of them paused before eating to consider what they were taking in. She tried to emulate them. It didn't feel as unnatural as she thought it would.

Growing up with just her mother, their eating habits were generally wholesome but very informal. They had weekly sit-down dinners to make sure Eva knew how to set a proper table, use the right forks, and dine with others, engaging in appropriate conversation. All the things she imagined her grandmother had taught her mother. But the rest of the time, it was casual, and though they might chat a bit about their day or plans for the week, they ate breakfast at different times, took lunch to school and work, and for weekday dinners, they settled in front of the television to watch Jeopardy. But they were never purposefully silent when they were together.

When they had their weekly formal dinner date, her mother had always asked her to slow down instead of gobbling down her food, as if to get the meal over with. "Pace yourself," she would tell her. But pacing herself sounded like running a marathon. And if so, didn't she want to win? She was uncomfortable with the enforced nature of this weekly meal. It felt phony, as if she and her mother were trying to be people they were not. And as a teenager, she often found a way to be busy on that night. Her mother had understood. "If you don't know how to set a table and eat properly by now, I've failed."

"You haven't failed, Mom. I make you proud when I'm out and about. Honest."

"Well, I appreciate that. We can't have the town librarian's daughter bringing shame to the family name, can we?" They both laughed. As if! Eva had never been rebellious and was, if anything, overly protective of her mother's good name. It was hard enough to grow up in a single-parent household in a small community without adding fuel to any potential gossip. She realized that now, with her mother dead, she had gone and become a source of gossip. *Oh dear.*

Ack! She couldn't tame her thoughts. Now her mind was back down the hill, far away from this place and time. So she refocused on the delicious soup, noticing each ingredient and considering all that had gone into each bite of food. All the way back to the seeds and then forward again, she watched the whole process as if it were a vision. The seedlings sown in the soil sprouted leaves and flowers. She could see the vegetables growing and ripening in the sun. She envisioned the fields and gardens where they grew, the farmers who cultivated them, and all the workers who played an essential role in bringing the food to market. Then she looked over at Allie, Sara, and Connor, who had apparently bought them and carried them all the way up here, then chopped them up and added them to the pot. And of Minna, who had stirred it all to combine into a more delicious soup than she would have imagined. She smiled, settled in, and savored each spoonful. She was so grateful to them all. Wasn't life, after all, amazing?

When they finished, she got up to help Minna take the bowls to the kitchen, where a dishpan of warm water awaited.

Minna washed and rinsed them, and Eva toweled them dry. Connor returned everything to its proper place, stacked just so at the far end of the counter. Eddie filled the clean pot with water and returned it to the campfire for tea.

Eva asked Minna how she had come to be there. It felt less weird than asking what this retreat was about.

Minna smiled. "Well, it's a bit of a story, if you're up for it."

"Sure!"

"I'm a nurse in an orthopedic surgery ward. So I see a lot of people in a lot of pain. And I also see people suffering."

"What's the difference? Isn't pain suffering?" Eva asked.

"People come in with physical pain, but their fear, anger, impatience, frustration, worry, etc., cause suffering that exacerbates physical pain. We can generally lessen the physical pain for them, but there's not much we can do about the suffering.

"About ten years ago, two patients sharing a room had almost identical surgical procedures done. But one had been looking forward to the surgery. She'd been waiting for it for months and knew it would relieve her ongoing pain. The other hadn't expected to be in the hospital. She'd been thrown off a horse, and suddenly, there she was, not knowing what the future held for her. Would she heal? Could she ever ride again? Would her insurance cover this procedure? How long would she be in such pain? The poor thing was frantic with worry.

"All through the night, she moaned and groaned, though we gave her as high a dosage of morphine as we could. She wailed and cried out, and we were helpless. There was nothing more we could do. It was a rough night for everyone. And, of course, we also felt sorry for her roommate, who was stuck beside her, trying to sleep. After all, she had a whole lot of physical pain, too. But she didn't have the mental anguish her roommate was experiencing. And that made all the difference! She wasn't compounding the pain and causing herself more suffering."

The dishes were done, and Connor had put everything away and left the kitchen, but Minna hadn't finished her story. "We can sit. We have a little while before the bell."

So Eva sat down at a picnic table, appreciating that Minna was taking the time to share all this.

"The Buddha used a helpful metaphor: Imagine experiencing physical pain. That's the first dart. Ouch! Right? It hurts!"

Ah! The Buddha! Eva thought, relieved. So, this was a Buddhist retreat. That was great. She remembered a term paper she'd written for a World Religions course that she came upon recently during the painful lonely experience of sorting through her mother's storage locker.

She had taken the paper out into the sunlight and read through it, remembering that her professor advised her to just choose just one school to focus on. She had chosen the school of the Elders, the Theravadan school, since, as she understood it, it stayed closest to what the Buddha taught. She also appreciated that it seemed more of a psychology than a typical religion with deities. She'd never been big on the idea of some old, white-bearded man in the sky looking down and judging her. Replacing him with more festive colorful figures didn't change how she felt.

She had set that paper aside, thinking it would be of interest to Heather, but then got interested in reading it herself, and it was still on her bedside table. What a coincidence!

Minna was saying, "So, with the first dart, we feel pain. But then, what do we do? We activate suffering with a second dart of our own making. The mental activity -- anger, distress, worry, remembering similar past experiences -- takes that physical pain and compounds it into a complex of mental suffering."

"Wow," Eva said, "I see that happening with my students all the time. With some kids, every little scratch or bump turns into a big drama. Others get hurt and just say ouch before moving on."

"Yes! Exactly. And what the Buddha taught is to see that pattern in our own experience. To notice that maybe we're caught up in thinking about who caused this pain, and we make ourselves miserable because we feel victimized, or foolish, or we're plotting revenge. There are so many ways we shoot that second dart at ourselves, making what was pain into extreme suffering."

Eva nodded, mind properly blown.

Minna continued. "Many of us don't realize we are going through life actively seeking out the most annoying, insufferable things to pay attention to. Here's an example: Driving in traffic, who do you notice?"

"Bad drivers."

"Exactly. And how do you feel when someone does something that you feel puts you or others in danger?"

"Angry, annoyed, sometimes outraged."

"Of course, and then, just when you need to be most present and attentive, those reactions activate a distracted mind that, combined with tension and emotions from clinging to the scary or annoying experience, cause a miserable ride, possibly poor driving, and in the worst case…"

"An accident." Eva finished the sentence, remembering her recent almost-accident due to her having been so upset and distracted that she'd forgotten to turn on her headlights.

Minna nodded and continued. "And, of course, it's not just driving. We all do that, or variations of it, until we realize that we are shooting ourselves with a second dart. Once we see that the first dart happened *to* us, but the second one *we* cause ourselves, it almost becomes laughable. We see it and we recognize how human we are. Then we can let it go."

"Wow, that's huge. I've never thought about it that way."

Minna smiled, then looked off into the fairy-lit forest beyond the kitchen. "But back to your original question about how I joined this group: Those two patients I mentioned? The one that was there on purpose and the other by accident?"

Eva nodded.

"Well, I actually owe the one who was there for scheduled surgery a debt of gratitude. In the early morning hours, after she'd regained some strength, I could hear her quietly asking the suffering roommate if she wanted to do some pain-relieving exercises. And the poor accident victim was desperate and said yes. So they did some breathwork together, enough for her to drift off to sleep for several hours.

"Ah, so you all got some relief."

Minna smiled. "Yes! But then later when I was talking with the patient who offered the breathing exercises, it turned out that she taught meditation. I was curious to learn more about it, and we exchanged contact information to meet again after her recovery. And when we did, she told me all about Insight meditation and helped me find a sangha near me. This sangha! And the practice, the teachings, and these wonderful people—my sangha. I should mention that there are many more of us in the sangha. These are just the ones who were game for a dedicated retreat focused on the Eightfold Path in nature in a cool season when anything could happen. That narrowed it down quite a lot." Minna smiled.

"Anyway, after I had been attending weekly meetings for a while and had developed my daily practice, other nurses noticed the difference it was making in the way I dealt with the stresses of our work. And they asked me to teach them. Well, I wasn't quite up to that, but I did convince the administration to bring in a mindfulness program. You're a schoolteacher, right? So maybe they have a mindfulness program in your school?"

"They did! Our school counselor initiated the program, and it helped, but the funding was cut, so…"

Minna sighed. "Well, that's a shame. However, there's nothing to stop teachers from pausing at the beginning of class to have a moment of silent awareness, noticing their breath and coming into the present moment, perhaps setting a kind intention for the day. Something suitable for anyone, regardless of religion or beliefs.

"It's obviously not the same. And I prefer the whole of the Buddha's teachings for myself, not just the sterilized version for institutional acceptance," Minna added.

"And Connor learned about it from you?"

"No. His best friend growing up was Korean American, and Connor would occasionally go with him to the Buddhist temple his family attended. Connor disliked the crowds but enjoyed the chanting. Then he was offered a scholarship to attend a private tech-focused high school, and unfortunately, the two friends lost touch. But I think his attendance at the temple planted a seed. After graduating from college, he joined the Peace Corps and served in Thailand.

"Oops, I realize this is not my story to tell. But, oh well, not to leave you hanging. After his service, Connor stayed for a few months in a forest monastery. He wanted to experience what the Buddha had experienced. He sat at the base of trees every day and meditated. For like hours!

"I was concerned when he got so gung-ho about it. If he does anything, he does it full on. Upon returning home, he secured a job in the tech industry. He's hoping to help ensure that AI is ethical. But most of his spare time is spent reading the Pali Canon. He never does anything halfway."

"Thanks in part to our shared love of the Triple Gem—the Buddha, Dharma, and Sangha—Connor and I are closer than ever. He still lives at home. We built a little ADU in our backyard. My husband was insistent on that. But for me, it's just a treat to have him home."

Just then, Connor appeared, "Mom, I know you're talking about me. There are no walls here."

Minna looked a little sheepish but giggled. Clearly, their bond was strong. Eva felt an ache in her chest. First, she thought about how lucky Connor was to have his mother. And then how lucky Minna was to have raised a child, something that had been at least a possibility for Eva, was now going to be off the table.

She took a breath, closed her eyes, and could see so clearly how she was creating suffering with these thoughts. She took another calmer breath and opened her eyes. Connor was gone, and Minna was getting up from the table. And then she heard the bell ring.

"Well, it was great talking with you. We'll be going into silence after this, so I wish you a wonderful retreat."

"Oh. You, too." She hadn't planned to stay for the retreat, just for the night, but it was nice to feel welcome. Then she worried that if they were in silence, she wouldn't be able to say goodbye, that she would just disappear, leaving them all to wonder.

*　　*　　*

As they returned to the circle, she saw Lily walk over and place a blanket on Eva's back jack. Appreciating her thoughtfulness, she wrapped it around her and smiled across at Lily, who nodded. Then she settled in, Trusty at her side.

As everyone assembled, Eva tested herself to see if she could remember their names. As a schoolteacher, she was excellent at learning names quickly. Going clockwise, there was Lily, Vicente, Eddie, Eva, Minna, Connor, Sara, and Allie. Eight of them. A nice number. Also, the symbol for infinity. She looked up into the night sky through the trees. But Eddie was right about the fairy lights. She couldn't quite see the night sky.

Vicente sat with his eyes closed, and when a calm settled, he opened them and began.

"So here we are on the first night of our retreat focused on the Buddha's Noble Eightfold Path, and I'm delighted that we have eight of us here, even though Isaac couldn't join us. I can't help but think it's ironic, but perhaps not surprising, that the sangha member who took on Wise Intention as his focus, and intended to come, ultimately didn't. Let's send him some *Metta* for whatever is keeping him from this retreat."

They paused and closed their eyes, so Eva did the same. She didn't know Isaac, didn't know what this Metta was, but she felt sorry for him, missing this. So she hoped he would be well.

Vicente continued, "And I want to extend a warm welcome to Eva, who has agreed to join us, making our numbers complete. And because Eva is new to this, I'll share some of the basics of how we gather.

"On a Buddhist Insight retreat, it is traditional to be in silence the whole time, except when invited to speak in the circle as part of Dharma exploration, and, if absolutely necessary, during our yogi jobs.

"It becomes self-evident why we choose silence, but it may seem odd if you haven't experienced it. This rule is not meant to shut us up, but to open us up to what is present in any given moment, beyond words. And even if we have words swarming within us, thinking, thinking, it's a kindness not to invade each other's experience with them. We can become somewhat tender and vulnerable. So silence is our gift to each other and ourselves. Please don't think of it as something being imposed upon you. Let it be the sweet promise you make to yourself. Obviously, we'll be out and about, and there will be many opportunities to break noble silence without external repercussions. No one will be shushing you. We are all adults here, and we undertake this silent retreat with glad hearts, joyful in the opportunity to quiet down and become centered.

"Each of us will have our own unique experience. There will probably be many commonalities, but we'll be in different places and stages of the experience at any given moment.

"Lily and I will be available to any of you at any time, if you experience anything that concerns you or are unsure about what to do.

"Because we are up in the hills on this nature retreat, not in an established retreat center where everything is taken care of and seems to run seamlessly thanks to the retreat manager and years of experience, there will undoubtedly be some things that we'll need to address. But let's see if we can maintain as much silence as possible.

"Traditionally, noble silence includes no eye contact. Why? We might not realize how much we communicate with our eyes, our smiles, our hands, and our wanting to be polite. So when our gaze steers clear of such contact, we are not being rude. We are respectful and help each other maintain our meditative experience. Silence allows us to be in community more intuitively, without the need for words or any other kind of signal.

"We each have our own reasons for being here, but in general, we are here to cultivate skillfulness and recognize and release the habitual patterns that keep us from sensing into this moment. Even though we are all in silence, our minds will likely chatter away in their habitual way. But with Wise Intention, we gently but firmly bring our attention back to the felt sense of being alive in this moment. Here. Now. Just being.

"Months of planning by almost all of you have resulted in this opportunity to be together in this lovely place. Lily and I wholeheartedly thank you for all your Wise Effort in putting it together. I know we were naysayers in the beginning, but you saw what was possible and you made it happen. Every concern we had, you addressed. For every potential problem, you found a solution. It's quite remarkable! So deep bows to you.

"Please turn off your cell phones and put them in this basket. This is one of the greatest gifts you can give yourself. There are bedside clocks, and the bells will ring to wake, for meals, and for sitting.

"So, that's all the practical aspects. Before we go into silence, are there any questions about this retreat? Does everyone remember which aspect of the Eightfold Noble Path you will be presenting? If you're struggling with it, just let me know. I'll be happy to help."

What? Eva thought. Was she supposed to…? *No, of course not, don't be ridiculous.* She was just a visitor for the night. None of this applied to her. How could it?

Lily added, "I'm happy to help as well. However, I trust in your ability to share your own experience with the aspect you've taken on. Remember, we've each taken the aspects that we struggle with. So no one is expecting great expertise. We've all read Bhikku Bodhi's book. We've all explored the Path before. This retreat is an opportunity to delve a little deeper, allowing the Path to come alive in your own experience. And of course, we'll begin with meditation."

She looked around at each face in the circle, smiling warmly. She was like a queen in her benevolence. But when she came upon Eva's face, she laughed. Why did she laugh?

"Oh, Eva, dear, don't worry. Relax and enjoy. Just be respectful and follow the rules of silence. But again, if you have questions, feel free to ask Vicente or me anything that concerns you."

Phew! Eva realized she must have said that out loud, because everyone laughed. She blushed and looked down. But she felt relieved. When she looked up, she noticed that everyone had their eyes closed, so she closed hers as well. The usually persistent tight knot she experienced in daily life seemed to be much easier to loosen here. Maybe it was the mountain air. Or maybe it was the knock on her head when she fell. Or maybe it was this lovely group of people.

Whatever it was, she appreciated the fresh air and the fresh perspective. Even if this was just a brief time out for her, it was exactly what she needed. She didn't feel lost in the tangle. She didn't feel like she was drowning in anxiety.

As for meditation, it wasn't alien to her. A counselor at the elementary school gave a presentation on how to calm students with breathing practice. Heather meditated at the end of her yoga practice. The church her mom had attended had a meditation prayer group. And she knew lots of people who used one of the various meditation apps.

But she couldn't honestly say that she had meditated before. She sometimes just sat and closed her eyes. Or took a tub and released all thoughts. She wasn't sure she could really call it 'meditation', at least not in the sense of what she assumed meditation was - going off into some blissful state. Was she doing it right? Who knew? And really, who cared? She was here and she was glad to be here. She settled in and just sat.

She felt Trusty by her side. He knew how to meditate, for sure. Although she imagined he was just sleeping, and there were telltale signs that he was dreaming, probably chasing something…a rabbit?

Thinking of a rabbit, she found her thoughts chasing the white rabbit from *Alice in Wonderland.* Was this experience all that different? Curiouser and curiouser.

*   *   *

After a while, the bell rang, and she opened her eyes, feeling refreshed. She didn't think she'd fallen asleep, but… *Oh dear, what if I snored?*

The aroma of cinnamon herbal tea wafted through the night air.

Vicente looked around at everyone, smiling.

"To start our investigation of the Buddha's Noble Eightfold Path, Lily's going to give us an overview so we're all clear on what we're doing here. Lily?"

Lily thanked him and smiled at them all. Eva could see how her smile nourished them. Expecting a sermon of sorts, Eva felt a creeping dread. But she was in for a surprise.

"The Eightfold Path is the Buddha's prescription to end the suffering he recognized in himself and the world. The *Dukkha* that we cause ourselves.

"I confess, I love that word 'Dukkha', don't you? It really nails it. 'Doo-doo, kah-kah'. There's no English word that could capture it so well. Think about it. When we complain, we may say, 'I feel shitty.'"

Eva was surprised at the language Lily was using but could hardly believe her ears when she burst into a playful rendition of Maria's song from Westside Story, replacing the word 'pretty' with 'shitty'. "I feel shitty, oh so shitty…"

This couldn't be happening, could it? It seemed so irreverent, so inappropriate, so…

But everyone else laughed, relaxing a bit into the evening. And then, as a teacher, Eva saw how Lily had created a soft entry, an engaging container for the evening's exploration. Of course, Eva couldn't use such language in her elementary school classroom. But she could start a challenging topic with something lighthearted to allay students' fears about learning.

She also realized how the use of potty language to remember a foreign word made it memorable, and, apparently, accurate. Eva wasn't likely to forget the nature of Dukkha anytime soon!

As the laughter subsided, Lily continued, "The literal translation of Dukkha is an ill-fitting axle hole."

"Ill-fitting axle hole," she repeated. "Just imagine how that would feel. Living your life riding around in a wooden cart, and there's this one wobbly wheel that goes 'kerplunk, kerplunk'. Maybe you complain about it. Maybe after a while, you stop paying attention to it. However, it remains just beneath the surface of your awareness, the backdrop of your entire life. This annoyance. This sense of life not being perfect. Not what you would choose. But it feels like you have no choice!"

"This Dukkha, which is often a subtle underlying suffering, is what the Buddha recognized and what he set about to cure. I won't retell the story most of you know so well about how he went about to do this, and if you don't know it, you can easily find out, but what was the prescription he came up with for dealing with dukkha?"

Here she looked around the circle, and everyone but Eva chimed in, "The Noble Eightfold Path!"

"Exactly. It's a vital guide to living and provides a perfect foundation for exploring all the Buddha's teachings. However, to use it and benefit from it, we must remember it. Otherwise, it's just one more of the Buddha's many lists! That man did love his lists!"

Everyone nodded and laughed. Clearly, they all respected the Buddha and were grateful to him for his insights and teachings. But they didn't seem to worship him like a god. That was a relief for Eva. She wasn't particularly religious. She thought of herself as open to possibilities, but, lacking any proof, she'd just wait and see. She didn't want to be persuaded to believe in any deity. But she knew enough about the historical Buddha, who lived 2,600 years ago, to know that he was of high birth in his Indian community yet still suffered. So he searched and ultimately found what he was looking for. Now she wanted to learn more.

Lily went on. "Lists, lists, and more lists! Each one is so valuable, but how do we remember all these lists? We must experience them. They must bloom within us! We need to have our own aha moments. Of course, we'll each have our favorites, the ones that we see more clearly, the ones that resonate. But the Eightfold Path is not just another list. It is the container through which we can understand all the other lists we explore.

"So it's always felt to me to be the central list, this prescription that addresses the dukkha we all experience.

"Sitting here earlier this evening, it came to me that we have a handy metaphor we can use to explore the Eightfold Path. Feel free to use it or not, but the more I think about it, the more helpful it seems."

She looked around, and everyone seemed intrigued.

"The beauty is we don't even have to use our imaginations! We can just look at the center of our circle."

Now, everyone looked puzzled. Lily laughed.

"The pot!" she said, as if that would make it clear. But everyone looked more puzzled.

"Okay, let's explore and see if this makes as much sense to you as it did to me earlier. Let's call it the Cooking Pot Analogy. When Minna was stirring our delicious evening soup, I noticed how the pot, the fire, the spoon, and the plumes of steam rising all work in relation to each other. The aspects of the Eightfold Path do as well.

"First, let's look at the pot. We'll call it Wise View because it is the container for consciousness, where we can cultivate wisdom.

"The spoon handle is Mindfulness, stirring steadily. There's a quality of spacious awareness to the dedicated stirring, awareness of everything.

"The part of the spoon that is submerged is Concentration, the single pointedness that touches the pot of Wise View, and stirs up insights, wisdom, and awakening.

"But nothing gets cooked up in the pot of Wise View if there's no fire, right? The initial flame of the match is Wise Intention. And the well-laid logs and kindling represent Wise Effort.

"Now, as you know, traditionally, Wise Speech, Wise Action, and Wise Livelihood are taught after Wise Intention. However, as I understand it, the Buddha was teaching mostly young men who lived as monks in community, and I imagine, as such, they needed a great deal of moral guidance. But our parents taught us right from wrong, and whether we behaved well when we were young or not, we wouldn't be on this retreat now, as adults, if we were inclined to go out and rob banks or kill anyone.

"If anything, many of us are dealing with inner voices, inner critics, judging us, and even beating us up about what we should or shouldn't do. We've internalized society's explanation of right and wrong, all tangled up with shame and punishment. Perhaps during your meditation and contemplation, you've started to notice those voices. Maybe you've noticed that they want you to do the 'right' things for all the wrong reasons. And without Wise Intention and Wise View, our efforts to appease them in our words and actions come out all wrong. We can have compassion for these inner critics, recognizing how deeply submerged they are in greed, aversion, and delusion. But when we let them guide us, we lose our way and get into trouble.

"So we're cultivating awareness, and we're recognizing the ill-conceived ideas that crop up, just as young Siddhartha, after six years of grueling practice, sat under that Bodhi tree and began to recognize Mara, the seducer. And instead of going into battle with Mara, he met each temptation with clear recognition. Whether the images were demons to scare him or dancing girls to seduce him, he knew they were illusions to distract him from his purpose of awakening. Out of the depths of his wisdom and compassion, at each encounter, he would say, 'Ah, Mara, I know you.' And the images would disappear.

"Now imagine that this awareness that we're cultivating is what we're cooking in the pot of Wise View. Consciousness gains clarity through the stirring of Mindfulness and Concentration; and through the steady heat of Wise Effort, which is sparked by the flame of Wise Intention.

"But what about Wise Speech, Action, and Livelihood? The *Sila*.

Where do our words and actions come from? They rise, like the steam from the cooking pot, directly from the other aspects -- our view, our level of awareness, our effort, and our intention. If they are wise, the steam will have a delightful aroma that will be wholesome and beneficial. If they are unskillful, that steam will be a foul stench, wafting out and polluting the air with misery.

"And that's it. That's all the aspects of the Eightfold Path! Voila!"

Everyone stared at the center of the circle, at the Eightfold Path metaphor dancing before them. Eva thought it was an impressive 3-D visual presentation.

"Thank you, Lily," Vicente said, clearly meaning it. "I can just envision it all. And I can see how it would really help not only to remember the aspects but to see how they work together. Because although it's called the Eightfold *Path*, it's not linear, is it? A circle or a wheel is usually used to represent it, but this makes it even more memorable and understandable. And given this metaphor, we might consider rearranging the order in which we explore them, putting Wise Speech, Wise Action, and Wise Livelihood at the end of the retreat."

"I'm for that!" said Sara. Allie agreed happily. *Why did they care?* Eva wondered.

"That's not right," said Connor. "I know Sara and Allie would rather have their presentations last, but that's not the right order." *Ah, yes*, Eva remembered, each of them would be presenting one of the aspects of this Eightfold Path. Well, it didn't make any difference to her one way or another, as she probably wouldn't be here.

Vicente said, "Let's not worry about that right now. It was just a thought." He looked at Connor and the young man seemed somewhat mollified. Vicente looked around the circle and said, "But right now we'll do our traditional opening of the retreat by taking vows to follow the Five Precepts." Then he looked at Eva and said, "As we do so, Eva, you can listen and decide if they are right for you. Connor, would you like to lead us?"

Connor nodded, pulled himself up straight, took a breath, and asked everyone to close their eyes. Then, in a slightly more formal voice, he said:

"We vow not to harm any living thing.
"We vow to refrain from taking what is not freely given.
"We vow to refrain from misusing sexuality.
"We vow to refrain from false and harmful speech.

"We vow to refrain from consuming intoxicants that lead to mindlessness."

Then Vicente rang the bell beside him. And they all bowed.

All the precepts felt reasonable to Eva, certainly something she could agree to in her short time here, so she bowed too.

"Thanks, Connor. And, Eva, I hope these all feel basic and reasonable."

Eva nodded. "Yes, but I thought the Eightfold Path would be like the Ten Commandments. But it sounds like the Precepts are more like that."

Vicente replied, "The Eightfold Path is a companion to living in a way that is wholesome and wise. The aspects are reminders of where we can easily stray from the Eightfold Path and end up with a great deal of pain and regret. No external deity will punish us. Experience itself causes suffering, both to ourselves and all beings directly or indirectly. We cultivate ways to refrain from unskillfulness and methods to self-correct without causing further harm. We will no doubt look at the Precepts more closely when we study Wise Action.

"To summarize our purpose on this retreat: The Noble Eightfold Path is the Buddha's prescription for the end of suffering. The Path consists of Right View, Right Intention, Right Speech, Right Action, Right Livelihood, Right Effort, Right Mindfulness, and Right Concentration.

"So that is what we will be exploring and practicing on this retreat. We agreed to use the translation of 'wise' rather than 'right' for this retreat. We'll walk the Eightfold Path together. May it be of benefit to all beings.

"Now, we're going to do a walking meditation. Then, we'll come back for our sitting practice, and we can end the evening with stargazing in the meadow, if you'd like."

Walking meditation? Eva hadn't heard of that. How was it different from just walking?

Everyone was getting up and heading in the direction of the tents, but then turning to the right, to a small meadow that was remarkably level for being up in the hills. They all lined up, giving each other space, and they stood there, eyes closed.

What was going on? Eva wondered. It seemed a little creepy, so she snuck away. Trusty was okay with that. She went up to the fancy tent and into her little anteroom. Ah. She would lie down for just a little bit.

When the bell rang, it startled her. She hadn't planned to fall asleep. She felt rested and returned to the circle, where, feeling a little guilty that she'd not done the walking meditation, she made a concerted effort to do the sitting meditation with sincerity.

She closed her eyes, ready for silence, but then heard the welcome voice of Lily, gently guiding the meditation.

"Relax into the felt sense of being alive in this body…. with each breath, releasing any tightness, any tension, any withholding from this moment, just as it is."

Eva followed along with the instructions gratefully. Indeed, each exhalation was a release, taking with it the pent-up emotions she hadn't realized she was still carrying around. Like a burden. Afraid to let go. But now, with this invitation, simply opening, blooming, like a flower in the sun.

Thoughts rose and fell away like clouds drifting across a clear blue sky. Eva wasn't entangled in them or blinded by them. Just aware that they were there, floating through. Just random threads of thought. And because she recognized it was just thinking, she could choose to shift her attention to her breath instead. She didn't have to chase down every thought to its conclusion. There was no conclusion. Just a pattern of random thoughts drifting through. Whatever thoughts arose had more space around them, and she could see them as just thoughts and emotions dancing in the air in patterns that were timeless and ephemeral.

She was surprised when the bell rang forty minutes later. She found herself pressing her hands together in gratitude, listening to the resonating sound of the bell as it rang out into the night air.

When she opened her eyes, she could see that everyone else seemed more peaceful and centered. This moment felt like the true beginning of the retreat. The entry point into a spacious, almost timeless, experience. Beyond the beyond.

Lily said, "Sweet dreams for those of you who are ready for bed. If you prefer to stay up a bit, Vicente and Connor will lead some chanting. Alternatively, you can bring a mat or blanket and lie out in the meadow to gaze at the stars. It's a clear night!"

Eva stood and stretched. Since she'd had a little nap earlier, she was looking forward to stargazing. She noticed a small pile of yoga mats leaning against a tree, and several people were taking them and heading for the wider meadow across the hiking trail where they had entered earlier in the day. She followed suit, and Trusty was happy to tag along.

On her back, with the yoga mat under her and her blanket on top, and Trusty cozy up against her, she felt so fortunate, so free. As she gazed at the sky, she breathed in the fresh, cool night air.

She loved stargazing. Her mother was always pointing out planets and constellations. Eva loved looking. She enjoyed being able to distinguish the planets, but not so much the name of constellations. She couldn't get past the fact that the stars might resemble familiar animals or objects from Earth; however, the stars themselves were not actually in those formations. From outer space, those designs would disappear. It was just the human brain imprinting something familiar on points of light.

When she was little, sometimes she would make up other formations: "Look, Mommy, there's a giraffe!" But while her mother thought that the creative game was fine for fluffy clouds, with stars, she explained, it was different.

But even now, Eva couldn't see the difference. The stars and planets were amazing, just as they were. She didn't need to claim them. But then, feeling like a traitor to something her mother cared about, she found the Big Dipper and made a wish upon the North Star to send her spirit love and ease. Tears filled Eva's eyes. She muffled her sobs in her hands. Trusty leaned in closer.

"I'm okay, T. I really am. Don't worry."

Then she heard chanting in the distance, back in the camp as the fire burned out. Those earnest voices singing a foreign language could have sounded strange or even scary.

Namo tassa Bhagavato Arahato Sammāsambuddhassa.

But they comforted her. She didn't want to join them. At least not right now. But she appreciated knowing they were there.

With renewed enthusiasm, she stared into the moonless night sky. Soon she had that feeling she often had in childhood, of looking down into vast space, held to the earth by gravity so she wouldn't fall off. She giggled with delight.

After a while, a chill made her rise, roll up the mat, and make her way to the tent. She and Trusty crept through the dark main room where Lily was already asleep, softly snoring, and into their cozy quarters. Eva climbed under the covers, petted Trusty, settled on a folded blanket on the floor beside the bed, and fell immediately to sleep.

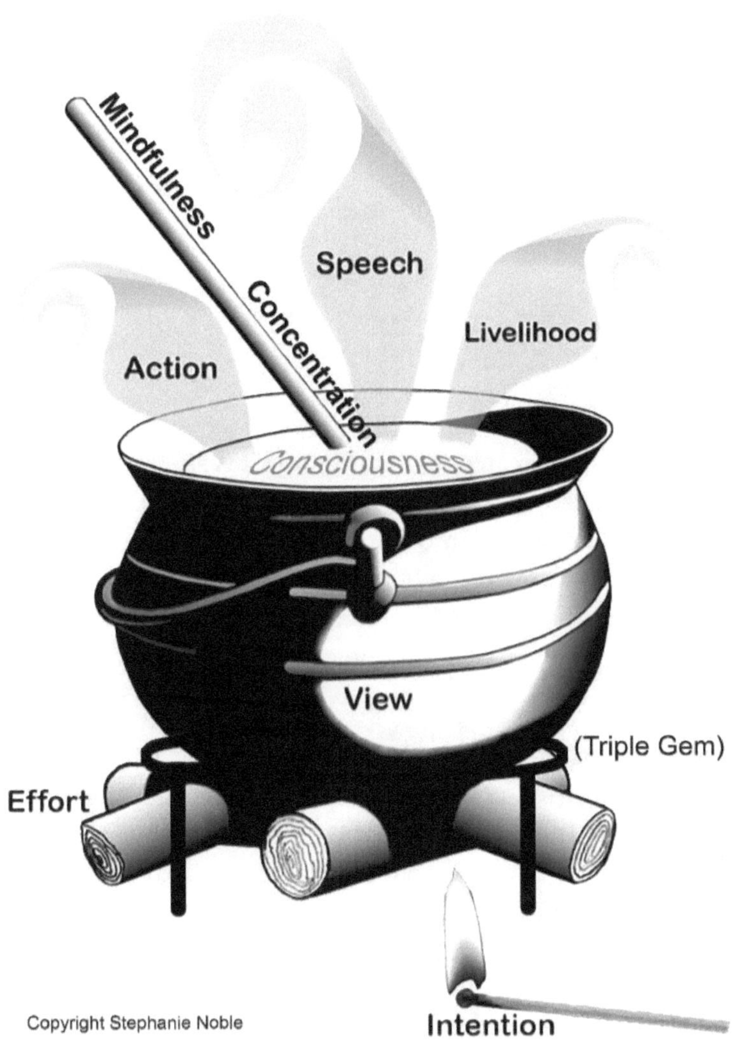

Mindfulness
Concentration
Speech
Livelihood
Action
Consciousness
View
(Triple Gem)
Effort
Intention

7 Wise View

Eva woke early, feeling well-rested. When she and Trusty left the tent, she saw that Lily was already gone. She realized she had no clue where the bathroom was. She imagined an outhouse up the hill with a quarter moon cut in the wooden door. But when she looked around the camp, now she could see behind a couple of trees one of those very large, very fancy porta-potties exactly like the one at her friend Emily's wedding.

Wow! How had she missed that? And how in the world had it gotten here? Had they had it airlifted in? As she stepped inside, she saw that it was spacious and clean but had no mirrors. The shower had a little dressing area with a bench, and she went in, closed the curtain, stripped down, and took a quick shower, using the soap, shampoo, and conditioner provided. She felt clean and refreshed. Her clothes from the day before were fine, and she was grateful that she always kept an extra pair of briefs in a little bag in her daypack for emergencies, as her mother had taught her when she got her first period. She washed out the pair she had been wearing, wrapped them in a towel, and took them back to the tent to hang dry.

Trusty was waiting for her when she came out of the tent but walked quickly ahead to the kitchen area. It was bustling with activity, but the counter, with an assortment of teas and hot water, was to the left of the entrance, near the picnic tables, well out of the way of the kitchen crew who bustled around the counter-height tables.

Off to the right of the entry, she noticed a pair of bowls on the ground, one filled with water and one with kibble. How thoughtful! Trusty zeroed in on them with gusto.

Cup in hand, Eva wandered to the edge of the camp and looked out over the dew-sparkling meadow. The sun had just come over the eastern hill of this valley that, strangely, she didn't recognize. How far had she wandered? When she was young, she thought she knew every inch of these hills, but apparently not.

Interesting. Every moment of this little overnight getaway was an unexpected treat.

She didn't need to leave right away, though. Maybe after breakfast? Or maybe after the morning gathering? No one was expecting her at home until much later.

*　　*　　*

When Connor rang the kitchen bell, she returned and lined up at the ample buffet, which included oatmeal, warm muffins, apples from local orchards, Fuyu persimmons, and nuts. Yum! She hadn't felt hungry, but suddenly she was ravenous. *Pace yourself. Pace yourself.* Her mother's voice, repeating a phrase she'd heard often.

Sitting at one of the two picnic tables, she thought about her conversation with Minna the night before. Now they were all in silence. Not awkward silences that need to be filled, but a purposeful silence that was a presence itself. An enveloping blanket of ease. No expectations. Ah. She sat with her food, the thoughtful plate she had composed of the lovely offerings. A piece of art. An almost frameable still life. Except that she planned to eat it. And she did. Bite by conscious bite.

Afterwards, she had another cup of tea. She watched as others rose and returned their dishes, scraping the remains into a compost bin, and submerging the plates, cups, and silverware into a wash basin. Then she did the same.

She wanted to help, but it looked like everything was under control. So, she went back to the bathroom and brushed her teeth with the travel toothbrush she always carried. Not quite her electric toothbrush, but it would do. Then she ran her fingers through her long brown hair and pulled it back in a ponytail. There was no mirror to confirm or deny how she was looking. It didn't matter. Did anyone care? Was anyone judging? Did she care if they were? She would never see them again after today.

When she returned, she noticed that those who had no chores were already seated in the circle, meditating. So she did the same. The simple sitting felt very different from the night before, less magical but still pleasant. Soon, the bell rang, and she opened her eyes to see Vicente setting down the ringer. Then he looked up and smiled at them all.

"Good morning, everyone. I hope you had a good night's rest."

They all nodded, including Eva.

"This morning, we will be exploring the first aspect of Buddha's Noble Eightfold Path: Wise View. If you all liked Lily's Cooking Pot Analogy…" He looked around and, seeing that everyone was nodding and smiling, said, "Then Wise View is still a good place to start. You can't cook much without a pot!"

They laughed, delighted. So true!

"When I woke up this morning, I remembered back—WAY back— when my college roommate and I had our first apartment. We had no idea what we were doing, and very little money to outfit the place. We gave barely any thought to the kitchen, assuming we'd just survive on ramen and taco stands. A banged-up saucepan tossed in with a box of other kitchen stuff at a garage sale seemed fine to us. We didn't care that it was made of thin metal, and we figured it wouldn't make much of a difference. But we found that that pan was worse than worthless. Everything we cooked burned and stuck to it and was impossible to clean. We tossed it. Lesson learned."

"So the aspect of Wise View, our cooking pot, is the container of our practice. Without it, our attention spills out in all directions, flooding every thought and emotion, even a tsunami of speculation, rumination, resentment, calculation, or retribution. Without Wise View, we may see enemies everywhere and react accordingly."

Well, that painted quite a picture, thought Eva. Was all her recent thoughtless behavior simply due to misperception? Was she just looking at things all wrong?

Vicente asked them, "What assumptions do we make about our view? Our view of life, of the world, and of ourselves? Are we like bumbling first-time apartment dwellers who think any old pot will do? Any old view will do? Isn't a pot just a pot? Isn't the world just the way it is? Aren't I just the way I am? Aren't my views valid? And aren't my views an important part of who I am? What makes me '*me*'?

"Probably most people feel that way. And, even if they have a feeling maybe there's more to it than that, they may be afraid to find out anything different.

"But some people sense there's another way of seeing. Maybe they've had glimpses, moments of freedom from the suffering of such limiting view. And they start looking about, seeking, exploring, and perhaps they discover the *Dharma*, the teachings. So let's give the Buddha a chance to make a case for examining our heretofore cherished view more closely.

"Here we are in the hills. Yesterday we came up from the valley. Later today, perhaps you'll have the experience of standing on a high peak. So many different vantage points. So many different views. Now, let me ask you this: is any of them the 'right' view? More correct than all the others?"

Several people shook their heads thoughtfully.

"No, of course not. Each one offered a different vista. A different perspective on things. A different understanding of what makes up this beautiful area, where we are so fortunate to spend a few days.

"We can learn from all the views, all the experiences, and all the senses. And we learn different things from each of them. We who walk the Buddha's Noble Eightfold Path are coming in touch with a way of seeing that promotes well-being, peace, and harmony. A Wise View that will keep us from causing suffering to ourselves and others.

"That doesn't mean that we judge others who hold different views. As we cultivate wisdom, we can see how people come to hold their views, what life experiences might have caused them to adopt a view that may be very limiting and painful, both to themselves and those around them. We can also see others who have more expansive views but use different language, symbols, and mythology to define it, and have various ways of exploring it. As a university professor of religion and philosophy, I've spent my life learning and examining these closely.

"When we meditate we practice softening the tight hold we have on all our opinions and judgments of ourselves and whoever is causing some distracting or discomfort in our experience. We begin to see the arising and falling away of thoughts and moods rooted in greed, hatred, and delusion. These do not define us. They are not who we are. They are visitors. They come and go. Our practice in meditation is to notice them coming and going.

"In moments where we are on the mountain peak, we feel we can see forever and understand so much. But to find a way to plant seeds that will nurture our growth and benefit all beings, we go to the rich soil of the valley floor. So Wise View is neither just at the top of a mountain peak nor in a deep valley. It's all-pervading. Wherever we are, we cultivate a way of being present with all that's arising."

He paused and looked around at them all. Eva was fascinated by what he was sharing. She loved that he acknowledged the value of the valley where the rich soil nourished seeds and growth. She was proud of her small agricultural valley and all it could produce, proud that it wasn't a monoculture crop, but a community of independent farms, mostly organic.

Vicente continued, "Just so, we cultivate Wise View, which holds room for spacious awareness and in-depth concentration, both of which season the pot of Wise View."

He looked over at Lily, and she glowed with the recognition that he had taken her analogy and enriched it with his own exploration.

"Our meditation practice, our vows to honor the Five Precepts, our exploration of the Buddha's teachings, and our steady willingness to follow the Eightfold Path, all support us in cultivating Wise View.

"We typically hold a variety of opinions about a variety of things, don't we? Wise View is about skillfully *holding* all that arises. We all have experiences of clinging, chasing, clutching, longing, and battling whatever occurs in our experience, at every turn, reacting with despair or anger when something in life doesn't meet our expectations, hopes, or demands.

Eva recognized so much of her own experience in what he was sharing. It was like he had read her journal! Of course, he hadn't. So this was just normal? This was just the way it was? Well, that sucked. But then what was the answer?

As if on cue, Vicente said, "So how might we hold our experience more skillfully? Well, what if we held it lightly? What if we hold it with loving kindness? What if we really pay attention to what happens when we cling to it? And what happens when we don't? Seeing the difference for ourselves is vital. Recognizing that these experiences and these responses don't define us. We allow ourselves to remain open, to be available to feel awe-struck, and maybe, just maybe, filled with delight.

"Now, most of us have been meeting together for a long time, so none of this is completely unfamiliar to you."

"But still a bit of a mystery," someone murmured, and others laughed.

"Yes, a mystery worthy of our attention," Vicente agreed. "But the Buddha offered guidance that has been passed down through generations and written in the Pali Canon. And when it comes to Wise View, he provides three important clues. Does anyone care to speculate on what they might be?"

"*Anicca, Anatta,* and *Dukkha,*" Connor called out.

"Ah, our scholar speaks. Exactly. Thank you, Connor. Lily discussed *Dukkha* last night. In a more, uh, colorful way than I might have, though my college students would have loved it. I'm afraid I couldn't pull it off."

Everyone laughed, remembering Lily's doo-doo, kah-kah description, then, imagining this elegant elderly man describing anything that way. As a teacher, Eva knew full well that connecting with students required being authentic, letting yourself be known, and being where they expect to find you. Vicente's students would likely feel distracted rather than delighted by his explaining anything in that way.

She briefly thought about her own students. Was she bringing her authentic self to her teaching? Was she connecting with them? Not lately, she hated to admit.

"So," he continued, "since everyone now understands *Dukkha* perfectly..."

Laughter.

"...now we will look at *Anicca.*

"This is actually a wonderful time of year to look at our assumptions that make up some of our views about life and the way things are. The autumn air is crisp, such a contrast to the recent summer's sweltering heat. Leaves are changing their colors and falling to the ground, leaving the branches bare so that the trees can survive the winter cold.

"We know this is the way of things, don't we? It doesn't surprise us. Just so, impermanence is an intrinsic aspect of life. It makes it all possible. In Pali, the word for this universal impermanence is *Anicca.* Ah-knee-cha.

"Last week, I attended a memorial service for the child of a friend. It was, of course, extremely sad, and later that day, back home, I couldn't help falling into a funk, questioning the fairness of why that young life, so full of joy and promise, died much too soon. I found myself staring out a sliding glass door at raindrops dripping down the glass, matching the tears in my eyes. Some of the raindrops were stationary, while others slid down the glass at a very slow pace, some more rapidly, but all at a steady rate. And then, as if out of nowhere, one darted down to the bottom of the window.

"It was like a gift, that insight. Just that single racing drop reminded me that there is no set time for any of us. We can rail against death and call it unfair, but no promises were made about the length of any life."

He looked around at them, checking to see if this had registered. He had such a look of compassion when he came to the younger ones, as if seeing that these potentially painful personal discoveries of impermanence were still ahead of them. And when his eyes came to Eva, it was like he could see the pain she was in. The impermanence she was railing against.

"Railing against impermanence makes life much more difficult when we cling to the past or wish away a challenging present in the rush toward a possibly more promising future. Noting and accepting impermanence can lead to appreciating it, finding the wonder of this moment just as it is. Over and over again. It also allows us to accept that whatever future we might be looking forward to will not be solid, but, of course, impermanent. There is no absolute goal of perfect conditions. 'If only…' or 'After I get this…' or 'Once I've done that…' are just ways to put off being fully present and allowing this moment to be known and perhaps appreciated. Our practice helps us to learn to accept this moment on its own terms. This moment is temporal. Fleeting. We can't catch it, stop it, frame it, or cast it in bronze for future reference. We can only live with as much awareness and wisdom as we can muster.

"So, where in your life might you be wrestling with the nature of impermanence? And then how is it keeping you from living this moment?"

He gave them a minute to consider that question. Eva thought of two areas she could look at where she was wrestling with impermanence: Obviously, the loss of her mother and the loss of her ability to give birth. But she didn't want to think about them, dwell on them. She wanted to be here now. Wasn't that the point?

Vicente added, "No need to go into details and try to solve anything. Take a moment to cultivate some compassion for yourself and your possible reluctance to acknowledge the amazing cyclical nature of life. If nothing changed, there would be no cause for awe and wonder.

"And without impermanence and the cycles of nature, we would all starve. It's all so obvious, and yet we often choose to pretend it doesn't apply to our challenges. And that causes us suffering."

As Vicente paused, took a sip of his water, and looked over his notes, Eva felt tension in her body around the topic of impermanence. Why did he have to go and bring this up? She had been feeling good but now felt worse off in a way. This wasn't helping. It was time to leave.

But obviously, she couldn't get up and leave in the middle of this session. So she did the next best thing. She took a conscious breath. She released, as best she could, the tension. She petted Trusty, leaned down, and kissed him on the nose.

The thoughts kept flowing as if Vicente had turned on a faucet and she didn't have access to the handle. Of course, she knew that everything changes, but she didn't have to like it! She felt it was a significant flaw in the whole system. Why did her mother have to die? Why were errant gray hairs showing up on her head? Why were advertisers telling her she could be young forever? She looked at Lily with her silky white hair and her face aglow. Her age was part of her beauty.

She imagined Lily had lost her parents and maybe other family members and friends. She had no doubt experienced heartache, perhaps illness — who knew? Yet there she was, just living, greeting each moment with kind attention. *Was she delusional? Or was she insightful?* Eva wondered.

Then she thought of the scene in the movie *When Harry Met Sally* when the woman at a nearby table said, "I'll have what she's having."

Yes. I'll have whatever Lily's having. And somehow that thought calmed her, like she'd been struggling to find her foothold. Now she saw a footprint on a path that led the way.

Vicente was speaking. "Now, I'd like to open the conversation up for you to share your own experience with impermanence. Please turn to the person next to you and take a few minutes each to share what comes up for you. Where do you feel resistance to the nature of impermanence? Where do you struggle? And/or how have you come to terms with it?

And please remember, this is not a conversation. The listener just listens without commentary."

Everyone began shifting in their seats, and since Eddie turned toward Vicente, Eva turned the other way, toward Minna. They smiled at each other. It would be so easy to just return to the conversational nature of their talk the night before, but she wasn't sure how to approach this more formal conversation. She would be happy to let Minna go first. But just then, Vicente added, "The person whose name comes first in the alphabet can go first."

"Oh dear," Eva said. She gulped and looked down. "Um, well, I have to say I'm not a big fan of impermanence." She didn't want to talk about it. What would she say? That she just lost her mother a few months ago? She didn't want to go there. No.

She pet Trusty to build her confidence but then realized he was a part of her dislike of impermanence. So she said, "I know a dog's lifespan, especially a large dog's lifespan, isn't usually much more than a decade or so. I celebrate each of Trusty's birthdays, making a big deal of it. I make him special cake-shaped birthday treats, and last year, I invited other friends with dogs to a party. Great fun."

Now she realized that she had put off planning this year's party because of Chad. But the biggest gift she could give Trusty was to ensure that he would not have to suffer one more day of seeing him. Life was short, and a dog's life was even shorter, making every day much more precious.

"Anyway, every year I put a bigger number of candles on the birthday cake, and it makes me so sad. I love him so much." She put her face down and cried into his fur.

When she didn't say anything else, Minna put her hands together and bowed. And that felt right. It was different from someone rushing to comfort her, saying how everything would be all right, or to look on the bright side.

The bell rang to signal it was time to switch. Minna paused and then said, "I'm not a fan of impermanence either. My work as a nurse is to fight against it. I appreciate that in my ward, I rarely deal with it. It's a recovery ward, a way station on the way home after surgery. The patients are generally healthy when they go into surgery, and in almost all cases, are alive and well when they come out. But then there was COVID. All elective surgery was postponed, and we were all hands on deck. Suddenly, our quiet ward was full of people struggling against death, and we were helpless to save them.

"That was a horrific battle with impermanence. And Vicente can be all poetic about it, and gain insight from raindrops, but I…well, I'm not there yet."

She paused. She looked like she was deliberating over something. "I've been very fortunate that most of our family is still intact, our parents and friends…but…" Then she leaned in and whispered to Eva, "Connor doesn't remember this, but he had an older sister. He was so young when she…and he wouldn't have understood. But it's a secret that tears me apart. And I can't help but rail against impermanence. Some small children died on my watch during COVID, and it kept reminding me. Not that I would ever forget."

Eva drew a breath in shock. This was more sharing than she had bargained for. She didn't want to know a secret, carry it with her, imagine a little girl dying, which now she would probably do every time she looked at Minna or Connor. Maybe she should leave today, face her own troubles, and not take on anyone else's.

Then she remembered how her mother had carried a secret, too. What was it with mothers and their secrets? It must be part of the protective motherly instinct. She felt compassion for Minna now. She just hoped she wouldn't tell Connor on her deathbed that, as well as losing his mother, he had lost a big sister too.

The bell rang. They bowed to each other and returned to face the circle.

Vicente said, "As we share and as we listen, let's remember two things. One is that this is not a place to be guarded, nor is it a confessional. It is an exploration of a particular aspect of the Dharma. In this case, impermanence is a topic that often triggers challenging emotions for many of us. If this is true for you, please see Lily or me. We won't have answers, but we are a safe place to 'download'. In our dyad and circle sharing, we explore and investigate in a safe space. And, when listening, to simply be a witness, without comment or response. This can be challenging, of course. But that is our practice. And I think you'll find it valuable and come to understand its importance.

Eva appreciated this clarification and only wished that he'd given this little lecture before the exercise. But now that he had, she felt safer. Minna overstepped. It happens. All was forgiven.

Vicente spoke again, looking at the little clock on his table. "Let's take a little break. You can do walking meditation in the meadow behind me or find an isolated spot nearby to meditate. I know the kitchen crew needs to attend to a few things, and I don't want them to miss the talks, so we'll meet back here when they ring the bell to indicate they're done."

Eva was curious about this walking meditation, but it looked like zombie-walking to her. As she considered going over to the walking field, Lily caught her attention. When Eva approached, Lily said in a low voice, "I just wanted to check in on you. How are you doing?"

"Overall, very well, thank you!"

"Wonderful. I hope you're planning to stay with us for the whole retreat?"

The very thought of it filled Eva with a sense of ease. But wasn't there something she needed to do or someone she needed to tell?

Then she realized she should text Heather, of course. She and Chelsea would be worried about her if she didn't get home this afternoon. How could she have forgotten? And she'd have to let the school know. Oh, dear. Maybe she should just go. But no. Chelsea could contact the school easily enough. But hopefully her housemates won't worry or demand an explanation. How could she explain this?

"If you don't mind, I would love to. But I need to let my friends know I won't be home until…? Um, when does this end?"

"Friday morning. If you need to use your phone, do it in the tent. In fact, let's go there now. I have something else to talk to you about."

They made their way to the tent. Eva entered her little haven and dug out her phone from the bottom of her daypack. It still had power, so she texted Heather and Chelsea, not sure what to say, but began with *"Left Chad!!! Good riddance. No worries, but I'm on a little getaway. Out of phone range. Back Friday. Let the school know? Sorry. XOXOXO"*

Then she turned the phone off and buried it deep in her pack again, satisfied she had nothing to stop her from enjoying her retreat. She entered the central area of the tent, where Lily was thumbing through a slender, brown paperback book.

"Ah, good. Well, now that you are officially on this retreat, there are a couple of tasks that fall to you. The first is a yogi job. As you can see, everyone has one. Some are more visible than others, but we're all doing our part."

"Of course, I'm happy to. What's my yogi job?"

"All that's left is someone to keep the bathroom clean."

Eva groaned inside. She couldn't help it. Cleaning up the bathroom after a whole group of people, including guys? But she accepted as gracefully as she could.

"Okay, is there a set time I should do it?"

"Well, preferably at a time when others aren't using it, but also when you won't miss a Dharma talk or other activity. So, hmm, what I've found in the past works well is to do the cleaning after lunch. Others will have their yogi jobs cleaning up in the kitchen, and those who don't might walk or nap. So the bathroom should be relatively free."

"Okay."

"You should see the look on your face. Honestly, it's not that bad, and you might be surprised by what you learn in the process!"

Eva knew she looked skeptical, but she couldn't help it. That made Lily laugh even more. Then she quieted down and said, "Now, you might remember that Isaac, the fellow whose seat you are filling, was going to give a presentation on Wise Intention. He took it because it's a challenge for him. And, clearly, it remains a challenge. But he's not here, and so, my dear, it falls to you."

"What do you mean?"

"You don't have to give a formal Dharma talk. That would be asking too much, but we need you to just hold the seat for Wise Intention and lead the discussion."

"How could I do that? I have no idea what Wise Intention is, and I'm pretty sure I don't live up to it!"

"I have a book here with the chapter on Wise Intention marked. You could look it over and then later this afternoon…"

"This afternoon?"

"Well, yes, it's the next aspect we want to explore. Think about the analogy of the cooking pot. Intention is the spark that starts the fire!"

"But Eddie had to build the fire first."

"Good point, and, coincidentally, he's doing Wise Effort. But without Wise Intention, all the effort in the world could be destructive. So we really need Intention to be first."

Eva thought about that moment when she lit the fire. Suddenly, it all became very clear to her. She saw how that struck match representing Wise Intention could spark a campfire for warmth and to cook a meal, or it could start a forest fire.

"Okay," she said. *In for a penny, in for a pound*, her mother whispered.

"Okay?"

"Yes. I'll do it."

"Well, that's great! You're a lifesaver."

"Well, actually, you're a lifesaver. You all are. And I'm happy to play my part."

"Oh, we hardly saved your life! We helped you up, that's all."

"And welcomed me and are now helping to enlighten me!"

Lily laughed. "Okay, well, let me or Vicente know if there's anything we can do, anything you need help with."

"Oh, I will! Believe me."

She took the book, a slender brown volume, and slipped it into her daypack. Then they headed toward the walking meditation field. Trusty followed along, ready to run around in the field. But he paused when he sensed something different about this field.

Eddie was there, slowly walking. So slowly, Eva wasn't sure he wasn't just standing at first. Connor arrived and was about to begin, but seeing her standing there, he asked her if she needed any guidance. She nodded. They walked further away from Eddie so Connor could give instructions without disturbing him. Trusty settled down at the edge of the field to watch. Somehow Eva sensed he wouldn't suddenly chase after a critter if he saw one. Such a wise considerate sweetheart.

Connor began his instruction. "Okay, now what we're doing is creating a set space for our movement. In a group, it would be chaos if we were walking in all directions, crossing paths with each other. So first we assess the space, see what others are doing, and if no one's started, just see what would be the most natural division that wouldn't be disruptive to any flow of traffic."

Good grief, Eva thought. *This was quite the maneuver.*

As if reading her mind, Connor said, "I know this seems complex, but once you have your 'lane', then you can let go of anything else and just be present, walking as slowly as you need to go to be fully present with all the sensations of moving: The foot touching the ground, the muscles in the leg, how all the muscles are interconnected and affected by each movement. The eyes can be downcast or raised, but the focus is on the simple movement. The endpoint is not a destination. Just a turning point for the continuation of walking meditation."

"To what end? I mean, what am I trying to accomplish here? How will I know when I'm done?"

Connor just laughed. "No end. No accomplishment. Never done."

Hmm. Okay, well, that sort of made sense in a way, Eva thought. And after Connor stood aside and made a gesture for her to begin, she found she was willing, even eager now, to give it a go.

"How slow should I go?"

"As slow as you need to go to be fully present with the experience. If you go only two steps or twenty or forty, it doesn't matter. You're not trying to get anywhere. Just be sure you stay in your lane and ignore whatever others are doing. They are walking at their own pace."

Pace yourself, her mother would say. But now she understood it to mean slow down, be conscious. That's what her mother meant all along. And, though it took a bit to get started, she was able to settle in and pay attention to the most subtle sensations of her foot pressing the ground, then lifting off, the shift of her body, and the simple sense of being alive.

The process was restful and enlivening at the same time.

"Okay, I think I have it, thank you, Connor."

He bowed and moved to a 'lane' equidistant between Eddie and Eva.

She centered in, took a few breaths, and brought her attention to her left foot, lifting it ever so slowly. She moved very slowly across the small field, then turned around and retraced her steps. She decided that to experience it fully, she would take off her shoes and socks. When she stood again and began to walk, her feet and toes had a celebratory reunion with the earth, the sensations of the cool green blades, and occasionally crunchy, dry leaves, keeping her attention fully present.

*   *   *

Sooner than Eva expected, the bell rang. She pulled on her socks and shoes and returned to the circle. Trusty settled by her side. She hugged him and whispered, "We're in this together, T. Hope you're okay with it!" He seemed more than okay with the idea. And they settled in.

Vicente continued his talk.

"So we took a little glimpse into Anicca, impermanence. Now we're going to look at its companion: *Anatta*. While understanding the nature of impermanence allows us to release our clinging to this moment or yearning for another, understanding Anatta helps us to release the fear and sense of isolation that causes us so much suffering. It basically means no separate self. But that's too simplistic and creates confusion.

"When the Buddha taught this, he didn't have the benefit of modern science to back up his teachings. But we do. And even though it may be challenging for some of us to understand, the science is basic and clear. And I've asked Connor to speak from a scientist's perspective. Connor?"

"Okay. I won't go into any advanced theories. I'll keep it super simple: All matter, whether it's solid, liquid, or gas, is made up of atoms. These atoms are composed of subatomic particles called protons, neutrons, and electrons. The central nucleus of an atom contains positively charged protons and neutral neutrons. Negatively charged electrons orbit the nucleus in an electron cloud. There's much more, and they're discovering new things all the time, but Vicente asked me to keep it simple for you, and that's as simple as it gets."

They all smiled at Connor appreciatively. Eva was familiar with what Connor shared but unclear how it applied to these Buddhist concepts.

"Thanks, Connor." Vicente looked around to see how the circle was responding to this. They looked thoughtful but also relieved to have Connor's sharing so short.

Vicente elaborated in terms they might understand. "We might imagine all the elements that make up life—earth, water, fire, and air—as the stuff from which life's building blocks, just like children's plastic building blocks, are made. And, thanks to electrons, atoms bond together into molecules, just the way the little holes and plugs of the blocks allow them to connect. And, very important, they break apart just as the blocks do when we finish with that session of play. You can see the impermanence there, as well as the interconnection.

"So I'm made up of atoms, as is the air I breathe, the solid, liquid, and gas all around me, and every life form. All atoms all the time, all interconnected, all coming together and falling apart, in an ever-changing state of being. So there are no edges to being. There is fundamentally no separate self." He smiled at them. "When I taught about Buddhism and the concept of impermanence, one of my students at the university said, 'Oh, that's just like the *Lego Movie*!'"

Everyone laughed. "It just shows we can discover the *Dharma* everywhere. It's always available. Just waiting, it seems, for us to notice.

"That said, I know this is a challenging concept for even experienced students of the *Dharma*."

Eva knew about atoms. But why had she never given a thought to the idea that she wasn't solid? At this moment, the idea made sense. And she could see how much suffering she experienced in her life, believing she was separate, isolated, and very vulnerable. She worried about how people saw her. Could she possibly go through life another way? But wouldn't that cause boundary issues? And wouldn't she just disappear?

Vicente continued. "Understanding the science of it doesn't automatically make us feel that it is true. Our habit of mind is strongly in favor of the separate-self version of being. Our culture emphasizes it for profit. Buying their products helps us compete to promote this separate self. It works great for them, but how is that working for us? "Look around! We humans are incessantly 'other making' in our personal relationships, and in how we treat the earth as a resource instead of the source of all life. We get stuck in an alienated mode of misery that doesn't serve us.

"To help us understand 'no separate self' on a deeper level, we practice quieting down and being fully present, softening our habitual need to fortify our identity as 'me' and 'I'.

"The Buddha knew this part was challenging, but he also knew that these teachings led to the end of suffering, so he persevered. He came up with a list. I know, I know. No surprise there! This list, the Five Aggregates, helps us understand the concept of 'no separate self' and, in incremental doses, cultivates a Wise View. It is traditionally taught as part of Wise Mindfulness, but Minna asked me to share it, so I will.

"We begin by asking ourselves a simple question, a child's question really, but also the question that forms the foundation of many philosophical discussions throughout the ages: Who am I?

"Pause for a moment, close your eyes, and ask it again, as if for the first time. 'Who am I?' You might repeat it like a mantra that goes deeper and deeper with each repetition.

"Where is this solid, dependable sense of self that you call 'I' and 'me'?

"The first thing that might suggest itself is this physical body, this material form. This is who I am, or at least part of who I am.

"But is this true? Let's explore: What are the edges of this body? Is it the skin that is so porous, allowing moisture to enter and exit throughout the day? That very skin sheds itself constantly. Is it still 'me' when it's dust on the floor?

"What about the breath? Is it 'me' when it is in my lungs, but then no longer 'me' when it has been exhaled? Where exactly does air become breath, and breath become air?

"Most of the cells in the body are regenerating and replicating over time. Very few are the same as when we were born.

"So, this seemingly permanent body is neither solid nor separate from the rest of life.

"The Buddha said, 'This body is not mine or anyone else's. It has arisen from past causes and conditions.'

"Clearly, this body we see as separate and an essential part of our identity is an intrinsic part of the pattern of life, ever-changing and evolving. Getting caught up in labeling and claiming it, feeling pride or shame in it, is just another habituated pattern that entangles us.

"How liberating it is to recognize that this body—whatever its shape or shade—is simply the fleeting expression of life temporarily taking human form. Can we appreciate the benefits of being embodied—mobility, sensations, etc. without attachment? Can we take good care of this wondrous temporal vessel of being without wishing it to be other than it is?"

Eva felt overwhelmed, but then she heard her mother's voice: *Here today, gone tomorrow.*

"But if we think that life is all just atoms and energy coming together and coming apart, we miss the beauty of the intrinsic interconnection of all life, the unique patterns, expressions, and interactions, the stories, dances, and songs of all species, and the interweaving of all life. So we look for balance. Life is neither all science, defining and dissecting, nor all art, connecting and celebrating; it is a beautiful amalgam of both.

"There are an estimated nine million species of plants, animals, fungi, and other organisms on Earth. Probably more. All are intrinsically interconnected and interdependent in this web of life. I love to picture it all as part of Indra's Net, all connected. And who am I? Where am I? I am. I exist. This being I call 'me' is intrinsically connected and valuable. But not exceptional! Our species is not even the smartest one. We just choose to think of the way we think and interpret information as smart. We do have a particular kind of intelligence but we clearly lack other types. We've lost our sense of connection that would guide and inform our actions more wisely."

He paused. Eva sensed he had a lot more to say on the subject but didn't want to overwhelm them.

He took a sip of water and continued. "So with our exploration of Anicca, no separate self, we are practicing how to be liberated not from life—not at all! —but from our attachment, our clinging to the solid separate-self sense of being that causes suffering in the world.

"I remember reading that Einstein considered the feeling of individual separateness as a sort of delusion that keeps us confined, creating boundaries where there are none. And his prescription to overcome this delusion is very Buddhist indeed. He believed we could only be liberated by expanding our sense of compassion to all beings, the whole universe. Which is what we do with our Metta and Karuna practice, isn't it?

"At this moment, we are humans having a human experience. That's all. What is it to be human? Is it to hate and kill and cause suffering? Or is it to be present, to cultivate kindness, compassion, joy, and generosity?

"When Lily mentioned the ill-fitting axle hole, the literal meaning of the word dukkha, there is the implication that with attention and wise effort, the cart is fixable. That we can pause and address the problem. And that's what we are doing here. Let me be clear, we are not fixing ourselves the way all the advertisers promote. We probably do too much of that already with poor results. We are fixing our *way of seeing*. We are adjusting our lens through which we look at life. We are acknowledging and releasing the delusion.

"Once we see and address the nature of our suffering, we can end our mindless habit of causing suffering to ourselves, to others, and to the planet. The Eightfold Path lights the way.

"So, you might want to spend some time throughout our retreat noticing your own experience of being embodied. After meditating, you can engage in self-inquiry about the body and your thoughts regarding it. Notice any thoughts, words, or actions during the day that reveal your perceptions. You can ask, 'Is this true?' And let the automatic answers arise and be acknowledged, leaving room for quiet wisdom with nothing to fear and nothing to prove."

He looked around at the circle of faces, and Eva did too. A delightful bouquet of a variety of body shapes, sizes, and colors, and just as she'd thought at first sight of them all encircling her after she'd fallen, together they seemed to represent the various continents of the world. Allie had Chinese features. Sara was from somewhere in Africa, her dark skin and height could indicate she was from Sudan, or?? Anyway, not a fourteenth-generation black American, like Chelsea, whose ancestors built much of this country.

Vicente was Latino, more Spanish than indigenous. Minna and Connor were likely of Irish descent. And Lily? Probably a hodgepodge of Euro ethnicities like Eva herself, but more northern than her own southern and eastern European heritage. Eddie was at least partly of indigenous American descent. A most eclectic group! Wouldn't it be fun to invite them to her classroom, bringing the 'Our Little Family' poster to life?

Seeing how far her mind had wandered, into speculating, imagining, and even planning, she reigned herself in. Their differences were fascinating, but in this conversation, very much beside the point.

Could she let go of the idea that their bodies defined them? Or that, given how they looked, they must be from someplace or act a certain way? Could she let go of the idea that her body defined her? She thought about how much time she spent bemoaning and belittling her looks. But it was just a body. Very serviceable. How liberating a thought that was. But also limiting! Because in this circle there were also other species. Trusty, of course, but also untold numbers of plants, insects, and underneath them, fungi, making life on earth possible. All life is interconnected. Not separate topics to teach, but life itself.

Vicente spoke again. "So we have the first of the Buddha's Five Aggregates: I am not my body. This body is not me. All these bones, skin, hair, organs, and systems do not define me. So consider that. Investigate it experientially. See for yourself, as the Buddha advised.

"Does anyone remember the second of the Five?"

Allie raised her hand and said, "Senses?"
"Very good," Vicente said, nodding. "The senses or 'feeling tones.' What are these?"

People called out in rapid succession:
    "Seeing!"
            "Hearing!"
                "Touching!"
                    "Smelling!"
                        "Tasting!"

"Yes, thank you, that's correct. Very tangible stuff, right? Just pause and notice each one with the sense of Consciousness."

Eva looked around, aware of all the sights. She listened to some jays in the trees. She touched Trusty's fur. She caught a whiff of some piney scent. But taste? There was no distinct flavor she could identify. But now she felt hungry.

"Okay," Vicente continued. "These are the feeling tones related to the physical senses. Are any of those feeling tones you? Or unique to you? Do you think others are seeing and hearing and touching and smelling and tasting things much differently?"

They shook their heads.

"No, we may have different tastes. I certainly must add hot sauce to make dishes more palatable, but so do many others. It's not unique to me. We also have our preferences for what we consider pleasant or discordant sounds, sights, and so on. But so do billions of other people. It certainly doesn't define us.

"Now, the third on the list of Five Aggregates is Perception. Perception is just our agreement about the names we give to everything in the world. We have many different languages, but none of us has a unique language of our own. It wouldn't be language or communication if that were the case. So how we name what the world around us is not unique to any one of us.

"So far, so good. Do we agree?" He looked around at everyone, and they nodded, some with more certainty than others. Eva wasn't sure she liked this seeming erasure of who she believed herself to be, but she couldn't disagree with him on the list so far. But where was this going?

"The fourth you might find a little more debatable: Mental formations. All those thoughts and emotions."

Eva agreed that she found that debatable. Her thoughts and feelings were her very own. Nobody else's! And she could see a little squirming around the circle, as if some others—not Connor, of course—found this an uncomfortable suggestion.

But Vicente went on. "Do you really think the pattern of your thoughts is unique? Never thought before? If that is the case, then why, when you see a movie, a play, or read a novel, do you resonate with some of the characters? Why, when you read a poem, does it speak for you in words you might never think of, but once written, resonate so fully?

"Now, not everyone is having the same thoughts or emotions at the same time, except perhaps in a theatre when a scene evokes some extreme emotion. Everyone is startled and screams. The fact that a movie director can make that happen tells us that we are not as unique as we think. And that our thoughts and emotions are easily manipulated. Advertisers know this. So do potential dictators."

Eva almost gasped, thinking of what she had seen on Chad's whiteboard, how he and his group were purposely manipulating people, making phone calls, activating fear. She shivered. She hated that what Vicente was saying was true.

He continued. "Now, this doesn't mean we aren't special. We love certain people and they become special to us, don't they? Of course they do. But that connection has more to do with recognizing our commonalities than with seeing the ones we love as unique. A space alien arriving on our planet would not evoke love, would it?

"Love naturally arises from the intrinsic web of life and the patterns of experience passed down through generations. The stuff we are made of is the same stuff we are all made of! As a species and as animals in a complex network of life.

"It's a lot to take in, isn't it? But fortunately, the fifth and final of the Aggregates is Consciousness. The awareness to perceive, examine, etc. But--and this will come as no surprise--the Buddha says that even this does not define us. How could it? Sometimes we aren't conscious. We faint. We sleep. In surgery, we are blissfully unconscious. We don't suddenly disappear. We don't suddenly lose our identity. So, even consciousness is not who we are. It is the awareness of the four other Aggregates.

"So there you have it. Or, more accurately, there you DON'T have it. The list of who you are not. And if it makes you uncomfortable, it's just the conditioning from a culture that emphasizes, celebrates, and glorifies the separate self. But only to sell products that will make us feel more special, more admirable, more lovable, as if we are products ourselves. So take all of that with a big grain of salt.

"Let's sit for a minute and let this all settle in."

So they sat. And all the spinning busyness of Eva's thoughts circled like dust and settled, then drifted away. There was just the felt sense of the earth supporting her, the autumn air on her skin…and…wait, where was Trusty? She opened her eyes and saw that he was still happily sitting beside Vicente. *Why that turncoat! What a traitor!* And then she smiled. She was happy he was comfortable here. And she realized that she was, too. There was no place else she'd rather be.

Eva thought of the scene in *The Wizard of Oz* when Toto pulls back the curtain to reveal the man pulling the levers to create the monstrous, scary Wizard. Dogs are more intuitive at telling the truth about people. So, as she watched Trusty with Vicente, she felt sure that staying on this retreat was a wise choice.

The bell rang, and when she opened her eyes, Vicente looked at them brightly, and said, "The time has come for us to go on an adventure! Go get freshened up, stop in at the kitchen and pick up your lunch, and let's meet over there at the trail in ten minutes."

He bowed to them all, and they bowed back. Then he rang the bell and rose to leave the circle. The rest held back until both he and Lily were gone before getting up.

8 Exploring Vantage Points

Everyone was standing around, stretching, and looking happy to be going on a hike. Vicente gave brief instructions about spacing themselves, maintaining their noble silence. Then he said, "Let the awareness of interconnection permeate you, letting go of any sense of destination and just being present with the experience of being alive. And notice how many different valuable vantage points there are to experience."

Vicente let Eddie take the lead, then Sara, Allie, Connor, Minna, and herself. Then he followed a good twenty yards behind. Lily had stayed behind in camp. Clearly not a big fan of serious hiking.

As they walked, she could see that this was not like any hike she had ever been on with her friends, where the whole point was to catch up on what was going on in their lives and get some exercise.

Here, each person explored at their own pace, while keeping each other within sight. It was less of a hike and more of a meander. People would step off the path to stare at the patterns of lichen on a tree trunk or squat to look more closely at something on the ground.

She thought about how, if they had their phones with them, they might be framing what they were seeing into a perfect photo to share on social media. Capturing it. But that capture was false. Photography was an amazing art medium and a meaningful way to share history, as she discovered in her teaching—a picture was really worth a thousand words. Sometimes even more. But this habit that she and many others had of wanting to capture a sight or a moment, she could see now, was a little dysfunctional and disconnected. A two-dimensional rectangle couldn't capture even the complete sense of sight, let alone all the other senses that were part of this experience.

She noticed how her thoughts had wandered so readily into opinions and judgments, and she brought her attention back to the feel of her feet on the ground, her muscles working, the fresh autumn air wafting on her skin, and the warmth of the sun, so much kinder than it had been in the summer. Ahh.

Again, unlike her typical hikes, the group didn't seem to have any destination in mind.

She couldn't help whispering to Minna, "When do we get to the first vantage point?"

Minna smiled and whispered back, "It's all vantage points."

All vantage points? What? And then she understood: Of course. This moment's experience of awareness of all the senses in this place was as good a vantage point as any. There wasn't anything better around the next bend. No 'perfect view' to seek. This was it! This was being alive, *fully* alive in this moment.

They veered off the fire road onto a shady coniferous trail. Eva walked more slowly and saw more. She didn't strain her brain to think of plant names, which was good, because she didn't have her phone with its handy app to identify them. Now that seemed like yet another distraction, a mental game of naming and claiming, bolstering her sense of being knowledgeable, but taking her out of the moment.

The plants vibrated in the dappled light—pale green heart-shaped leaves nestled in with tiny curls of deeper green. A hidden trickle of water sang from the depths of a ravine. The air was cool on her skin.

Trusty checked out everything while staying close to the path.

They climbed higher than she'd ever imagined she could go up into these hills. They reached a peak with flat-topped boulders that seemed like a natural resting spot where there was room for everyone to sit on the flat surfaces. They all settled in and soon started pulling sandwiches from their packs. Hers was labeled 'Eva - avocado, cheese, lettuce, and tomato on whole wheat, light on the mayo,' which was, amazingly, exactly what she always ordered at the deli.

She pulled out her water bottle and Trusty's water bowl, and they both drank deeply.

A couple of people had finished their lunch and were either lying down to rest in the sun, meditating, or jotting down notes in their journals.

Not hungry, Eva got up and walked around the perimeter of this peak, in part to appreciate its beauty, but also out of curiosity. From here, surely, she would be able to see her valley, her town, her life. She should see at least the hospital, the tallest building in town.

Thinking of the hospital, she was suddenly back in a moment a few months before when her mother was dying. Eva was returning to the hospital room when she heard her mother and aunt talking. She hadn't wanted to interrupt, so she waited outside, not meaning to eavesdrop, but she couldn't help it when it was clear they were talking about her.

"Has she never asked about him?" her aunt asked in a husky whisper.

"Sure, from time to time. And for each simple question, I gave an equally simple age-appropriate answer. I didn't want to do what mom did to us when we were curious about sex. Remember how we came home from school one day, asking about where babies came from?"

Aunt Evelyn laughed, "Oh yes, she was cooking dinner and she turned the burners off, whipped out a piece of paper and started drawing diagrams—stick figures doing very weird contortions. It was like she'd been waiting for that moment forever."

"Her explanation left us with more questions than we had to start." They both laughed. But her mother's laughter turned into a cough.

Evelyn said, "Our question was more along the lines of 'what store sells babies, and can we get one?' We just wanted an upgrade on our baby dolls. But Mom, being Mom…"

A pause in the conversation as Eva imagined them each thinking about their mother.

Her mother's voice resumed. "Anyway, I didn't want to over-tell but just give the answers she was seeking. So she knew she had a father, biologically, but that he couldn't be with us. I didn't go into the reasons -- the secret I'd kept from him and why -- that would have been too much when she was little. And then when she was thirteen, she was complaining because some of her friends were having Bat and Bar Mitzvahs, and she said she wished she were Jewish."

"What did you say to that? *Oh, but you are!?*"

"Kind of. I think I told her that her birthfather was Jewish, and that if she was interested in attending our local temple and seeing if it was for her, I had no objection, but that it would look self-serving to show up at the age of thirteen, so why not wait a few years."

"Remember our friend Judy? We were so envious because she had both Christian and Jewish parents and got to celebrate both Hanukkah and Christmas. Kids are such practical little creatures, like little animals looking for more food…"

A pause in the conversation.

Aunt Evelyn said, "But you haven't told her you've been in touch with her father?"

"Oh, God…I wanted to, but…" her mother replied weakly.

What??? Eva's heart jumped. *Mom is in communication with my father? And she didn't tell me?* She pressed one hand to her chest and the other to her mouth to stop the gasp she felt rising in her throat. She leaned against the cool wall of the wide hallway and listened.

"I thought I'd have time. I kept thinking I'd tell her when I feel stronger, but every day…I guess I was fooling myself. I just don't want it to be our last conversation, you know? We've always been so close. So happy together, so fortunate to have each other."

"Sis, you've been a great mom. She's lucky to have you."

"Thanks, but I see now I failed her in this. I've been selfish seeking him out and keeping him to myself. It felt protective at the time. She hadn't expressed any more curiosity. I was the one feeling there were loose ends…"

Eva felt frustrated then. Should she have asked more? She hadn't wanted to hurt her mother's feelings, to make her feel like she wasn't enough. But of course she was curious. Of course she wanted to know her father.

Her mother continued, her voice significantly weaker, "At least for now, in these early stages. When I did that search, I didn't really expect…I doubted I'd find him, and if I did, I doubted he'd be available or even remember me."

"But you did find him, and he is widowed, and of course, he remembers you. I mean, how could he not? So how long?"

"About six months. Just conversations. No visits."

"And you told him about his daughter?"

Eva stopped breathing, listening in suspense.

Silence.

Say something, Mom! Yes, and he can't wait to meet me? No, because you wanted to consult me first? Which is it?

But there were no more words. Had her mother nodded *yes* at Evelyn? Had she shaken her head?

After it was clear the conversation was over, Eva had tiptoed a few yards back down the hallway to make a louder entrance, ready to greet the two sisters, the two conspirators who held this secret, *her* secret! *After all, he was just an old boyfriend to Mom, but to me, he is blood. He's my father! How could Mom keep this from me?*

Erasing the distress from her face as best she could, she entered the room. But her mother had nodded off, her pale face painfully gaunt, and Aunt Evelyn just looked up at her with compassion.

Then, in the middle of the night, the hospital called to inform her that her mother had died.

She remembered how the community swelled in mourning over the loss of their beloved librarian. They were some comfort to Eva, but utter strangers to Evelyn, so she quietly exited and flew home to mourn her sister on her own. And Eva hadn't reached out to her since. Why? she wondered now. The one person who knew her mother in some ways better than she did. The one person who mourned her deeply. They could comfort each other. But Eva had tried to set her grieving aside, as if that was possible, and focused on handling the mountain of responsibilities—all the death certificates, funeral arrangements, accessing accounts and passwords. And having to prove she was indeed her mother's daughter in the middle of it all. Time consuming, but also infuriating.

In the process, Eva had also set aside her thoughts about her father. She'd lived without him for more than three decades after all. But, as she combed through her mother's things—dividing them into piles to keep, donation, recycle, dump, gift to friends—she kept her eye out for any signs of communication. But there was nothing. No letters, no emails. And her mother's phone was inaccessible without her thumb print, so Eva couldn't check her call records without making a big deal with a death certificate and proof of her role, etc. So she let it go.

But now she was left with a sense of having lost both her parents: the one who loved her more than anyone in the world, and the one who may or may not even know of her existence.

She sighed. And that sigh brought her back to the moment. She could see how the mystery of the missing hospital had taken her on a painful memory journey. Now she looked around her—the resting campers, the wildflowers so unexpected in autumn, the vast sky. She returned to her boulder and put the uneaten half of her sandwich away in her pack. She made a vow to put all thoughts of the past or future away as well.

Others were lying on their back looking up. So Eva gave it a try.

From this vantage point, the sky was crystal clear, the richest blue she'd ever seen. And then out of thin air, she watched a cloud form. A little wisp curled into a puff. The puff grew and evolved into a bright white cumulus cloud that drifted away. She closed her eyes. Then, she noticed the intense color on her eyelids backlit by the sun.

*　　　*　　　*

When everyone had had a chance to eat and rest, Vicente called them together. "Quite a view, isn't it?" he asked them, looking around.

They all nodded in agreement and appreciation.

"It's nice to come up here and get this expansive perspective, isn't it? It refreshes our view when we return to the valley where we set the wise intention to plant the seeds of loving kindness and generosity, knowing that we reap what we sow."

He paused as they all looked into the distance thoughtfully. When they looked back toward him, he continued. "Ah, views. We might think about how, in conversation, we say 'In my view…' It acknowledges that this is just our opinion, and others are free to think differently.

"But in another way, we may be claiming a particular vantage point, building our sense of identity upon our unique view of things, the way we see the world, the beliefs we align with or rail against, and the people we see as like-minded allies or enemies.

"We might say, 'From my perspective…'

"Perhaps we were born into this perspective, having been raised with a comfortable sense of belonging to these inherited beliefs, and we feel obligated to hold these beliefs and perhaps live up to them to honor or validate our history.

"Or maybe we found this perch on our own and feel pride in our individual stake in the rich vein we have claimed. The ego thrives on being king, or queen, of the mountain, so to speak.

"How we come to a perspective plays a role in how attached we are to it. Our 'story' is our identity. We rely on our story. It comforts us. Even a terrible tale, full of misery and woe, is *our* tale, and we hold it dear, and defend it as we share it with others by word or deed.

"Sometimes our story seems incomplete, and we are in a state of seeking something or someone who can tell us who we are. We search for some kind of confirmation, a deserved perch, a deed to this life we are living. 'Who am I?' we may ask with the same urgency as a baby bird clambering blindly in a nest, cheeping for worms.

"How does this attachment to our identity and this quest for a defining story affect our ability to access Wise View? When we so rigidly align with a personal viewpoint, we naturally feel compelled to defend it, to build a fortress of self. We may seek distinguishing marks that align and separate us, friend and foe.

"In this state, I ask you, how can we access or value a more spacious view, where there are no sides, no mine, no yours, no theirs? How do we discover this moment just at it is, without craving or claiming? How do we access the infinite field of interconnection and compassionate understanding?

"That's what we are learning, isn't it? How to recognize our fear-based tendency to isolate and defend a separate-seeming self. We can see the way we cling to our story because we are terrified that we are nothing without our beliefs, our thoughts, our personality, our behavioral quirks that distinguish us from others, and our ways of being that mark us as part of this tribe and not that one. Just that noticing—without condemning, clinging, or claiming—is cause for rejoicing. We are finding our way along the Eightfold Path. We're discovering the joy of taking refuge in the Buddha, Dharma, and Sangha.

"Through the practice of meditation, we may begin to see the patterns of thoughts and emotions. Arising out of the stillness and inner silence, attachments, judgments, beliefs—everything that we mistakenly thought makes us who we are—become visible in the spacious field of awareness that is infinite and generous. We relax, and begin to see that the clinging, hunger, and thirst for something else is universal—not me, not mine. We see how the naming and claiming, and the holding on tight to this moment, causes suffering. We accept the fleeting nature of being.

"If you notice any sense of defeat when I say this, as you judge your own experience of meditation, know that Spacious View has room to hold that defeat and any lingering judgments. It has room for all thoughts and feelings that arise to be seen, heard, felt, and acknowledged.

"As this meditative practice of quieting down becomes a natural and regular part of our lives, insights naturally arise. We didn't invent them, but we are ready for them. We begin to see where views came from, how they became ingrained or calcified in our patterns of thinking. What we thought was something solid becomes softer and airier.

"Through this inner exploration, we realize there's no reason to defend our views. We do not have to hold them like a shield or armor. And we don't have to make someone else wrong or take sides to exist with joy in the world. Quite the contrary! When someone says something, perhaps something hurtful to us, we can, with a more spacious view, see their patterns, all the inherited perspectives, words, experiences, and cultural norms that shape those patterns."

Vicente paused and took a sip of water. Eva took the opportunity to close her eyes. At some level, she understood exactly what he had been saying. She could see patterns from her family, culture, news, friends, and other influences. And instead of being the tight knot of her troubled solid self, they were dancing freely in the sky, a pattern of wafting clouds coming together and drifting apart. *Not me. Not mine.*

It could be overwhelming to see this, but it wasn't! She could see how the threads of thoughts wove together into veils – a veil for each belief about herself, each person she knew, and so much more – woven of experiences, traumas, opinions, and beliefs.

Vicente continued. "When we use the word 'spacious' instead of 'right' or 'wise,' it reminds us to look at the space between things instead of just focusing on the things themselves. On a universal level, this involves seeing the interconnectivity and the fluidity of being. On a personal level, we notice how we are relating to the object in question. We can examine how we perceive the world and listen to how we discuss it. Instead of simply accepting everything we say as truth, we can notice our thoughts, emotions, judgments, and beliefs, uncluttered by our layers of opinions about them. We see that 'the world' is not some solid, clearly definable thing but a whirling collection of amorphous opinions that we may have accepted as truth without bothering to question them.

"When it comes to how we see people, instead of focusing our thoughts on the person as if they are a solid, separate unchanging entity, we realize that our idea of them is an ever-changing flux of memories, beliefs, thoughts, emotions, judgments, assumptions, and opinions. And because there's nothing to cling to there, we can gently release our assumptions and be present, open, and filled with loving kindness unclouded by grudges.

"Another benefit is that we can see the degree to which we react when they say something or do something that sets off particular patterns in our behavior. Instead of focusing on them and how they should be different, as we might have done, now we notice the pattern of thoughts arising that are full of judgments. We notice the complex emotions and physical sensations, often painful sensations, associated with these thoughts. We see the interrelated nature of this inner storm system that sets in, spawned by a behavior that perhaps irritates us. We see the Three Poisons showing up: Greed, Aversion, and Delusion.

He paused and looked around. Then he pointed into the distance and said, "See that smog over there?"

Smog? Eva thought. *We don't have smog! And I didn't see any smog anywhere when we got up here.* But she looked where he was pointing, and, sure enough, there was a heavy layer of brownish smog. It wasn't smoke. She knew the difference. *But that doesn't make sense,* she thought. The sky had been clear for decades, not like back when gas engines with low mileage were all that was available, and the few factories at one end of the valley spewed unfiltered exhaust. *But now. Was it changing back that fast? Oh no!*

Vicente was saying, "When you see smog from afar or from a plane, you recognize how thick it is, and how unhealthy. The Three Poisons are like that smog. From this vantage point, on retreat, slowing down, practicing mindfulness, it's easy to recognize. But when we're going about our daily lives, caught up in rushing and over-reacting, it's more challenging to notice the thick smog of Greed, Aversion, and Delusion. Yet it's affecting us just the same. Just as the smog causes lung disease, the Three Poisons create significant problems in our way of being in the world."

Again, Eva couldn't help feeling defensive. *There's no smog in my town!* But then she recognized the irritation that popped up so quickly. And the fear-based reactivity! Both were signs of aversion, weren't they?

Vicente continued. "Now in the absence of the smog of greed, aversion, and delusion, we have the luminous clear sky of wisdom, generosity, and loving kindness."

As quickly as it appeared, the smog disappeared, and the sky was once again a radiant blue. *Wow, that was fast!* Eva thought relieved. Then she had to wonder at Vicente's ability to conjure. Was he a magician who could summon smog at will? Who would want to do that?

She answered her own question: *Someone teaching the Dharma and illustrating a point. Hmm. Well, point taken. Maybe there is no smog there, but how about in here, in my way of thinking? Aha! Oh, was that an insight?* She felt excitement and a sense of pride. *Oh wait, that's craving and self-making. But I'm seeing it! I can be happy about seeing it, can't I?*

Vicente continued. "Wisdom, generosity, and loving kindness are our natural states. But we need to be vigilant to recognize the smog of greed, aversion, and delusion polluting our minds. And the most effective way to do that is to meditate regularly, adhere to the Precepts, and explore the Noble Eightfold Path with all its benefits. In this way the mind becomes luminous like the sky, able to hold temporary weather patterns passing through. If we hold all that arises with the wisdom, generosity, and loving kindness that is the nature of our luminous mind, then those thoughts and emotions will be as beneficial as the clouds that provide shade and rain.

"And with Wise View, we can see the world as it is: a rich web of interconnection – alive, fresh, and wholesome. How different this feels than the calcified and rigid views we have held in the smog of greed, aversion, and delusion. With our vision blurred by the smog, we stumble and say and do harsh things, causing harm to ourselves and others.

"No doubt at some time in your life you have felt someone else's calcified view of you. You have felt the stranglehold of being seen as something solid and unchanging. Perhaps someone who has known you all your life and still treats you as a child. Or someone who only knows you in one role and can't make room in their view for all of who you are. So you know how irritating and exhausting it can be to feel viewed this way, how it brings up feelings of having to prove their view wrong, and has the potential to set off a whole series of unskillful interactions. Noticing this, we can begin to release the painful way of perceiving ourselves as a solid, separate fortress that needs to be defined and defended.

"Very gently, we can begin to open to the more wholesome and life-affirming way of seeing how this self, made up of the Five very impermanent Aggregates, is intrinsically interconnected with all life.

"This gentle shift allows us to understand we have nothing to defend because this whole experience of existence is our home. This dance of microcosmic points in a macrocosmic web of infinite interconnectivity is present, whether we are aware of it or not. However, when we follow the Buddha's Noble Eightfold Path, we learn how to discern all the interwoven threads of thought, emotion, and sensation that pulsate and vibrate throughout life. That is Wise View."

He paused, letting his words settle in. Eva looked around and saw the radiant faces of her fellow travelers on this Path she hadn't even known existed yesterday. It was all new to her, yes, but it was also so familiar.

Vicente continued. "We might notice that there may be something familiar here, something that sounds perhaps a lot like what people say they experience when they experience the presence of God. They talk about having a sense of being deemed okay as they are, forgiven for their human imperfections. Accepting a higher power is a response to an awareness of there being a vantage point that is infinite and all-encompassing. How does God, for those who believe in God, seem to be able to hold all the mess without getting dirtied by it? God by nature is transcendent and intrinsically personal, infinite yet never distant.

"Every earnest accounting of an experience of the presence of God suggests this spacious awareness, this spacious presence that arises when we quiet down and open our hearts to what is, whether we are in a place of worship, out in nature, or on our meditation cushion noting the arising of greed, aversion, or delusion.

"My mother was a devout Catholic. I can still hear her in the night saying the rosary. Sometimes it made me feel safe, like I knew she was praying for me and would keep me safe. But at other times, her voice sounded so desperate, so pleading, that I worried there was some terrible threat to us that she didn't tell me about.

"Growing up, I noticed how she seemed so burdened on the way to mass and so refreshed when she returned. As a young person, I found the church's rigidity regarding certain matters frustrating. On the one hand, it promised that God loves all of us. But the priests made it clear that the love was conditional. Many of us were not welcome.

"As I began to explore on my own, I realized I didn't need to go into battle with God, and I didn't need to defend him. I simply had to focus, be still, and listen. And I found that I was in God and God was in me. Because it was all one infinite system of being. I am not a devout person, but I have a spiritual inclination. Hence, my career as a professor of comparative religion. My rich exploration led me to meditation, and Buddhist Insight meditation in particular, because it doesn't point to a separate divinity.

"At my mother's funeral, an aunt pulled me aside and scolded me for breaking my mother's heart with my acts against God. I assured her that I am living a wholesome life and that my mother and I had come to an agreement to respect each other's beliefs and needs.

"I didn't bother to tell her about the conversation we had about Mother Theresa, but I'll share it with you. It was a real turning point for us, where we really came to understand each other.

"As the story goes, someone asked Mother Theresa, 'When you pray, what do you say to God?' And she replied, 'I don't say anything. I listen.'

And when they asked her what God says, she smiled and said, 'He doesn't say anything. He listens.'"

Wow, thought Eva, feeling a gentle release in her whole body.

Vicente looked around the circle. "That state of listening is very much like the bare attention of mindfulness, isn't it? Awareness without expectation, explanation, categorization. Just open and receptive. Listening.

"My mother had come to a point in her life where she was no longer begging God but opening to the stillness of the infinite presence that her devotion brought her. So we could both appreciate Mother Theresa's words of wisdom."

He took a sip of water from his bottle. "I've met Catholics who have discovered that meditation and Buddhist teachings enrich their experience of their faith, deepening their understanding of Jesus' core teachings, which are best read in direct translations from the original Aramaic language in which he spoke.

"Training in letting go and simply being available for the spacious sense of 'union with the divine' is revitalizing for any spiritual life.

"Many Buddhists consider Jesus to be a Buddha, an awakened being. Others firmly disagree. I imagine the Buddha might say that the whole conversation is a waste of time, based on speculation rather than exploring the gifts of the Dharma. And all these gifts reveal themselves, opening like buds, flowering at just the right time, from simply sitting, opening to the infinite nature of being, letting it reveal what there is for us to learn in each moment."

Then he closed his eyes for a moment, and everyone did the same.

For Eva, much of what Vicente shared felt beyond her understanding. But that filled her with a sense of promise, that there was a whole journey, a big adventure, a rich inner exploration, and she was just at the beginning of it all.

Vicente opened his eyes and smiled at them all. "Okay, I know that was a lot to take in. But I want to be sure that I've answered any questions to the best of my ability."

Allie raised her hand. "It all sounds amazing and I'm excited, but at the same time I'm still struggling with this Anicca and Anatta."

Vicente nodded. "Thank you for saying that, Allie. We haven't been raised with these concepts—quite the opposite! —so we all struggle with the concepts of impermanence and no separate self.

"Okay, we're on the beach building a sandcastle, fully engaged in the moment. We know that our castle is temporary. It will dry out and be blown away or washed away with the incoming tide. Right?"

She nodded.

"So, why do we have such difficulty understanding that this is the nature of all life? That all, including what we call self, is impermanent. And that to insist otherwise is the cause of great suffering.

"Again, I appreciate your asking, because we may need to look at it from many different angles, and we need to be ready to let go of some debilitating misconceptions.

"We can't force our understanding. It unfolds on its own timeline, not according to our expectations, plans, or even diligence. We tend to cling hard to our cherished views, our celebration of 'me' as uniquely correct, or our pity party of 'me' as uniquely unacceptable.

"The Buddha used the metaphor of sandcastles to talk about the Five Aggregates of Clinging, which are again:

"Form—this body, this physical plane of existence.

"Feeling—the senses.

"Perception—agreed-upon names for everything.

"Mental formations—all those thoughts and emotions! And,

"Consciousness—awareness of the first four aggregates.

"Now, this looks like the basic recipe for making a self. This is ME! But as we explored this morning, when we looked closer we see that, much the way a sandcastle is a temporary assembly of grains of sand, this self is an assembly of fundamental elements that come together and fall apart: earthy bones, skin, and organs; watery blood, sweat, and tears; the air we breathe; and the fiery process of turning food into energy and synaptic brain activity.

"The Buddha's teachings center on these Aggregates to reveal the way the habit of naming and claiming a solid sense of separate deludes us. The word 'aggregate' means conglomeration. The Pali word for it is *khanda*, often translated as heap. So this body we think of as solid is a temporal ever-changing heap of molecular formations. These sensations arise and fall away. These perceptions are culturally informed and change over time. And thoughts! They change depending on causes, conditions, and other factors.

"The assembly of this body usually lasts longer than an afternoon's sandcastle, but we know there is a tide, a natural rhythm, to this human life. Railing against the nature of impermanence is like having a tantrum when a turret of the carefully constructed sandcastle crumbles.

"And to insist that we are separate, that we need to keep fortifying this isolating castle, this fortress, of I, me, and mine, with labels, features, awards, accomplishments, etc., and the demand to be seen as unique, is to not only be delusional but misery-making. Whatever our shape, our interests, our accomplishments, we are temporal.

"But having this temporal experience can be meaningful. We may feel there is something we are here to learn, here to do, some contribution to the whole -- not to prove how unique or special we are. We can let go of our fear of failure or appearing foolish, and we tap into this sandcastle nature, this being alive in a temporal human form. We cultivate the beneficial qualities and skills to contribute to the symphony of life.

"But notice that this list is called the Five Aggregates of *Clinging*. Why?"

He looked around the circle, but when no one jumped in to answer his question, he continued. "Because most of us cling to the idea that this body, feelings, perceptions, thoughts, and consciousness are who we are."

Minna raised her hand, and when Vicente nodded, she said, "It reminds me of that scene in *Alice in Wonderland* when the hookah-smoking caterpillar asks Alice, 'WHO are YOU?' And she answered something like, 'I hardly know, sir. I know who I WAS when I got up this morning, but I think I must have changed several times since then.'"

"Ah, yes, thank you, Minna," said Vicente. "The caterpillar's question is a bit like the Buddha's night of awakening when Mara, the demon, kept taunting Siddhartha, asking him, 'Who are you?' and more pointedly, 'Who do you think you are?'

"Most of us can relate to this. Our self-talk is populated with inner voices that either demean us or inflate our self-image to protect ourselves. Noticing them is an essential part of cultivating awareness and loving kindness. We can, of course, have skillful conversations with these inner critics who nag, seduce, confuse, and label us. But most of us just accept the abuse they dole out and then suffer and make those around us suffer.

"When these inner critics ask *WHO are YOU*? What do we answer? It's unnerving, isn't it?

"Siddhartha, having meditated for years, had cultivated a level of awareness that allowed him to recognize that he had a right to liberate himself from Mara's seductive delusions and vicious taunts. He put his hand on the ground and called on the earth as his witness.

"The earth is our witness as well! We are fleeting expressions of all the elements coming together in this time and place. We can cultivate awareness and loving kindness to meet whatever arises. With Wise Intention and Wise Effort, we can use whatever interests, inclinations, skills, and knowledge we have for the benefit of all beings.

"Freed from all this clinging and need for finding the perfect labels, we can participate without self-doubt or self-aggrandizement. We can live!"

Vicente beamed at them all. And they beamed back, inspired.

"Let's close our eyes for a moment and ask ourselves: *Am I this body? These sensations? These perceptions? These thoughts? This consciousness?*"

Eva closed her eyes. Again, she noticed all the sensations, but the questions Vicente wanted her to ask herself still seemed foreign and maybe a little scary. *If this is not who I am, then...*She noticed how fear made her body tense up, her jaw tighten.

"Take a breath," Vicente advised. "The body may not define you, but it does need oxygen."

As her breath returned to normal and her fearful thoughts quieted down, she tried to follow the instructions. She asked herself, *Am I this body? Is this body really 'me'? I didn't create it.* Some aspects of it were not to her liking. If she created it, why wouldn't she have made it better? And it keeps changing! All the changes over the past decades, none of which were her choosing. Who would have chosen to get a period and pimples? Who would have chosen to gain weight from eating their favorite foods? Who would have chosen to have a gene that would make it likely to get cancer? And this body will continue to change, won't it? *There's nothing I can do about that. I can only make the best of it.*

What was the next one she was supposed to consider?

And just as she was wondering, Vicente repeated the list. "Am I this body? These sensations? These perceptions? These thoughts? This consciousness?"

Eva thought, *Sensations? No, they aren't who I am. They come and go.*

Perceptions? Well, it feels like they are me, but then they change. Like how I thought Chad was such a great guy, and now...Don't go there, she reminded herself.

Thoughts? I hope I'm not my thoughts! They seemed like wild horses running free. Eva couldn't stop them if she wanted to.

Consciousness? Well, SOMETHING has to be me, right? That felt like her last hope. *But then again, where was I when I blacked out? Hmm.*

Vicente began again. "The Buddha taught that to claim any one of these is to suggest that we had independent choice in the matter, that we have control over them, that we are isolated and unaffected by the flow of life all around us, that we are unaffected by time, preconditions, genetics, culture, social influences, the ebb and flow of the tides of existence."

"In your exploration, did you find yourself? Or did you experience what most of us do who are being honest: The labels don't fit! Not because they are the wrong labels and we need to find better ones, but because there is no separate self to label. Imagine that sandcastle covered in labels. A fortress of self. But it's all a delusion.

"Think about it. This body is a product of a series of marriages between ancestors. We can experiment with it a bit, if you'd like. Food intake, exercise, and other factors will have an impact on the body, but only to a certain extent. And even those decisions to make changes are influenced by the cultural norms around us. The belief that this body is not okay just as it is doesn't arise independently.

"Do we have control over the senses? We all have varying abilities to see, hear, touch, smell, and taste. These abilities may change over time, and we may be able to improve some of them with modern technology. But if they were us, we'd have more volition over them. If we were born without vision or hearing, was that a choice we made? And wouldn't we have ordered a nose that could smell flowers but not a skunk? Wouldn't we have ordered a body impervious to pain?

"And perception? We didn't think up these culturally agreed-upon labels for things. Our parents and society told us the names of objects and how everything works. Scientific research reveals that other species perceive things in entirely different ways. Perception is not who we are; it's just a way to experience life.

"And what about thoughts? We like to think our thoughts are our own, but even the most creative writers draw from the culture and styles available. They weave stories out of what they observe and use the skills they inherited or developed. Even fantasy writers draw from the limited well of human imagination.

"In truth, most of the time, most of our thoughts could just as easily be thought by the person next to us, given similar causes and conditions. Maybe that bothers us. Maybe we want our thoughts to be unique. Special. But why? To gain approval? To get a better label to plaster on the sandcastle we call 'me'?

"And consciousness is just awareness. It's not who we are. It's like a navigational compass of being, orienting us, overseeing all the rest. It steers the boat of being me in this moment.

Whoa, thought Eva. *This is a lot to take in!*

She closed her eyes and took a deep breath. And it felt like the world slowed down. It was silent and peaceful. She let herself settle and soften.

When she opened her eyes, refreshed, she was ready to hear more. And as if waiting for her permission to continue, Vicente picked up where he left off. *How odd!* she thought. She almost wanted to close her eyes again to see if closing her eyes was like hitting a pause button on a recording. But she didn't, because she was curious to hear what else he was going to say. Even if she didn't understand it all.

"So then who are we?" Vicente looked around at their faces, some thoughtful, some concerned, like they should have an answer.

Vicente smiled. "Relax! This is not a disappearing act. It's an act of liberation! It's a gentle practice of letting go of the need to be solid, separate, and seen in that way. It's questioning our need for the nouns we use to define ourselves and seeing if verbs are more accurate.

"Let's do a little exercise. Find a term you use to describe yourself."

Everyone thought for a bit. Then Allie raised her hand and said, "I am a problem solver."

"Thanks, Allie. Now, how might you change the language from a noun that defines you to a verb that expresses the way you enjoy engaging?"

Allie closed her eyes and pursed her lips in concentration. When she opened her eyes, she smiled and declared, "I enjoy identifying challenges and finding solutions."

"And how does that feel any different?" Vicente asked her.

"Hmm. Using a verb feels liberating."

"Yes. A verb-based pattern of thought offers more freedom and can evolve without a sense of loss of identity or self-diminishment. If someday you lose interest in or the ability to problem-solve, it won't be a loss of identity. Just a different way of being in the world."

"Interesting. I like it! It feels more life-affirming. I can solve problems, but it's not who I am. I wouldn't be lost without it."

Vicente nodded. "We tend to find ourselves on a painful chase to 'be' someone, grasping at and clinging to this isolated self whose walls must be constantly fortified and defended. But what we're really doing is cutting ourselves off from life, from being, and from recognizing our intrinsic interconnection."

Others nodded.

"We may think we're building some impenetrable permanent 'self,' but we're only creating misery. And if we're aware that all is ever-changing, including this 'self', we can be a bit more playful. We can be in the world as if playing on the beach, building sandcastles, and engaged in the moment, while at the same time understanding that what has our attention is temporary and will fall apart with the incoming tide, dissolving in the wind and rain of life. Whole civilizations rise and fall. There is no final perfection."

"But does that make life meaningless?" Sara asked.

Vicente looked at her and said, "I can't answer that for you, of course. But we can notice the clinging nature of our ideas about ourselves. What happens if we hold our heritage, our ethnicity, our features, our family, our culture, our personality, our talents, our knowledge, etc. a little more lightly? With both compassion and delight, but with less tension and judgment?

"Again, I can't answer how that would be for you, but for me it makes life more vital, and gives me the option to do meaningful life-supporting actions, to live by the Buddha's Noble Eightfold Path in each fleeting moment. And instead of making me sad, understanding the Five Aggregates frees me from unreasonable expectations in life – in this body, my loved ones, and the world. I like to think of it as being better able to hold all of life in an open embrace and engage in wholesome, beneficial ways to offer loving kindness to myself and all beings.

"From this vantage point, the world is not a scary mess. It is a wondrous mystery: a rich, vital, and volatile mix of cause and effect, patterns of cycles and seasons. All that birth, death, decay, and rebirth! From this vantage point, awe increases, and harsh judgments and the need to be right fall away.

"Yet from this vantage point, we are better equipped to be powerful agents of change. Through our practice, we embody loving kindness and compassion that ripples out into the world.

"The vantage point for Wise View is both deeper and more expansive than the limited surface view of life we often have. From this vantage point, we feel more embodied, more present with whatever sensation arises."

Everyone nodded thoughtfully. Some had their eyes closed, taking it all in, meditating, or nodding off in an after-lunch nap. Eva wasn't sure.

*   *   *

After a while, Vicente rang the bell, and they opened their eyes.

Everyone looked refreshed.

Vicente looked around at them and said, "We hiked up to this peak to get a vaster view in the same way we come on retreat. But the valley is where the seeds of the Dharma are planted and nurtured, where the Eightfold Path is rooted and grows, in our daily lives and relationships. Let's keep that in mind when we return home."

Eva appreciated that advice, and everyone else looked thoughtful as they took it in. This airy perspective was restful and refreshing, but it was time out from her life, an opportunity to see it from this vantage point, and set a wiser intention going forward.

Vicente said, "Let's gather our things and head back down to our camp. We have more of the Eightfold Path to look forward to, starting with Wise Intention. Then this evening we'll look at Wise Effort."

Eva, startled, remembered that she needed to read something from the book Lily had given her if she was going to lead a discussion group on Wise Intention, whatever that was! *Oh, dear.* So she pulled out the book and opened the book to the page Lily had marked. She could see the chapter was very short, so she was relieved. But then she panicked, because as she began to read, the words looked like gobbledygook! Just a dancing jumble of symbols.

Oh no! Had she given her the wrong book? In a foreign language? No. That wasn't it. She could see random words, but just as she began to read them, they softened up and floated away. It was the weirdest thing! It was as if the words on the page were clouds in the sky! How could she possibly decipher them? She was both fascinated and horrified. She wanted to linger to watch the dancing cloud words.

Maybe they would settle down. Eva took a deep breath, closed her eyes, and released all thoughts. She followed her breath, kept releasing any tension that came up, and then, when she felt her panic subside, she felt confident that when she opened her eyes, there would be standard text on the pages and she could read it.

But when she looked again, the text was blurred as if someone had rubbed petroleum jelly into her eyes. She couldn't make out a single thing. She looked up to see if her vision was impaired while looking at other things. No. It was all perfectly normal. *What the…?*

She looked at her hands and could see every little detail. She could, she noticed, see better than usual. In fact, her hands were quite fascinating. She looked and looked, and the more she looked, the more like a little landscape her hand became, her fingers like little peninsulas, her palms like lacy trails in a field. But the book? Still gobbledygook.

She panicked and got up to speak with Vicente.

Connor was already in conversation with him, so she waited a discreet distance away. She heard Connor say, "Why are we going to Wise Effort after Wise Intention? *Sila* is next."

"I know that's traditional, and I know you object. But we're shaking things up a bit. We will explain why to the whole group later. For now, let's just get back down the hill."

"But Vicente…" Connor was getting upset.

"Connor, we must be careful in our explorations not to let the living *Dhamma* turn into dogma. We are exploring, that is all. When we explore, we try to look at things in different ways to see what else we can discover. We investigate from different angles. There's no harm in that, and we may discover value in it. Shall we give it a try?"

"But it's not right. It's always taught in a certain order for a reason."

"What reason?"

Connor looked frustrated. "I don't know the reason, but there must be a reason, or it wouldn't be taught that way."

"Remember what Lily suggested? That the Buddha was teaching young men, boys even, who needed moral guidance to live in community, and they needed ethical guidance before they could even begin to explore the rest of the teachings? But we're all adults here. Our parents raised us with strong moral values. Did they not?"

"Yes. Well, mine did. But that doesn't mean we can just rearrange the traditional…"

"Okay, Connor, let me appeal to you as a scientist. Let's talk about evolution. Nature has never been unwilling to try doing things differently, has it? Everywhere you look, there's a new species or variation. Let's just say that on this retreat, just this one time, we're going to experiment. It's natural."

"Yes, but the Buddha wasn't a scientist."

Vicente looked thoughtful, then asked, "Wasn't he? He investigated. He tried things out. He tried out all the techniques of the day, putting them to the test, didn't he? That's something for you to consider."

Connor looked as if a light had suddenly turned on in the darkness. It was a light Eva recognized from her students when they finally understood a concept she was presenting.

Vicente had briefly turned away from Connor to smile at Eva, obviously thanking her for her patience, so he hadn't seen that light. When he turned back to Connor, he continued, "Clearly this is uncomfortable for you. But learning to live with discomfort without turning it into suffering is our practice, is it not?"

Connor smiled, "Yes, of course. We'll wait and see. Like scientists. Thanks, Vicente." And with that he went off to join his mother who was waiting at the path's edge.

When Eva approached Vicente, he asked her what he could help her with, anticipating many questions. "I know this was way too much to take in, so just let it go for now."

"Well, it was amazing, very rich, mostly beyond me, but still…But, um, about my presentation on Wise Intention. Lily gave me a book to study, but I can't…this is so weird…I can't read the words."

"Really? The Pali words? That's not important. Or? I'm sorry. We always make assumptions about people's abilities and never consider that…"

"No, God no! I'm literate! It's *my job* to teach children to read! It's not that. And it's not a matter of vision. I can see everything else, even close. I don't understand it."

"Well, don't worry. You don't need the book to lead a discussion, really, although it would certainly help. I'm so sorry about that request. It was unreasonable, and now look at you, all in a panic. If you don't feel up to leading a little discussion about Wise Intention, you don't have to."

"Really?" Eva felt a wash of relief. But then she remembered she had willingly taken it on, and that all she had to do was get the group talking about it, much like the discussion they had just had before Vicente resumed his talk. She could do it. And she would learn something in the process. "No, I'll do it."

"Alright, but let's just check in with your intention in doing it. Are you doing it because you feel cornered and you must come through?"

"Oh, no. Well, at first, but no. My intention is…"

Seeing she was struggling, Vicente said, "Just be present with the experience, not trying to change anything, not trying to make it all better. Just be a witness to this experience. Take whatever time you need."

Eva closed her eyes and felt calmer. Her breath slowed down, her chest rising and falling gently. It felt very peaceful.

"Now, whenever you're ready, ask yourself, 'What is my truest intention for this afternoon's gathering?' Words might come up, or it might just be something visual. And if you're judging yourself, remember you can switch to the verb form as we did earlier."

Since Vicente seemed to have all the time in the world to wait with her for the answer to come, she relaxed and allowed herself to access that spaciousness she had experienced several times since arriving here. She could even relax into the nature of impermanence and interconnection.

She realized she didn't have to perform. She saw that letting go of needing to be seen as good and worthy freed her to find instead the verb that best suited the occasion. Instead of telling herself, "I'm a teacher, I can do this." she looked for the verb within: "I enjoy creating opportunities for people to learn in fresh ways."

That seemed right. And she now realized that she was occasionally put in the position of presenting new material she wasn't completely familiar with. Granted, she was usually able to read about it, at least skim it over, but sometimes there wasn't even time for that. And, even so, she still could create space for exploration. Her own innate curiosity created a sense of enthusiasm that was contagious.

She opened her eyes and told Vicente, "My intention is to create a safe space to explore the topic of Wise Intention, about which I currently know ABSOLUTELY NOTHING but am eager to learn."

"Excellent!" exclaimed Vicente, clapping with clear delight.

She thanked him, gave him the book that was of no use to her at this time, looked around to be sure she wasn't leaving anything behind, and, with Trusty by her side, followed the others down the hill.

9 Wise Intention

Returning to the camp, she realized she had her yogi job to do. But everyone was using the facilities, taking showers after the hike. She would have to do it later. She had hoped doing the scrubbing would take her mind off anticipating leading a discussion. She had felt confident earlier but now doubt filled her. *Who am I to…?*

Wait a minute, she told herself. She knew how that thread of thinking went. This was a discussion about intention, so she paused and asked herself, *what is my intention?*

My intention is to not make a fool of myself. My intention is to be a good sport and go with the flow, to not let these lovely people down.

She could see that these were intentions rooted in a sense of separate self, defending that fortress of self. So she walked a little further into the woods, close enough to camp to hear the bell. She put her hand on the bark of a birch tree and sensed into the rough and smooth of it. It didn't have anything to prove, and neither did she.

She remembered the intention she had told Vicente, which embraced her lack of knowledge. Then she took a deep breath and released everything but loving kindness for all beings, including herself.

As the circle assembled for the afternoon sit and Dharma exploration, Eva felt more at home. She was part of this sangha, a word she hadn't been familiar with but now felt natural. She settled in and meditated. When the bell rang forty minutes later, she felt as clear as a mountain pool. And after a brief break, when the group reassembled, she was as ready as she would ever be to lead a discussion on a topic that she knew absolutely nothing about.

"Okay, to be clear, I know nothing about Wise Intention," she began. "I don't know what the Buddha advised. I had no intention of being here! I fell and you all helped me up and welcomed me into this circle of friends, this...um... sangha." The word felt a little foreign, but everyone nodded, smiling encouragingly. She closed her eyes briefly, letting her breath guide her. "I feel grateful. And intrigued by all this discussion. I am curious about the nature of Wise Intention, because I'm certain my intentions of late have been very unwise.

"But when I lit the match last night, I felt the power of the flame, as small as it was, the way it could be used for benefit—providing warmth and cooking. And the way it could be used for destruction, burning down the whole forest. Fire is powerful! And so is our intention. So the match does make a great metaphor for it.

"But that's the extent of my understanding. So, my intention is just to hold the space for the rest of you to share your understanding, thoughts, and experiences with Intention. Please raise your hand if you have something to say, and perhaps together we'll clarify our understanding. So who would like to go first?"

Lily and Vicente were smiling and nodding. Neither was going to be the first to speak. And Eva thought that was wise. When no one else spoke up, she started to get nervous but then realized she knew how to lead a discussion, even with reluctant participants. She knew how to read a face that was ready to say something but was shy about doing so. Her eyes landed on Sara, who had that thoughtful look in her eye. Surely there was a story there.

"Sara, would you be willing to share your understanding of Wise Intention?"

Sara smiled, surprised to be called upon. "Well…I know that we all have intentions, whether they're wise or not. Whether they're conscious or not. And all intentions lead to words and actions that are either skillful or unskillful." She paused and thought a bit. "What I notice is that when I remember to pause before I say or do something to ask myself what my intention is, it really makes a difference.

"Last night and this morning, we were exploring Wise View. It's easy to see that Wise Intention is rooted in Wise View. But so often I only recognize my intention looking back on it. I can see that my intention was reactive, fear-based, and rooted in the thought that I must defend myself. Now I am learning to ask myself before I do or say something, 'Is my intention kind?' It's like a safety checkpoint before entering the potential landmine of interactions. Checking in this way helps me stay out of trouble!"

"Do you have an example we might relate to?" Eva asked.

"Oh, too many! But I would rather just stay present rather than bring up the embarrassments of past words and actions."

"Oh, I get that! Believe me!" Eva laughed. She looked around the circle to see who else was percolating. Connor seemed about to burst. When she looked at him, he started right in.

"My job in tech is focused on AI. Artificial Intelligence is amazing, but just like fire, as you said, Eva, it can be used for benefit or harm. When I'm staring into the flames of the campfire, I'm dazzled by the sight of it all. And AI is like that. Dazzling. Enthralling. Just to think of all the possibilities. And not just convenience, but breakthroughs in medicine and other areas. It is mindboggling, really.

"But if the developers of AI are not rooted in Wise View and Wise Intention, then…well, I don't even want to bring the potential consequences into our peaceful circle. But it's powerful. Like playing with fire. And I'm doing my best to provide a Wise View perspective, but I'm only one guy. And the lure of greed threatens even the most well intentioned developers."

"Thank you, Connor," said Eva. "Both for your words and your work."

Several people put their hands together and bowed to Connor with appreciation. Others looked spooked.

Eddie caught Eva's eye. She nodded.

He said, "For me, it's important to recognize the difference between an intention and a goal. Wise Intention is a way of being in the world right now. If I intend to make a million dollars, that's a goal. It's off in the distance, and focusing on it makes us blind to what is here and now. Chances are with that focus, we're also not being kind, because the goal is all-pervading, and we'll be annoyed or worse if anyone 'gets in our way.'"

"So goal setting is wrong?" Eva asked.

"Well, I think it's more that it can set you up to be unskillful. Let's say you set your sights on something you want. A house, a job, a mate, etc. The standard message in this culture is to 'go for it! But what happens when you get it?

"We can get so in the habit of chasing after some distant goal that we don't know how to be present with what we achieve. In my own experience, adulthood was like a checklist. I got the wife, check! I got a good paying job, check! I got the house! Check! It was all going exactly as I'd planned it. But there was still this restlessness, this feeling of what next?

"I talked with a friend, and they recommended meditation. So I started doing the practice, and I felt like I was pretty good at it. I learned about the jhanas, and…"

"Jhanas?"

Connor leaned toward her and whispered, "Stages of concentration. Kind of altered states, but…"

"Okay, thanks, Connor. Go on, Eddie. Sorry to interrupt you."

"No problem. Connor's right. I thought I'd prove what a great meditator I could be, maybe even an enlightened being. I went at it exactly the way

I'd gone after everything and completely believed I would attain it with my 'eye on the prize' mentality."

"And?"

"And I crashed and burned. That's when Vicente gave me some valuable advice, and reminded me of the importance of Wise Intention, and what it really is."

"Wow! Why aren't you leading this discussion?"

"Because I'm leading Wise Effort. I still have a lot to learn in that area!"

"Ah, so that's kind of a coincidence, isn't it? Lily's Cooking Pot analogy had the match of Wise Intention, and you asked me to light the match for the fire last night. The campfire you so skillfully built. Were you practicing Wise Effort?"

"That was my intention!"

Everyone laughed.

Allie raised her hand, and when Eva acknowledged her with a smile, she said, "I find it helps me to ask, 'Who am I trying to please, here?' Because it seems like my intention is to live up to impossible standards that my mother set for me.

"Then it just came to me on this retreat to, like, look a little closer and ask, 'Who was my mother trying to please?' Because now I can see how it goes back generations of people-pleasing. And it seems like no one was ever pleased.

"Of course, some of the things my mother taught me were important, and not that different from the Five Precepts in Buddhism. But most of the rules had to do with the etiquette of being *seen* as a good person, not about doing good in the world. You know, like: *Don't let the neighbors see you doing that.* Or *What would Grandma say if she saw you doing that?* Or *your friends won't like you if you...* Or *What will the boy think if you let him...*you know.

"I think many of us were brought up this way. And I know it's all well-meaning, but, really, it feels like the opposite of Wise Intention. I want to do things because they are wholesome and beneficial for myself and all beings. That may seem like a high bar compared to the one my mother set me, and maybe less attainable, but it feels authentic and loving. It fills me with joy. And if my effort and action don't match my intention, it's something for me to investigate, not something for the neighbors to gossip about."

Eva nodded, smiling thoughtfully, so impressed with this young woman's wisdom.

Vicente raised his hand, and, when Eva nodded, he said, "An important aspect of Wise Intention is renunciation. I know that sounds like deprivation, but it's not. It's really a gift. It keeps things simple and keeps us in touch with the essence of each moment. We can see what we do out of habit and ask ourselves if we'd miss it. We can experiment with letting go of mindless habits in our lives and in our thoughts. Maybe we don't need to obsess over every little thing."

The discussion was launched, and after others shared with the group, Eva paired them off to further discuss their own experiences with intention, suggesting five minutes each.

She and Minna turned toward each other.

"You go first," Eva said.

"Okay, well, I'm glad you created dyads, because I wouldn't talk about this with the whole group. What came up for me around Wise Intention was a time about ten years ago. I didn't lose weight after Connor was born. Then perimenopause came on, and I started gaining more. As you know, I'm a nurse, so I knew the health risks, but I also had a blind spot about seeing myself as that heavy. I have a challenging job that requires me to eat sporadically, and as you enter the hospital cafeteria, there is a bakery display right in front of you that's hard to resist. I know, it makes no sense for a hospital to be pushing sweet, fatty, high-carb food, but there you have it.

"Anyway, it was challenging to find a compelling motivation. My husband didn't seem to have a problem with my size. He was matching me anyway, and we were both becoming couch potatoes. The strongest motivation I had was that I wanted to fit into the clothes I already had and not have to go out and buy the next size up. I also didn't want people to think that I had no willpower. I mean if I'd always been heavyset, that would have been different. But it was just me mindlessly gorging. Anyway, my intention was rooted in shame about how I was perceived. It was rooted in a sense of separate self and a fear of being judged. That's not Wise Intention. But I didn't see that at the time.

"I also had some fear-based motivations that kept me from losing weight: I knew people who got cancer and lost a lot of weight, and one patient had lost twenty pounds in a few weeks from some rare disease and was just skin and bones. And of course, we see anorexia patients and must watch them like hawks to make sure they eat.

"So, excuses, excuses, I could make a convincing argument that it was a good idea to have extra pounds to spare. Additionally, I have seen people at the end of their lives, sometimes with regrets. One ninety-year-old woman, when asked what she would have done differently, said she would have eaten more ice cream. That stayed with me. And the awareness that, as we age, our sense of taste and smell can dull down or even disappear. I figured I would indulge now, so I wouldn't later regret not having done so while I had the chance to truly enjoy the taste of my favorite treats.

"But then I had a medical scare and ended up as a patient in the cardiac ward of my hospital. Fortunately, everything turned out to be fine, but the cardiologist said something that really spoke to me. She told me that *as a kindness to my heart,* I should lose some weight.

"Kindness is one of my intentions in meditation and in life. And I have more opportunities than most to send *Metta* to people in great need, people who are in pain and fear. So it is an important part of my daily practice. But we're taught that the practice of Metta always begins with ourselves. And at first that was challenging, but over time I found I could begin my meditation with 'May I be well. May I be safe and free from harm.' And eventually, I found myself meaning it. Then I go on to my family and friends, then out into the community, then out into the world, encircling the whole planet. It's my favorite thing to do! Sending Metta!

"So when the doctor used the word *kindness*, it struck me. I had never thought of being kind to my heart before. Her phrase *as a kindness to your heart* stayed with me and helped me. It was very different from the negative shame-making thoughts I'd had about indulging in sweets or potato chips. You know, *Why are you such a pig? Why can't you control yourself?*"

"Once I started using her phrase, I began to see that the other intention that is wise—to be present in the moment, anchored in physical sensation—is often lacking from my mindless grazing.

"So I set these two intentions, and gradually over the years I've lost the excess weight. I'm still sufficiently padded, and I still have the occasional treat, and I enjoy it more because I'm really paying attention. And if I don't enjoy it as much as I thought I would, I notice that, too, and can let go of my craving for it."

Then Minna put her hands together and bowed. Eva did the same.

She was touched by the depth of Minna's sharing. She wasn't sure she could be that revealing, especially with her recent activity. What had her intention been with Chad?

"Okay," she began. "I'm not sure what to say. It's all so new to me." She closed her eyes and took a breath.

"I feel like I had Wise Intention in choosing a career as a teacher. I wanted to help children. But lately I can see that I haven't been living from that intention. I've been distracted. I'm grateful to have the chance to think about that. My students deserve my best intentions and my best effort."

She paused, thinking about the truth of what she'd said. "Yes, I've been distracted. Mindless. So, if Wise Intention is to be mindful, to be present, then all I can say is that I've been unwise indeed." Eva paused and tried to be present. It was so much easier on this retreat, up here in the hills. Down below, it was all a shambles. She'd made a mess of things, and she felt like she was struggling to fit together a jigsaw puzzle without looking at the photo on the box. She looked up and out through the trees at the hills and clouds in a loving dance. She was sure she had put together a jigsaw puzzle much like that last Christmas. If only life were that simple. If there were only clearer directions.

Minna seemed to sense her getting lost in troubled thought. "It's Wise Intention to notice if our intentions are driven by any of the Three Poisons: Greed, Aversion, and Delusion."

"Ah, yes, that makes sense," Eva said, relieved to get some clues. She could see how, over recent weeks, her intention had been driven by all three. A craving to lose herself in mindless sex, an aversion to feeling the grief and worry that her mother's death and her upcoming surgery caused her. And the delusion that she could avoid any of it.

She could see Minna waiting patiently, expecting her to share. Could she? Was it required? And what would she say? So she just said, "So how do we get Wise Intention when we're caught up in the Three Poisons?"

Minna smiled. "Well, the counterpoint to greed is Renunciation."

"Renunciation? Like, become a nun?"

"Not necessarily. Just vowing to look clearly at what's going on and how it causes suffering. In the case of desire, you might ask yourself if it's bringing you the happiness you thought it would. We don't have to strong-arm ourselves into anything. That's just a short-term unsatisfactory solution that doesn't cure the core problem, and the repression creates more problems."

Eva sighed. It sounded so promising. But whenever her mind revisited all the foolishness of the past weeks, she shuddered with self-loathing. When she thought back further, to her mother's death, her heart broke all over again. And if she thought forward to her hysterectomy and its possible ramifications…well, she couldn't even go there for a second without feeling drenched in dread. But what did this have to do with intention?

"Everything about this is new to me. I am an absolute bottom-rung beginner here."

"That's excellent! Beginner's mind is best."

Yes, Eva had always heard that expression about beginner's mind. She thought about her first grade students, almost all beginner readers. Probably eager and afraid in equal parts. She encouraged them to just have fun learning. The letters and words will reveal themselves at their own pace if they just stay with it.

She took a breath and said, "My intention now is to give myself this completely unexpected gift of exploring, learning, meditating, and being in nature. And it is a gift! You all are such a gift to me! I am so grateful!"

And then she closed her eyes again, pretty sure there was nothing more she needed to say. After a while, she opened them. Minna's eyes were closed, too. Eva noticed that the intense buzzing conversations had quieted down a bit.

Only then did she remember that she was leading this discussion! She had the bell! So she carefully took the bell bowl and the ringer and gently knocked it against the inside of the bowl as she'd seen Vicente do. It wasn't very loud, but everyone responded, opening their eyes or pausing in their conversation.

"Alright," she said to them, "Let's thank our partners and come back into the circle." People shuffled around to face the center again.

"So, I hope you had as rich an experience as Minna and I did."

Everyone smiled, affirming that they did. "Does anyone want to share how their experience was? Obviously, only share from your experience, not from your partner's."

After a moment, Allie raised her hand. Eva nodded at her warmly.

"I really appreciated the chance to talk one-on-one about something I'm going through that I wouldn't feel comfortable sharing with the group, so thank you."

Eva nodded. "Yes, dyads are good. We use them sometimes in the school where I teach. For a child, speaking their truth in a larger group can be terrifying, but with one person, it feels safer. It can become a testing ground or a gateway to speaking up in class. I've also noticed it can become the start of a friendship."

She saw Connor raise his hand, and she nodded at him, glad to see that he seemed at ease and not stressed about the rearrangement of the presentation order.

"I guess I was one of those terrified kids. I still am in some ways. But, looking back, I can see that my intention has always been like a turtle staying protected in its shell, only sticking its neck out when necessary. I was always on guard. However, the more I meditate and the more I open within the sangha, the easier it becomes for me to trust. I don't always assume there's danger everywhere. I mean, I still prefer to be alone a lot of the time, but it's not hiding away. It's just following my interests. And now I've found others who share those interests."

"You mean this sangha?"

"Oh, uh, no. Well, yes, this sangha, too. But I was talking about an online community of people who are really interested in the same nerdy stuff I am. They don't even know I meditate. Right now, they think I'm off visiting family somewhere that doesn't have Wi-Fi."

"They wouldn't understand, or they wouldn't approve?"

"I don't know. I just like to keep things separate."

Minna laughed, then covered her mouth.

Connor smiled. "She's laughing because I do the same thing with food on my plate, and it used to drive her crazy."

"Ah, yes. I have students who do that as well. All I care about is that they don't get into food fights when I'm on cafeteria duty."

Everyone laughed.

"Thank you, Connor. Who else has something to share?"

Allie said, "Well, here's something I can share with the whole group: I feel like I'm always rushing around and forgetting things. Last week I challenged myself to use Wise Intention. And I couldn't believe what a difference it made. I don't know why I was surprised, but I was.

"As I was driving home from class the other day, I set my intention to be present and kind. There was this moment when it felt like dancing. I wasn't rushing, or trying to outsmart other drivers, or beat the lights. It was like we were all on a dance floor moving together, responding to each other. We were courteous, because we cared that we all be safe and get there. I discovered that when I am present and kind, others respond the same way. And if they're rushing around mindlessly, I understand how that is, and I feel compassion for them because it's an awful way to be. So instead of getting angry, I send them Metta."

Sara nodded enthusiastically, and without checking in for permission (which to Eva only meant that the conversation was on a real roll! Yay!) said, "Oh me too! At least whenever I can remember. Especially when I normally feel awkward because I'm so tall. Also, probably because my complexion is much darker than most people here are used to. Some get startled, but then they adjust and they're fine. Even so, that's such an awfully awkward moment for me, you know? What am I supposed to do with those feelings of being judged or causing alarm? I felt awkward and so unbearably visible when people gawked.

"So usually, in stores, anticipating comments, either direct or overheard, I got into the habit of whipping past people, in a big rush to get out of there. I'd even rush past short people who could have used a tall person like me to reach the top shelf. I never even had eye contact or said hello.

"But thanks to my practice, I've gained a richer and kinder perspective. I make sure I have enough time to shop without rushing. I set the intention to be fully present and filled with loving kindness. Not the syrupy kind. That's just annoying. But the kind Vicente was sharing in the discussion of Wise View—a profound understanding of the interconnectedness of all life. Or as profound as I get at this point. Enough to relax a bit.

"Now I often feel that sense of being in the flow of humanity. I'm not even thrown off of my game by having to wait in line. I just practice being present, seeing all the festive colors and shapes of the packaging, noticing the people, not to judge them, but to send Metta. And especially to someone who's struggling at the checkout counter. And, of course, to the cashier.

"And then, when I get home, I might even feel refreshed by my adventure rather than ready to climb back into bed."

"Thank you, Sara and Allie," said Eva. "Rich sharing. And food for thought for me, for sure."

Then Vicente raised his hand and when she nodded, he said. "I'm reminded how much of the *Dharma* we can learn from driving. I remember the first time I attended a meditation class, and on the way home, I came to a stop sign. I'd always been a bit of a speed demon. But at that moment, maybe for the first time, I felt that it wasn't there to annoy me but as a reminder to pause, take a breath, and be present."

Lily chimed in, "Yes, same here. I used to live near a hospital, and it wasn't hard to realize that the terrible driving that people did on that stretch had to do with their worries about a patient or their exhaustion from being up all night, or even that perhaps they had just lost a loved one. So if someone was racing, I would send them Metta because they might be racing to be at the bedside of someone they loved or rushing a very pregnant woman to the delivery room. We don't know!"

"What about slow drivers?" said Allie.

"Oh," Lily smiled, "I just imagine they have a seven-tiered wedding cake in the back, and they have to drive very, very carefully to get it to the event in one piece."

Everyone laughed.

"But what about when they're nowhere near a hospital?" Eva asked. "Say a few guys in different cars are chasing each other in and out of the traffic. How can we not be upset about that? How do we justify their actions? And do we want to?"

Lily answered, "Well, first we need to have compassion for ourselves. We're feeling vulnerable, and their reckless driving is putting us in danger. So we just remind ourselves to stay present with the emotions and sensations that are arising and do our best to be skillful in our own driving. However, at some point along the Eightfold Path, our cultivation of Wise View enables us to recognize that those reckless drivers either believe they are invincible, which renders them delusional, or they don't care if they live or die. Understanding that, we may be able to muster some compassion for them."

People nodded in agreement. Then there was a lull.

Eva looked around at the group, "I have learned so much about Wise Intention! Thank you. I look forward to exploring it myself. Is there anything else that I should consider?"

Vicente said, "When we get to Wise Action and Wise Speech, especially, we'll see how Wise Intention plays an important role. But for now, I think we've explored it sufficiently. Thanks so much for being a good sport and leading the discussion, Eva."

Everyone in the circle nodded their heads, and a few said, "Here, here!"

Eva felt appreciated and smiled at them all. How was it possible that she hadn't even known them yesterday afternoon, and yet here she felt like the Buddha's teachings had bonded them?

Vicente said, "Well, it's time to transition into whatever's next for you. If you don't have a yogi job, you can rest, do a little yoga, meditate, or do walking meditation." With that he rang the bell, and they all put their hands together and bowed slightly. Eva did the same, and it felt quite natural, just courteous and acknowledging the transition.

10 The Yogi Job

Eva did some walking meditation in the level meadow. As awkward as it had seemed at first, she was beginning to appreciate the simple moment-by-moment movement.

Unfortunately, Trusty didn't understand it at all. She could see that his meadow actions could be a distraction for the walkers, so she settled him into the tent for a snooze, which he was happy to take.

As she returned to the tent, she looked forward to a little nap. Then she remembered her yogi job. This was probably a good time to do it. Ugh, dreaded bathroom duty! But then she realized that she could bring the same level of calm attention from walking meditation into this work meditation. So she peeked into the bathroom to see if it was clear. Those who took showers after the vantage point hike were gone. She entered and found the cleaning products, along with gloves and a bucket, in the closet. It was also well-stocked with towels, toilet paper, liquid soap, shampoo, and conditioner, all of which were scent-free, to refill the dispensers located by the sinks and in the showers. Against the wall was a mop and broom.

She put the orange 'Cleaning in Progress' sign outside the door and paused to consider the best place to begin—the toilets. Get them over with, she thought. But it wasn't bad. She gave the interiors a thorough scrub and wiped down the seats. She swept the floor and emptied the waste baskets into a larger bin outside.

As she continued cleaning, she felt the need to prove herself a good team player, not a slacker.

They worked so hard. Yet they didn't make it seem like hard work. They went about their chores with a kind of ease and cheer that made Eva think about intentions. What was her intention in doing her yogi job? Was she just trying not to feel guilty? Was she trying to make a good impression? Was she trying to earn approval? What might a Wise Intention be in this situation?

To be present. And to be kind. Well, she was here, and she wasn't daydreaming about anything else, just doing the job. But could she do it with loving kindness? As a service to those who were doing so much to keep the camp running and the campers fed? Not a tit-for-tat kind of obligation, but rather out of genuine caring and appreciation? Yes, she could do that.

She wiped down the shower, checking the drain for loose hairs. Then she cleaned the sinks, faucets, and counter, grateful there were no mirrors to deal with.

After checking to see if any of the dispensers needed refilling and ensuring there was sufficient toilet paper, she swept the floor and then mopped it. When she finished, she was exhausted. But in a good way. All that hiking! All those concepts to think about! And then having to lead a discussion group without any idea of the topic! What a day!

She returned to the tent to rest until supper. Trusty was happy to see her. She closed her eyes and just as she was about to drift off, the bell rang.

*   *   *

Sara, Connor, and Allie had prepared rice and beans with a festive salad. They set up a buffet in the kitchen area, and everyone sat at a table to eat. Eva was accustomed to conversation at meals, but again, there was quiet, everyone attending their meal in a relaxed and peaceful silence. And again, she found herself fully present with the food, aware not only of the flavors and smells but of all it took to provide her with this nourishment. She was filled with gratitude.

After dinner, they returned to the circle. The fire was welcoming, as was the aroma of whatever tea was steeping in a large China teapot on a low table set by the fire. Cardamom maybe? Minna was, quite appropriately, being "mother", and poured her a cup. She took a tentative sip. It was somewhat minty, with a hint of citrus. Delicious.

They all sat together, drinking their tea, with their eyes mostly closed, but some stared into the fire. Eva enjoyed the dancing flames, as well as the variety of their shapes and movement. After a while, she set her cup down and closed her eyes. Now the sound of the crackling flames and the feel of the difference between the warmth on her face and the cool air on the back of her neck caught her attention. There was no place else she would rather be. Nothing else she would rather be doing.

11 Wise Effort

The bell rang and Eva opened her eyes. Eddie was setting the ringer down. He waited for everyone to make any adjustments and then began his Dharma talk.

"On our hike today, after lunch—thanks for those delicious sandwiches, Sara, Connor, and Allie—I was sitting on a rock ledge looking out over the valley. Quite a vantage point! So spacious, freeing, and easeful.

"I noticed a hawk at the top of a towering tree, surveying his world with a sharp eye for something tasty, no doubt. He took off and soared up and up, held aloft by the air currents. Circling on the thermals.

"I envied that freedom. It made me wish I'd taken up hang gliding. And of course, that set me off on a whole set of thoughts about life choices and roads not taken.

"But it also made me think about how Wise Effort is like that. If we are present and aware when we are with life rather than at odds with it, then we attune to the currents, the elements, the way of all beings doing what comes naturally to the way they are.

"So how are we? So often, it feels like we are way off track with our natural beingness. We feel anxious, depressed, and isolated. We've created systems that don't support us and cause harm to ourselves and the rest of nature, rooted in a disconnected, destructive, and very unwise view of the world and our place in it."

People nodded grimly.

"But it doesn't have to be that way, does it? Our innate sense of natural interconnection with all life can hold us aloft. We can trust the invisible currents that carry us. We're not alone and solely responsible for carrying the weight of the world on our shoulders.

"We can develop a level of awareness that supports us. We can be like sailors who know the tides and the ways of the winds, and how to make slight adjustments to get where they need to go. We can cultivate Wise Effort by sensing the energy of the universe as it courses through our bodies, feeling the support of that vibrant, invisible web of life.

*　　*　　*

"At first, when Isaac suggested I join this sangha, I wondered why I would do that. Buddhism? It's not my heritage. I wanted a sense of community and connection. But I didn't feel like I could find that in an Asian religion appropriated by a bunch of white people. How was it not different from them wanting to learn the sacred tribal dances?

"But a mindfulness meditation app offered through work was helpful with my stress. So I tagged along with Isaac to a meeting. After all, I had nothing to lose. I felt welcome and discovered that sitting together in a sangha to meditate is quite different from listening to an app. There is something about the communal energy. So I came back as often as I could, when family commitments allowed. And I continued my daily meditation, setting up a spot on our back porch where I could sit with the sunrise. It made a huge difference in how I met the day. But the sangha became a significant part of my life, and I missed the communal practice, the teachings, and the steady kindness of the sangha when I couldn't attend.

"Finding the sangha, I began to see that it's not about any one tribe or ethnicity. We all find our own way to wisdom and understanding."

He paused and lowered his voice. "Sometimes I wonder how much effort I put into reconnecting with my heritage, whether I should be doing more, or whether I could just let it go, and just focus on the here and now. I recently learned that my ancestors in the late 19th century had their tribal lands divided and distributed to create individual homesteads in exchange for citizenship, disrupting the communal self-governance of the tribe and often causing chaos and ill will. I'd always known that children were removed from their tribes and forced to assimilate. That happened to my grandparents. But I hadn't heard this other part of the shameful story.

"I always felt cut off from the wisdom, from the language, and from my personal history. And since my older relatives have passed away, I don't have anyone to ask. I feel in my bones how important ancestors are, but it also feels hopeless."

His eyes welled up. "You know what it feels like?" he asked them, with such a look of despair that Eva's heart felt it was about to break. "It feels like someone took a can of toxic yellow jacket killer and sprayed it into our cultural nest. Some hives were overlooked for the most part, while others were smothered but managed to survive. And some were totally decimated, leaving the few survivors wandering around, wondering. That's how I feel. Cut off from my nest, my tribe, my community.

"Maybe someday I'll try harder to explore my roots, do a DNA search, and maybe connect with other tribes. Go to powwows. Who knows? There's a lot of stuff going on. Joyful stuff. But I don't feel ready to go there right now. Maybe when my kids are older and I have more time.

"But for now, as I learn more about the Buddha's teachings and practice just being aware, especially in nature, I feel I am reconnecting. I am being held by my ancestors. So I thank you all, and the Buddha, for that."

He paused, then chuckled. "If I shared all this with my buddies at work or on the basketball court, they'd think I'd lost it…Until a few years ago, I would have agreed with them. Talk about unwise effort! I was like a horse with blinders, eyes straight ahead. At work I neither my intention nor my efforts were wise. I felt I had something to prove to my boss, my fellow employees, customers, and pretty much everyone. I also had to deal with clueless people who projected stuff onto me, thinking they were being clever when they said, 'Oh, let me guess, you must be for the Atlanta Braves or the Cleveland Indians.' Or 'How's it going, Chief?' or

'Tonto'. Silly stuff. Even among my buddies, you know how guys like to tease each other. But it piles up. It takes a toll.

"Then at home, I was wiped out. I became a couch potato, glued to the TV, too exhausted to do much around the house, or with the kids, or even enjoy a night out. So I was either adrenaline-charged or an empty tank. There was no happy medium, and I didn't know how to fix it.

"The mindfulness app took the edge off. But it was like nibbling at some popcorn when I needed a wholesome meal." He looked around the group, and there were nods and smiles of recognition. "Yum!"

Everyone laughed.

Eddie smiled. "And the first thing I learned was about the Buddha's realization of the Middle Way. That really spoke to me.

"As you know, when he was a child and then a young man, Siddhartha was coddled by his wealthy family. He was being trained as a leader, a warrior prince of some kind. He was surrounded by luxury and had everything his heart desired. But being waited on hand and foot didn't cut it.

"And I get that. Not that I've got servants waiting on me! Far from it! But when I just lie around with the Sunday paper, a choice of games to watch, and things to eat and drink, in a home, with a family, and a retirement plan, I have that same feeling. *Is this it?* And instead of making me feel well-rested, I feel depleted.

"Even with all that luxury, Siddhartha wasn't happy, and when he saw that he wasn't the only one suffering, that there was, in fact, significant suffering in the world beyond his gates, he decided to be an ascetic. So he gave it all up and left his cushy life. For six years, he tried all the popular methods of wandering ascetics who practiced deprivation to become enlightened. Siddhartha was exceptionally gifted at self-denial and sometimes torturous practices, until he was skin and bones. But they didn't fulfill what he was seeking. Finally, he remembered a time in his childhood when he'd experienced what he was seeking. He had just been sitting under a tree. So adult Siddhartha went and sat under the tree and had insights that changed him and changed the world. He rejected both extremes of self-indulgence and asceticism. He discovered the Middle Way and found it to be the clearest path to the end of suffering.

"So here we are—seekers like Siddhartha, but with a significant advantage. We don't have to wander for six years of homelessness and self-deprivation. He spent his life ensuring that his students and followers, for generations to come, wouldn't have to suffer as he did. He continued to practice, refine his approach, and share his findings. And because he lived a long life and had a very organized mind, and his teachings were of such value to his followers and their followers over the centuries, here we are 2600 years later, finding the deep value of his teachings.

"We come to these teachings because we each have been suffering in our own way. That's what turned us into seekers and brought us to this sangha, and now to this retreat.

"And I think that that shows very Wise Effort! So kudos to us all."

Everyone smiled.

"But Wise Effort is more than just remembering to meditate each day and attend sangha meetings. There's Wise Effort or the potential for unwise effort in every moment, isn't there?

"With Wise Effort, we learn to check in, and if we're suffering, we can look to see which of the Five Hindrances we are succumbing to: Sensual desire? Ill-will? Sloth and torpor? Restlessness and worry? Doubt?

"At any given moment, we might be experiencing one or more of these. It's also helpful to know that it's just human nature to experience them. We don't have to waste time beating ourselves up about whatever we find. That's not the point. And we don't take them on as our identity. They are not 'personality types.' They are just part of the experience of being alive in human form.

"Each of the Hindrances causes us suffering. When we learn to recognize them, we can reset our intention and effort to meet them — not in a battle, but in compassionate clarity.

"If we pay attention to sensation, we see the clues. For example, when we feel ourselves straining, putting our well-being at risk, this is not Wise Effort, is it? When we slip into oblivion, this is not Wise Effort. Wise Effort is fully conscious, alert, yet relaxed and buoyant."

Eddie smiled. "I try not to talk too much about my kids, but, next to drivers, they can provide some pretty interesting examples for exploring Wise Action, and, in this case, Wise Effort.

"My daughter started studying the violin. I was proud of her when she went to her room and practiced each day. But, as you know, it's a painful instrument when played by a beginner. Still, I figured she'd either improve or abandon the instrument. She'd play the same piece over and over again, making the same mistakes each time. But she was dedicated! So we were proud of her even though it didn't seem like she was making any 'progress.'

"But one Saturday morning, I had to interrupt her practice to ask if she had anything else for the laundry. I knocked, but since she was practicing, I felt okay with opening the door. The playing continued, but she was sitting on the floor, happily explaining something of great importance to one of her dolls. It turned out that she had recorded herself practicing. That explained her lack of improvement. But talk about unwise effort!

"After she turned off the recording, I asked her why she did it. She said that she thought it was a good use of time. She was making us happy by practicing while doing what she wanted to do. Of course, I explained that no one was making her play the violin. That taking lessons had been her idea. It seems she'd forgotten that. She said, 'But you were so proud of me! I didn't want to hurt your feelings.'

Fortunately, the violin was a rental and easy to return. It was also an opportunity for a clarifying conversation.

"That reminds me of the violin analogy for Wise Effort: If the violin strings are too tight, they might break. If they are too loose, the instrument will be out of tune. A violin can only make beautiful music when its strings are neither too tight nor too loose. And the same is true with us as well. With spacious awareness, we can tune in to Wise Effort."

"When I began to see the value of the Middle Way, when I let go of the voice in me that was merciless, and when I discovered Wise Intention, then I found the real meaning of Wise Effort. We know all these aspects of the Eightfold Path are intrinsically interconnected, but when we discover it for ourselves, that's when the teachings become real, right?

"So Wise Effort made its way off the cushion and into my daily life. Even the most challenging chores, I try to do with a sense of presence. If I catch myself in an unwise effort, I remember I can pause and reset. And it makes all the difference."

Eva nodded, having just done her yogi job in a more conscious way than she usually would do a distasteful chore.

Eddie admitted, "There are still times, though much less often, when I feel so tight and anxious about all that's on my plate, like something's got to give, and I feel like I need to ditch my daily meditation practice. But when I come home to my intention, I make wiser effort. I see how my thoughts are just that: thoughts. They come and go. Maybe something will pop into my head that tells me my whole practice is just self-indulgent navel-gazing. That I'm just fooling myself, even posturing at becoming wise. And that my wife is thinking, 'Oh, isn't that nice for him. He gets to sit and close his eyes, while I…'

"And maybe she did feel that at first, but now, seeing the effect of it, she's begun to appreciate my meditation practice. She notices how much more balanced, engaged, and authentic I have become. And the chores are all done! And done with Wise Intention and Wise Effort—not just to get it over with and get onto something more pleasant, not to get her off my back about it, and not just to prove I'm a standup guy.

"And if I think about not coming to Sangha meetings because there's this other thing or I'm tired, she's the first to say, 'No, you should go!'

"So I see Wise Effort as being fully present, aware, and engaged in whatever project it is. It's about letting go of the idea that certain chores are drudgery or obligations. It's mindfulness in action.

"True confessions here, I didn't think I was dad material. I didn't understand kids, and making a family was the biggest leap into the unknown I've ever taken. Then those first weeks, dealing with a baby that wouldn't settle and a wife who was recovering and who said she felt like a cow, only good for milking…I felt kind of helpless. We were both exhausted, and even though family kept offering help, we were too tired to think about what help to ask for!

"Looking back, I see that there were many moments when I felt those sneaky, insidious messages. You know that tendency of mind to take this very sucky moment and stretch it indefinitely into the future?"

Lots of nods in the circle, including Eva's own.

"So there I was in this kind of homemade hell, not having a clue, despite all the books and lessons and advice.

"But between daily practice, even when I can only get in ten minutes here and there, sometimes with a child resting on my lap, and coming to our sangha meetings, being a dad has become a joy. We have fun together, we get the housework done together, and they know I'm there for them. So they trust that when I say it's time to do homework or go to bed, I have their best interests at heart. Well, mostly. Obviously, it's not perfect. I mean, they're kids. Sometimes they're amped up and just want their way. But it's just part of their nature. And I'm learning to read them kind of the way that the hawk today was reading the air currents or the way a sailor reads the wind and waves."

Eddie paused and looked around. Then he noticed the fire was getting low, so he got up and used a thick branch to poke at the logs. Once he was satisfied, he sat back down and continued.

"Wise Effort comes from a deeper connected place within us. Quieting down and settling in, we find this calm connection, and from there, at least in my experience, anything we do can feel almost effortless because it rises from within us.

"Think about the ocean. Does the tidal water try to rise? No, it is naturally arising out of its nature and the surrounding conditions.

"This may seem all well and good if we are in touch with our deep connection. But what if we are not aware of it? How do we become aware of it to experience Wise Effort? Where do we begin?

"The fundamental Wise Effort is simply to get ourselves to the cushion to sit. Once there, our Wise Effort is to follow our breath and notice. It's not helpful to harshly criticize ourselves when our mind starts to drift. We just nudge our attention back to the breath. It's a lot like raising a child. Firm but compassionate. And we can then let go of any ambition for achievement or fear of failure.

"We don't waste our energy with tension, regrets, or recriminations. We accept our humanity and celebrate awakening to this moment, and then this one. That's Wise Effort."

He closed his eyes, and others did the same, so Eva followed suit. His words inspired her to notice the breath entering her nostrils. The inhale and exhale were equally easy and natural.

When she opened them, she noticed Eddie was looking over his notes. His sharing had been so natural, she was surprised. He asked, "Is everybody good? Does anyone need a break?"

Everyone shook their heads.

"Okay, because when I talked with Connor just before we sat, he felt it was important that I include that the Buddha taught Wise Effort in the context of ultimate spiritual awakening, not just living better. And he gave me this little list." He held up a half-sheet of paper. "It seems to me this would fit better in tomorrow's explorations?" He looked hopefully at Vicente and Lily, but they didn't know what was on his little sheet, so they shrugged. Then he looked at Connor, who said, "It's part of Wise Effort."

Lily took pity on Eddie. "You're doing such a great job. Why not take your own advice and take a moment to let the wind hold you aloft? And, if it doesn't, then Connor will include it in his exploration of Wise Concentration tomorrow."

Eddie looked relieved, but Connor looked upset. "It's part of Wise Effort," he said again.

Vicente said, "Well, why not include it in the discussion. That way, Connor can make sure it gets shared to his satisfaction. Maybe you can discuss it over a little break?"

"Okay," both men agreed, one reluctantly and one with gratitude. Everyone in the circle was relieved.

"Well then," said Eddie, "Time for a break. Let's take a few breaths, let the dust settle, and then feel free to meditate, do walking meditation, or whatever is a Wise Effort for you right now."

Eva closed her eyes, letting go of all the visual and auditory stimulation of the past few minutes. She sensed the elements, running through them one by one: the earth supporting her, the air caressing her face, the heat of her cozy blanket, and the moisture in her mouth. Ahhh. Then she asked herself, *What would be Wise Effort for me right now?*

When the bell rang, she had her answer.

She and Trusty got up and, as they left the circle, she could see Connor and Eddie conferring. As she passed Lily and Vicente, she overheard him say, "Well, it's just part of the experiment, isn't it?"

That word experiment sounded a little creepy. But Eva reasoned that he was just referring to the experimental arrangement of having the students teach aspects of the Eightfold Path. There were bound to be glitches. And the question of who would share which aspect seemed a very minor snafu to Eva, if whatever was shared was of value.

Eva and Trusty circumambulated the camping area, Trusty sniffing away, then veering toward the kitchen where he refreshed himself at his bowls. How quickly he made himself at home here. Once he seemed satisfied, Eva picked up a yoga mat, and they crossed the trail into the meadow where she had recently encountered a minute but vast world in the grass. Now she lay on her back and stared up into space. It felt like a perfect counterpart.

She thought about what Eddie had shared about exploring his roots, finding his tribe. She, too, was part of a tribe, but disconnected from it. Her father was Jewish, so she was part of the tribe of Israel. Her mother had told her that she wasn't Jewish because it was passed down through the mother. Was that true? How could she not be part Jewish? She had tabled her curiosity out of respect for her mother, but now she was gone. Eva sighed.

She realized she was caught up in thought rather than being present. She looked up at the stars, which made her think of her mom. Apparently, her father was still very much on this earth. Somewhere. And maybe she would find him. But for now, she would just enjoy this moment of awareness that, thanks to gravity, she felt the earth clinging to her, holding her to its bosom, as she looked down, down, down, into infinite space.

When she heard the bell ringing, she rolled up her mat and headed back to camp, noticing that several others had been lying in the field as well. There were no fairy lights, and flashlights would be too bright, so they moved slowly toward what appeared to be a fairy circle across the trail. She noticed that the big pot was back on the refreshed fire, heating some water for tea.

Once they settled in, Eddie shared the verdict. "So, Connor is going to take a few minutes to explore how we use Wise Effort in our meditative practice and our mental states. Then I'll take over at a certain point where I feel more comfortable. No biggie." He nodded at Connor.

"Okay. Thank you, Eddie." Connor looked around at the circle.

"First, let me say I'm glad that in all this reordering of the Eightfold Path, at least the *Samadhi*, the mental discipline factors of Wise Effort, Mindfulness, and Concentration, are still together.

"Okay, it's important to understand that there are four fundamental actions of Wise Effort. They are, first to prevent unskillful states. Then to eradicate unskillful states. Third, to develop skillful states And, finally to maintain skillful states.

"Maybe you, like Eddie, bristle at words like 'prevent' and 'eradicate', but they feel accurate to me.

"These words help us to recognize the various unskillful states within our meditation practice. Are we lost in thought? Nodding off? Judging ourselves harshly? Complaining about aches, pains, or itches? Being so caught up in desire that we are impatient to become enlightened and wonder why this is taking so long.

"How do we prevent them?" He looked around. "First, we make sure we're sitting with Wise Intention, right? If we meditate out of habit or as a chore to get through, we won't be fully present. We each find our own way to settle into a sitting position. I find that chanting the *Namo Tassa* chant helps center me and reminds me of my intention. But we each find different ways. And we'll learn more about them tomorrow, when I give my talk on Wise Concentration.

"Eradication may seem like a powerful word for simply noticing the thoughts that arise and letting them go. But that's basically what we're doing. If we have Wise Intention, we won't beat ourselves up about unwise thoughts. Remember how the Buddha didn't go into battle with Mara, the tempter, but just said, 'Mara, I know you.'

"So we don't go into battle, beat ourselves up, tell ourselves we're hopeless, compare ourselves to the person next to us who must be in a state of pure bliss. No. We just recognize and briefly name whatever arises, take a breath, and shift back to simply being present. And if at the end of the meditation, we feel like that is all we have done, we can recognize that we were following the directions: doing our best to prevent and eradicate these states. Scientifically speaking, the brain is creating new neuro pathways.

"Developing and maintaining skillful states is very similar. We're building the muscles of mindfulness, and, as we learn how to handle distractions, we can develop deeper states of presence. I will go more into this tomorrow."

Connor nodded at Eddie, who said, "Okay, thanks, Connor. Appreciate it, man." He put his hands together and gave a little bow of respect.

Then Eddie looked around at the circle and picked up the thread. "So, our Wise Effort in meditation practice helps us to cultivate awareness in our lives. And that's where I notice Wise Effort the most. Whatever I am doing, I see if I can slow down enough to be present. For example, I can attune to the texture of the logs as I lay the fire. And without getting lost in thinking, I can acknowledge the original tree nature the logs. This helps remind me of impermanence and interconnection.

"Attuning to all the elements as they present themselves in my work helps me to connect with them, to see myself as part of the continuum of life as I do whatever I'm doing. I'm not lost in thought, or rushing to get whatever I'm doing done so I can move on to my next chore. Wise Effort is a sense of aliveness in this moment. And connection.

"To do this, we rest our awareness at the six sense doors where we experience the world: Seeing, hearing, tasting, smelling, touching, and consciousness of the mental interpretation of the senses.

"If we are cultivating awareness, we start to see unwise effort and all the pain involved.

"In meditation, we may imagine that thoughts are just clouds floating through the blue sky of awareness. But it's challenging to get our heads out of the clouds and see that that's what's happening, isn't it?"

Everyone nodded in agreement.

"In the same way, we can reset our Wise Intention and use Wise Effort to come back to the present moment. It's not wise to scold and berate. It doesn't work with kids, and it doesn't work with us. Firm and compassionate, again and again. That's how we train this wild brain of ours. But most importantly, really resting in awareness of the interconnection of all life, all beings throughout all generations.

"So what keeps us from that sense? One or another of the Five Hindrances the Buddha taught about.

"The Five Hindrances are:
- Craving for material goods and sense pleasures
- Hatred, anger, annoyance, intolerance
- Restlessness and anxiety
- Sloth, torpor, inertia, stagnation
- Doubt, indecisiveness

"Any or all of these arise at times during meditation, as they do during the rest of life. The Buddha compared the mind to water, beautiful but easily contaminated. He talked about a pond, but apparently, according to Connor, at another time he talked about a pot. That ties in with Lily's Cooking Pot Analogy, so let's picture the water in our pot in the various states. The Buddha said:

"Craving is like colored dyes staining the water, attractive but impure. Can't you just picture the pretty swirls, like bright lights in Las Vegas?

"Hatred is like boiling water. And isn't that how it feels when we're angry? Uncontrollable, bubbling over, hot and dangerous. Like we want to blow off steam?

"Restlessness is the water being whipped into waves by wind. Choppy, challenging, wanting to get somewhere, but thwarted somehow.

"Sloth is like a stagnant pond choked with weeds. You can't move. It's too much effort. It feels like you're being dragged down to the bottom.

"Doubt is muddy water. You can't see even an inch ahead of you, and you think you never will, that you don't have it in you, and maybe these teachings aren't of value anyway."

Eddie looked around at the circle and asked, "Can you relate to any of these?"

"All of them!" someone called out, and everyone nodded.

Eddie smiled, and asked, "Then, how do we clear the water?

"The Buddha offered these four methods:

"First, we pause and consider the consequences of any unskillful state. That pause alone could help, but the willingness to look closely and acknowledge what it might lead to is huge.

"Second, we see if we can cultivate a positive counterpart. For example, if we feel hatred, we practice loving kindness. Kind of like when we get a dish that's too spicy, we can add yogurt to balance it out.

"Third, let the state pass through like a cloud, reminding us that the thoughts are just thoughts, not *my* thoughts.

"If none of those works, he advised forcible suppression. 'Just say no.' As a parent, I know sometimes that's the only way to go. But I hadn't ever really tried it on myself. And I realized my mind has been an overgrown, undisciplined kid most of my life!

"And then, what if none of that works? We are advised to take refuge in the Buddha and rest there."

To Eva, that sounded more comforting than forcible suppression, even though she knew as a teacher that 'no' was not a dirty word. She realized that over the past weeks it would have been good if she'd said that to herself a little more often.

Eddie finished, "Okay, well, I hope the thought of all that in the water didn't spoil your appetite for a mug of hot tea on a cool night! Then we'll open it up for a discussion."

12 Wise Effort Discussion

Minna served all who wanted one a cup of tea, and there were some tea biscuits, as well. Eva took her cup and two cookies back to her seat.

When everyone who wanted one had a cup in hand, Eddie began, "Alright, thank you, Minna." He held up his cup. "Now, who wants to begin with questions and comments on Wise Effort?"

Sara raised her hand, and when Eddie nodded at her, said, "I've noticed that when I'm trying to 'be good', and especially to be *seen* as good, it's not Wise Effort. To please someone. To be liked. To be loved. It's exhausting. And then, if someone seems to love me, I'm not sure if they truly love me or if they just appreciate all the effort I've put in on their behalf. Or if they'd love me if I wasn't trying so hard all the time. And that makes me feel like I must keep doing more and giving more than I really have the energy to do. I don't feel like I can just be me. I must live up to some ideal I've foolishly promoted and they've bought into, just assuming this is who I am. I know now that no one asked me to do it. I just assume. And then I'm doomed."

"Thank you, Sara," Eddie said.

Eva thought 'When we assume, we're doomed' was a good thing to remember. But she was still a little uncomfortable with how the group sharing worked. She was accustomed to conversations where, when a person said something, someone else would jump in and try to make them feel better, offer advice, or say, "That reminds me of the time I had the same experience." That Sara could share so deeply and then everyone could sit with it, nodding warmly, was, in one way, refreshing, but she had to suppress her impulse to say something to help Sara.

But then she realized that the practice itself, this retreat itself, this learning to be present with whatever's arising—that's what was helping. They didn't have each other's answers, and it could be intrusive to offer advice in this deep sharing space.

She thought about Eddie's mention of being a go-getter overachiever, and it made her think of Chad. She didn't want to think of him -- not now, not ever!

She closed her eyes to shut him out, but something different happened. She felt as if she was still stargazing and seeing constellations. But in their patterns, she could see a complex network of Chad's ancestors, culture, and experiences that shaped his intentions, his efforts, his actions, and everything about how he viewed the world and his place in it. She had never met his dad, but from his description, she knew he expected, even demanded, a lot from his son. The bar was set high, and kept getting raised as he grew, so it was always beyond his reach. He could never satisfy the man. And now, somehow, she could see the father and his inner voices whispering that *he* wasn't good enough. She felt such sorrow for the burden they all carried, for the blindness, and for how cruel it made them.

Now that she saw this about him, it didn't make her want to go back to him. No, not ever. But she felt an inkling of compassion for him, seeing how he suffers. The First Noble Truth was revealed clearly in her own life and understanding. We all suffer.

And what was the cure for this suffering? The Noble Eightfold Path, these lovely people were saying. How lucky she felt to have literally fallen into this group, this sangha, and to have the opportunity to see things with fresh eyes and an open heart. She felt as if a great weight was being lifted. No, it was more like an unbearable boulder was gently dissolving into the atmosphere, becoming just microbial stardust drifting off harmlessly into outer space. Ah.

*　　*　　*

Lily's voice broke the silence. "I don't think I have shared this with any of you before, except Vicente. But it's a good example of unwise effort. When I was in my early forties, I was so unskillful in my striving that my body rebelled and staged a sit-down strike—or more of a lie-down strike—a lie-in while I recovered from a medical crisis.

"I was so out of touch with any understanding of anything wise! I had learned to meditate in my twenties and found it nourishing, but when I rose to a high-powered job in public relations, I told myself that I 'didn't have time' to meditate. My intention was to be seen as a superwoman mother and rising star at work. I could do it all, I thought.

"And maybe I could have if I'd had Wise Intention and Wise Effort. However, my understanding of the way things work was fundamentally flawed. My View was very unwise. I saw myself as entirely separate. Even separate from myself! I was playing different roles and was a different person in each one. My different wardrobes gave me different powers.

"But I wasn't a superwoman. I was just a confused, vulnerable being trying hard to be seen. I was exerting so much energy fortifying the walls of my sense of separate self, worried about what others thought of me, that I fell… like Humpty Dumpty. And all the king's horses, and all the king's men…

"But in my broken state, I had time for meditation. Flat on my back, there wasn't much else to do unless I truly went vegetative watching television. Fortunately, I didn't go that route.

"And through many hours of meditation over many months, I discovered that there is no separate self to fortify, and no value in promoting myself like one of my client's products.

"When I was feeling a little better, I found a sangha, and that made an amazing difference in being able to explore and gain clarity. That's when I learned about taking refuge. We take refuge in the Buddha and our own ability to awaken. We take refuge in the Dharma, the teachings, the Pali Canon." She looked at Eva and explained, "The Pali Canon is the oldest surviving record of the Buddha's teachings."

Eva appreciated the information but hoped she wasn't going to be singled out every time there was something she didn't know, because she knew nothing!

Lily continued, "And we take refuge in the Sangha, the community of meditation practitioners and students of the Dharma—*the Triple Gem.*

"So now I'd like to amend my Cooking Pot Analogy a bit. As I stared at the fire, I noticed the trivet that held the pot, and wondered what role it plays in all this. All the aspects of the Eightfold Path are represented. Now I realize that the trivet, with its three legs, represents the Buddha, Dharma, and Sangha. Without these three, the pot of Wise View would rest directly on the burning logs. And as we saw when Eddie got up to adjust the fire, logs shift and are unreliable. The pot could easily tip over, and the contents could douse the flames."

Vicente was smiling and nodding. "Oh, I'm so glad that you found a place for the Triple Gem, Lily! It's perfect."

Then, looking at them all, he added, "What's come up for me is to remind ourselves that it's not just Wise Intention but Wise View that supports Wise Effort. Each aspect of the Eightfold Path relies on and supports the others. And in our growing analogy here," he said, nodding toward the center of the circle, "we can see that there would be no point in effort if there were no pot to cook in. We might build a fire to stay warm, but we'd go hungry, wouldn't we? And the teachings of the Buddha are our nourishment."

He looked around, pleased, and everyone was smiling. So he went on.

"When we believe we're solid separate selves, it makes us feel isolated and lonely, and in need of defending and fortifying, as Lily said. This sense of separation triggers such intense fear and confusion that it throws us off balance. We have no center, no inner gyroscope keeping us oriented to all that is. And when we have no center, we can't connect with others because we're not where they expect us to be. They may try to get to know us, but we are too busy trying to figure out what would make them like us or admire us, to let them in! We are imagining how they see us and making constant adjustments to feel safe."

Lily nodded and said, "I definitely could have found an easier way, but we learn from whatever happens to us. Sometimes the worst things are exactly what catapult us into where we need to be. Take Eva here. She tripped and fell, and it could have been bad. But here she is, seeming to be taking all this in and glowing with joy."

Eva was startled to be called out. But yes, she was grateful, and if that made her glow, then it was the first time in a long time, maybe ever, that that was truly the case. She just smiled at them all, holding each of their eyes briefly in gratitude. Then she pet Trusty, and he rolled over for a belly rub. They all laughed.

Lily went on, "My healing took longer, almost a year, but it was a rich period of both physical and emotional recovery. Over that time, I began to get to know myself, my own preferences, opinions, and feelings, without the until-then all-important feedback of others. It wasn't to fortify a sense of separate self. It was just a gentle series of observations without judgment, a homecoming to this experience of being alive in this body.

"The unskillful effort from having seen myself as object rather than subject of my own life probably led to or at least fed into my illness. It is very stressful always trying to figure out what others want from you and how to please them! So part of my healing was coming back to center, coming back to acknowledging that the only person I can be is me, even if others don't like what they find, even if I lose people I love.

"But what happened was quite the opposite. When I was well enough to socialize, I chose my companions instead of hoping to be chosen by them. I was simply being myself, rather than the person I thought people wanted me to be. Not surprisingly, it improved all my relationships. I was who I was, and they could find me where they expected to find me and understand me in a way that they couldn't before, back when I was a shape-shifting blob of desire to please them."

Eddie looked at her with admiration, "I'm so grateful you found yourself and that I found you, and this sangha." Then he turned to the circle and asked if anyone else had other examples of either wise or unwise effort.

"Well," said Minna, "I notice how unwise my effort gets when I pick up my cell phone. First, I get lost in social media, and we all know that's a bottomless pit of unskillfulness. Second, it seems that there's always some new 'upgrade' that needs to be assimilated and understood. So annoying! And all my effort to learn it or fix it is unwise because I'm so annoyed both at the makers of the devices and at myself for not being able to figure it out."

"That's what I'm here for, Mom," said Connor.

"I know, dear, but I shouldn't have to rely on you for every little technical difficulty. And I apologize for reminding you of your phones!"

"No worries, Minna," said Eddie. "We've all dealt with it, and technology is a part of our lives."

"Not part of mine," said Vicente.

"Ah, yes, the Luddite in our midst. Well, someone must hold down the fort of sanity against the onslaught of techno chaos."

"I take my assignment very seriously," replied Vicente. People laughed. But he added, "Still, my not having a phone sometimes puts other people in difficult positions. And I own that. But on balance…"

Lily said, "We've had this conversation many times. We can move on."

Eddie looked around, waiting to see if anyone else had anything they wanted to say. When no one spoke up, he asked, "So, how do we cultivate Wise Effort?"

Connor spoke up. "We can pause."

Eddie nodded, and then, when Connor didn't continue, he added, "So often we jump right from one activity to another without giving ourselves even a moment to realign with our deepest intentions or give ourselves needed rest. Suppose you lead a busy life and schedule appointments one after another. What if we schedule in these pauses as well? And let these pauses be restful and mindful, nourishing yourself.

"Anything else we can do to cultivate Wise Effort?" he asked them.

Allie said, "We can reframe our self-talk—Just check in with the language we're using to describe our experience and see how it affects our effort: 'I'm struggling with…,' 'I'm wrestling with…,' 'I'm up against a wall,' 'This is a tough hurdle,' 'I have to jump through hoops.' Sometimes the words just make it feel impossible, so why even bother?"

Eddie said, "Yes! Does that sound familiar? Perception is key! When we notice how we talk about effort, we see how, just through our choice of words, we create difficulty where it doesn't need to be."

Sara said, "We can work together. On this retreat, we work together, making easy work for all. That's wise effort. And it doesn't have to stop when the retreat ends. In the sangha, we have several project groups that work together for various beneficial purposes for the community and the earth."

Eva was delighted to hear that the sangha had an environmental group and wondered what they did.

Minna spoke up. "We can stay tuned into the body. When working on a project, whether it's on the phone, at the computer, or engaging in physical labor, it can be easy to become so focused on the project at hand that we forget to attend to our own bodily needs. For example, working in the garden, bent over pulling weeds, we may ignore our backs' messages of pain and suffer the consequences. Keeping the senses alive in the moment will make the experience more whole and healthier."

When no one else spoke up, Vicente added, "And of course, finally, we can discover a lot about whether our efforts are wise by looking over the Buddha's list of Five Hindrances of Desire, Aversion, Restlessness & Worry, Sloth & Torpor, and Doubt."

Eddie beamed. " Thank you, everyone. That covers it! Now, to end the evening, I've asked Lily to share a story I love about Wise Effort, and she's agreed."

Lily was caught off guard but smiled. "Thank you, that was all very inspiring, Eddie. Are all of you still up for more exploration? Some of you have heard this before."

All nodded, and Eva was particularly curious because she definitely hadn't heard whatever it was before. And maybe Lily sensed that, because she smiled even more strongly when she looked at her.

"I'm sure you can think of many things that give you joy in doing. But no doubt, you can make an equal list of chores you avoid, or when you're doing them, they give you anything but joy.

"When I told Eva what her yogi job would be, I had to laugh at the look on her face. Cleaning the bathroom is rarely a first choice. However, I now want to share why I laughed by telling a story about my experience on a retreat many years ago, which still stays with me. When I was asked what yogi job I wanted, I replied, 'One that will let me stay in total silence.'

"'Okay, here you go,' the volunteer said with a gleam in his eye. And he signed me up to scrub the shower stall in the men's dormitory. Okay, I thought, I asked for it!

"The next afternoon, after lunch, as I took the provided box of non-toxic cleaner, sponge, rags, gloves, and scrub brush into the white-tiled enclosure, I felt claustrophobic. My task seemed insurmountably difficult and uncomfortable, all that repetitive arm movement and bending. Honestly, I was doing the job only because I would feel terrible if I didn't fulfill my commitment, even though no one would check up on me to see if I did it. I had an interior drill sergeant who said 'hup two', and my miserable platoon of one scrubbed away. I've heard tales from past actual army privates admitting they did their assigned tasks in a slapdash way, just good enough to fulfill the order. And that's probably how I cleaned the shower that first day, just wanting to be done and out of there."

She looked around the circle, and asked, "Is there any job you do in your life that fills you with aversion, but you do it because you would feel terrible, or be fired or shunned, if you didn't do it?"

A few people nodded. "Now notice how your self-talk in this state is full of words like 'should', 'must', 'have to', etc. See if you find a harsh internal drill sergeant who gets angry if not obeyed. That voice, instilled in us early on in life, drains us of any possibility of joy in the doing. In fact, we may feel angry at the injustice of having to do this task when it should be someone else's turn, and so on. How does this kind of effort affect relationships at home or work? Adversely, of course.

"We may ignore the inner drill sergeant altogether as a show of resistance against the injustice of it all, and the task doesn't get done as we stew in toxic emotions, as that inner voice gets more abusive, and we feel worse and worse. And how does that work out? The chore, already unpleasant, just gets larger, doesn't it? The dishes in the sink pile up, the carpet gets grungier and harder to clean, and the clutter becomes impenetrable. Planned projects don't get done, dreams of writing the great American novel don't get written, family gatherings don't happen, friends don't get called, and we lose touch with people we love and enjoy. What a mess!

"Back at that retreat shower: On the second day, as I took up my scrub brush, I was more accepting of the task at hand. If I were going to do this thing, I would make the best of it and do it well. My own sense of self-respect demanded this, but there may also have been a little bit of ambition to be the best shower scrubber ever.

"Does that sound familiar?" she asked the group. "Are there efforts you make that bring up a sense of competitiveness or a focus on a potential reward? Perhaps there actually are rewards for some of the efforts you make. Awards, trophies, bonuses, raises, advancement, praise, or fame. But the retreat center offered none of that. At the end of the retreat, there was no hope that the teachers would pass out ribbons, including one to 'good girl' Lily for her excellent efforts at shower scrubbing. So, it was easy not to get caught up in chasing such goals, as they were not key to my efforts. But many of us spend a lifetime in such a state. And if the rewards and praise are not forthcoming and are doled out to others, we may become bitter, forlorn, despondent, and full of self-doubt.

"On the third day, I realized that the retreat teachers used these showers I was scrubbing, so I shifted from proving my worth to expressing my gratitude for their teachings. *May you be well. May you have a nice shower.*

"Are there any efforts you make in your life that are done for the benefit of others because you feel grateful? Often, explorations of effort come back to asking ourselves exactly what we've been exploring this evening: What is my intention here?

"But on the fourth day of the retreat, I experienced a shift into a deeper, more connected state. When it came to my yogi job, I was able to let go of all the mental reasoning and trying so hard to make my experience okay. Instead, I sensed the movement of my arms and body as I wielded the scrub brush, sponge, and spray bottle. The pleasure of being alive, whatever I was doing, filled me.

"Have you ever had that sensation? You are using the same muscles, but now there is pleasure in it. It's interesting to notice that the body is not averse to movement at all. It is our mindset that creates any aversion. We might object to strenuous movement in some situations but then dance all night if the music moves us. Explain that! Yoga often provides a profound sense of pleasure in the awareness of the body being alive, moving through space, stretching, and resting. A yogi job is another form of yoga, once the mind lets go of all that confusion of purpose.

"On the fifth day of scrubbing I had the same sensory awareness, but I also became aware of being part of a continuum of shower scrubbing yogis — all who had been here in this sweet little, white-tiled stall before me, and all those who would be here day after day, retreat after retreat, scrubbing earnestly, dealing with their own vast range of thoughts and emotions. I sent them all *Metta* and opened to the possibility that past yogis had sent *Metta* forward to me. In that isolated space, there was a joyful sense of community, camaraderie, and a relief that it wasn't all up to me to keep this tile shining. If I missed a spot, it wasn't the end of the world. Others would follow up, just as I had done for ones before me. Although we each did the best we could, it wasn't about perfection! It wasn't really even about the tile! I woke up to the realization of what it means to be alive and to participate fully in life, whatever I am doing.

"As you go about your day, doing or not doing whatever is on your plate, can you be fully present with the effort itself? Can we all awaken to the joy in the doing? Can we feel loved and loving as we fully participate in the ongoing cycles of life?

"Can we notice the thoughts that arise in relation to tasks we do, plan to do, or avoid doing? See if you can pause, relax, and ground yourself in being alive in the moment, then approach the task as a meditation.

"No doubt you're familiar with the Zen expression 'chop wood, carry water'? Can we let go of all sense of accomplishment, reward, praise, aversion, and avoidance, and just do the needed chore with as much awareness and compassion as possible?

"There are so many reasons why we don't make an effort. Perhaps the task just looks too daunting. On a family holiday in a rental home, my little granddaughter took one look at all the jigsaw puzzle pieces laid out on the table and said, 'This is too much, we can't do it, it's 500 pieces.' But, as the adults went about assembling the puzzle over the coming days, she began to see it in a different light. She noticed where a piece might fit. She became excited when she was able to put the pieces together, and she discovered joy in doing so.

"If you have a big project to tackle, think of that puzzle. It looks daunting at first, but simply setting out to do it, in incremental work periods over a series of days or weeks, or however long it takes, really makes a difference in how you relate to the project at hand.

"The retreat yogi job is a good model for getting things done. Choosing 40 minutes a day to work on a particular task helps get it done and done wisely and effectively. Then you don't have to think about it for the rest of the day!

"Out of fear, there are tasks that we need to do that we avoid. For example, estate planning and emergency preparedness both raise issues we may not want to think about: the inevitability of our own demise and the possibility of natural disasters. Facing our fears frees us to prepare without despair.

"In our meditation practice, we learn how to cultivate wise effort by actively bringing our attention to the breath and other sensations, noting how they rise and fall away. We notice any thoughts or emotions, including those self-condemning voices that tell us we can't do this, we're no good at it, we're hopeless. We practice compassion and return to the breath.

"Just so, we go about living our lives, we can keep that sense of being fully present, anchored in physical sensation, aware of thoughts and emotions that pass through, but not sabotaged by them. We can attune to our natural rhythm and discover the joy in doing."

Lily then nodded to Eddie, indicating that she had finished sharing her thoughts.

"Thank you, Lily! Anyone else?" Eddie asked the circle.

Sara raised her hand and then said, "Yes! Joy in the doing. I like to live in a clean home, but I used to dread my weekly cleaning day. But then, through my meditation practice and developing a greater ability to be present, feeling the aliveness of the body moving in space, being in relationship with surfaces, I discovered I do find joy in doing. I might turn on some dance music. So maybe Wise Effort is bringing that aliveness to everything we do, recognizing that this is not a 'chore' that we have to get through but an embodiment of aliveness. I'm grateful to have an apartment to clean. I'm grateful to be able-bodied enough to clean it myself. And I'm *so* grateful for the practice and for this sangha."

Connor raised his hand and, with a nod from Eddie, shared, "When I think about Wise Effort, at first I thought my effort was as wise as it could be. When I'm doing anything, I'm 100% there. However, that means I have a difficult time switching gears if something comes up while I'm in the middle of a project. I get upset. Then I can't do anything.

"I see that more clearly now. I'm not sure what it will entail, but I think it's an important part of my exploration. Perhaps I can relax a little and try to cultivate a more spacious awareness, rather than maintaining such a tight focus. Maybe it would help in relationships, too."

When Connor seemed to be finished and was absorbed in thought, Eddie thanked him and said, "Wise effort is learning to be with, or as Sara says, even to *dance* with all that arises in all life's amazing variations.

When we approach things we do in this way, our effort feels effortless. And each moment of wise effort is its own reward."

Allie raised her hand, and Eddie nodded at her. She said, "And Wise Effort is healthy effort. It's a natural effort akin to that made by all species of animals and plants, each true to its own abilities and needs. You don't see animals gorging until they are sick. Nor do they starve to look better in the mirror.

"Wise Effort is fully present in the moment, ready for whatever arises, playful at times, and purposeful as needed. It is about tuning into the body's own wisdom and natural rhythms, rather than going on autopilot and ignoring when the body needs to shift positions, get up and walk around, or rest. It's eating when the stomach dictates instead of when the restless mind starts craving candy or chips. It's finding joy in doing whatever wholesome activity we're engaged in right now, instead of calculating what's on the to-do list."

She laughed. "I just imagined a deer or raccoon walking around with a to-do list. Pretty funny."

Everyone laughed and nodded.

Eva appreciated everything she heard. It was a lot to consider.

Eddie said, "Okay, so unless anyone has anything else to add, I'll just turn the talking stick over to you, Vicente."

Vicente smiled. "What great sharing. Thanks so much, Eddie, for your in-depth exploration of Wise Effort, and to all who spoke. A very insightful discussion.

"Let's just take a few minutes to close our eyes and see what Wise Effort would be for you now. Maybe you're ready for bed. Or you'd like to sit or do walking meditation. Possibly you'd like to do some stargazing. Or perhaps you'd like to try some chanting.

Everyone closed their eyes. After a short while, Vicente rang the bell gently.

And with that, several people rose, bowed, and headed in various directions. Others closed their eyes and shifted their positions for meditation and chanting.

Eva was ready for bed. But she was also curious about the chanting. What was Wise Effort in this situation?

Trusty rose and headed onto the path toward their tent, looking back to see if she was with him. Well, she promised herself to learn to trust him more, so she followed him.

13 Wise Mindfulness

Eva woke refreshed and rose with the bell. After sunrise meditation and tidying up, she heard the breakfast bell and slowly made her way to the kitchen. The bells were both beautiful and relaxing. By now, she could distinguish between the sounds of the waking bell that wandered through the camp, ringing outside each tent, the kitchen bell before each meal, and the Tibetan bell bowl held by whoever was giving a Dharma talk. And she enjoyed the freedom of not having to check the time. She would not have thought there could be freedom in what, at first, seemed a very regimented schedule. She wouldn't want to live like this forever, but she appreciated it for this retreat.

She noticed that only Allie and Sara were in the kitchen. She imagined that Minna and Connor were preparing their Dharma presentations for the day.

At the picnic table, she ate slowly, savoring each bite. Gratitude filled her. Gratitude for the oat grasses and the orange trees, the farmers and laborers, the people who made the equipment, those who drove it to market, those who sold it to whoever bought it, and to those who carried it here, and those here who prepared the meal. And to the earth and the sun and the rain! Oh my, she realized, her gratitude was boundless!

After breakfast, she visited the bathroom to brush her teeth and check up on anything that might need to be done later. It was amazing how clean it stayed. She thought of a recent field trip to a kid-friendly science activity venue where cleaning staff had to be constantly near the men's room, because little boys could be so messy and prone to water fights. Well, people grow up, and at least these sangha members take responsibility for themselves and are extra considerate of others. Wise Effort! She had thought this would be a challenging yogi job, but it was clearly one of the easiest. Still, she hadn't scrubbed the shower yet.

Feeling as if she was getting off too easily, she poked her head in the kitchen to see if she could help with the cleanup, but the two young women waved her away. So, she and Trusty set out to take a little walk. She followed his wagging tail as he trotted along a narrow trail that led past the star-gazing meadow and along the rim of a steep little valley, its hills densely packed with evergreens and ferns. She noticed two different kinds of lichen: one pale green, like paper curled up at the edges, and the other, like threads of pale green tinsel.

She could hear the trickle of water somewhere, and soon she came upon a little waterfall with a shallow pool that released the water into a longer falls below. Trusty walked into the water and splashed around, then pounced at a water skate that darted out of his way. This made him bark—a great game.

Since he wanted to hang out there, she sat down and felt the coolness of the rocks, how different the air felt in this little canyon. She touched the moss, which was like furry, emerald-green curls. The ferns leaned gracefully over the rocks. She noticed several different kinds of ferns. So many species of everything in the world! Were they in competition for space? Or did they support each other, nurture each other?

She sighed. She longed for a world where all species, including her own, especially her own, nurtured and supported one another. Was it possible? Or was that just a fantasy? After all, many species eat each other or destroy each other. There was perhaps something growing on that very tree that was sucking the life right out of it. Oh dear.

But then a nearby tree, as if hearing her concern, explained: —*Life is amorphous and ever changing. A collaboration and competition and combat, just atoms rearranging themselves.*

—But, what about disease? What about death? Eva asked.

The tree answered, —*these things are your ideas, not life's. Life is all transition, seeding, budding, leafing, blooming, offering life to life in nectar, and then fungi feeding on the remains, creating soil to nourish plants. All that flies, runs, or swims is also cycling through, infinitely nourishing itself. Around and around it goes.*

—Whoa!

—Woe? As in sad?

—No…I mean, wow! Overwhelmed!

She silently thanked the tree and closed her eyes, noticing her breath, her lungs like billows. Every cell of her being, vibrating with life, and the dead cells sloughing off here and there -- not gross -- just feeding life. How intrinsically this body she thought of as 'me' was connected through the air — through all the elements — with all the species of animals that were breathing the same air, sharing the same space. And then all the plants that were giving out oxygen, and how they benefited from her breath, in this lovely exchange that none of them had to think about. It was just natural. And it wasn't even a give-and-take, because that implied separation. It would be like expecting a nursing baby to say 'thank you, mommy' for every suck at the breast. The natural interconnection…no, not just interconnection, this universal symbiosis, this…life! This web of life was, in fact, deathless!

There were no endings, just infinite transitions, just as the tree said.

"Just as the tree said!" Girl, listen to yourself!!!!

She tightened up, but then remembered about Mara, the seductor.

Ah, Mara! I know you! she answered, testing the Buddha's phrase tentatively. And, amazingly, that mean-girl inner voice settled down, and Eva rested in the awareness of being an intrinsic, fleeting expression of one infinitely expansive living organism.

She would have liked to sit here longer but sensed it was time to return. "C'mon, T."

Reluctantly, Trusty shook himself off and followed her back to the campsite. As she approached the camp, she heard the bell for the morning's gathering on Mindfulness. So she headed straight for her familiar spot in the circle and settled in. She closed her eyes and let her energy calm down.

*   *   *

Soon, the bell rang, and Minna began sharing.

"First, I want to thank Vicente for sharing the Five Aggregates of Clinging that are essential to Wise Mindfulness, but a little beyond what I felt confident enough to share."

She bowed to Vicente and he smiled and bowed back. Then she looked around at the circle and said, "We hear this term 'mindfulness' a lot, don't we? It's a bit confusing because it sounds like the mind is full, doesn't it: Mind-*full*ness. That's the opposite of what most people think it is: an empty mind off in the void. But neither is Mindfulness, is it?" she asked them, looking around.

"So how can we more accurately describe it? We might say it is the refined quality of awareness of whatever is arising in the current experience of being alive. It is simply noticing whatever is arising without judging, wondering, analyzing, storytelling, etc. Being fully present in this moment just as it is. Bare attention is another way to talk about the experience. But for me that's awfully close to *bare*ly paying attention. Still, if we understand it, bare attention can be a helpful way to think about it.

"I'm very fond of the word 'presence'. A sense of being fully present. And that it's a gift we give ourselves. Of course, this fondness for a concept creates attachment and confusion. I know. Past, present, and future are all concepts of the thinking mind making things linear.

"In his discussion of Wise View, Vicente took us on an exploration into Mindfulness when he talked about the Aggregates. And, in our sangha in the past few weeks, we have been exploring the aggregates of who we believe ourselves to be, so I'm not going to go through each of those. But I did notice that in general everybody seemed ready to let go of the idea that the body is who we are, and the feeling tones, etc. But when it came to our thoughts, some of us bristled. So I'm going to focus on that aggregate and how we deal with it in our practice.

"Using the spoon analogy, I like the idea that what we're stirring is disrupting our patterns of erroneously thinking that our thoughts are who we are, our moods are who we are. A spoon stirring disrupts the unwholesome tendency of *self-ing*, and at the same time creates a smoother, clearer, calmer, more cohesive way of seeing and being.

"When we were up the hill on our hike, I was reminded of the meditation of imagining thoughts as clouds passing through. Our moods, thoughts, impressions etc. are not who we are. Not I. Not me. Just clouds passing through: wisps of nothing coming together, coming apart, and floating on.

"Maybe we find ourselves feeling down for 'no reason'. What happened? Good question! With our mindfulness practice, we develop the ability to notice how a seemingly random thought triggers an emotion. Then we see how an emotion triggers a mood. And then how moods can trigger thoughts. Just the way a cloud starts from nothing and grows bigger, maybe filling the whole sky of our mind.

"Let's pause and consider this in our own experience."

Eva closed her eyes. She loved the idea of a cloud meditation but definitely bristled like a porcupine at the idea that her thoughts were not hers, not who she was. She felt like she would dissolve into a puddle of nothingness if she wasn't the thoughts, moods, and emotions that coursed through every moment of her life. Maybe she wasn't quite ready for this. She tucked the idea Minna had presented away for future consideration.

*   *   *

After a bit, Minna continued. "Whether we are meditating or living mindfully in all we do, we practice mindfulness for our own benefit and for the benefit of all beings.

"As a nurse, I'm trained to be compassionate with patients, and to be precise in how I administer the prescribed dosages and keep exacting records. Compassion and precision pair up very well in our mindfulness practice, too. When we meditate, we can bring precision to our posture. And we cultivate compassion. For ourselves, and for anyone who shows up in our thoughts, or makes a sound that we might feel is disruptive. This is our practice."

"Mindfulness is the nature of consciousness when it becomes clear and spacious, alert, attentive, present, and relaxed.

"With this steady practice, we may become aware of interconnection, how what we say and do impacts all around us and beyond through a rippling effect. Knowing this, we understand the importance of all the aspects of the Eightfold Path, so that what ripples out from us isn't harmful. When we speak or act unskillfully, we can see the patterns of suffering to us and others. With practice, this awareness doesn't make us afraid to speak or act. Instead, we meditate and develop the awareness and skills to stay present, feel that interconnection, and cultivate loving kindness for all beings, including ourselves.

"I remember when I first started meditating that practicing mindfulness was like dancing on the head of a pin. Rarely was I able to stay present. But over time, the pin became a much larger and more stable space, and eventually it became the ground under my feet. I could walk about, live my life feeling fully present in every moment. My daily practice and going on retreats have given me that, and I am grateful. It is not a gift I take for granted. I treasure it and take care of it through steady meditative practice. And of course there are times when I realize I have fallen out of being lovingly present in the moment, when fear activates unskillfulness. But I am grateful to say that it happens less often, as I stay steady on the Path.

"The Eightfold Path guides me, guides us, and grounds us in wisdom, concentration, and virtue practices so that we may cultivate this awareness in our lives and live mindfully, able to deal skillfully with all that arises in our experience.

"Spacious Mindfulness is held in Spacious View, the infinite understanding of the universe as one pulsing being instead of a hodgepodge collection of solid parts jumbled together in some cosmic tumble-dryer, banging and clashing against each other.

"But how is mindfulness different from view? A spacious view shapes our perception of the experience. Mindfulness, together with Concentration, is the steady stirring and clarifying of our murky consciousness into wisdom. As we meditate, we begin to see our own thoughts and emotions, recognize and release the belief that they define us, and become aware of the Five Hindrances that affect us and all humans. We question and soften previously unquestioned judgments and assumptions about ourselves and the world around us. This clarification process expands our ability to feel compassion because it melts the assumed barriers between people. When we see someone in difficulty, instead of thinking, "There but for the grace of God go I," we think, "There go I," for we know that person is not separate from us in the deepest sense.

"How is mindfulness different from concentration? Concentration is the practice of centering. In Lily's cooking pot analogy, Mindfulness is the upper handle of the spoon, open to the air, attuned to all the senses. The lower part of the spoon has a single-pointed focus, steeped in the vortex of insight and wisdom.

"Mindfulness cultivates clarity. With that clarity comes a release of urgency or impatience. We have the time to notice all that is arising in our experience.

"We often think that if only circumstances were different, we could relax and find peace. Whether it's our body, relationships, work, or the world, we may believe everything has to be just so before we can be happy. But here's a reminder from the ancient Buddhist texts that helps us see through the lie we keep telling ourselves:

"A seeker of peace should drop the world's bait."
  - Vagga III of the Samyutta Nikaya of the *Pali Canon*

"Just like a fish would live a happier life if it didn't fall for the lure of the fisherperson's bait, so too can we be happier if we can see the shimmering bait for what it is, and swim on by. But how do we identify the bait in our lives?

"Whether it's tasty treats, affection, praise, variety, the next cool thing, the fear of missing out, the world offers up a bounty of lures, doesn't it? Instead of using these lures to define us (I'm a restless person; I'm a needy person; I have a sweet tooth; I have an addictive personality, etc.), we can use awareness of worldly baits to liberate ourselves.

A skillful practice we can use in meditation and all through the day is to be aware of Feeling Tones: pleasant, unpleasant, and neutral. Because it's really the pleasant feeling, in whatever form we can attain it, that we crave. And it's the unpleasant feeling, in whatever form it may come, that we dread. Staying mindful of the arising and falling away of pleasant, unpleasant, and neutral —noticing and naming them without getting entangled —is the key to staying present.

"You'll find this practice readily available for those moments when you think, 'if only'. For example, 'This would be a perfect experience, if only that woodpecker would stop hammering away at the tree.'

"The sound is just a sound. Our attention is reaching out, blaming the bird, getting our feathers all ruffled, but it's actually our anger that makes us miserable. That's the internal noise we need to recognize. And that we have all the power to release!

"It's not what's happening that we want or don't want, it's the pleasant or unpleasant feeling.

"As we do this practice of noticing pleasant, unpleasant, and neutral, we begin to see the impermanence of the feelings. They are empty and ever-changing. When we see that for ourselves, we no longer cling to them.

"So let's just take a few minutes now to investigate for ourselves the truth of this teaching. Just close your eyes, sit, and notice any sensations, moods, thoughts, etc. that arise, and just note them as either pleasant, unpleasant, or neutral."

Eva closed her eyes and did the practice, not expecting much. It seemed too simple. But she followed the instructions, noticing sensations, and then judging them as pleasant, unpleasant, or neutral.

When the bell rang a few minutes later, she was surprised at the power of the simple practice to not only bring her into the present moment, but to release all the inner commentary. 'Unpleasant' was enough to stem the flow of commentary. 'Pleasant' was enough to curb the desire for more. She hadn't noticed anything neutral, but maybe that was an advanced practice.

Minna looked around at them all, smiling. "How was that?"

"Pleasant!" several called out. Then they laughed.

"Yes!" she replied. "Even when not all of the experiences are pleasant, it's still pleasant to simply note them without becoming entangled and to recognize their impermanent nature, isn't it?"

Nods all around.

She looked over her index cards, then said, "With mindfulness practice, we begin to discern between skillful ways of living, rooted in wise ethical teachings of the Buddha's Eightfold Path, and unskillful ways, rooted in fear that promotes greed, aversion, and delusion.

"We're cultivating kindness and awareness so that we can see, through our own experience, that all is impermanent and interconnected. We can know from our own experience that thinking otherwise causes suffering to ourselves and those around us, extending out in radiant circles of contagious pain. And conversely, how a growing understanding of the nature of all life radiates infectious joy! We choose at every moment what we are spreading. This does not require us to plaster on a happy face. Instead, we are learning to come home to this moment just as it is. Instead of reacting out of fear, we can respond from that more profound understanding.

"From this refreshed perspective, we might see life as a dance of interconnections, causes, and conditions. Can we dance with all we encounter, greeting whatever arises with kindness and joy?

"As with any dance, the music changes. The tempo, partners, and conditions change. Can we greet each moment of the dance without longing for a past dance or fearing or dreaming of some future dance?

"The world is rarely at peace, but with Mindfulness, we can be more skillful in how we respond to the world's conditions. Even when all the news seems bad, we stay centered and balanced. Like sailors who know how to get about on a ship even in the roughest seas. Because it doesn't do the world much good if we're all hanging over the railings puking our guts out, does it?"

Minna looked around and all shook their heads in agreement.

"So we might think of it this way: with the steady practice of Mindfulness, we have the sea legs to see that the sea of life is not the enemy. The waves are not the enemy. These are all just the conditions of life.

"We can see that even the most odious person is not the enemy, but someone who is suffering from the universal forces of greed, hatred, and delusion that take over and lead to violence and suffering, stirring up and fueling the *Eight Worldly Winds*: pleasure, pain, gain, loss, praise, censure, status, and disgrace.

"A big part of my practice has been letting go of burdensome and even poisonous lists of 'if onlys'—how things would have been different if only that hadn't happened. And demands I make on myself, my loved ones, and the rest of the world —like ransom demands that if they aren't met, I won't participate. Who suffers from this list? Everyone. Who benefits? No one.

"My mindfulness practice allows me to dance with each moment as it comes. Sure, sometimes the music of our lives is a dirge. Still, if we stay with the dance, we discover endless opportunities to share the vibrant interconnected awareness of being alive in this moment just as it is."

With that, she looked around at the circle.

"Mindfulness is not viewing things from a lofty, remote location as an observer, separate from life. We don't make anything 'other' or 'enemy.'

We are not pushing away, blaming, or punishing any aspect of self, or making any person or situation a scapegoat for the challenges we are facing at this moment. Of course, this goes against a lifetime of habits and cultural norms.

"But it becomes easier when we can really see the patterns and rhythms of life. We discover the most skillful way to deal with antagonism is to engulf it in the power of infinite loving-kindness. When we slip into the old, toxic pattern of other making, we feel stuck in the sludge of fear that drags us down and closes our eyes to the true nature of life.

"In every moment, we have the option to make skillful choices by staying present, anchoring our awareness in noting the feeling tone of the moment. We can be responsive rather than reactive. We can dance with all that arises rather than let it keep us on the sidelines or engaged in a battle. We see that every moment is a pivotal point of power, where we can act on our wisest intention with wise effort, or we can go mindless and fall into habitual behavior, driven by fear.

"With mindfulness, life doesn't become 'perfect'. Conditions of all kinds still arise. But what we may have labeled as difficulties become more permeable, more manageable, and we see bridges and networks revealed where we thought there were only walls.

"With mindfulness, there's enough space between the thoughts to not be constantly in conflict. And there's room for the 'Don't know' mind to hold all life with reverence and awe. Is this a problem? Maybe yes, maybe no."

"Some of you are probably familiar with the old story of the farmer. But I always think it's worth repeating. It goes like this:

"A farmer's horse gets loose from the corral and disappears. The farmer's neighbor says, 'What a calamity! Poor you, stuck without a horse to plow your fields.' He was surprised when the farmer shrugged and said, 'Maybe yes, maybe no.'

"A few days later, the horse returns with six wild horses in tow. Wow! Now the neighbor said, 'That's fantastic! What great luck!' The farmer again says, 'Maybe yes, maybe no.'

"Then the farmer's son falls off the horse while trying to tame it, and he breaks his leg. 'How terrible!' the neighbor sympathizes. The farmer seems heartless in his unwillingness to claim this as a catastrophe. "Maybe yes, maybe no.""

"The next week, the army comes and takes all non-disabled young men, but not the son hobbling around on crutches. The neighbor cannot believe the farmer's good fortune."

"The story could go on and on. The neighbor is locked into assumptions, while the farmer is open to the possibility that the story is at the very least incomplete, even when it seems evident to the neighbor what the truth of each situation is.

"Most of us can relate more to the neighbor, reacting to every change of fortune as a disaster or a stroke of luck. How often do we say, "Thank God!" or "Oh no!" when we hear news? It's part of being in a civil society. But there is a gift in allowing ourselves to pause in our automatic reactions to ask, 'Is this true?' and to see that the verdict is never in.

"We all have stories of misfortune that turned into great gifts. Many of us are here in this sangha because of some loss or difficulty that challenged us to sink or swim. And we chose to swim!

"So rushing to judgment is always premature. We don't know! And far from being scary or weak in some way, living in the 'I don't know' mind is a joyful state, opening a world of wonder.

"Again and again the Buddha invites us to 'not take his word for it' but to explore for ourselves. It's a rich invitation. And in this sangha and on this retreat, we take him up on it.

"With mindfulness, we can appreciate this gift of life, in whatever form it has taken, through whatever experiences we find ourselves in. We notice that our tendency to compare our lives, appearances, or anything else with others stems from fear—and as we maintain our practice, this pattern gradually fades away.

"Mindfulness also softens and releases the 'if only' mindset that may have trapped us in the belief that causes and conditions are the source of our happiness, when in fact joy arises simply out of being present, aware, and compassionate with ourselves and all beings.

"The gift of mindfulness is priceless. So, I'll leave you with that and look forward to our discussion after lunch."

She bowed to the circle, and everyone bowed back.

Vicente spoke. "Thank you so much for that, Minna. What a beautiful morning talk. And now, as promised, I encourage you to have a solo, mindful experience, taking the time to be fully present in nature. To be in touch with all senses. To notice when you're getting lost in thought and gently return to this moment. Feel free to wander or stay close. You can mindfully walk or lie on the ground looking up or down. Discover all that we miss when we 'take a hike' with the idea of a destination or the achievement of exercise. Just be present. What a gift!"

"Oh, and be sure to pick up your lunch to take with you."

14 Belly on the Ground

Eva sat for a bit to let all of Minna's sharing about Mindfulness sink in. She had been feeling increasingly aware, but now she appreciated that it was a central part of this whole experience, not just a fluke of having hit her head. Yes, it did happen quickly, but maybe she was just ready for it. Or maybe this was just the nature of an intensive silent retreat. Whatever it was, she was grateful.

When she got up, she stopped by the kitchen to pick up her lunch. But instead of sandwiches, there were wooden bento boxes and the artful arrangement of rice, tofu, beans, and delicately sliced vegetables. Ah, this was probably why Sara and Allie had shooed her away. They were preparing a surprise.

She appreciated that there wasn't anything on the table that would end up in the trash. She took a box, a pair of chopsticks, and a cloth napkin. She also saw a stack of blanket squares and took one of those. Sara saw her and held out a little pack of kibble and dog treats. So thoughtful. So loving. She was so grateful.

Leaving camp, she let Trusty go his own way, keeping an eye out for him, but not following him unthinkingly as she often did. She wanted to have a truly mindful experience. As she walked up the trail slowly, she noticed purple thistles and white spheres of dandelion puffs like constellations, tiny star-studded universes unto themselves.

She paused and scanned the hills and valleys. The sun felt warm on her skin, and the wind came in little gusts. She closed her eyes to see if it would push her in one direction or another. Would that be mindful? To just go wherever the wind blew her?

She took a breath and centered herself. What was her wisest intention at that moment? To practice being fully present. Just that simple. Just that challenging!

Since she had taken a lovely little walk that morning, she realized there was nowhere she needed to go, nowhere she needed to get to. She saw a spot nearby in the upper meadow that drew her. It was off the trail, a little sheltered from the wind and sun. She would be like her first-grade students on little nature walks. She loved watching them squat down to see a bug or a flower, or a bug on a flower. She allowed them to have their way, within the circumference of the field. Now she could give herself the same. She imagined being six years old. Open to awe and wonder.

When she eventually made her way to her designated spot, she put the blanket square down and sat cross-legged. She looked at the nearby trees and bushes, noticing patterns and gentle movement in the breeze. She raised her face to the sky and felt her chest expand, aware of the fresh air coursing through her lungs. She felt utterly at home.

Now she wanted to be closer to the earth. She wanted to lie on her belly and look into the depths of all that was happening in the grass. So she did. And the longer she stared into the grass, the more amazed she was. There was a whole world in there. Insects of all kinds and sizes were making their way around the grass: an ant rushing through on a mission, a ladybug landing on a blade and walking up one side, pausing at the tip, and then just as slowly down the other. The longer Eva watched, the more she could see. Insects no bigger than a pinprick had busy lives in this amazing metropolis of skyscraper grasses.

She didn't know how long she stayed on her belly, gazing down into this little world, but eventually her back ached from the slight arching, and she realized she felt hungry, so she sat up. The transition made her feel somewhat woozy. She had been a giant and now she was…well…better not to overthink it. Being six years old had turned her into Alice in Wonderland.

And just then, as if on cue, a jack rabbit ran across the meadow, and Trusty jumped to chase, but she grabbed hold of his collar. "Let it be, let it be." And that reminded her of the Beatles song, those words of wisdom. Ah.

To distract him from the rabbit, Eva opened his little packet of kibble and treats, which he gobbled up. She set out his bowl from her pack and shared some of the water from her metal bottle.

Then she opened her bento box and found rice, edamame, spinach, mushrooms, broccoli, pumpkin, bell pepper, cucumber, and tofu. She pulled out the chopsticks and nibbled thoughtfully, savoring the flavors and the crunchy and smooth textures.

When she finished, she thought she would do a little walking meditation since this part of the meadow was more level. But as she began, she felt so aware of the little worlds she was crushing beneath her feet that she headed back to camp with Trusty leading the way.

She returned her bento box to the kitchen, following written instructions for cleaning. Then she headed back to the tent to rest. But heat had built up inside, and she felt confined. So she got up and headed over to the bathroom to clean something, anything. When she got there, it was tidy and well-stocked. But she decided she would scrub the shower anyway to see what Lily had been talking about.

Twenty minutes later, the shower looked pretty much the same, but she felt she'd done her job. It wasn't filling her with the kind of insights Lily had talked about, but she felt a warm sense of contributing as a member of the sangha.

*   *   *

The bell rang for the afternoon session.

As Eva walked back past the kitchen area to the center ring, she couldn't help but feel there was an imbalance in the yogi jobs. Her responsibility was nothing compared to all the labor of providing three meals a day.

Yet Sara and Allie, especially, seemed to be enjoying the creativity and each other's quiet company. She thought of Heather and herself at that age. Yes, they would have much preferred spending time in the kitchen together, away from the older people. But it still seemed like a lot of work. Wise Effort, she reminded herself. Yes, but what if they signed up for it beforehand, not realizing all that it entailed? And what about Vicente and Lily? She had no idea what their yogi jobs entailed. She supposed that on a normal retreat where they did all the teaching, they wouldn't have yogi jobs, but...

Stop, she told herself. *Just stop*. She paused, took a breath, and looked around. She reached out and touched the bark of a nearby tree. "Let it be," Was that her inner wisdom or the tree talking? She smiled. Who could tell?

15 Mindfulness Discussion

Minna had rung the bell, and everyone was returning to the circle, looking refreshed. "Welcome back. I can see how present you all are. That's the benefit of a retreat. We become more and more present each moment of each hour of each day."

I'd love to hear from you about your experience with mindfulness. Or any questions you may have about it."

After a minute or two of silence, Lily, clearly sensing the reluctance to speak after such a rich experience, spoke up. "For me, it feels important to focus on how I am in relation to what happens. Whether it's a traffic jam, disappointing news, or potentially frustrating experiences, I have plenty of opportunities to practice noticing how I engage with all that arises. As I cultivate awareness and compassion, I feel like I'm clearing the way for the luminous mind to shine, the one that was there all along, but hidden behind all the stories I was telling myself about the world around me, and about myself. More and more often now, and especially on this retreat, my awareness is radiating a deeper understanding. A yellow jacket is not the enemy, not the other. Nor is the driver who is weaving dangerously in traffic. Nor is the politician using power for reasons rooted in Greed, Aversion, and Delusion.

"Life is full of potential enemies, but my practice allows me to pause, recognize, and stop drinking poison. It allows me to see the intrinsic interconnection of all life, the nature of impermanence, the power of loving kindness, and the wisdom of awareness."

Once again, quiet settled in—a cherished stillness that leads to deeper sharing.

Eddie raised his hand. Minna nodded, and he said, "A friend of mine died recently, unexpectedly. It was such a shock. He was on a beach vacation with his family. He and his kids were swept away on a sneaker wave that surged. He was able to save one of the children, but when he swam back out to find the second, unsuccessfully, he drowned.

"So, while I appreciate what was said about focusing on how we are in relationship with everything, part of that has to be mindful of potential dangers. The world is not a benign place. My friend knew better than to turn his back on the ocean, but he was more compelled to stand between the ocean and his children to keep an eye on them. They weren't anywhere close to the water. It just…" Eddie hung his head and put his hands on his face to shelter his sobs.

Eva felt the impulse to rush to comfort him, but everyone simply closed their eyes and breathed. But then Eddie said, "Thanks so much for holding this space for me to simply be with my feelings." He pulled out a napkin and wiped his face. "You know how sometimes people think they're comforting someone when really they're just uncomfortable and want those uncomfortable feelings to go away? Their words try to fix what can't be fixed. And even their hugs have a 'hush, hush' quality. I found myself wanting to do that with my friend's wife, but she seemed besieged with people doing the same. So, I stood back and sent Metta, and when we talked later, I really thought she could feel that loving kindness. I tried to be present with her grief and my own, instead of just wanting to make it all go away."

Some nodded, clearly having experienced the same themselves. Eva wondered if she would rather people hold the space rather than hug her in such a situation. She really couldn't remember at her mother's funeral what all who had so appreciated her mother's dedication to the town library did to express their sympathy. It was all a blur.

Minna said. "We just don't know, do we? We don't know what will happen in the next moment. Life is fleeting, no matter how long we live. And we don't know which moment is our last. That not knowing can be quite unnerving. We struggle so hard to feel in control of things, and we fool ourselves into thinking we've got it covered. Then, the reality of being alive in this temporal body becomes clear in one way or another.

"We may have little control over what arises in our experience, but we can cultivate a skillful way of being with it. In our meditation practice and by incorporating the Buddha's Eightfold Path into our lives, we have many more skills.

"Whatever happens, Mindfulness allows us to check in to see 'What is my intention here?' and 'Am I using wise effort?' We are cultivating a skillset to help us handle what arises. It may not be all we are doing, but it is the most immediately appreciated part of our practice.

"Has anyone noticed the mind's tendency to dwell on the most painful experiences in our lives? I find myself doing that, and it came to me that it's just like how we rub achy parts of the body, seeking comfort. We mentally massage the most tender painful memories in our lives. Does it bring comfort though? Or is it just chasing suffering? That's a question I live with.

Eva realized the truth in Minna's sharing and noticed others nodding as well.

After a couple of minutes of silence, Lily, looking around at the circle of people who now seemed to be massaging their saddest moments, said, "Shifting gears here, I'll just share one silly story from my long and checkered life, shall I?"

Everyone perked up and nodded.

She began, "When I was growing up, my mother hadn't wanted to stifle my creativity, so she just let me 'play' in the kitchen. And whatever I tossed in the pot and cooked up, she insisted my brothers and father eat. Can you imagine?

"But although it had been fun as a child to torture my brothers in this way, when I got married, I didn't want to torture my husband. I recently came across an old letter of mine among my mother's things. (Back in the day, we wrote these things called letters with pen on paper in cursive and we sent them in stamped envelopes through the mail.)

"In my letter, I mentioned a 'successful' meal I'd made, which consisted of chopped-up cooked chicken and hard-boiled eggs combined with some chicken and rice soup mix, and then topped with more Minute Rice, all served on toast. Ugh! Sounds dreadful, doesn't it?

"But I'm glad to report that in a letter a month later, I shared that I had decided to learn to cook. (What a good idea!) I sat down one day and read *Joy of Cooking* through and through, then went out and bought some necessary spices, and instantly I was a thousand times better at cooking than I had been the week before. My husband was absolutely astounded and extremely pleased. I even made a decent loaf of bread!

"I admit, I'm still not a great cook, but I certainly learned something important back then: With a little wise intention and wise effort, we can learn new skills.

"And that's all we are doing in our practice, isn't it? Developing our skills. Learning to notice. Learning awareness. Learning to open to receive infinite loving kindness, and then, once we feel it fully, naturally radiating it out to all beings. This is the joy of mindfulness."

"Thank you, Lily!" said Minna. Then she turned to the whole circle. "Unless anyone else has something to say, I'd like to do a little exercise." She looked around at their faces, all quiet and receptive. "Okay, then. Let's begin."

"Take a moment now to sit and just look around you. Use all the sensations to anchor your attention in this moment. With your eyes closed, you might notice light and darkness, colors, shapes, and movement. Let go of labels of objects, opinions, and judgments. Okay, now imagine this scene as a framed painting in a museum, trusting there is something here, even in this most ordinary scene, to appreciate, just as it is."

Everyone did as they were told. Eva looked up at the dappled patterns of light on the trees that surrounded their circle, then the colors of the clothes of everyone in the circle, as if they were daubs of paint from the brush of an unknown artist.

After a bit, Minna continued. "Now notice the sounds arising in this moment. Again, letting go of imagining the source of the sounds, just sounds, just notes in the Symphony of Now, never to be repeated in just this way."

Eva closed her eyes and listened. The afternoon had a stillness to it, but then she heard jays squawking nearby; a throat cleared, a sniffle. Could she experience them as just sounds, just part of this moment's symphony? This seemed somewhat trickier.

Minna continued, "Wise Mindfulness has room for all that arises, even if, maybe especially if, the sounds are ones you have strong opinions about. Perhaps you love songbirds but not the cawing of crows. Wise Mindfulness has compassion for the habituated judging, too.

"Now, if you like, send Metta, that it may lighten the burden all beings bear. Can you do this without adopting their burden as your own? Can you stay present in this moment, radiating loving kindness and not chase after stories that entwine and resonate with your own?

"Now, eyes closed, sense into the textures under your fingers.

"Wiggle your toes to bring your awareness fully into the body.

"Notice other internal sensations: breath, overall energy, any internal processes like digestion, pain, an itch, etc.

"Welcome to this moment, just as it is. Welcome to Wise Mindfulness!

"Mindfulness is not just meditation. Meditation cultivates the *habit* of mindfulness, allowing us to be present in all moments of life. Every moment is precious, never to be repeated! It may not be the moment we expected, planned, or hoped for, but it's the moment we've got, and only we can imbue it with real value by being fully present to experience it.

"Okay, now, with your eyes still closed, how about we each come up with a few words that sum up what mindfulness is for us. Just call out popcorn style."

Eva thought about it. It was such a new concept that she didn't feel she would have anything to share, but she was delighted to listen to the voices as they began slowly and picked up speed, calling out:

"Embracing the ordinary with delight expands and enriches each moment."

"Letting go of the need to be or experience anything unique or special is liberating."

"This moment contains the whole universe; it is always enough."

"There is nothing that needs changing here."

"Inner silence does not rely on the world quieting down."

"Pleasant and unpleasant sensations don't need to be springboards to mental proliferation, *papancha*."

"I can feel compassion for myself and all beings, despite judgments and opinions I may habitually experience."

"Every breath, every sensation is different from the last. In this way, I can better understand the nature of Impermanence."

"Thoughts and emotions arise and fall away. I don't need to fight them, chase them, or cling to them."

"Thoughts and emotions do not define me: Feeling angry does not make me "an angry person.""

"Patterns of speech and behavior passed down through generations don't define me."

Eva realized this last voice was her own! But it was true. That's what resonated with her right now, and how it helps to hold it all with greater ease and less anger and judgment.

And having said that, it set something free within her. A capacity to breathe more fully, to inhabit space as if she deserved to be there. She realized how much she had been shrinking inside herself, protecting herself, but she was just making herself more vulnerable. Now she felt expansive.

And then she heard Minna say, "You might think of mindfulness as allowing yourself to fall in love with this moment just as it is, again and again. Not the wild ride of romantic love with all its drama, nor the ecstatic feeling that may come at certain stages of deep concentration. Just a consistent, easy open love. We can hold each moment the way a parent holds their infant, with tenderness and delight, even if they are squalling or have a smelly diaper. Just so, we embrace this moment as it is, not comparing it to any other moment, not wishing it away, but meeting it with our full attention and love.

"Mindfulness is being up close and personal with this moment, knowing it is unique and lovable, just the way it is. Like the Buddha, we can recognize the patterns of illusion without claiming them, chasing them, or battling them. We just acknowledge them and let them go. They are not strangers to us. And they are not a danger to us, as long as we see them for what they are.

"When we believe these thoughts to be who *we* are, we attach great significance to them. They become precious to us, and we hold them up to be admired or deplored. With mindfulness, we begin to recognize that this is just part of the illusion. We greet whatever arises with clarity, compassion, insight, gratitude, connection, and, perhaps, a sense of release.

"To think of any of what we are learning here as just another piece of knowledge we can claim to know, stow away, or forget, would be doing such a disservice to ourselves when this is the Buddha's finest gift to us. He spent six years making space for the wisdom to be well received when it came to him. Maybe we can honor his efforts with gratitude and generosity to ourselves by cultivating a receptive space to receive it."

Eva felt such gratitude for this teaching that she was speechless. She just hoped she could hold onto it. No, that was the wrong word. That would be clinging. She just hoped she would be inspired to continue this journey when she returned home.

She opened her eyes, took her journal out of her daypack, and made a note to herself. She hoped she would be able to read it later when she got home.

As she tucked the journal back in her pack, Connor asked, "Can I add one more thing, Mom?"

With a nod from Minna, Connor looked at the circle and then lowered his eyes to speak. "So, I read this article the other day about how, by using powerful magnetic fields and infrared light, some physicists found a never-before-seen quasiparticle. Unlike anything observed before, this particle behaves in a way that makes no sense."

Well, if it made no sense to Connor, it certainly made no sense to Eva, but she trusted him to explain.

He went on, "Okay, imagine a tiny train speeding down a track, moving as if it had no mass at all. Effortless. But then, the moment it tries to turn, it suddenly gains weight and resistance, as if hitting an invisible wall. That's exactly how this new quasiparticle behaves—massless in one direction, but heavy in another."

"Now I know most of you aren't as interested in quantum physics as I am, but it's a huge deal. And when I read the article, it made me think about the Eightfold Path. When we follow the Path, after a while, it begins to feel almost effortless. But when we turn the other way, when we mindlessly act out of greed, aversion, and delusion, it's like we're stuck in a heavy slog of resistance. We suffer!"

Then he looked up and looked around. Everyone had astonished looks on their faces.

"Wow," Eddie said. "That's brilliant, Connor!" The others nodded and laughed. "That's what I was going for when I talked about the soaring bird and Wise Effort. In many ways, it feels effortless, even though people might think it's a huge amount of effort to meditate every day and follow the guidelines of the Eightfold Path. But it frees us from the weight of anxiety, shame, regret, and all that complicated stuff that comes with it. Just brilliant."

Connor smiled a huge smile, clearly so happy that something that meant something to him also resonated with the group.

Minna looked at her son with such deep affection and pride. She clearly wanted to give him a big hug, but between the retreat rules and probably Connor's own, she held back. Instead, she put her hands together and bowed to him, and then to the whole circle, and they all bowed back, deeply grateful for all that had been shared.

Now Eva noticed that the sky was clouding over and a wind had picked up. Was a storm coming? She shivered and pulled her sweatshirt closer.

She saw Vicente looking up as well. He said, "After our rich exploration of Mindfulness with a presentation, our solo explorations, the delicious bento box lunch, and now this discussion, I think we are quite ready to explore another aspect of the Eightfold Path: Concentration. And, given the weather, I'm glad that we had already decided to do that part of the afternoon in the yurt."

Yurt? What yurt? Eva wondered. She had not seen anything beyond the areas of the camp she had already explored. But, of course, she hadn't wandered through the 'bedroom' area where there was an assortment of pup tents. But certainly, she would have noticed a yurt.

However, as they all headed up the hill, sure enough, off to the right was a path leading up to a knoll with a beautiful, round structure. Surely, she would have noticed that before! But, once again, she had to let go of her assumptions and expectations and just go with it.

16 Wise Concentration

They took off their shoes outside the yurt before entering the space, and Eva asked Lily if Trusty should stay outside.

"If he wants to come in, he can. Trusty is welcome anywhere. We checked, and no one has allergies."

"That's great. Thank you."

Trusty very clearly wanted to come in. Not only did he decide to enter, but he made a beeline to sit next to Connor, who was seated by Vicente at the front of the space. The rest of the cushions were laid out in a half circle facing them. It seemed like a more formal arrangement than the egalitarian circle around the campfire. As she settled into one of the cushions, she noticed that in front of each of them was a shallow bowl filled with water. Would they rinse their fingers?

Most of them closed their eyes, but Eva kept hers open. This was a new space filled with interesting things. There were a few intricate Tibetan thangkas on some of the walls that she wanted to look at more closely. There was a statue of the Buddha on a raised platform behind Vicente and Connor.

After thoroughly reviewing the decor of the yurt, she looked at the men at the front of the room. She noticed how Connor sat straighter than he had when he was down by the fire circle, next to his mother. His shock of red hair, blue-green eyes, and stocky build were a contrast to Vicente's greying thin hair, olive skin, and dark eyes. However, there was a sense of a father-son rapport, and Connor wanted to please Vicente.

Even Trusty took on a wiser air, sitting sphinxlike, his triangular ears sleeked back, his eyes partially closed sagely, and his mouth open, as if smiling, panting a little from their hike up to the yurt. *Such a handsome boy*, she mused.

This triumvirate—Trusty, Connor, and Vicente—expressed in their aspects the finest qualities of masculinity. They were noble, reliable, adventurous, all seekers in various ways. And they were genuine, wise, generous, good-hearted, and kind.

She felt her eyes well up with tears of joy at the proof that men were not all bastards, not by a long shot. She had just fallen for the wrong one. She now saw that, of course, she'd had an unwise intention, driven by sensual desire, mindlessness, and emptiness that craved to be filled. Mara had seduced her. And beating herself up about it now would be just more engagement with Mara.

A real relationship, she knew, would come about from the fullness of her own generous spirit, cultivated through Mindfulness. It would be a relationship with someone aligned with her values and vision. A vision that was expanding and clarifying moment by moment on this amazing retreat. She felt no yearning for this relationship. She just took comfort in knowing that it could happen because there were wonderful men in the world. And she promised herself that, if it happened, she would not be fooled again.

Vicente rang the bell, looked around at them all, and began.

"Connor is the youngest in our sangha, but probably the most experienced meditator among us. Although Lily and I have been meditating for decades and have attended and led many retreats, Connor took his cue from the Buddha and went straight to the source. He was ordained as a monk in the Thai forest tradition and spent six months in deep practice. After that, he read the entire Pali Canon in its English translation and has been studying Pali so he can read the original. I think he doesn't trust the early Western interpreters. And he's wise not to take their words for it, since they brought their inherent cultural bias.

"He's traveled around Southeast Asia, visiting other monasteries and temples, and he has visited the four sacred sites where the Buddha was born, awakened, first taught, and died. Now, many people have done that as part of a standard tour, but Connor didn't want to go on a tour. He went on his own, and he stayed close to the spots, meditating—all this to say that he is deeply dedicated to exploring the Dhamma.

"So, it's my great honor to introduce you to our sangha brother and teacher for the afternoon, Connor, as he shares his understanding of the aspect of Concentration."

Connor had looked confident before, but now he was squirming and blushing. All the build-up clearly made him uncomfortable. He was faltering under so much praise and maybe worrying about blame if he didn't deliver on Vicente's high expectations.

Connor took a breath, closed his eyes, opened them, and looked around. Everyone smiled encouragingly. He nodded, acknowledging he felt supported, and no matter how flustered he might get, that this was a safe space. Eva thought how brave he was to do this! What an inspiration already!

"Okay, well, all that Vicente said makes me sound like a know-it-all, but it's just part of the way I like to process information." He rustled his notes on his lap nervously. "I know that makes me a nerd, but that's okay. I've always been a nerd, and now I'm a Dhamma nerd."

Then he paused, thought for a moment, and rephrased. "Okay, wait! It's not WHO I am, but it's HOW I tend to function. I am *not* a nerd. I *nerd*. I am *nerd-ing*. As a verb. Get it?"

Their smiles and nods clearly gave him the strength to continue. "First, I wanted to explain why we're gathering in the yurt instead of our usual spot. I read that it's better to meditate inside to avoid all the natural noises that occur, so you can really concentrate on one focus, which is what we'll be doing today. The Buddha and his followers were outside most of the time, and his great awakening was at the base of the Bodhi

Tree. I spent as much time as I could in the forest monastery outside. But I thought it might be a good experiment. Let's see if being inside helps us in our concentration practice. Anyway, we have this beautiful structure, so why not use it?

"Okay, well, um, let me get started. But first, or I guess that's second, I want to say that I like Lily's Cooking Pot Analogy a lot. When I heard it, it didn't feel right because it wasn't part of the Theravada tradition. But then I thought about all the similes and metaphors the Buddha used. They seemed to come up spontaneously for him, and it was an important part of how he taught. The word 'path' is a metaphor, but it's misleading, right? We're not going from one place to another. The traditional symbol of the wheel is circular, and we see that all its parts work together, being interdependent. But it doesn't show *how* they work together, does it? Lily's metaphor shows how they work together, and I appreciate that.

"I did have a hard time changing the regular order of the eight aspects. I really dislike change. Especially when done to teachings that are over two millennia old!

"But now I can see how maybe putting Speech, Action, and Livelihood before Mindfulness and Concentration might have disturbed the peace of the silence we've cultivated together. By putting the Sila, the virtues, at the end, we can better take what we have learned and practice when we return to our daily lives.

"I think the Buddha, who came up with creative ways of sharing the Dhamma with stories and metaphors, would probably have approved of your Cooking Pot Analogy, Lily, so thank you."

Lily nodded with a smile.

Connor went on, "That said, even though the overall analogy makes sense, I was uncomfortable with Concentration being the submerged part of the spoon. I mean, it made sense that Mindfulness was more in the world, in the open air, but to submerge Concentration -- it made me feel like I was drowning.

"But then when I began to think about it a little more, I thought how when you're underwater, you're cut off from all the sensory stuff happening above the surface.

"I tried to imagine having an oxygen tank, etc., but that got in the way. And then I decided I could just have gills. I mean, why not? Well, obviously, I know why not. But in a metaphor." His voice trailed off, and he looked down at his notes that he hadn't been using.

"Anyway, when I imagined having gills, I felt like a superhero who could sit at the bottom of the cooking pot and use my magic gills to be able to sit there. But then I had to figure out how to survive as the liquid heats up."

Minna gave Connor a look that conveyed he was getting off topic. He said, "I know, I know, I get carried away. But I just needed to think all through this so I could incorporate it into my sharing."

Lily said, "It's okay, Connor. You don't need to use the metaphor."

"Really? Okay, thanks, Lily. I didn't want to hurt your feelings."

Lily laughed, "You haven't at all. Thank you for being so thoughtful."

Connor took a breath. "Okay, good, because I had this all prepared at home," he said, displaying his stack of notes, "and then trying to put a Cooking Pot in it was just…"

He took another breath, as if air was in short supply. Then he closed his eyes and visibly settled himself.

Eva, being a schoolteacher, knew how much effort Connor was putting into this. Even though she hardly knew him, she felt inordinately proud of him. Tears came to her eyes.

Connor cleared his throat and began.

"Okay, here it is: The most important distinction between Mindfulness practice and Concentration practice is that Mindfulness is more global and Concentration is single pointed. But the two work together, and Concentration helps cultivate Mindfulness."

Eva couldn't help but think that perhaps Concentration was like a hunter mode of following a particular prey, while Mindfulness had a global awareness necessary to raise children, gather food, clean the home, and cook dinner, and…*Hush,* she told herself…*just listen!*

Connor continued, "There are many possible points where we could focus our concentration practice, and I'll share some of them. I wanted to talk about the Four Jhanas, the first four stages of meditation. But Vicente said I wouldn't have time to talk through them *and* do the experiential practices.

"I hope you'll explore them in your own practice they help us let go of the constant pursuit of sensual pleasures and find freedom from overwhelming choices, which brings a peaceful mind and acceptance of not having — or needing — all the answers.

"This is good for me because I have always been hungry for knowledge. I want to accumulate it, box it up, organize it. When I'm struggling, I just assume it's because I don't have enough information. So I do a deep dive into the well of accumulated knowledge. And I get fascinated, enchanted even. Then I recognize that I'm caught up in greed for knowledge. Facts, theories, it all becomes a kind of addiction.

"My challenge is to accept that there is much I can never know, and then to rest in that don't know mind with gratitude. To let go of the idea that life is a mystery I have to solve. To allow a sense of wonder in. To rest in awe and gratitude for simply being present to experience it in this moment, just as it is. I admit I am not there yet.

"This challenge hasn't stopped me from exploring and researching, but it has changed the goal of accumulating information into the Wise Intention of joyful exploration.

"I recognized that my need to know everything was one aspect of my need to be in control of the situation. Maybe we all have that need. But through our practice, we understand that we are not in control here! We equip ourselves with information to deal with whatever life might present us but let go of the false belief that there is any armor out there that will truly protect us from the nature of impermanence.

"No one knows everything. We might rely on the experts or AI, thinking they have superpowers. But it's all 'garbage in/garbage out'. Maybe it was true ten years ago, but things are always changing. With Wise Concentration, we open to Wise View. And if we understand that we don't need to know everything, we suffer less. And we can learn to love the question itself. Who said that?"

Vicente said, "Rainer Maria Rilke in his letters to a student: 'Be patient toward all that is unsolved in your heart and try to love the questions themselves, liked locked rooms and like books that are now written in a very foreign tongue…'"

"Okay, thanks, Vicente," said Connor, though it seemed Vicente wasn't done with his recitation. "Now, since many of us practice meditation by focusing on our breath, I thought we'd try something different. With Mindfulness, we may be aware of the presence of all the elements in the body—earth, water, fire, air, and consciousness—but in Concentration practice, we choose just one to meditate on. So I've set up small bowls of water in front of each of you. And it's very traditional for us to simply focus on our water bowl."

Eva wasn't quite sure how this worked. She'd only ever practiced meditation by sitting with her eyes closed, focusing on her breath. But then she remembered that she had focused on the campfire flames: the element of fire. And, of course, she had focused on the breath, which was the air element. She had at times in her life become mesmerized while sitting on a beach, watching the ocean waves or the ripples in a mountain lake. She could do this.

Connor's voice broke through her thoughts. "Let's begin with a little *Metta* practice to ease our way. We create a safe space to practice. Feel free to use your own wording. The simplest "May I be well. May I be free from harm." is fine.

Eva took a breath and thought of these words of well-wishing. She felt relaxed. She felt supported by the radiant sense of loving kindness.

After a few minutes, Connor said, "Now, whenever you are ready, open your eyes and focus only on the water in the bowl before you.

"Remember our exploration of Wise Intention and Wise Effort. They will support you. Remember, Wise View to help you hold this practice without a goal or the need to prove anything. Let go of everything but this, just this…"

The bowl was small and dark, and the surface of the water was still. At first, it was hard to distinguish the water from the bowl itself. Eva felt herself tense up; afraid she would not be able to 'meet the challenge.' Then she remembered Wise Effort. She would just be present. There was no challenge. There was just this opportunity to be present in this moment, just as it is. With the support of the Metta practice and with the invitation to simply stare at the water, Eva felt herself releasing any concerns.

Then she noticed subtle reflections of light on the water. At first, it was just a thin line of white on the curve of the bowl. Then she saw a more subtle, softer smudge of light to the right and above it. Then she noticed an even more subtle hint of light at the bottom of the bowl, all of them holding the same curve, but at different levels of intensity.

A waft of afternoon breeze came through the yurt's open windows. Eva felt it on her skin, but she focused on how it affected the surface of the water. The lines of light danced about. She shifted ever so slightly on her cushion and could see more light playing on the water.

After a bit, she couldn't resist picking up the bowl and holding it in her open palms and tilting it slightly this way and that, bringing it closer to her face and further away. She didn't do this stealthily, but quietly, so as not to disturb anyone. The light danced and shifted in shape on the surface; her gentle breath was powerful, causing the water's surface to ripple. Her hands encircling the little bowl were like embracing the whole planet, this small, fragile Earth. She felt a profound love within her—such a deep sense of connection.

She realized as she observed it all that it wasn't possible to focus on only one element. All the elements are always present. The earth element of the bowl holds the water. The air element in the breeze makes it ripple. The light element makes the water visible—and that fifth element, Consciousness—her awareness, holding it all.

She closed her eyes and felt a sense of something beyond happiness. A deep connection. This body wasn't separate either. This consciousness was not separate either. No matter how many edges there are in the world, this is all one being, and all our thoughts and opinions and judgments are just patterns that soften with awareness, with clear seeing, with understanding. This was the same message she kept getting from every meditative experience she had.
How many ways there were to remind her!

She was so grateful for them all.

She hadn't even realized how much she had been trying to fit in, to do this right, to prove herself in some way, but why? And now, some inner voice rose within her and reminded her of what Minna had told her: "I have nothing to prove. I have nothing to hide. I have nothing to fear."

And then, when she'd really taken that in, there was a deep reminder: "I have something to give."

She was filled with radiant loving kindness. She opened her eyes and found she was sending Metta to this sangha and then radiating out into the entire world without exception.

At that very moment, Connor had opened his eyes and was about to ring the bell. So she closed her eyes again and let herself hear it fully, resonating out into every corner of the universe and beyond with loving-kindness.

And then she bowed with gratitude for this gift of presence.

*   *   *

After a minute or two, Connor invited them to stand and take a brief break in silence, just to give whatever had come up for them room to be felt even more fully.

So Eva went outside and walked into this area she hadn't seen before. It was full of life. All manner of insects, birds, and lizards-- all dancing in their own patterns in the afternoon sunshine and light, billowy breeze. And she now knew she was not an invader here. At the very least, she was a generous producer of CO_2 and moisture, and who knows what else that was beneficial to life, and intrinsically interconnected. She was…how else to put it? She was home.

Soon the bell rang again, and she returned to the yurt where Connor had removed the bowls and arranged the cushions back into an egalitarian circle. He still made room for Trusty at his side, but he clearly felt more confident and in his element.

Once everyone was settled and looking at him, he said, "I mentioned earlier that there are forty places to put your attention. I won't list all forty. These are available for study from multiple sources, including Bhikku Bodhi's book on the Eightfold Path, which most of you have read. But they basically break down into seven groups. And we just did a meditation from the first grouping, the *kasinas*. Well, actually, *kasinas* are colored disks, but I couldn't find those, so I used the little bowls. Anyway, they represent different qualities. Four represent the primary elements--the earth, water, fire, and air.

"So that's what we just did, focusing on the element of water. And now I'll open the floor so anyone who wants to can share a few words about your experience focusing on water."

Eva just wanted to stay with the resonant effects of her mindful meander and this water meditation. She felt like it would be too quickly diluted by her natural engagement with others and curiosity about their experiences.

As if in immediate obedience, her hearing shifted. She kept her eyes closed, and the sound of everyone's voices was garbled, as if she were underwater and could hear people talking but not their words. It was strange. But also strangely comforting, as if she had a self-protective superpower that she hadn't been aware of. She didn't suppose it was very mindful, and really, it was kind of weird, but also cool. Maybe the underwater hearing was a direct reaction to Connor's earlier mention of Concentration being underwater in Lily's Cooking Pot metaphor.

Eva's ears perked up when she heard Conner saying something about the distracted mind being like a fish flapping about on dry land. What a coincidence. Maybe she should pay attention to what he was saying.

Connor continued. "Awakening through concentration has three parts: Seeing the selfless nature of phenomena, abandoning signs of permanence, and recognizing the unsatisfying nature of phenomena."

Everyone looked thoughtful, some nodding, some puzzled. *Oh good, I'm not alone in not getting all this*, thought Eva.

"I know that's a lot to take in. For some it will be nonsense. To others it will be compelling concepts. And to some, perhaps, it will be fully understood. That's the aim of our Concentration practice. Because with those three understandings we become freed from greed, hatred, and delusion. That's *Nibbana*!"

Eva could see a glow in his eyes that looked like hunger, as if he could see what he was after on the horizon and was ready to pounce.

Connor looked down at his notes. "Okay, after the ten *kasinas*, the list includes ten 'unattractive objects.' Historically, this included hanging out with decomposing corpses. In our culture we immediately bury or burn our dead, often without even seeing them in that state, let alone watching them decompose."

Eva noticed she wasn't the only one who shifted a little uncomfortably. A state of deathlessness was all well and good, but it just felt too soon. She wanted to escape her mother's death, not relive her funeral.

Connor went on, unaware of any discomfort. "I've kept my eyes open while hiking to see if I could come across any decomposing remains of voles, moles, or birds that I could bring for us to sit with. But between the bobcats, coyotes, and vultures, nature keeps a very tidy camp."

People couldn't help but laugh. Partly at Connor being Connor, and partly in relief that his hunt had been unsuccessful.

"The benefit of sitting with decay is to come face to face with the reality of impermanence. Most of us have so much resistance to the concept of impermanence, *Anicca*. We think we can keep things from changing, keep ourselves and those we love from aging and dying, but if we pause for even just a minute, we know it's not true. Right?"

They all nod with acceptance.

"The teachings tell us that sitting with a human corpse puts impermanence front and center, making it feel very personal. We recognize that this 'me' I see in the mirror is not only changing but is going to die. Who knows when? But it's going to happen.

He lowered his gaze. "I know I'm young, but I've lost classmates to car crashes and overdoses. I was never old enough or 'cool' enough to know them well, but they were in my world and then not. It was shocking. And in school, our teachers had to train us to be prepared to protect ourselves from a madman with a gun. So, I may look young, but death is not abstract to me."

"So even though we can't sit with decaying remains, we can sit with our experiences of coming face to face with our own mortality through whatever losses we've experienced. Or maybe you've come close to death yourself. Let's sit with that awareness for a bit."

Every relaxed part of Eva's body screamed 'no!' And yet, she knew it was time. Look what avoiding the pain of the loss of her mother had gotten her into. If not now, when? So, she sighed, sat, and cried.

She thought her crying was silent, but perhaps she was sobbing a bit, because soon there were several sobs and gulps around the room. It didn't really matter who they were crying for. It was a funeral without a specific casket. It was grief. Pure and simple. And there couldn't have been anything more consoling than the sounds of others sobbing and sniffing. No arm around her shoulder would comfort her as much. Because she was not alone here, this was not her isolated grief. It was universal. They all had lost someone, and if they hadn't, they knew they would, because all was impermanent. Anicca.

Yet she sensed that her mother was with her now. Not as a ghost, but as the continuing expression of life living through generations. This body, these genes, and all the memories they shared. There wasn't anything in her life that didn't contain her mother in some way.

As the sobbing subsided, laughter ensued. It seemed funny that these lovely people could cry together spontaneously. And laughter and tears seemed as married as any two expressions of emotion could be. Eva opened her eyes, looked around at all the tear-stained faces now chuckling, and she felt an incredible release from any last withholding and a deep sense of connection with this sangha and all life.

Eventually, Vicente cleared his throat. "Thank you, Connor. Clearly, you successfully communicated your point! I know the concept of death is challenging for many of us. It seems in this culture, there is a preference for concealment and looking away. However, my experiences with death started so young that it was woven into the fabric of my life. In my community in Mexico, right next to the grocery store was a coffin store, and there were children's coffins in the window. My mother would cross herself as we walked by, and I knew she was asking the blessed Virgin of Guadalupe not to let her lose another child to the rages of measles or polio or whatever else was rampant, not just in our community, but in the world before vaccines.

"Funerals were such a common thing, I just accepted them as a part of life. You turn a corner and there's a street full of people walking with a flower-decked coffin. And sometimes I was part of the funeral procession, and maybe I wasn't always aware of which relative or family friend was in the big box. But I remember one time, it was a little box, a box of my size, with my cousin in it, and I understood that we would never play ball in the street again, and I cried.

"Naturally, I remember and cherish the annual *Día de los Muertos*, when we spent the night in the cemetery, decorating our dearly departed's gravestones with *cempasúchiles*—what is that orange flower called in English? Mary-gold?—it doesn't matter. For days beforehand, the ladies would use the flowers to create beautiful wreaths and other decorative items. There were other flowers, but it was said that one had the most pungent scent to draw the ancestors' spirits into the mortal world.

"There was drinking and music, but all very respectful, not like a saloon. Everyone was always aware of the loved ones the family had lost, but they believed with great fervor that on that night, the thinning of the veils made it possible for them to be together with the living in a wonderful celebration. My mother believed, as so many do, that the soul lives on as long as we remember them. And she firmly believed there is heaven and hell. If that is so, I assure you *mi madre está en el cielo.*

"Putting this into context, Buddhism came into being in India, into a culture where reincarnation was universally accepted. And Siddhartha Gautama accepted it. He was a man of his time.

"But the Buddha wasn't interested in questions of philosophy, of origins and final destinations. When asked about such things, his standard answer was that we can't know, and not only can't we know, but it's all beside the point. What he cared about was ending suffering in the here and now, for himself and all beings. Awakening! That this rested on an assumption that the beliefs he inherited about reincarnation were true is not surprising. But his mind was as open as any mind could be. Those who kept the Buddha's teachings alive orally for hundreds of years before they were all written down, and many of those who followed, accepted reincarnation as the way of things as unquestioningly as we assume that the sun rises in the east.

"But does the sun rise in the east? No, of course, the sun doesn't 'rise' at all. Instead, it is revealed by Earth's rotation. Our distant ancestors had no clue about that, so for them, the sun's rising and setting was an unequivocal fact. Perhaps the same is true with reincarnation. We don't know. Maybe the same is true with heaven and hell. We don't know. Someday, when we transition, we may know, but it is not something we can be certain of in this life.

"Our focus has to be on living. We're not doing this practice to get into heaven or reincarnate into a cushier life. We're here to release our blinders so we can stop making a mess of things in our own lives and in the world. We are here for the benefit of all beings.

"Not knowing the answers to these eternal philosophical questions may seem scary, but for me, there's a greater ease in resting in the state of not knowing. *Que sera, sera.* Acceptance of death is fundamental to life. Knowing exactly what happens is beyond our jurisdiction."

Vicente looked over at Connor and nodded.

Eva found Vicente's sharing fascinating. Her students loved the animated movie *Encanto*, so she had watched it and found it delightful. She had watched it again after her mother died and allowed herself to fantasize about seeing her mother again. It was comforting. But she felt like it would be cultural appropriation to create an altar on the Day of the Dead. Was it? Maybe, instead, she could make her version of a little altar — a photo of her mom and a few of her favorite things — and light a candle, then sit and think about her. But she will do it on the anniversary of her birthday. That felt more natural for her.

"Anyone else?" said Connor now.

Minna raised her hand, and when Connor nodded, she said. "Well, as a nurse, I am not unfamiliar with death. It is not alien to me. It is part of life in a hospital. During the pandemic, as you can imagine, it was a living hell. I have never felt so helpless or exhausted. And I felt so cut off from my family. However, we did feel the whole community, and the entire world community, showing its support for all of us on the 'front lines'. The nightly banging of pots and applause as we entered and exited the hospital. It made a difference. It didn't eliminate the danger, fear, frustration, or exhaustion, but it gave us a sense of community beyond the hospital walls that we'd never known. And that's stayed with me."

Eva noticed that everyone was looking at Minna with the same warmth and appreciation she was feeling, tinged with the complex emotions from the memory of the worldwide experience they'd all lived through. If ever anyone thought we were isolated fortresses of self, COVID should have set them straight. And yet, the world returned to its old ways, didn't it? She certainly had.

Minna nodded that she'd finished sharing. Connor thanked her. Then Vicente leaned over to Connor, and they quietly conferred. Connor nodded and looked at the circle.

"Okay, the decomposing corpse is one of the forty places to meditate on, but it's not to obsess about it or get all morbid. It's the opposite. It's to acknowledge the impermanence of life and let it go."

He looked down at his notes and read: 'Luminous is this mind brightly shining, but it is obscured by attachments." [AN 1.49-51]

"I really like that quote from the Buddha. Concentration is a practice of such pure focus that it burns away attachments. It's also a reminder that this aspect of the Eightfold Path shouldn't be undertaken without guidance from a qualified teacher. To delve into it entirely on your own, without a teacher, without a sangha, without understanding, is like playing with fire.

"For example, without guidance, we might misunderstand the word 'attachment'. Releasing attachment is not turning away from life or our connection to the people we care about. It's only the clinging that causes us to suffer, not the interaction. Through the practice, I've found I can recognize attachment by how it feels in the body. The tension, the exhaustion of mental exertion, and all kinds of other subtle and not-so-subtle effects of how our attachments obscure our view.

"Most of you are familiar with many of the Ten Recollections. These are the fundamental Buddhist concepts that we explore and discover through our own practice—for example, the Triple Gem: the Buddha, the Dharma, and the Sangha. Lily shared how, in her Cooking Pot Analogy, the trivet that holds up the pot is the stabilizing factor for the pot of Wise View.

"The word Buddha means awakened, a reminder that we have the capacity to awaken. Without exception. Again, not a distant goal, but a moment-by-moment practice. A willingness to be here now, no matter how many times we get distracted.

"It's a reminder to meditate regularly. I find comfort in having a regular schedule, which makes it easy for me to fit meditation into my day. The day feels lopsided and uncomfortable without it. But I know others find it challenging to find time. And all we can do, in that case, is to do the best we can. To really understand its value. To imagine Lily's metaphoric pot tilting without the trivet.

"The pot would also tilt if we didn't have the teachings. I encourage you to read the Pali Canon, which holds the original teachings. You don't have to read everything. There's a lot of repetition. But at least you get a sense of it. There are numerous books and recorded Dharma talks from various teachers, so you can study the Dharma on your own schedule even if you can't attend meetings.

"So that's the Buddha and the Dharma. What about Sangha?

"With this, he looked around the room and smiled. "Of the three, Sangha is considered the most important. Even if you don't meditate, even if you don't study, even if you're zoning out when listening to a Dharma talk, being in community with others who earnestly practice is of great value.

"I know people who meditate and listen to audio talks while they're jogging or whatever. And they seem to think they've got it covered, that they don't need sangha. And maybe it's true for them. I'm no fan of gatherings, but what I began to see was that without the sangha, when I falter in my effort, or start to have doubts, when I fall into one of the Five Hindrances, it's the sangha that helps me.

"The Buddha, Dharma, and Sangha are equally important and make up the Triple Gem."

"There's so much to share, but I don't want to dump it on you. So let's go outside and do some walking meditation, which is another form of concentration practice."

Eva decided to stay in the yurt to do her walking practice. The meadow up here seemed too uneven, and she still felt like she would be trampling the creatures in the grass. Okay, and yes, she wanted to examine the artwork more closely.

At one point, she found she was wondering about the floor of the yurt. It was made of wood; she could see that. But she didn't know what kind of wood it was. She didn't know who built the yurt. Where the lumber came from. What was under the floor? She assumed there were posts, but were the posts sitting in the dirt, resting on stone or concrete? It didn't really matter, of course, but she was fascinated by how, with every assumption she made about what she knew, there were a million unknowns. The canvas of the yurt walls came from somewhere, grew from something—cotton fields maybe, and if so, how was the process different from cotton sheets with such a different texture? But anyway, it was woven somehow, transported, and all these things were unknown to her.

She looked up and saw the tree branches swaying in the breeze through the skylight. She had always thought she knew trees because she was familiar with the names of most species and could differentiate one from another. This was the information she shared with her students on nature walks. But what did that even mean? She knew nothing! She could talk about what went on inside the trees, but it was just words describing processes she'd never experienced. The tree was rooted in the ground, but she didn't know where the roots went. She could picture them, but she didn't know. She didn't know.

"I don't know!" she said to herself. Somehow, this was the most freeing thought she felt she'd ever had in her life. I DON'T KNOW!!!! Wow!

She felt she had come to the end of her natural walking meditation and decided to make a trip to the bathroom. When she returned, others were finishing up. Lily came up to her and said, "So how are you doing?"

"Good! I realized something."

"What's that?"

"I realized that I don't know!"

"Hooray!!!"

Eva laughed. That was exactly right. *Hooray!*

They re-entered the yurt and settled themselves onto their cushions, closing their eyes. She noticed that Trusty hadn't returned. He had better things to do. She knew he wouldn't venture far.

Connor rang the bell, and they opened their eyes. The energy in the yurt was different now, alive and alert. Eva would have to remember how to shift the energy in a classroom. But this was not a teacher training retreat. This was…what was this? Well, whatever it was, it was, as far as she was concerned, just for her. Just what she needed. She would let go of expectations and preferences and just open to what Connor had to share. He was indeed wise beyond his years.

Connor began, "When we are meditating, our attention is zeroed in, locked in place. The way a birder might look through binoculars at a rare bird, perhaps. It becomes so interesting that all thoughts fall away. There's just the focus.

"But then thoughts and emotions arise. *Oh no!* We may think. *What to do?* One thing we can do is categorize the thought as one of the Five Hindrances and adjust accordingly. We might think of these Hindrances as the tools of Mara, the one who kept seducing Siddhartha. Gently but firmly acknowledging Mara, seeing the seduction, helps us to release it in a skillful way. We don't have to beat ourselves up or think it's part of who we are. It's just Mara, who would like nothing more than causing inner turmoil.

"Now Eddie did an excellent job of going over each of Hindrances, using the Buddha's metaphor of water. Can anyone tell me what they are?"

Eddie raised his hand.

"Besides Eddie, obviously," said Connor. "Everyone, just think of one. Maybe one that has come up for you sometime today. It's excellent practice."

"Okay," said Sara, "Craving!"

"Yes," said Connor. "Craving, you'll remember, is like colored dye—so attractive on the surface of the water but not something you'd want to drink."

He looked around. "What else, what other Hindrance have you experienced lately?"

"Aversion," said Lily. "I was sitting out, minding my own business, when a bee started antagonizing me. Of course, I wanted to be kind, and, of course, I wouldn't kill it, but I did very much want it to leave me in peace. Then I realized he was attracted to the scent of my chamomile tea. So it was a situation of his craving colliding with my aversion!"

Everyone laughed.

"Thanks, Lily. What else?" asked Connor.

"Restlessness," said Allie. "I was excited to have you all open your bento boxes for lunch, and it made me restless this morning."

"Yes, thank you, both of you, for those. They were delicious and beautiful," said Connor. "And do you remember what the Buddha likened restlessness to?"

Allie looked thoughtful, then said with uncertainty, "Like waves? Whipped by the wind?"

"Yes, correct," Connor smiled.

"Can't I at least do one?" asked Eddie.

"Okay, go ahead."

"Sloth. I'm the first one up every morning to light the fire and do other tasks, and this morning I just wanted to stay in my sleeping bag."

"And did it feel like a stagnant pond, choked with weeds?" asked Connor.

"Well, not physically, but mentally, yes. Pretty accurate."

"And the fifth Hindrance?" asked Connor.

When no one answered, Minna said, "The fifth one is Doubt, and I have no doubt that our newest member might have some doubts. Not to put you on the spot, Eva."

Well, Eva did feel put on the spot. But at the same time, she was grateful to be included. "Yes, of course. I doubt I'll ever be able to remember all these lists!"

Connor said, "No worries. No one remembers them all. But they are there for us when we need them. Now, Doubt is likened to muddy water. How do you get out of it?"

"Keep on keeping on?" she asked.

"Yes, but what do you keep on doing to clarify that muddy water?"

"Ah," said Eva. "Meditate!"

"Yes!" Connor beamed at her. "Okay, everyone, now think of the contents of the pot as consciousness, the thinking mind. When it is calm, peaceful, and spacious, then the contents are pure and clear. That's wisdom. Not a collection of knowledge, but spacious awareness.

"Now, let's go deeper into this metaphor of the Five Hindrances.

"With Sensual Desire, if food coloring has been poured into the pot, it would color our view of what is happening, right? Those colors are alluring, but they blind us. This sensual desire refers to any craving for something that we experience through our senses.

"For example: Our eyes might desire only the most beautiful things, whatever our idea of beauty may be. We want to surround ourselves with it. Clothes, homes, cars, and so on. All eye candy that may drive us to spend more than we can afford.

"Our sense of taste might be addicted to sweet, salty, or fatty foods. We get cravings, we go mindless. We cause our bodies to suffer the consequences.

"Our sense of touch may crave surfaces that are soft, smooth, or silky, as well as warm. Or cool. Now I like to pet Trusty here. His fur is delightful. But I don't crave it, and I think that's an important distinction for us to notice. When I was living in a monastery, it was a good thing I wasn't picky about thread count!

"Our ears might crave pleasant sounds. We might feel we need to have our favorite music to set the mood and enjoy the moment. We might have a variety of playlists to suit every aspect of our lives.

"Desire for pleasure colors our experience. If we're really paying attention, we see that desire is painful. We see everything through the filter of whether it fulfills our craving or not. All else falls away, and we get out of balance. This desire sets up a dependency on everything being a certain way. At its extreme, desire creates a driven quality, so our lives are shot through with desperation, helplessness, and sometimes self-loathing. In this way, one Hindrance can easily lead to another."

Connor looked around the room to make sure everyone was taking in the full horror of this Hindrance. Eva certainly was. She'd always thought of her preferences as pleasant and harmless. But now she could see that under certain recent conditions, desire had become the monster that ruled and was ruining her life.

"It might help to remember that a gas leak into a pond would create a pretty swirling, colorful effect, but be deadly." He looked around sternly.

Eva had to smile because he was so sincere. But he caught her smile and gave her an extra stern look, as if he thought she wasn't taking this seriously enough. But she was. She really, really was. She lowered her eyes, feeling chastened. She imagined that some of his teaching style was rooted in his time in the monastery, where the monks might have been very strict.

Connor continued with the metaphor. "Now let's imagine the pot boiling. This bubbling quality represents the Hindrance of aversion. If we hate something, it might erupt in anger, violence, or rage.

"In this mind state, when the water is boiling, can we see anything else but the bubbles? No. We are just focused on the bubbles, the aversion, the anger, the hatred. It is all-consuming. It is the only thing that exists. And we can't see that our speech and actions cause harm." He looked around the room. "Maybe you can think of a time recently or in the past when you felt really upset about something."

Eva did not have to think back far. She thought of the rage within her that sent her storming up into the hills. She had been so blind that she tripped and fell. It turned out well, but it could have been disastrous! Yes, she could see how dangerous the Hindrance of aversion could be.

Connor seemed satisfied with their thoughtful consideration.

"For the third Hindrance, imagine the pot filled with disgusting muck, as if campers from last week forgot to clean it. It's stagnant. This hindrance is sloth and torpor. Moving muscles in the body or mind would be too much of a slog. I imagine we've all experienced this at times. Maybe we're coming down with or just getting over an illness, or we're dealing with some difficult emotions that we want to hide from.

"But some of us live in states of severe depression. In that case, meditation isn't a quick fix, but rather part of what we may need to do, including seeking professional psychological help. But for most of us, most of the time, it's just recognizing that something's amiss. We're not just resting; we've fallen into the disgusting muck of sloth and torpor. It happens! No judgment. But it's an opportunity to reset our intention and effort to make them wise."

Again, he looked around. He clearly cared that what he was sharing was being fully received. Eva hadn't experienced much sloth. But torpor felt somehow like more of a mental fog, a cloaking device she might use to keep from thinking about things that she'd rather avoid.

"For the fourth Hindrance," Connor continued, "imagine wind blowing through the camp and across the surface of the liquid in the pot, creating a lot of ripples and obscuring whatever is beneath the surface, and making it impossible to see any reflection. This is the hindrance of restlessness and worry. We are glued to the future of our imagination. Maybe we're restless for the next thing, or we're worried something bad will happen. Either way, when we feel restless or worried, how can we be mindful of the present moment?"

Hmm, Eva was a little worried about the world, but she wasn't overly concerned about herself right now. She had made a big decision and felt solid in it. She was a little concerned that Chad would cause her trouble but couldn't see why he would bother. Still…

And she was maybe a little restless to see what life would be now that her head was much clearer, and she had these teachings to turn to. Was that a bad thing?

As she looked around the room, though, she could see that others recognized themselves in this Hindrance. Some of them were parents, so they were naturally concerned. And some were so young they were probably restless to see how their lives would unfold.

Connor spoke. "For the Fifth (and final) Hindrance, imagine the contents of the pot being thick, offering no reflection and obscuring our view. This represents doubt. Maybe we doubt our ability to meditate. We might think everyone else seems so into it, but our thoughts are all over the place. Or we might doubt the teacher's ability to teach, or maybe the value of the Buddha's teachings. Or maybe we question our self-worth or our ability to do something that everyone else has told us we can do.

"This kind of doubt isn't just questioning and exploration -- that's wholesome and worthwhile -- but a habituated state of doubt that undermines every Wise Intention and Wise Effort."

"Remember that these Five Hindrances of sensual desire, aversion, sloth and torpor, restlessness and worry, and doubt are states of mind, not to label ourselves or get attached to yet another aspect of identity. They are universal human tendencies that we can recognize as they arise. We don't judge ourselves for experiencing a state of mind but acknowledge that it is universally experienced by all of us at one time or another, to one degree or another.

"Recognition without judgment is key. Remember how the Buddha was able to deflect the tempter Mara by saying with compassionate awareness, 'I see you, Mara. I know you.'?

"We can see and know these Hindrances for what they are. We can say, 'Ah, desire, I know you.' or 'Ah, aversion, I know you.' or 'Ah, sloth and torpor, I know you.' or 'Ah, restlessness and worry, I know you.' or 'Ah, doubt, I know you.' That recognition is the bright light of awareness that dissolves the suffering caused by these Hindrances.

"Maybe you find you have been having more challenges with one or more Hindrance. They can be like pack animals! But each seen and recognized can be tamed.

"The Concentration aspect of the Eightfold Path is huge, much more than any one Dharma talk could ever cover. We have set something up for this evening. Vicente will explain."

Vicente nodded and thanked Connor. Then he looked around the circle. "As Connor said, there is much to the aspect of Concentration, more than any one lifetime's worth of exploration and practice for most of us. But that's okay. We're in no rush.

"This evening after supper we will form two groups. One will explore and practice the Four *Brahma Viharas*, the Devine Abodes. The other group will practice the first Four Jhanas, those levels of Concentration. So, think about which of those calls to you."

"Lily and Minna will lead the Brahma Viharas in Lily's tent. Those who wanted to explore and practice the Jhanas, led by Connor and me, will return here to the yurt after supper.

Eva decided to attend the Four Brahma Viharas. Divine Abodes sounded, well, heavenly. Much more inviting. And it would be cozy.

"Speaking of supper," Vicente continued. "Whoever needs to can head out now. The rest of us can enjoy the quiet of the yurt in meditation."

Then he bowed, and everyone bowed back. Sara, Connor, Minna, and Allie got up and left the yurt. Trusty left with them. Then Eva remembered she should check the bathroom to see if it needed anything. So, she left as well.

As she restocked the soap dispensers, wiped down the sinks and fixtures, and replaced some toilet paper rolls, she tried to use Wise Effort and to notice when one of the Hindrances arose.

She looked around to see if there was anything else she should do. She worried she wasn't doing a good enough job.

Ah, worry! That was one of the Hindrances. She remembered it was paired with Restlessness. But she didn't feel that way. *Hmm.* She was pretty sure she would never be able to remember them, that she wouldn't be able to continue meditating when she got home. That this retreat was like a dream that she'd wake up from with nothing to show for it.

Hmm, which Hindrance are you? she asked. *Ah, Doubt!*

She could see how labeling threads of thoughts and emotions as they came up helped to short-circuit them! What an excellent skill to have. And weren't these the tools of Mara? *Hello, Mara, I know you.*

17 The Four Brahma Viharas

Later, after the sun had gone behind the hills, Eva peeked into the kitchen area to see if they needed any help. Sara nodded with a big smile of gratitude.

She saw that Eddie was also in the kitchen. That was unusual. After directing Eva to help Connor, both Sara and Allie took off their aprons and headed toward their tent. *Ah, right*, Eva remembered. *They will be leading the talks tomorrow on the three remaining aspects of the Eightfold Path and will need time to prepare.*

She donned a clean chef's white apron that had been hanging on a tree branch, washed her hands in the metal sink, and followed the quiet assembly directions offered by Connor. Eddie ladled the lentil soup into bowls, and Eva cut the warm whole wheat bread. Trusty stayed discreetly out of the way, but now she could see that he and Connor had some kind of deal. Aha, she knew it! That made her smile.

Soon they had the simple meal warmed and ready, and Connor rang the bell for the rest of the sangha to come to the buffet. The soup must have been made earlier in the day, or perhaps earlier in the week? Eva was still amazed at the bounty of this camp kitchen. She'd stopped bothering to wonder how they managed it all. What did it matter? The food was delicious, and she was grateful.

After everyone brought back their dishes and poured some herbal tea for themselves, she and Eddie washed everything and wiped down the surfaces. Minna and Lily had taken their meals to the tent. She imagined they needed to confer on how to present the Divine Abodes, which, by camping standards, was indeed a divine abode. Conner took the clean dishes and stacked them in his special way.

Eddie went to turn on all the fairy lights around the campground, as well as a set of ones leading up to the yurt.

Eva stood in the center of camp, feeling at loose ends. What bell would ring next? If they weren't sitting around the fire, everything felt very different. Unsettling. But Eddie came back along with Allie and Sara. They each had flashlights, and even in silence, couldn't help but shine lights up under their chins and make ghoulish faces at each other. The mood was light, and they laughed.

Vicente arrived and invited those who wanted to go to the yurt to learn about the Jhanas and try deeper concentration practice to follow him.

Minna appeared and invited those who wanted to learn more about the Four Brahma Viharas and practice Metta meditation to follow her.

Two short lines along fairy-lit paths splashed by the beams of flashlight-waving retreatants headed in two different directions.

When Eva entered the tent after Minna, she was surprised to see the seating area transformed into something even more special and welcoming. The curtain to Lily's bed area was closed. But there were flowers, candlelight, and more upholstered seats. How?

Only when they were seated could she see that they were all women. Lily, Minna, Allie, and herself. So those who followed Vicente and Connor to the yurt were Eddie and Sara. Equally divided.

That Sara chose Concentration wasn't surprising. She seemed very focused. A silent retreat certainly left many gaps in people's stories. Eva had had to dampen her curiosity many times. *Which of the Hindrances was curiosity? Restlessness? Hmm.*

They sat together, Trusty by Eva's side. She pet him appreciatively. He clearly didn't want to abandon her at night. She closed her eyes and took a few slow easy breaths. There was no place else she'd rather be.

*   *   *

After a few minutes, the bell rang and they opened their eyes.

Lily smiled at them. "Minna and I have been talking, and we've found, not surprisingly, that we both incorporate Metta practice into our daily lives. She will share her experience, because I love her story."

Minna smiled at Lily and looked at them all. The warmth of the candlelight in the tent made Eva feel as if they were about to hear tales from the Arabian Nights. But it was just Minna sharing the Buddha's teachings. And that was more than enough.

Minna began, "These Four Brahma Viharas are not so much to study, but to be allowed to bloom and grow within us. Just as we can observe the Hindrances we learned about this afternoon, we can notice these mental states that come with our dedicated meditation practice.

"The first Brahma Vihara is *Metta*. Loving kindness. This loving kindness is very different from being nice, being polite, or minding our manners. This quality of infinite loving kindness is received, absorbed into every cell of our being, and then radiates to all beings everywhere.

"When I first learned about it, I thought 'Oh, that's what I do already!' because I used to do a little blessing every time my husband or Connor would leave the house. I'd say, "White light, all around, keep my baby safe and sound." That freed me from the worrying thoughts that would otherwise plague me throughout the day. It's a scary world out there, and I wanted them both to come home safely to me. I also did it every time we got in the car together.

"Then one day we were riding across a bridge, and I remembered I hadn't done my little blessing. So I did it silently, right then and there.

"I'd been meditating for a while by then, and was familiar with the word Metta, and I just assumed it was just different wording for what I was already doing. But between my personal meditation practice and attending Dharma talks, something had shifted within me. And at that moment on the bridge, having secured protection for our car and my family, I realized that my blessing was a little selfish. Yes, of course, I didn't want our car to be in an accident, but what about all these other cars on the bridge? Didn't I want them to be safe?

"Well, of course, I did. So, I started to do my 'white light' chant in my mind, but then I thought, 'Why stop there? Why not protect everyone who was traveling on the freeway beyond the bridge?'

"And my answer horrified me. I thought about how statistically not everyone could be safe. Someone will be in an accident at some point.

"What a dreadful thought! As if I had the power to decide who would be sacrificed to the gods of the underworld or something. I had an inflated sense of my own power, but a paltry understanding of Metta.

"And, since I had been practicing Mindfulness and knew firsthand the value of being fully present in every moment, I realized that statistics aren't necessarily predictive. Past patterns don't have to be repeated. If everyone on the freeway was paying attention — not looking at the view, not texting, not distracted, not nodding off, or arguing, or whatever — then everyone could arrive at their destinations safely.

"So, I wrapped them all in the white light and then beyond and beyond and beyond. All up and down the freeway as far as I could imagine.

"And then I understood the true nature of Metta: It's infinite."

She paused, letting her story sink in.

Eva thought it was sweet that Minna had her magical-thinking way of dealing with life's dangers. But really, wasn't Metta just more magic?

Minna resumed her talk. "Connor says he likes to imagine that every atom is vibrating Metta, that our awareness of it makes it vibrate even more. Our sense of interconnection and openness to Metta enlivens our being. Then, when we recall someone in need of loving kindness, we don't 'send' it to them so much as amplify what already exists.

"Metta is all-inclusive, no one is excluded. In the sangha, we've had so many conversations about the challenges of sending Metta to politicians whose policies or behavior we abhor. It's easier to send it to unknown people, just the world in general, than to send it to someone whose face makes us cringe, whose policies frighten us. But it's essential to do so.

"It helps me to remember that Metta is not a reward for good behavior. People who behave badly, even do horrendous things, are lost and entangled in the tangled veils of tight, twisted thoughts. They are suffering. Sending Metta isn't saying we want everyone to achieve their terrible goals. It's more of a clarifier to help them recognize the Three Poisons of greed, aversion, and delusion that are driving them to do the things they do. With Metta, we offer freedom to release fear, to take a breath, to see the world anew with Wise View.

"The wording for Metta varies. The most traditional I've heard from many teachers is *May you be well. May you be free from harm.* And that's very similar to my white light all around, isn't it? It's protective. But over the years of my practice, my wording for the Metta that I send has evolved. As a nurse, of course, I don't have a problem with the 'May you be well' part. But the second sentence 'May you be free from harm' for me activates all the fear of all the things that might harm us. It creates this defensive mode that seems counter to the true nature of Metta as I understand and experience it.

"So I say, *May you be well. May you be at ease. May your mind be peaceful. May you know the joy of being fully present in this moment, just as it is.*

"You can develop your own wording. I truly believe we each have access to just the right words we need to hear and need to say, if we are sensing that infinite connection. Connor and I use different words, but we are ultimately saying the same thing."

"Would you lead us in Metta practice?" asked Lily.

"Of course. But for this practice, we'll just use one sentence, not all of them, just to get the way to proceed."

Eva had every intention to follow along with the instructions, but she was stumped when Minna said, "We always begin with ourselves because we can't share what we haven't opened to, haven't received, haven't cultivated. We close our eyes and say, "May I be well.""

"May I be well," Eva thought. Yes, she very much wanted to be well. Cured of her sick addiction to Chad or anyone else who might activate that kind of desire that made her feel lost. She wanted to be done with grieving but knew now that she couldn't be done with it, that it would just evolve, and that fighting wasn't working. She felt she was a failure at emotions all around. Love and grief.

Minna, as if sensing her discomfort, said, "For many of us, this may be the hardest part of all. We may feel we don't deserve loving kindness. But it's not something to be earned. It's like sunlight that falls on everyone without regard to their behavior. It's not a reward. When we think of it that way, then we might be able to say, well, why not me? Why would I be the only exception?

"If it is too difficult, we can start by bringing to mind someone it's easy to send loving kindness to, like a child for whom we harbor no ill will."

Eva was relieved to have the focus off herself. She could easily think of many children she could choose. But instead of picking any of those in her classroom, she found herself focusing on the adorable eighteen-month-old baby of a coworker. It made her smile just to think of him.

"May you be well." She envisioned him, smiling, laughing, and playing. Yes, she very much wanted to send him this loving kindness. Of course, she wanted him to be well.

After a minute, Minna spoke again. "Good! Now, keeping your eyes closed, notice the feeling arising within you for the person you chose."

Eva felt warmth and welling up in her heart, sweetness, a tenderness. She felt a sense of loving kindness.

"Now use that feeling and bring yourself into the center of your awareness, and once again, but this time with more heart, more clarity, more understanding of the true nature of Metta, say, 'May I be well.'"

And Eva did.

After a minute or so, Minna continued, "As challenging as it may be to give Metta to ourselves, this practice also asks us to send loving kindness to difficult people. So bring to mind someone you may have strong negative feelings about. Someone you know or someone you've never met but who activates negative emotions in you."

Allie asked, "What if they're evil and powerful? What if they're ruining the world and destroying our future?"

Minna gently nodded, saying, "Even then."

"I just can't…"

"I understand, really I do. But Metta isn't wishing that everyone gets what they think they want. It's a well-wishing, a healing, a liberation from greed, aversion, and delusion."

Allie didn't look convinced, but she did look thoughtful.

Minna went on to explain that we send out Metta in radiating circles to those we know.

"We envision Metta expanding all the way out until it encircles the whole planet in its open and loving embrace, and beyond, and beyond."

They were silent for a bit, just letting the words resonate. Eva could sense how the addition of this practice enhanced meditation. All the benefits of the practice were shared immediately. And not diminished in the sharing but amplified.

Minna continued. "And if the words feel clunky, just rest in awareness. For me it feels like infinite radiant light is centered in this temporal self and easily, naturally, radiates out to all beings without exception."

That addition made all the difference to Eva. She was weary of words!

They all closed their eyes and let that sink in. Eva felt worries and anxiety dissolving as the light infused her heart. She was happy to become a light being centered in this seemingly solid self, not imprisoned by it. In this way she could love this dear little fleeting Eva and all beings everywhere.

*   *   *

After a few minutes, the bell rang. Eva opened her eyes that were filled with tears of gratitude.

Lily smiled. "Beautiful, Minna. Just beautiful. Thank you for sharing your insight and wisdom. Why don't we take a brief break."

Allie pulled her journal out of her daypack and wrote something down. But Eva felt content simply closing her eyes and resting in awareness.

When they resumed, Minna said, "The second of the Four Brahma Viharas is *Karuna*. Compassion. Once we feel Metta, once we feel that infinite unbreakable field of being—atoms and all—then we feel empathy. As a nurse, of course, I am in the constant presence of people in pain. Empathy and the desire to help sparked my interest in nursing.

"But empathy can be debilitating. We take on the pain as if it is our own. The practice of Karuna is not to succumb to the negative emotions someone may be feeling, but to access this universal compassion.

"Karuna has been a lifesaver for me. I become a conduit for loving kindness and a vehicle of compassion. My purpose is to deliver help as needed, listen as wanted, and be a strong, abiding presence in a fraught situation. That is very different from when I started nursing and was taught to 'not get too involved,' or 'create a protective barrier,' or 'don't give yourself away.' I understand the reason for that advice. A nurse can't be of service when depleted by empathy.

"But Karuna is action rooted in understanding our intrinsic interconnection. We help in whatever way we can, while staying centered and focused. We rely on the Eightfold Path to guide us. We can check in with our intention to ensure we are acting out of true compassion. We can check in with our effort and see if we are giving from our bounty or depleting our own energy from a feeling that we 'should' do something. We can recognize whether we give from genuine compassion or from guilt. Or, in my case, 'just doing my job. Just phoning it in.' This isn't good in any profession, but for a caregiver, it's particularly harmful.

"You may remember that earlier in the retreat, Vicente talked about the feeling tones, the senses. These are the *worldly* feeling tones we're familiar with. They are pleasant, unpleasant, or neutral. But each of them tends to activate one of the Three Poisons: greed, aversion, or delusion. If it's pleasant, we want more. If it's unpleasant, we want it to stop. And if the sensation is neutral, we may be drifting into daydreaming, not noticing anything, and that is part of delusion.

"But there are also wholesome feeling tones that don't activate the Three Poisons. We can rest in them indefinitely!"

Eva immediately felt a strong desire for whatever would bring that on.

Minna and Lily both smiled at the interest that statement evoked in everyone. "So, I imagine you're wondering, how do we access those feeling tones?"

Everyone nodded.

"Through acts of generosity and loving kindness. You know how good you feel when you give someone something and their delight warms your heart?" Everyone nodded again. "Well, that's a non-worldly feeling tone. And practicing Metta is a direct way to access it and bring it fully into our lives."

Minna looked around, pleased to see everyone's excitement about something she cared about so deeply.

Lily raised her hand and when Minna nodded, said, "I just want to add what an important discovery this was for the Buddha, what a difference it made for him when he was slogging away at starving himself to achieve Nirvana without any luck.

"After years of every kind of hardship practice, he remembered an experience he had as a young boy, sitting under a tree and just enjoying being fully present. Nothing to do. Nothing to achieve. Just that sense of being. Remembering that experience, he decided he was going about this enlightenment thing all wrong. And aren't we grateful he switched course! Because joy is at the heart of Buddhism. Not fleeting happiness of getting what we want, but the joy of living fully present, participating

in life in loving kindness, experiencing a sense of interconnection."

With that, Lily closed her eyes, and the others, inspired, did the same.

After a few minutes, Minna asked, "Are there any questions about Metta or Karuna? Or about the differences between them?"

Eva was so moved by the idea of non-worldly feeling tones, and she was about to ask how she might apply any of this to teaching children without being all woo-woo or creepy, when Trusty, who'd been napping at her side, suddenly sat up, then jumped up and barked.

Eva shushed him, embarrassed at his poor manners. But then they all heard the pounding of feet. At first, she thought it must be some hoofed animal, but no, it sounded human, just so out of place in this quiet retreat that it made her heart pound too.

Then the flap opened! Startled, then relieved, she saw it was Sara. But she looked so frantic that they all rose with concern.

"Minna, we need you," she said, not looking at anyone else.

Minna jumped up, grabbed her shoes by the opening, and was out of the tent before the rest of them had a chance to take in what just happened.

Oh my God! Eva thought.

The three of them looked at each other and started talking all at once.

"What do you think has happened?" Eva asked Lily.

"I don't know. There's only so much Minna could do as a nurse without any…Oh, I hope it's not Vicente's heart. Oh my, this climbing up and down hills…" Lily looked like she was going to be ill.

"Well, where are the cell phones? Someone should call 911."

"Vicente has them in his tent."

"Vicente?"

Lily smiled weakly. "He was the only one we could trust to absolutely not turn one on."

Allie said, "Okay, well, where's his tent? I'll run and find mine and…"

Lily shook her head, "Oh, no. We can't. We don't know anything yet. Let's not jump to…"

"But every minute counts if it's an emergency. Lily, please!" Eva wasn't a nurse, but as a teacher, she was prepared to take charge in an emergency. And it looked like this was one. What would they do up here in the hills? If Vicente had a heart attack or a stroke or whatever, how would the emergency crew rescue him? And if she made the call, could she even tell them where in the world they were? The landscape was very different from the one she knew so well. She felt very far from home.

Then Allie said, "But what if it's not about Vicente. Minna's not just a nurse, she's Connor's mother."

"Sure, but even so…"

"And what if it's not a medical emergency. What if…"

"Well," Lily said, "there's only one way to find out. Off to the yurt, ladies."

*   *   *

When they arrived at the opening to the meadow with a view of the yurt, Lily nearly fainted with relief to see Vicente standing on the porch by the door. Sara was standing next to Vicente, looking unsure where she should be. Minna was sitting with Connor on the top step, her arms around his shoulder. He seemed to be in no physical pain, but Eva could hear his sobs and muffled words as he talked to his mother. "I remembered her! I saw her! What happened to her?"

Minna murmured something to him and he settled down. Once he was calmer, he turned to Vicente, who stepped forward and bent down. Connor said, "I was doing a scientific investigation into the higher jhanas, and I guess I forgot the first lesson of the Buddha: to follow the Middle Way."

Vicente put his hand on Connor's shoulder, and said, "Well, Siddhartha almost starved himself to death for years before he had his realization, so I think you're doing very well. These things happen."

Seeing that everyone was okay, Lily, Allie, and Eva retreated back into the woods, not wanting to intrude. Eva imagined Eddie was probably still inside, meditating, not wanting to intrude from his end either.

After it was clear that Minna had the situation well in hand, Sara joined them the three women as they retreated to Lily's tent.

After they settled in, Lily explained to Sara that they'd already looked at Metta and Karuna. "You're familiar with both, so we'll just go on, though you missed Minna's wonderful story of her insight, how she came home to a deeper understanding of Metta. But I trust you had a good experience exploring the Jhanas?"

Sara nodded. She still seemed a little shaken.

"Dear, do you want to share your experience? Would that help?"

Sara shook her head, "No, I'm fine."

"Alright, then we'll just proceed as planned." She retrieved her notes and began, "The third Brahma Vihara is *Mudita*, sympathetic joy. It relies on the first two. Without those, when we are with someone who is happy, we may feel envy. This comes from our sense of separation, which leads to competition for what we perceive as limited resources. Happiness is not a limited resource! It's bountiful and contagious!

"This idea of sympathetic joy can be challenging if someone else got what you had hoped for. Envy may crop up. It's only human to want good things to happen. But it's joyful to feel so connected with all life that we can celebrate another's happiness with our whole being.

"You're probably familiar with the German word *Schadenfreude*, which is taking pleasure in the misfortune of others. Mudita is the direct opposite. If you experience *Schadenfreude,* you might stop and notice which of the Five Hindrances is present. And you might want to check in on that feeling of separateness that sets us up for all kinds of lonely, negative emotions.

"Does this bring up any questions or thoughts? It's challenging. It's not something we usually drop right into. We progress into it. It becomes so apparent. But its absence is very painful, and we can acknowledge that, can't we? We can accept that we are human beings with human emotions. Remember how we give Metta first to ourselves? This is also true with compassion. If you can't feel happiness for the happiness of others in certain situations, have compassion for yourself!

"Does that make sense? I don't want anyone to feel that you aren't 'achieving' something here. Just as Minna shared her earlier limited perception of Metta and then had an insight that changed everything, we each come to these teachings in our own time, in our own way."

Then Lily looked around at them: Two very young women, and one edging up to middle age. Eva could see the compassion in her eyes. She imagined that she had gone through a lot of turmoil in her younger years. She would love to know Lily's whole story, but she never would. She would probably never see her again after this retreat. And that made her sad. Very, very sad. Tears welled up, and she could feel them streaming down her cheeks. Trusty looked up, concerned. She started laughing. Why on earth was she crying? This was ridiculous.

"Can you say what's going through your mind right now, Eva? Or…"

Eva shook her head. She really didn't know. If she knew she would share it with them, but…

Then she blubbered, "I was just thinking how this retreat is going to end, and I won't see you again, Lily. You know, or maybe you don't, I don't think I shared it, but I recently lost my mother. I mean, I didn't *lose* her. She died. And I feel way too young to be motherless. And you've been so kind, inspiring, and helpful. I feel so fortunate to have been found by you."

"Ah," said Lily. "You're mourning. So, this retreat has offered you an opportunity to be with your grief. I'm so glad you happened upon us!"

Eva laughed. "Well, as I've said before, you all happened upon me. I was flat on the ground!"

Now the air in the small space lightened, and Eva was relieved.

"I hope Connor's okay. Should we send him some Metta?" Everyone smiled. So they sat together, ready to send Metta to Connor up the hill in the yurt, sobbing in his mother's arms. That was easy to do."

Then Eva remembered she was supposed to start with herself. Oh dear. But she did it. She saw that she didn't have a mother to cry to, and she could easily find it in her heart to send Metta to this suddenly motherless child, unskillful as she had been lately. And then she recalled the image of Connor, as he had just been, but also as he was when sitting before them, teaching Wise Concentration, and throughout the retreat, in the kitchen, taking care of meal prep and cleanup, and his growing bond with Trusty.

She imagined the Metta radiating in the night, like an infinite aurora borealis, encircling all the beings nestled asleep or alert to hunt. Metta permeated even the darkest places and grew and grew. Then it encircled the whole planet in its open embrace. And beyond and beyond. Ahh. Lily rang a tiny bell. They all bowed into the center of their circle. Then they opened their eyes and smiled at each other.

"Okay," Lily began, "The Fourth Brahma Vihara is *Uppekha*, equanimity. And we can see the value of cultivating the ability to be centered and at ease regardless of circumstances.

"But it doesn't arise by itself. It comes from our deepening practice and the first three of the Divine Abodes. We've tapped into an infinite source, and we find ourselves rooted so deeply that no storm can knock us down.

"We're not impervious to pain. That first dart is a part of life with all its joys and sorrows. But we are so supported by the Four Brahma Viharas and our Insight practice that we don't stab ourselves with a second dart.

"Our awareness becomes so spacious that we can hold great sorrow and great joy in the same moment. We can be fully present for whatever arises and see it as it is.

"The Vicissitudes, as the Eight Worldly Winds are also known, still whirl around, but our awareness can be spacious like the sky instead of being blown around and knocked down by them.

"With Wise View, truly understanding the nature of impermanence, no separate self, and suffering, this equanimity arises in our experience.

"It's comforting to know that Uppekha is possible. As we continue our practice, we begin to experience periods where it arises. Then longer stretches. Then it may become our way of being in the world. However, it's essential to remember that it is rooted in Metta and Karuna. Neither Mudita nor Uppekha can arise without the first two. We can't just make ourselves happy for others who get what we want. And we can't just make ourselves feel at home in the moment, whatever is arising in our lives and in the world. These are the gifts of the practice and of the Noble Eightfold Path."

Lily paused and looked around. "Is that clear? Do you have questions?"

Eva felt there was something so pure at that moment. As all the teachings began to come together and become clear to her, it wasn't as if she understood it all, not by a long shot, but she understood why she was on the Path. And she felt so grateful.

Sara and Allie looked radiant in the candlelight. They, too, seemed grateful and contented.

"Well then, let's bring our little exploration to a close for now. Feel free to stay here and do some sitting, or whatever calls to you."

She rang the bell again, and they all bowed.

Allie and Sara both rose and left the tent. Trusty clearly wanted to go out as well, so Eva put him on a leash and left, bowing at Lily with gratitude.

The leash seemed like a good idea in the dark of night. Trusty was so at home here, but who knew what critters he might want to chase in the night. The last thing she needed was for him to entangle with a skunk. What would she do then?

They circled the camp and stood out under the stars that were so much brighter here. Just then, a warm glow lit the top of the distant hill. *What is that? Fire?* She felt her heart race. But then she saw the top edge of the full moon rising.

She relaxed and stared in appreciation.

When she eventually returned to the tent, she heard voices inside. Oh dear, she didn't want to intrude.

But Trusty had no such qualms and nosed right into the flap.

Eva hesitated, but Lily called out, "It's okay, Eva. You can come through."

She entered, noticed Minna sitting with Lily over what looked like tea and a little plate of chocolates. *Ah, sometimes chocolate is the best medicine.*

She just nodded at them both and went into her sleeping quarters.

Still, the canvas didn't prevent the conversation from being overheard.

Minna was telling Lily how Connor had wanted to recreate a meditative experience he'd had in the monastery, a sense of being light.

"Ah, not exactly Wise Intention. It sounds like he fell into craving instead of wholesome aspiration. Is he alright?" Lily asked.

"I think so. But because of the talk about death this afternoon, it brought up a memory he had forgotten. But deep in meditation, he suddenly remembered his sister."

"His sister? You had a daughter?"

"Yes." Minna paused. "She was older three years older than Connor. She died when she was six, after a long, losing battle with cancer. It was a miserable time. But Connor was my little light in the darkness. His dad and I confined our grief to after Connor's bedtime, when we let ourselves weep. We were fortunate we turned to each other and not apart. We stopped mentioning her when he began to forget, since his questions were hard to answer, and he wanted very exacting details. Even at the funeral, he wanted to know what was in the box."

"Do you think Vicente talking about those little coffins might have…?"

"Could be. But also he may have overheard me talking in the dyads. Me and my big mouth. She's just been on my mind a lot lately.

"Anyway, deep in meditation, Connor began to recall his sister, and he broke down. Whenever she was home and up to it, she played with him…mostly games of her choosing where he would be 'baby', but still. He said that the sense of loss rose like a tidal wave and he was drowning in his sorrow." At this, Minna broke down.

Eva could imagine Lily holding the space for her, allowing her to grieve. Grief for her long-lost daughter and grief for her son's grief that must have felt so fresh for him.

"We're considering leaving in the morning, depending on how he feels."

"I understand. But if you do, make sure you're doing it for yourselves. The sangha can hold your grief."

"Whatever Connor decides, I'll stay or go with him."

They were quiet then. Maybe they hugged. Maybe they meditated together. Maybe Minna quietly left. Eva sent her and Connor some more Metta, grateful for the gift of something to do from a distance, hoping they felt the loving kindness. Then she drifted off to sleep.

18 Up for Interpretation

The next morning, as Eva quietly made her way from her part of the tent through the seating area, Lily peeked out from behind the curtain and smiled. Then, seeming to pick up on something, she asked Eva, "How did you sleep?"

Eva paused. "Fine, I guess. But just now I had a weird dream that woke me up."

"Oh, do you want to explore a little dream interpretation?"

"Is that part of the Eightfold Path?"

"Oh, no, at least not that I've ever heard. It's just something I've always enjoyed and found helpful. And I'm not sure if the Buddha would approve. He was strongly opposed to soothsaying, but this isn't about predicting the future. It's just another way to investigate the mind. It's another door into our inner wisdom."

Then she pointed to a chair and said, "Come, sit down, tell me. But only if you want to…"

"Okay, yes. Well, there were spiders, lots of them… solid round spiders. They were very busy…Oh, I can't remember anything else."

"Let me grab my dream book," she said, reaching into a little bookcase Eva hadn't noticed before. She pulled out a well-worn paperback and flipped through the pages. "Ah, here it is." Then she read to herself, peeking Eva's curiosity.

"Oh, yes," Lily said, "I thought it was something like that. It says that we create our own web or life space; how you weave your life is up to you."

Well, that sounds good and empowering, Eva thought. "But what about the spider?"

Lily went on reading, "The eight legs of the spider represent the cosmic energy for weaving the life we choose." She looked over at Eva. "Isn't that interesting? Here we are exploring the Buddha's Noble Eightfold Path, and you have a dream about an eight-legged spider!"

She read more, "We easily get caught in our own webs, forgetting they are but illusions of our own making."

"Illusions of our own making," Eva said. "Isn't that?"

"Yes! It's very much what we've been exploring, what the Buddha taught. We forget the power we have to change our reality."

"Wow." Eva realized she had been doing just that with her relationship with Chad. She had been creating an altered reality, thinking it was real, but it was all an illusion. She hadn't escaped from the pain of loss. She had made it worse. But at least now she knew. She was getting clearer. She was starting to see through the veils, the spider webs. Hopefully, she wasn't just getting entangled in another!

"Thanks for sharing that," she said as Lily put away her little book.

Trusty had left the tent earlier but peeked in now. Did he think he might be missing a party, or did he just want her to come outside?

Lily laughed. "Trusty says it's time for breakfast!"

*   *   *

When Eva entered the kitchen area, she was relieved to see Connor and Minna going about their daily routines. It would have been sad if they had had to leave before the end of the retreat.

Sara and Allie weren't there. Eva assumed they were preparing their presentations today. She looked forward to hearing more from them.

She took a cup of tea and sat by the fire that Eddie was adjusting. The early morning air was cooler and moister than it had been the day before. She held the mug between her palms to warm them, breathed in the rich tea vapor, and closed her eyes.

She allowed herself to settle into the felt sense of being alive in this moment. After a few more sips of her tea, she set the mug down beside her and adjusted her posture to meditate in earnest.

A snide inner voice started up with *Look at you, acting all Buddhist-y!*

Hello, Mara, I know you, she responded, and, amazingly, the voice evaporated, leaving her to this moment.

19 Wise Speech

After everyone (including Connor and Minna, Eva was happy to see) settled in the circle for the morning's exploration, Lily rang the bell.

She smiled at each of them, and then announced, "Today is our final full day together, and I expect it will be illuminating and insightful.

"We will begin this morning with Sara leading us in the exploration of Wise Speech. I don't think I need to say anything more on that topic. So, let's get started. Sara?"

As Eva looked toward Sara, she couldn't help but notice again that each person who presented an aspect of the Eightfold Path gained a quiet nobility. Sara's spine was elongated and regal, not hunched in her sweatshirt as it often was when she sat in a canvas back-jack. Now she perched on a firm round cushion, a zafu, her long legs crossed, her knees and calves resting flat on her mat. But it was more than just a different seat. It must be that each person took their role seriously, understanding the value of what they were about to share. Each became a sacred vessel, carrying the ancient teachings.

"Good morning, dear sangha. It's so good to be here, to sit with you all, to have this amazing nature retreat together." Sara looked around at each of them. Her skin was warm in the dappled morning light; her face, elongated like her body, was framed by a patterned head wrap that was more elegant than the hoodie that hid her face when she was meditating.

"I volunteered to lead the discussion of Wise Speech because it is an aspect of the Eightfold Path that's particularly challenging for me. So, I wanted to delve into it more fully and find out for myself, as the Buddha advised. Preparing this talk was quite illuminating, as I guess it was meant to be, right? I hadn't realized how unclear I was about what makes Wise Speech. So, I'm grateful for the opportunity to explore it so deeply.

"And, thanks to how we reorganized the order of the aspects to fit in with Lily's Cooking Pot Analogy, I had time to reflect more deeply on it throughout the retreat as we looked at each of the other aspects. Each of your presentations and explorations of them has enriched my investigation into Wise Speech.

"As Lily said, our parents taught us ethical behavior as best they could. Whether we obeyed or not, we knew right from wrong. Parents, teachers, and religious leaders all had the same message. In my culture, some of those messages are quite rigid, especially for women. I have been fortunate that my mother wanted me to be educated and wanted to send me abroad to study. She convinced my father because it also kept me safe, as my country is sadly so war-torn.

"Still, even though the cultural messages might vary, the core messages of knowing right from wrong seem to be the same.

"I had assumed when I came here that girls my age would be free of the messages I received. So, I was surprised to discover that many are trying so hard to be good, just like me, that we tie ourselves up in knots. Others become so angry that they lash out or shut down. We may become so uncomfortable that we don't even realize what we're saying. Our difficult emotions, hidden from our view, take over and do the talking. Or silence us, as our inner voices make us feel worthless.

"But, as we follow the Eightfold Path, our words and deeds are informed by these other aspects and become naturally wiser and kinder. I find that my speech has become much less defensive. I don't have to prove anything to anyone. And that has been a great relief.

"My education has been, for the most part, financed by a basketball scholarship. I have been trained to compete, to believe that winning is everything. And for me to win, someone else had to lose. But now I understand that I don't have to compete in life as I do on the court. And a sangha is not a team competing against other teams but is inclusive, collaborative, radiating in all directions. Our sangha excludes no one."

She paused and looked appreciatively around the circle, smiling.

"Coming from a culture where speaking out in mixed company would not be tolerated, my arrival here had me bursting with unspoken opinions and repressed anger. I was raised to hold my tongue, not taught how to communicate skillfully. And that combination caused me and those around me a lot of pain.

"Now, when I slip back into hurtful patterns of speech, it hurts me. I'm quicker to recognize where I wasn't skillful, and correct, retract, or apologize. It's fun to see the surprise on friends' faces when I gracefully 'accept a loss,' because they see me as so competitive. I had carried that competitive mindset over into my relationships, wanting to win at all costs, even when I was outright wrong. I remember still trying to think of something—anything!—to support my argument. I could be so stubborn. And now that I've had a chance to reflect on it, I can see that when it was clear that I was wrong, it felt as if I was being erased.

"I've begun to notice that when my words and actions aren't skillful, it's just because I've gone mindless, not because I'm inherently worthless or a ticking time bomb waiting to explode. It's just because I'm human. Thanks to the practice of meditation and the Buddha's teachings, I can now let go of my defensive posture. I'm not my thoughts or my words, but I am responsible for them. If they are causing harm, I need to learn how to be more skillful in dealing with them. And that's why I chose Wise Speech as my focus for this retreat. I've come a long way, but old habits die hard, and I wanted to take a deep dive into this aspect so I can review it and inhabit it, making it more natural for me.

"Instead of strapping tape on my mouth and handcuffing myself to avoid saying or doing the wrong thing, which would feel like returning to my country's enforced ways for women—no tape or handcuffs, I don't mean to imply that! However, as I've been cultivating Wise View, Intention, Effort, Mindfulness, and Concentration, I've become more aware of my words and actions. Not in a nervous, self-conscious, or self-condemning way. That would be counter to Wise Intention. I see how awareness and pausing before speaking are helping both in my words to others and in the harsh things I've always said to myself."

Some in the group nodded with recognition. Eva was delighted to hear Sara speak after days of silence. It was interesting to see how much personality came through in the voice.

Sara continued, "I'm sure I'm not alone in having been clueless as to how my words and actions hold more power, more punch, and more range over space and time than I ever imagined, for better or worse.

"How can we be cruel to someone with whom we deeply understand we are intrinsically interconnected, made of the same stuff, regardless of tribe, race, or geographic origin?

"Our words matter. Our words matter when we're talking to a spider that we want to escort from the house carefully, or the lizard skittering across the path. Rooted in the most profound understanding of being, our words arise from loving kindness. Let's take a moment to think about some words someone said maybe years ago that hurt and keep coming back to haunt us. Perhaps we're giving that person too much power, but it's only human to feel vulnerable and filled with self-doubt, thinking maybe what they said is true."

Everyone closed their eyes, reviewing memories. Eva didn't have to review very far back, but she challenged herself to skip over recent history and find something in the past that still stung.

My mommy says you're a bastard because you don't have a daddy.

Oh yeah, that hurt. How old was she then? Seven or eight? It was hard to keep a low profile in a small town when your mother is the town librarian, a central figure appreciated by just about everyone who ever read a book. So, some adult, not realizing she was being overheard, said that about her. How cruel! How thoughtless! How…

Sara cut into her thoughts. "Okay, if you find something, feel the power of those words, the emotional toll they still have, the resonance across the years.

"Then, deeply knowing the potential power of words to cause harm, let's remember that *our* words are just as powerful. No matter who we are, or how little we think what we say matters, our words can pack the same nasty punch as anyone else's."

Eva saw that clearly. Decades ago, a random remark by a clueless child still hurt. Wow.

Sara continued, "It's so much easier to see the power of our words when we practice Mindfulness, isn't it? The insights from our Concentration practice also transform our speech. Awareness of impermanence reminds us that these might be our last words!

"How different this way of coming to Wise Speech is from a list of rules! This way it's an exploration, and perhaps a revelation. It's not just the same old scolding instructions we've all heard before in a different form. Blah, blah, blah! Be good! That just feels like a bucket full of 'shoulds' pulled from a polluted river of hate-filled traditions.

"Maybe we're trying so hard to be good because we believe that deep down, we're no good at all. But that belief sabotages us and undermines us at every turn."

Sara's rich, insightful offering spoke to Eva. She was grateful to hear that this was not just what she experienced, but something universal.

Sara lightened her voice and said, playfully, "I love Lily's Cooking Pot analogy, and thought of an added way that it works: When something is cooking, our first experience of it, even from a distance, is the aroma of the rising steam that wafts throughout the house. Isn't that just like our first experience of someone? Aren't their words and actions the first thing we notice? We learn so much about what's cooking from that steam, don't we? It either smells delicious or…it stinks!"

They all laughed.

"Let's use an example: Maybe I have an unsettled feeling, a little nagging state of discomfort in my mind. What is it? After a brief meditation practice, I can take even just a minute to check in and explore that discomfort through gentle self-inquiry. It might become clear that I'm feeling regret about something I said to someone. Maybe my words were unkind. Or maybe it wasn't my story to tell. Or I was in a hurry or distracted and didn't take the time to be as kind and considerate as I might have been.

"Just the simple act of noticing lifts me a bit, because I can recognize that 'something stinks' and now I know what caused it. I can't take the words back—the stench is out there in the air—but I can acknowledge it, and I can make sure I don't use that recipe again, or leave the kitchen —i.e., go mindless—when something's cooking.

"Before, if something like that happened, I could spend hours, days, or longer, telling myself what a rotten person I am. However, since joining the sangha, learning about Dharma, and practicing meditation, I have come to realize that I can turn to the Eightfold Path to help me understand what really happened. And the Cooking Pot Analogy makes that exploration much clearer.

"Okay, here's an example: Let's say that I recognized that my words were unskillful because I was rushing. Rushing is an unbalanced effort, isn't it? And why was I rushing? What was I hoping to accomplish? What was my intention? I might want to avoid the possibility of a professor thinking poorly of me for being three minutes late. My wise intention to be present and compassionate fell by the wayside. My unskillful intention took over, and instead of quietly settling in, I might say 'sorry, sorry, sorry' all the way to my seat, knocking against other students on the way and creating disruption. So it's easy to see that unwise intention leads to unskillful effort and speech.

"But let's not stop there. Why was my intention unskillful? Because my view at that moment became unwise. I forgot that there is no separate self that needs to be polished up to perfection and presented to others. And I wasn't steadily stirring the contents of the pot, cultivating mindfulness, staying in touch with Wise View and the insights of

Concentration. Now we know this stirring is neither tedious nor painful. It's engaging and enlightening, infused with loving kindness.

"With Metta-infused Mindfulness, sensing the intrinsic interconnection of all life cultivates wisdom and skillfulness in my speech and actions.

"I'm learning through the teachings and through my own experience that words tell people much more than we think they do. The language we use and the intonation. Even the way we hold silence speaks volumes. Whether our body language is tight and withholding, maybe even judging from a safe distance, or easeful and open, receptive, ready to listen."

She looked around the circle and smiled at them. "Thanks so much for falling into the second category!"

Now she pulled out a piece of paper she had wedged under her seat. She took a sip of water and reviewed it.

"But what did the Buddha say about Wise Speech?

"First, that our words be truthful. That sounds simple enough, but is it? And how do we know? Where did we hear it? Can we trust our sources? Everything has become a bit murky. There's so much misinformation, geared toward manipulating our thoughts, emotions, and buying habits.

"In the Buddha's day, there was no technology to communicate with millions in seconds. He spoke to hundreds, and his words carried weight throughout India and beyond through the centuries, because they were so meaningful, and continue to be. But now, look at how far our words—good, bad, and ugly—disperse into the world, in ways even our more recent ancestors could never have imagined, let alone the Buddha. His guidance for Wise Speech addressed in-person interactions, but the impact of our words—how they are received, passed along, and amplified—should give us even greater pause before speaking or writing, or hitting the record button.

"We should definitely double-check our sources, think it through, pause to reflect on the ramifications of, let's say, an angry or snide text, a rotten review, or any of the other ways our words are spread around, for better or worse. I recall having a bad experience at a restaurant and angrily giving them a one-star review. Later, someone explained to me about that star system and how a bad rating can significantly lower the overall rating, potentially causing the business to suffer. I thought back to my experience and remembered that I was just in a bad mood that day. The waiter wasn't as prompt as I thought he should be. Honestly, I can't remember. I do remember that the food was delicious. So, a one-star review was totally inappropriate. I was able to go back online and change the rating, but that's not always possible. That's the power of our outbursts, in ratings, comments, words spoken thoughtlessly."

She paused and took a swig of water from her metal bottle.

"When we aren't truthful, then trust falls away. If a person lies about one thing, how can we be certain they're not lying about everything? This is the way relationships fall apart, careers end, and we end up not even trusting ourselves. Sometimes people lie to be kind. That's very tricky, isn't it? But it's better to be silent than to lie outright.

"The second aspect of Wise Speech is to avoid slander. Essentially, this means not spreading gossip, particularly malicious rumors. Just not talking about other people is a good rule to follow.

"The third rule is to be kind in our speech. If we're upset and are about to blurt out something rude, we can remember how it always comes back at us, doesn't it? Our harsh, thoughtless, or cruel words cause a ricochet effect that never turns out well.

"Of course, if we are cultivating kind speech, we also avoid harsh speech. If we're angry and upset, it's not the time to spew out hateful words we will later regret, and that will be felt and remembered by whoever we're yelling at.

"Cultivating *Metta* makes all the difference in finding words that promote goodwill and harmony. This isn't just to 'make nice'. If there's a disagreement erupting, we don't need to rush around trying to make it seem like everyone's getting along. That's just our discomfort with difficult emotions.

"True loving kindness is rooted in a deep sense of interconnection. We're not defending this separate-seeming self, trying to get people to like us. We're creating space and openness for others to be heard and speaking from that same generosity.

"Another thing to consider before we speak is whether our words are beneficial. Do they really contribute to the conversation? Or are we just filling space or trying to prove something? Just because we're quiet doesn't mean we disappear. Silence is quite powerful in its own way.

"Of course, we all might define beneficial in different ways. We might think it's helpful to preach to someone on how to improve. If they haven't asked, then it's really not our role, is it? If they do ask, can we respond respectfully, remembering that we don't have their answers, but might have something that will be of value?

"The next rule is that the words should be timely. Even skillful words can be very wrong if it's not the right time! For example: *Do we really need to discuss this when I'm studying for finals?* This rule asks us to pause in our urgent need to share something and notice what's going on with the other person.

"And situations need to be taken into consideration, don't they? I can think of a dozen times that something that could be said in a certain place with a particular person at a specific time would be totally appropriate to the situation. However, if we said the same thing at a different time, even to the same person, but we were out to dinner with their boss, for example, it would be extremely wrong.

"A lot of this is obvious. And yet we all struggle with it. Why? Because Wise Speech relies on Mindfulness. And many of us have lifelong habitual patterns of speech, where we mindlessly toss words out, potentially causing unnecessary pain and suffering that we later regret.

She took a breath and smiled.

"Being silent on this retreat has helped me develop more awareness and ease. I hadn't realized how much effort it takes to participate in a conversation, skillfully or otherwise. Now I can see how much I worry about saying the right thing or worry about someone saying something that might hurt my feelings. It's exhausting, and I'm grateful for this big time out.

"I'll return to the busy world of conversation, trusting this break from talking will have a real impact. And, by being more aware of my own speech, I trust it will positively impact all my interactions. If my words carry Wise Intention, then I trust the conversations will be more wholesome. I can't control what others say, but I know the power of my own words. And I hope I will be able to see that unskillful words coming from others are just the habitual mindlessness that we humans tend to succumb to so much of the time.

"So how can we speak wisely without stopping the flow of conversation as we run through all these rules? As we cultivate spacious awareness, loving kindness, and compassion, we deepen our understanding that there's no separate self in need of defending, and that we have nothing to prove to anyone. All that we do here, together and in our own practice, deeply informs us how we shape our thoughts into words. Because it becomes so clear how words can hurt and words can heal.

"Now, let's just pause and close our eyes, letting these ideas sink in."

Eva did so and found, to her surprise, some silence. Ahh.

*　　*　　*

When the bell rang a few minutes later, she felt refreshed.

Sara spoke again. "So, those are the basics as I understand them. Perhaps you have a different perspective, or a specific part of the instructions that is challenging for you. Feel free to share to whatever degree you feel comfortable doing so."

As mellow as she felt, Eva doubted that, if she felt compelled to share something, she could formulate wise speech after learning all that it involved. Best not to say anything. She had nothing to prove, after all.

After a minute or two, Eddie said, "Well, I've noticed when my speech is unskillful, it's usually because I'm angry. And I've begun to see how my anger is rooted in fear. Fear for my family, my country, my culture, the Earth. The future scares me to be honest. I see things in the news that get me so agitated, I just go on with this whole spiel that gets me more and more wound up.

"My wife used to try to talk me down or 'talk some common sense' into me or point out that I'm always talking about things but not doing anything about them. Then we'd both be upset.

"So, I've been practicing Metta. And it isn't easy to practice Metta on some people, especially if they're in power and messing with things that matter to me. But Metta practice makes it possible for me to stay present. I seriously doubt that I'm producing -- or channeling, or whatever we're doing with Metta -- for anyone to feel it land. But the practice is helping to transform my unskillfulness. I've got a little phrase I say to myself. I'm embarrassed to share it because it's so corny. And I apologize in advance. But it works for me, so I'll share it. Okay, here goes: *Feeling upset? Do betta! Do Metta!*

"I know, bad, right? But it's so bad that I remember it, like an obnoxious jingle. And it's true. When I meditate regularly, I do feel better. And I like that it's not just for me. It feels less selfish and self-absorbed. I may be fooling myself about that! But I trust that someday, with practice, I'll start to feel more of the interconnection and less of the isolation and antagonism that fuels my fear and anger."

Everyone smiled and nodded. Eddie's sharing was very relatable. So maybe in this circle, speech didn't have to be perfect? Just honest and heartfelt? Hmm.

After a minute or two, Allie spoke up. "I wasn't going to speak. Maintaining silence is so refreshing! I love it! But I so appreciated both Sara's and Eddie's sharing, and I want to confess some very unwise speech, if that's okay."

Lily said, "Allie, no confessions are required, and any absolution is up to you. But feel free to share if you're quite sure you want to."

So she did. And Eva watched her, unable to tame her curiosity about this young woman with Chinese features who hadn't chosen a more traditionally Chinese form of Buddhism, such as Pure Land or Chan. Why had she rejected her heritage?

Hmm, how do I know about Buddhist schools? Eva wondered. Then she remembered a map from a reference book on the world's religions, one of the many things she pondered for hours during her childhood, waiting in the library after school for her mother to finish work. It was such an interesting map. It didn't explain anything about Buddhist concepts or history that she could remember, but it was visually enchanting. That's probably why she had been so intrigued with the cloth hangings in the yurt. That old full-color illustration in the library book had featured those, along with statuary and temples in a variety of architectural styles across the continent. The raked pebble Zen gardens of Japan. A Thai temple. A stupa.

Eva's attention snapped back to the present when Allie cleared her throat and began.

"One of my biggest regrets is how unwise my words were when I…Well, this won't make any sense without a bit of background.

"Some of you may not know that I was adopted from China during the period when girl babies were unwanted because there was a restriction on the number of children a couple could have, and boys were considered much more important.

"My father is white, and my mother is Latina, from El Salvador originally. At home, we speak both English and Spanish, and I am fluent in both languages. I am not fluent in Chinese at all. No Chinese people were living anywhere within fifty miles of us, as far as I know, but we celebrated the Lunar New Year, and my parents encouraged me to explore and study Chinese culture and language. I give them credit for that. But it kind of set me up to think that if I went to China, I'd feel a sense of homecoming.

"So last year, I went on a tour of China. A dream I'd had for years, and my parents financed it. But what can I say? It was…weird. I studied a little Chinese before the trip, but wherever we went, especially out in the rural areas, the locals would speak rapidly to me, expecting me to understand. And the words I did have were as awkward as any non-native speaker. I didn't belong there any more than anyone else on our tour. But the Chinese we met seemed…I don't know, maybe I'm projecting…but they seemed disappointed in me. Like resigned. Sad. Like I had failed them. Silly, right? But that's how it felt. And later, when I had time to reflect on the trip, I remembered some very kind people who were happy to see me exploring my roots. There was even one woman who insisted I must be looking for my mother, and how could she help make that happen? Fortunately, the tour moved on before I had to explain that that wasn't it at all.

"But I just had this nagging feeling that I was an intruder. I still enjoyed the sights, walked the Great Wall of China, and all of that. But just like any tourist. Not like a child of the country I was born in. I don't know what I hoped to feel, but when I got home, I fell into my mother's arms and started crying like an idiot. She wanted to know what happened, and I just babbled away about how awful it was. And that really hurt her feelings, because it was a gift that they had scraped and saved to give me.

"So, according to the rules of Wise Speech, in the first place, my outburst wasn't the whole truth. There were, in fact, many moments on the trip that were breathtaking, inspiring, beautiful, and unforgettable.

"Then, of course, it wasn't kind. I was so thoughtless. And my parents drove a long way to the airport in the middle of the night to pick me up. So rude!

"Third, it was definitely harsh speech.

"Fourth, it wasn't timely. If I had waited until after I'd had some rest after that long plane ride, I could have shared the truth of my experience in a way that put it into context.

"But, at least, major props to me, it wasn't gossip!" she joked.

"Honestly, I don't know why this particular example came up for me. There are plenty of others I could have shared with you. But it popped into my head. That's why I appreciate having this time to be in silence."

With that, she gave a little bow to Sara. And Sara bowed back, smiling.

Minna raised her hand, and when Sara gave her the nod, she said, "I confess I have a problem with the gossip rule. It's not that I talk about people behind their backs maliciously, but our family is spread apart, and when I get on the phone with one of my sisters, we want to know how every family member is doing. And it feels so natural just to say what we know and not hold back. It's within this circle of love. But afterwards, I often wonder who I am to tell that story? It's not my story to tell. It's Connor's or…"

"Wait, what? You talk about me?" Connor said in mock horror.

Everyone laughed, Eva included. She was glad to see that Connor was 'himself' again, not weeping in his mother's arms. But was he fully recovered?

Then she thought, *Was anyone really?*

Minna laughed too, and said, "Oh, you!"

Then she looked around the circle. "I'm scheduled for a phone conversation with one of my sisters next week, so this will be an opportunity for me to explore how to use Wise Speech within our long-held and cherished tradition. I think that if I focus my questions on how *she* is feeling and what *she* has been up to, we'll steer clear of potential landmines. We rarely talk about ourselves! It might be refreshing to acknowledge that we, too, have lives!

"Still, I don't expect to be completely successful in avoiding talking about our kids and grandchildren, but I will try to limit my sharing to words rooted in assurance that everyone is okay, rather than bragging about any of Connor's many achievements or getting drawn into a discussion about the flaws of some errant in-law.

"And I'll try not to encourage her to divulge more if she shares a juicy story. But she would kill me if I started inserting Buddhist wisdom into the conversation. I'll have to be very stealthy!"

Minna took a breath and thought for a moment. "It will be interesting to see how this shifts the conversation. Will it make it feel like we don't have anything to say? Or will it allow us to go a bit deeper in our conversation?"

She paused briefly and then added, "Okay, true confessions, I'm reluctant to let go of the way that we weave the family stories together as a way of holding the family together across the miles. If we lived close and could have Sunday dinner together, the aunts could ask Connor himself."

"No, thank you," said Connor, this time seriously.

"So what's the answer? How do any of you deal with that, and how does Wise Speech apply?"

Eddie raised his hand and Minna looked at him, nodding.

"Well, this might be just me, but I think this is more of a female thing," said Eddie. "It seems like you all like to solve all the problems of the family and celebrate all the little moments. But most of the guys I know don't share that kind of stuff. We talk about sports, movies, shows, work, news, trips, and politics if we're on the same page.

"Maybe we'll boast about a kid occasionally...I just think it's different. So, I bring this up because maybe the Buddha, being a guy, just didn't understand about this matriarchal weaving business."

Minna looked thoughtful. "So, it didn't get woven into the Dharma. Huh. Could it be as simple as that? The Buddha was a guy, and he didn't get it? That feels like an easy out. I'm not looking for an easy out. Because honestly, sometimes it does feel like I've overshared."

Lily looked at Minna. "We've known each other for a while now. I've never heard you engage in malicious gossip. The patterns we have with our siblings or old friends are challenging to change, and sometimes the 'success' of that change upsets the delicate balance of lifelong relationships. It's more helpful to think of all this as an exploration, open and noticing, not rigid and self-righteous.

"Real gossip is slanderous speech intended to create ill will and division. It might be rooted in aversion or resentment, or a desire to build us up by putting someone else down. And I'm sure that's not the case with you, and hopefully not with your sisters.

"But it's interesting to notice how an innocent conversation about someone else goes from what they've been up to and how they're doing to a discussion of their personality traits and what we think of them.

"We might consider how we would feel if we overheard family members or two friends talking about us. If it makes us unhappy and hurts our feelings, then we really don't want to have that conversation with anyone else about anyone else.

"But if they were to share achievements or anything positive, we would probably feel glad to be acknowledged. Of course, we'd rather hear it directly from a parent or grandparents rather than secondhand! But still.

"So it goes back to what our mothers always taught us: if you can't say something nice, don't say anything at all."

Minna gave Lily a little bow of gratitude.

Eva thought about how we tell children to use their words instead of fists to convey their message. But words can be weapons that leave a lifetime of scars. The childhood chant of "sticks and stones may break my bones, but names will never hurt me" is clueless. Bones mend more easily than minds, where painful words cause wounds that fester and contaminate every thread of thought and, in turn, every word we speak, no matter how well-intended.

The circle was silent, and Eva thought maybe she should fill the gap with her thought, but then Connor raised his hand and shared, "I realize my timing is off sometimes. If someone doesn't come to the point fast enough, I'll interrupt or talk over them. Like they're wasting my time, or I have something so urgent to share, or maybe they aren't saying it right. I see it's disrespectful impatience that is just a bad habit."

"Thanks, Connor," said Sara with a smile. Something in the way she looked at him made Eva sense that she was thinking that her friend Connor was indeed an acquired taste, but she understood him.

Vicente looked thoughtful, and Sara asked him if there was something he wanted to add.

He nodded and began, "Wise Speech, as some of you have noted, has as much to do with how we talk to ourselves as it does with how we talk to each other. Sara skillfully revised her self-talk around competition vs. collaboration.

"Another aspect of self-talk is the belief that our words define us. In fact, our thoughts are probably not all that different from those of the person sitting next to us, especially if we have been exposed to the same experience, such as watching a show.

"Three thousand years ago, Greeks would think you were delusional if you claimed the thoughts in your head were your own. Thoughts were believed to be the voices of the gods. Today, if you claim the thoughts in your head are the voice of God, you would be deemed delusional. That's just one example of how thoughts, individually and collectively, change all the time.

"In western culture, most people believe their thoughts are their own and reflect who they are. This belief is generally taken for granted, but if we pause to examine it, we can see where this kind of thinking could lead to trouble: *I have an evil thought; therefore, I am a bad person. My evil thoughts make me unworthy of happiness. I deserve to suffer.*

'Laid out so plainly, we might balk at that line of thinking, but when we notice the pattern of our own thinking, we might discover thoughts seasoned with just such unhelpful reasoning in one form or another.

"In coming to Wise View, it helps to unload the erroneous belief that we are what we think. Believing our thoughts are who we are traps us in a hoarder's house, constantly tripping over the clutter. It's not surprising that such thinking leads people to do unskillful things to themselves and others.

He smiled, "I talk as if this is something others do. But I'm not perfect or impervious. My speech is filled with habituated flaws and mindlessness. And there are, on occasion, people who irritate me beyond my ability to tolerate. But that's when the Buddha's teachings help me most. Those people are like catalysts to keep me anchored in the Dharma, helping me to recognize that it really has nothing to do with me. It's their mental activity mindlessly processing away, and unskillful words come out, not realizing how they will be received."

When Vicente didn't continue, Connor raised his hand, and Sara nodded for him to speak.

"When you think about it, what are thoughts anyway?" Then he answered his own question, knowing they wouldn't have the precise answer he was looking for. He explained, "Thoughts are electro-chemical reactions from neurons interconnected by synapses. Thinking is a cognitive process that involves receiving input from all the senses, assessing and categorizing it, and then retrieving similar experiences from the inner data bank for review and evaluation. A very cool tool, right? But no way can we claim the process or the output of them to be uniquely 'me'." He paused. "Even though, of course, we do claim it all the time. And since it's false, that's breaking the first rule of Wise Speech. Right?" He looked around at them, clearly wanting them to all have the same level of enthusiasm for this more scientific exploration.

"So with our practice of Mindfulness and Concentration, as we observe thoughts passing through — painful or pleasurable, creative or destructive, organized or chaotic, insightful or deceitful — we can see how they recur and how they can get entangled. Can you see it?" He looked so hopeful that Eva thought her heart would break if someone didn't see it as he did.

Lily said, "Yes, Connor, I see it! It's like twigs and leaves in a stream, stuck in a swirling vortex, sucked down and then spring up later or decay and get flushed downstream. Isn't it?"

Connor looked thoughtful, then pleased. "Yes, I guess that works. Anyway, thoughts and emotions are the results of biological activity reacting to past and present causes and conditions. And that's why they don't define us."

"Thanks, Connor, for clarifying that," said Sara. She looked around, waiting for any other comments, and then, seeing that no one had anything else to add, continued.

"While clearly there are benefits to talking less, storytelling is in our DNA. Sharing words is key to our survival as a species. We don't want to be completely silent any more than birds or other species do. Listen to all the chirps and chatter all around us!"

They all attuned to the sounds above them in the canopy of the trees that surrounded the camp. Eva hadn't noticed it until Sara mentioned it, but now, as if on cue, it was truly a cacophony! Did the birds worry about whether it was a 'Wise Chirp'? Eva wondered and smiled at the thought.

Sara continued. "Communication is important. But if our speech causes hard feelings, distrust, and discord, how will we survive?

"So, let's look again at unwise speech and all the ways we can go wrong. We can see how something we say could be true but unkind. Our words could be kind and true, but poorly timed so the other person is available to receive them with their full attention. Or they could seem kind but be untrue, like buttering someone up to get what we want from them.

"A lie is wrong and generally causes more trouble. However, something could be intentionally untrue but still be Wise Speech in some instances. Think of the people who didn't report hiding people escaping from slavery or death camps. If they valued truth alone, they would feel required to admit the presence of the persecuted whose lives were in danger. The Buddha acknowledged exceptional circumstances like these.

"So we bring all the wisdom of our practice, our investigation of the Dharma, and we reject rigid dogma that undermines the true meaning of all that we are learning about ourselves, about life, about the world, and about awakening."

After a moment, Sara said, "Okay, that's all for me. Thank you for your kind attention. Later this afternoon, Allie will speak on Wise Action. And then this evening, Lily will give a talk on Wise Livelihood. So it's a very full day! Lily or Vicente, do you want to give any announcements?"

Lily said, "Sara, thank you for your beautiful Dharma talk full of Wise Speech."

And all in the circle called out thanks to Sara with bows of gratitude.

Lily and Vicente consulted each other. He looked at his wristwatch, then looked at them all and said, "Alright, let's do some walking meditation for the next twenty minutes. Then we will reconvene here. Allie and Sara have an interesting addition to the exploration of their two aspects of the Eightfold Path.

Eva felt overwhelmed with all that had been shared. Everyone else seemed so much more advanced. None of this was new to them, or at least not wholly new. But for her, it was all brand new. She was surprised that she understood as much as she did. But she'd rather not try talking right now. Walking meditation sounded like just the thing.

20 Walking the Talk

A bell rang to summon them back from the walking meditation. Vicente and Lily were not in the circle, but the rest of them sat down.

When they were all assembled, Allie and Sara looked at each other and nodded.

Sara began. "Okay, we spent the morning exploring Wise Speech. Now let's see if we can put it into practice. Silence is such a gift of the retreat, but tomorrow we will return to the busy world, where we will be expected to engage in conversation once again. Can we do it skillfully?

"Maybe not every time, but at least we will be more present to notice."

Then she nodded at Allie, who took over.

"We want to practice talking a little bit before lunch. And when we considered what the topic might be, we agreed that it would be interesting to explore the idea of where our words and actions intersect. So arrange yourself in dyads." She paused to let them organize their seats.

Eva found she was facing Eddie.

Allie continued with the instructions. "Okay, here's the question: Where in your life do your words and actions not match? For example, you say one thing, but you don't follow through with your actions. "Is there some part of your life where you talk the talk but don't walk the walk?

"Or maybe your actions are truer than your speech. Maybe you have speaking habits you haven't paid attention to, just saying whatever bubbles up, without pausing to see if your words are true, while maybe your actions tell more than words ever could.

"Does any of that sound familiar? If nothing comes up, just be as skillful with your words as you can be for the next five minutes each."

The bell rang. Eva couldn't imagine what she would say. Fortunately, Eddie was willing to go first.

He began, "This is an interesting question. I wonder if I tell my kids one thing about how they should live their lives, but then live mine differently? I really don't want to be a 'do as I say, not as I do' kind of parent. I would feel like such a phony. And my kids wouldn't respect me. And worse, they wouldn't get the guidance they need from me. I'm going to try to pay more attention to see if there's a disconnect."

He sat with his eyes closed, seeming to rewind scenes from his parenting to see if he could find evidence of a disconnect. Eventually, he opened his eyes and said, "I'm trying to think of some examples…but honestly, I've just been so immersed in the silence of the retreat, and I don't feel quite ready to return…like I'm a cookie that's not quite baked yet. Hopefully by tomorrow, but for now…"

The bell rang. And Eddie put his hands together. So, Eva did too.

She smiled. His acknowledgement of the challenge of coming up with examples made her feel more comfortable. Obviously, this first conversation would be difficult after all this lovely silence and inner investigation, and being in nature, relaxed and at ease for the most part.

She realized that she just kept smiling. She should say something. But she had nothing to say. What was the question again? She couldn't remember, and just as she was about to ask Eddie, Allie gave the directions again.

"Where's the disconnect between my words and actions?"

So, ready or not, Eva began, feeling like she'd stumbled onto a stage where she was suddenly expected to perform.

"Um. Well. Ur. This has all been so…" She took a breath. "It's really difficult to put into words what all this means to me. And I can't bring myself to even think about my life other than here… It's like a haze beyond this hill, and I don't have complete access to it. Memories come and go. It's the strangest thing. But whatever it is, I sense that my words and actions were at odds.

"On this retreat, my thoughts and actions feel interwoven, of a piece. And because it feels so remarkable, I have to believe that I was completely out of sync with myself. There had been a disconnect that I hadn't understood. I sense that I didn't want to understand, because then I would have had to make a change that I wasn't ready for."

She paused and closed her eyes. She noticed that she had pressed her lips together, as if not wanting to speak the words, but then she sighed and said quietly, "My mother died…quite recently, a lingering, painful…I was her caregiver. It's always been just her and me. So, after she was gone… I haven't been skillful in the way I have been grieving. I think that's where my deep disconnection is. I haven't wanted to think about it, so I…um…distracted myself. I hope I didn't hurt anyone in the process. This is so weird. I wish I could remember.

"Or maybe I should be glad I've forgotten… It's like the Buddha's teachings and all of this…" she waved her hands around to indicate the camp, the trees, the sky, "…are my everything right now."

When she said no more, Eddie bowed with compassion on his face, and they wordlessly agreed to close their eyes and return to blissful silence.

When the bell rang, she was grateful. No more words!

Paying attention to the felt sense of being alive in this moment, she noticed her stomach felt empty. And, as if on cue, she heard Sara say, "And now we have a special treat. Our lunch cooks are Vicente and Lily!"

Vicente and Lily appeared at the opening of the kitchen area. They waited for everyone to arrive, then bowed, rang the kitchen bell, and welcomed them in with a flourish and smiles.

Eva was delighted to see a buffet of tacos, burritos, black beans, salsa, lettuce, avocado, tomatoes, hot sauces, cheeses, and tortillas. Delicious! She gladly accepted a glass of horchata from Vicente. She knew it was a perfect complement to spicy food with its milky cinnamon sweetness, but she'd always avoided it, figuring the calories of rice and sweet milk would do her no favor. Usually, she'd prefer a cerveza or even a margarita. But now she wanted nothing to even slightly impair her experience of being fully present for this moment with this lovely buffet, the dappled light, the lilting breeze rustling the leaves in the surrounding trees, and most especially this loving, supportive, wise group of people. Her sangha.

21 Wise Action

After lunch they could each choose to meander, meditate, rest, or do their yogi chore. Eva had cleaned the bathroom for the last time, and she wanted to leave it spotless.

Then, knowing this was the last daylight time for her to wander, she and Trusty headed further up the trail behind the yurt for a bit of exploration. They came upon an intersecting trail and had a choice, so she took the one that led into the shady canyon. It became a switchback trail padded with fallen needles. The air was filled with golden dust held aloft in the heat of the day as the trail led her down into the cool of a canyon. Soon she heard the trickle of water, and then the roaring of a spring-fed creek. She sat on one of the big boulders and watched as each droplet of water was flung forth in fleeting solitude.

Fleeting solitude. That was the nature of being, wasn't it? This seemingly isolated body and mind? Impermanent. A droplet of life soaring through the air of being, then rejoicing in reconnection with the river of all life.

She lay back on the boulder, appreciating the coolness of the stone. She gazed up at the rough spires of what felt like an ancient cathedral, with the lacy arc of its canopy casting a dappled glow on all below.

Trusty found his way into the water, and she decided to join him. She took off her shoes, rolled up her pants' legs, and carefully climbed down the rocks, gingerly stepping into the cool water.

Trusty bounced about and splashed her, so she scooped up water and poured it over him. Then he shook, and the droplets danced in the dappled light.

Soon she sensed it was time to return for the afternoon Dharma exploration. "Come on, T."

As she made her way back to camp, she felt she was coming home.

*   *   *

Eva settled into her cozy spot in the circle and closed her eyes. It would be easy to nod off in the heat, but she just kept bringing herself back to the breath and the felt sense of the earth supporting her.

When the bell rang she opened her eyes. Faces glowed with a sense of presence. Eva felt the power of these practices, as if she'd never really been alive before, so caught up in her planning, worrying, regretting, and ruminating. She was simply here, exactly where she needed to be.

Allie smiled at them. "Following up on the little assignment we gave you before lunch: to look at the conjunction or dysfunction between Speech and Action, I'll just share a few of my own thoughts before I begin exploring Wise Action.

"So, maybe we have strong opinions about something that we are only too happy to voice, but we don't act upon them. For example, we complain about the world or our lives, but we don't use whatever skills, time, and resources we have to help bring about the change we see as necessary.

"I confess this describes my experience at times. I complain about how things are, or I dream about the way I want them to be. But I feel paralyzed and make a million excuses, blaming everything and everyone. Then I'm not just ineffectual and inauthentic, I'm annoying.

"Being dissatisfied became like a black hole that sucked out my energy and left me feeling powerless. But now, as I look back, I see that my unhappiness was the belief that everything had to be perfect. That I had to be perfect. I had studied so hard, done all the right volunteer jobs to look good on my college applications.

"When I got on campus, I thought life would be perfect. It wasn't perfect. That first week was a living hell and I kept thinking I should have chosen a different school. First, I didn't get a couple of the courses I wanted. Then my roommate became increasingly difficult for me to tolerate. I guess she wasn't happy either, but at the time, I was, um, let's say, less than compassionate. I became depressed because all my striving didn't pay off. I felt like college was just an extension of high school. But it was a prestigious school that cost my parents a fortune, and I felt so ungrateful. I felt ashamed, helpless, and alone.

"That's when Sara and I became friends. We just clicked in our quirky way. Who can explain friendship? We bonded over stupid stuff…I won't go into that. And when she found the sangha, I could see that it was helping her. But I didn't think it would be for me.

"Fortunately, the next semester we managed to room together. That was a relief, but I was still struggling. Seeing Sara coming home from evening sangha meetings so at ease and balanced, I realized I had to check it out.

"And that was Wise Action."

Everyone smiled. A few clapped.

"I began to see that my pursuit of perfection was just one more lure of Mara trying to keep me in that trance of believing 'if only' everything was different, I would be happy.

"I started seeing that nothing can ever be perfect! Perfection is just a personal opinion, and my idea of perfect changes all the time. The goal, the prize, everything is constantly shifting, getting further away, getting murky, or being reached but not living up to its promise.

"So, thanks to the practice and the teachings, I started to recognize that mental pattern of chasing, of not being present for the gifts ever present in life that I'd been ignoring as I searched for something else.

"A big aha moment came when I realized that taking all these courses wasn't about making a better me, but about exercising thinking muscles, developing skills, creating connections, and recognizing how my actions might, in some way, benefit the world. Instead of beating myself up about how to be the best Allie ever, I was learning how to express loving kindness, using my skills and interests to serve in a way that benefits the community of all beings. Moment to moment."

Then Allie looked at them all with great affection, her face beaming.

"So for this retreat, I took on the aspect of Wise Action because I see how often I do things without pausing to consider the ramifications.

"I can't help thinking about how sometimes when I'm being particularly demanding, my parents say, 'It's not all about you, Allie.' And now I can see that they are right. It's not all about me. But back then I was like, 'Who else could it possibly be about?'

"Of course, it is my responsibility to take care of myself and not expect anyone else to do so. But what I'd been feeling was different. I wanted everyone to take care of me, to make me a top priority, and to see me in a way that let me know I was special, gifted, and unique. The way they told me I was when I was a toddler! As a teenager, I was getting a different message from them and from the world.

"Anyway, no matter how many trips to the mall to find the outfits that would make me shine, no matter how good my grades were, no matter all the foolish things I did to be popular, I wasn't happy. And I felt guilty about it because I knew how blessed I was. I knew there were children in the world who were starving and suffering in ways I didn't want to think about. But I couldn't help it. I felt sorry for myself.

"When I started going with Sara to the sangha, there were people I'd hung out with, partied with, gotten drunk with, who probably thought I'd been kidnapped into a cult, or whatever.

"But I was the opposite. I could see how delusional my thinking had been. How I'd been demanding and then, when my demands weren't met or were met but didn't satisfy, how I would escape into unskillful behavior. Go mindless.

"The more deeply I explored the teachings and the more I looked at my actions and my intentions in doing them…well, it was a real wake-up call. And I am so grateful to be on retreat with you all, to practice, to learn, and to sit with the Eightfold Path in such a focused and meaningful way. You've all done a great job in sharing your own experiences around the aspects of the Eightfold Path. So, thank you!!

"I don't know if seeing the cause of my unskillfulness will automatically make me skillful. There's always that habitual nature when I go mindless or fall back into craving attention. But with practice, can pause and reflect before acting. And with my meditation practice and Dharma exploration, I trust my understanding will deepen and infuse my actions with more wisdom. And I hope more people will explore and adopt the Eightfold Path as a way of being in the world, because I know I am not the only unskillful person out there!"

Eva knew the truth of that and noticed others nodding. She wished she had discovered these teachings and practices at Allie's age. But wishing wasn't helping. *Pay attention*, she told herself.

Allie continued, "As we all know, the news is filled with the unskillful, dangerous, and even deadly actions of people who are defending their misperceptions of a separate fortress of self. I would hear about these things and feel like the world is full of bad people. But now I'm beginning to see that their isolated belief causes them to act out of fear instead of a deep understanding of the intrinsic interconnection of all life. Understanding that, it's much easier to send Metta and to feel compassion. But I also recognize that I'm still vulnerable and need to take care of myself first and not fall in with their unskillfulness.

"I appreciate how Lily's Cooking Pot Analogy shows the value of the Eightfold Path, making it so clear that Wise Action is a direct result of Wise View, Wise Intention, Wise Effort, Wise Mindfulness, and Wise Concentration.

"So even if we do something 'good', if we do it for approval or applause, then it's not truly wise. Our motivation and our intention matter. Are we genuinely trying to help? Or are we looking for praise?

"My motivation and intention have been unskillful. It's not a harsh judgment. I didn't understand, that's all. So, while I take responsibility for my actions, I'm trying to let go of the thoughts that I'm a bad person who needs to be punished or sign up for a self-improvement course. I'm a human being, as subject to the Three Poisons of greed, aversion, and delusion as anyone. And the clearer I see it, the easier it becomes to walk the Eightfold Path, which for me is like walking with helpful guideposts that shed light showing me where I may have stumbled and offer a clearer way to be of benefit to life itself.

"I feel like before I found this sangha and the Buddha's teachings, and especially the Eightfold Path, I was walking blind with my phone telling me to turn left at the next stoplight. I had no clue of the whole picture, of my orientation in space! But now, through the practice and exploring the teachings, I feel present and at home in the world.

"What a difference it makes to be able to *see* the unskillful action and its consequences in context! Not to scold myself, which just creates inner turmoil, and keeps me from seeing what's going on. Instead, bringing loving kindness into the mix, my inner critics melt like grateful little puppies being petted instead of kicked.

"On this retreat, I've begun to see some patterns of fear that are still operative because they are stuck in the sludge at the bottom of the pot where the spoon of Wise Mindfulness and Wise Concentration haven't yet loosened and cleared it. I see that my desire to be perfectly enlightened is just another of Mara's manifestations. I will keep stirring! At my own pace and with Wise Intention.

"At some point, if I keep practicing and give myself as much loving kindness as possible, I trust that I will begin to see more clearly. Even now, I get glimpses. But each glimpse, if I make note of it and revisit it, seems to create a core of understanding that feels supportive."

Allie closed her eyes. Then she looked around at the sangha. "Now, no lie, sometimes I see that I'm digging too deep too fast. Insights arise from gentle consistent awareness. A very wise person in this circle once told me, 'If you have to put on an oxygen mask and dive into the depths, you may be forcing exploration beyond what is skillful for right now.'" She smiled at Lily, who smiled back.

Allie paused and looked at her notes. "Okay, I shared all this because I thought it might resonate with some of you, but I didn't mean to go on and on about me. Sorry about that!

"But now let's look at Wise Action. On our first night of the retreat, we took a vow, the Five Precepts of Buddhism. These are practices to cultivate awareness of the harm our actions can cause. One of them refers to speech, and we've covered that, but the other four are all about action. So let's review them:

"Refrain from killing or harming other beings.

"Take only what is freely given.

"Refrain from misusing our sexuality.

"Avoid ingesting anything that compromises clarity of mind.

"There are a lot of different wordings for these. But I like this translation. So, I'll go over each one, and then we can have discussion.

"Okay, 'Refrain from harming or killing.' At first glance, this seems easy for most of us. We have no wish to shoot or maim. But of course, as we sit with what this means, it unfolds to reveal all the ways we might be causing harm or even killing without intending to. We use the skillfulness and wisdom that we have developed through our practice and through life experience to help us see more clearly. We accept that sometimes our actions may be unskillful, momentarily unmindful, operating out of lifelong habits, or simply unable to see the harm we may have caused. We use each experience as a lesson to learn from, to increase our sense of connection and understanding. We make reparations as best we can, vow to do better, and then we let it go.

"Next, 'Refrain from taking what is not freely given.' Again, at first glance, this seems easy for most of us. We have no urge to rob a jewelry store. But as we sit with what this means, it unfolds to reveal the ways we might be taking from others without their having offered it. Maybe we take loved ones for granted and assume the right to take things without asking or even feel they have the obligation to give to us. Beyond immediate relationships, we might forget who we are harming by 'getting a great deal.' For example, if the working conditions in fields or factories are exploitive or unhealthy, or both.

"In a state of disconnection, we can't see how what we are doing hurts anyone. Or we may feel so helpless that we get depressed and feel like our actions don't matter. But our actions do matter! One example is how even 'minor' theft affects us all when businesses need to install safeguards to prevent such activity, creating hassles for everyone, raising prices to cover the cost. And stores may go out of business.

"Okay, the Third Precept is to refrain from misusing our sexuality. Maybe we've been careless, hormone-driven, and hard-hearted, harming others and ourselves through our actions. Sexuality can also be used to lure, promote, and satisfy an agenda, and all of these uses are unskillful. I appreciate that it doesn't say don't have sex, just to bring our brains and hearts into the mix, not just our raging hormones. It's so important to understand the role of power in relationships, how someone might feel coerced into sex by someone they work for or admire. So someone in power might assume that it's consensual, but it's not. *Really not!*

"The Fourth Precept will help many of us with the Third, because we can easily make really unskillful choices when we're drunk." She and Sara shared knowing looks, clearly remembering some college life event that would offer an example but was better left unsaid.

"This precept reminds us to refrain from ingesting anything that clouds the mind and judgment. And often intoxicants also inhibit our ability to end the very suffering we may be trying to escape from by using them.

"So those are the Four Precepts. Monastics have more, but these are challenging enough for many of us. At first, each of these precepts may seem simple. Then they seem more complex and challenging. But ultimately, each becomes a key to liberation. As we let go of behaviors that are harmful to ourselves and others, we are free from the guilt, shame, and anguish caused by unskillful, mindless, or habitual behavior.

"Yes, I know that this is a list of 'don'ts' or 'thou shalt nots'. But it comes out of seeing how harmful they are to ourselves, those we care about, our community, and the world. Just like all aspects of the 8FP, it offers valuable guidance to clarify how we create suffering and how, at the very least, we can refrain from doing so.

"It's important to remember that these are vows we take for ourselves, not to proselytize and get all self-righteous, which is a cause of suffering. I learned that the hard way when I first started exploring the Buddha's teachings and misunderstood that it wasn't up to me to monitor other people's behavior."

She smiled at everyone, then concluded, "So those are the four of the Buddha's Five Precepts that have to do with Wise Action. It's a lot all together, isn't it? But maybe certain ones resonate with you right now.

"So I'll open the floor to anyone who wants to share what comes up."

She put her hands together and bowed, and everyone bowed back.

Sara raised her hand, and Allie nodded for her to go ahead.

"There's a Swahili word that's illustrated in a wonderful story. Would you like to hear it?"

Everyone nodded. Who doesn't love to hear a story?

"The word is *Ujima*, and it means collective responsibility. And the story is about an old man who lived up on a hill overlooking his village. And one day, from his vantage point he could see that there was a big surge in the river upstream. It wouldn't affect him on the hill, but he knew that the villagers, his community, couldn't see it coming. It would flood the village, and they would drown.

"He tried yelling, but they couldn't hear him. He tried waving, but they didn't see him. And, even if he could, it wouldn't do any good to run down to tell them, because there was no time to turn around and bring them back up the hill. So what did he do?"

The circle was fascinated by this story, but no one had an answer.

"He lit his house on fire!"

Why in the world? Eva wondered.

"Yes, he lit his house on fire, and the blaze and smell of smoke got the attention of everyone in the village. And what did they do?"

"They ran to help!" someone called out.

"Exactly! To a person, they ran up the hill to help him, this member of their community in need of their assistance."

"And saved their own lives!" Eddie said, excited.

"Yes!" Sara laughed. "Isn't that a wonderful story? Isn't that a wonderful core value? I don't remember all the core values but that one is called *Ujima*, collective responsibility. Another core value is *Umoja*, community. And I share it with you now because we are so much about sangha, both our small sangha and the greater community of all beings."

"That's a great story," said Vicente. Everyone nodded happily.

Sara smiled. "So as we look at the list of Precepts, the 'thou shalt nots', I hope we can stay connected to the greater sense of community and collective responsibility to remind us why we care about this list."

Eva noticed how the circle seemed to glow with appreciation, people nodding, closing their eyes, breathing in the wisdom. It would be lovely to just stop here. But Allie had a discussion to lead and so she asked, "Does anyone want to clarify how they understand the first precept? Non-harming?"

Connor raised his hand, and Allie nodded at him.

"Well, it seems straightforward. Don't kill. So don't eat meat. But historically, the Buddha and his monks ate whatever was given to them, including meat. When I was staying in the monastery, there was a family who came every day to a covered shed nearby and offered us our daily meal, so we didn't go into the town with our begging bowls. Someone told me they did that before and almost everyone gave them spoonfuls of rice. But this family, at least for the time I was there, brought us lovely meals. And often there was chicken or some kind of meat mixed in.

"So at least for monks it's more "Don't do the killing yourself." But it was a quandary for me because I had been a vegetarian. But refusing to eat the only food offered was bad karma, and foolish because that would be the only food we would get that day. But by eating it, I worry that I'm contributing to the bad karma of someone else if we have them do the killing. Aren't I complicit?

"But in my studying of the Dharma, it seems there are lots of degrees of bad action. For example, it's much worse to kill a human than another kind of animal. It seems partly to do with intention, which makes sense. If you are killing an animal to eat because you are hungry, that's less bad karma than killing a person out of anger, jealousy, or greed. The Three Poisons are more in play in the second instance. Still, killing any sentient being is not good."

"But I read somewhere about the aborigines in the Australian outback who go hunting and when they come upon a herd of…well, I don't remember what it was a herd of. But anyway, they communicated silently, asking them, "Who wants to offer to be our dinner today?" And the weakest among them would, for the health of the herd, offer itself up.

"Of course, we're not as a society attuned to the herd. Native peoples in these lands were, I imagine. They knew how to cohabit with other species. They didn't hunt for sport but for survival. They knew how to harvest what was growing naturally and didn't create vast fields of one crop creating a nightmare of monoculture. I'm glad to see so many farmers' markets thriving, and the return of small, often organic farms. But most people are eating industrially produced food and it's unhealthy for the environment and in many cases for their bodies. You'll be happy to know that all the food you've been eating on this retreat was organic, local, and sustainable."

"And delicious!" added Vicente. "A big shout out of gratitude to our fabulous cooks!"

"Here, here!" all agreed, smiling at Connor, Allie, Sara, and Minna.

"Aw, thanks!" Connor said. "I'll add that at least some of the ingredients were foraged on this very land. Don't worry, I was very careful and have good reference material to tell me what's edible and what's poisonous."

At this Eva found herself suddenly concerned. Had she been relying on this young man, earnest and sweet as he was, to make decisions about what she ingested based on…oh well, she was fine.

Connor continued. "I've probably said enough, but I don't want to proselytize. Because the more I learn, the less rigid I become. I'm more open to the don't-know mind. And that's a huge leap for me! For example, I think about how animals eating other animals is part of life and how we humans are omnivores. We have teeth to handle both plants and animals.

"Vegans may say that if there's a choice, eat plants first. But now there's increasingly scientific proof that plants are sensate and intelligent. Though I suppose that depends on how you measure intelligence. And, taken to its logical conclusion, this thinking could lead to starvation!

"The original peoples of all continents had a better handle on it. But they weren't dealing with the size of our human population. They weren't living in cities with skyscrapers and no access to wild land. But even within the confines of a city there are creative ways to bring in nature, and to grow food. There are all those rooftops just sitting there, after all! And the parks could at least in part be communal gardens. Even abandoned big box stores are being turned into solar-powered micro-greens growing farms!

"Anyway, I'm trying not to accept inherited views without question." Then, as an afterthought, he turned to Minna, "No offense, Mom."

"None taken, Son. I appreciate your exploration and deep consideration."

Allie smiled. "And I appreciate that you put so much thought into it, Connor. Sounds like very Wise Intention."

Connor beamed. *Did he have a little crush on Allie?* Eva wondered.

Allie continued. "Anyone else have a challenge with a Precept?"

Eddie raised his hand. "I don't feel satisfied going completely vegetarian all the time, and my family doesn't either. But we've found more veggie meals that satisfy us. We all agree it feels better. And it's easier. Every other week, one of the kids claims they're vegetarian or vegan now. And they'll take huge offense if we forget and put butter on their veggies. Then they fall off the wagon and complain when there's no butter. 'Why don't *I* get any? Wah!!'"

Laughter.

Eddie went on, "But I'd like to talk about the non-drinking part of the Precepts. I was surprised by how little I missed beer. I thought it was an important part of the social experience, but I enjoy myself more when I'm sober. Maybe when I was young, drinking helped me get over my nervousness. But I'm just hanging out with friends. There's no 'edge' I need to take off by drinking. Instead, there's clarity. I get the jokes. I can engage in conversations on all levels without getting lost. I'm present! So part of that is not drinking, and the other part is my mindfulness practice. But the not drinking is a big part of it. And I think my friends are cool with it. Some of them drink less, not feeling the pressure or the habit of keeping up. In the group, they say there's no way they'll become teetotalers, but privately, they tell me they appreciate feeling less hungover.

"All in all, that precept has been a lot easier than I thought it would be. And my wife is delighted with how much money we're saving!" He smiled at the circle and nodded at Allie to say that's all he had to say.

Then Vicente raised his hand and shared, "This precept isn't just about alcohol, of course, but all kinds of mind-altering drugs. Recently, there has been research into psilocybin and other psychedelic compounds for therapeutic use, even at my university.

"I try to withhold judgment. I certainly partook when I was young, and I attribute part of my understanding of the Buddha's teachings to insights I had while on some psychedelic. But the potential for self-destruction is great. And to be honest, there were just as many moments of being high when I was completely delusional. Fortunately, I realized there's no quick, easy way to awaken. I started studying all the world's philosophies and exploring various religions. That led me to my career, and eventually to my personal resonance with Theravada Buddhism."

He looked over at Lily and whispered, "Do you want to share your psychedelic adventures in your hippie days in Haight Ashbury?"

Lily smiled. Then, with her index and thumb together, she zipped her lips shut. Everyone laughed.

"Okay," said Allie. "What about the Precept for sexuality? It doesn't forbid it, just asks us to be skillful." Looking around at their faces, she added, "And no, they're not talking about *those* skills…"

Eva felt the weight of her recent over-indulgence in all things sexual rise like a souring meal. She was ready to give up sex completely right now. Look where it got her! In a destructive relationship. But she knew she didn't want to give it up forever. How could she ensure that her enjoyment didn't entangle her in such a mess?

Allie continued, "There is so much going on within us. We can be careless, hormone-driven, and hard-hearted, harming others and ourselves through our actions. And we live in a society where sexuality is actively used to lure us, promote a product, and satisfy an agenda, and all these uses are unskillful. Any thoughts on that?"

Lily spoke up. "The wording in the Precept is not an exact translation but a Western version that evolved: We are advised to refrain from 'misusing our sexuality.' But what does that mean? It leaves room for interpretation. And consider the raised consciousness around sexuality in our culture, especially around consent. Two thousand years ago, a woman's consent was of no concern. Even a hundred years ago. Even now, in some cultures. She glanced at Sara, who nodded. Maybe in our culture, we have recently evolved a bit in our awareness, but that doesn't mean there isn't plenty of unskillfulness. As we know."

"I like the wording," said Connor. "It expects us to use the wisdom of the Eightfold Path as a whole to consider whether it is wise."

"The Three Poisons come into play here," said Minna. "But will we pause long enough to ask ourselves if we are acting out of desire, aversion, or delusion? And it would be so easy to say, "Desire, for sure, and I'm good with that!"

Eva recognized how much poison she had ingested to fall for Chad. Desire, oh yes, she had succumbed, again and again. And then right in the middle of succumbing to desire, she could see how aversion steps in. Repulsion, self-hatred, shame. It must be very confusing for the partner. So, when no one spoke up, she found herself giving voice to her thoughts.

"Yes, it's true, we are all floundering, men and women alike. Caught up in desire and hormones, oh the hormones!"

Connor laughed. "'Floundering' is a funny word. It makes me think of the way salmon rushes up rivers to spawn, not even caring that they will die soon after." He looked up, clearly thinking things out further. "Or the way males of many species strut their stuff, display their feathers, duke it out with their antlers. We humans aren't that different. We're just expected to know the rules, and the rules keep changing."

Eddie gasps. "There are rules? Oh no! This explains a lot about my many failures in my early years." Everyone laughed. "Actually, my wife was very clear from the start. *This? Yes, please! That? Maybe on your birthday. And that? Oh, hell no!!!*

More laughter. Then Sara said, "That's the other thing. With so much porn available, men have unrealistic expectations, both about the 'ideal' female body and the outrageous variety of ways to interact sexually."

"And of course it's not just heterosexual sex either," said Allie. "I'm grateful that the wording for this Precept doesn't exclude those who are attracted to the same sex or are bisexual, gender fluid, or asexual."

Everyone nodded. Vicente said, "Yes, that's so important. It wasn't that long ago, it feels like only yesterday to me, when for some, suicide felt like the only solution to the daily torture of being gay. Police raids. And the AIDS epidemic! Homophobes declared God was purposely punishing gay men. I lost several friends to AIDS, and my heart is still broken, all these decades later—such a waste.

"But I also take heart knowing that love in all its forms can now find wholesome connections instead of brief nameless encounters. Couples can marry and even have children if they want. Being out is not just a celebration of self —"look at me!"—No, it's life-affirming, it's acknowledging that all beings are worthy of respect.

"When I think back, what I recognize is that because of society's discomfort with homosexuality, it forced a whole segment of the population into hiding in bars and bathhouses, into sexual acts that were just nameless physical release. The things people hated about homosexuality, the very things that made it seem perverse, were forced upon the community by intolerance!

"Real relationships existed, of course, but they were mostly hidden. Some were accepted within families, but mostly barely tolerated, and the relationships were considered roommates, extra uncles or aunties, dear friends. The truth of sharing a bed, sharing a life, sharing a deep and abiding love -- that was kept hidden from all but the dearest and most open-minded friends.

"I would never have imagined in my lifetime that gay marriage would become legal. And I know there are those who, for who knows what reason, would like to make it illegal again. I don't know why the relationships of people they don't know are so threatening to them or why they think it's any of their damn business, but…"

There was a pause as everyone thought about the shifting political tides, the impermanence of it all.

Vicente's sharing touched Eva. She thought about her friends and extended family, and the freedom they had to love who they loved. She knew the history to some extent but hadn't thought about all that Vicente shared with such emotion.

The idea of things shifting back…it sent a chill down her spine. Could anyone do that? Could anyone be so cruel? And why? She found herself tearing up a bit, her heart tightening. She closed her eyes and took a few slow breaths. The word 'impermanence' came up. She didn't like it. She wanted everything in her life and her world to be perfect. And occasionally, many things felt pretty good, as if the world was finally coming to its senses. And then, just like that, things change.

Her mother, who had been quite political, once said, "The political pendulum swings. Sometimes it's a broom sweeping clean. Sometimes it's the chop of a guillotine."

Eva's thoughts went to the school library, the books, so many brilliant, loving books that made children feel seen, heard, and understood, but that some small-minded parents wanted to be banned. She wasn't going to lie down and give in. She would find a skillful way to address the mean-spirited thinking driven by greed and fear.

Allie finished her presentation by saying, "As we can see, at first each of these precepts may seem simple and straightforward. But the more we explore them and apply them in our lives, the more complex and challenging they become. But to whatever degree we can incorporate them into our lives and allow them to guide us; they provide a key to liberation. As we let go of harmful behaviors, we free ourselves from the guilt, shame, and anguish caused by unskillfulness, mindlessness, or habit.

"Yes, this is a list of 'don'ts', but it's also, importantly, a list that helps us to clarify how we create suffering and how we can refrain from doing so.

"Our meditation practice helps us to develop an understanding of connection, and to be responsible for how we impact others, as well as how we respond when the unskillfulness of others affects us.

"As people living in the busy world of infinite interactions, we have many more opportunities to err and rededicate ourselves to these vows, so it helps to keep them close."

There was a thoughtful silence.

Then Lily said, "I just want to add one other thing to this growing Cooking Pot analogy of ours: Though the steam of our words, actions, and livelihood may seem ephemeral and lacking substance, it's the part of the whole that we can't change or take back. The steam wafts here and there, and try as we might, we can't retract a harmful word or action. We can apologize, but we can't undo what's been said or done. So even though those faint tendrils of steam seem like nothing much, they are vitally important. Our words and actions reach out across space and time. So let's use them wisely. And that's my last word!" She nodded to Allie.

"Oh, that's a great addition! Thanks, Lily." Turning to the group she said, "Okay, that's all for this afternoon's session. Consider what is the wisest action for you right now. Check in with your body. Do your muscles want to move? Feel free to take a hike or use the yoga mats in the yurt to do some stretching. Or maybe your body is telling you to lie down, let the mind digest all this rich sharing, or go on a mindful exploration. Listen to your body and let its wisdom move you to Wise Action."

Then she put her palms together and bowed, and they all bowed back with gratitude.

22 Wise Livelihood

On her late afternoon walk with Trusty, Eva explored more parts of the area she hadn't realized were there. A rivulet of water trickling down a moss-covered waterfall was just enough for birds and squirrels to sip. She was pleased that Trusty sat quietly beside her as she watched them come and go. She already felt a sense of nostalgia for this place and this time. *Stay present*, she reminded herself.

Back in camp, she stopped in the tent to grab a raincoat. The weather had been so consistently pleasant, with light breezes that cooled her after a hike and a lovely chill in the night around the campfire. Idyllic really. But now dark clouds were rolling in.

It was tempting to lie down and rest a bit before the evening meal and the final Dharma talk. But Lily was busy preparing for her Dharma talk that night amid scattered papers all over her bed. Eva didn't want to distract her. So she headed for the kitchen to see if there was anything she could do to help with preparations for the evening meal. She was just in time to help Minna carry the big pot over to the fire, this time filled with lintel soup.

Eddie had laid the logs out almost ceremonially, and when he saw Minna and Eva, he smiled. Once they set the pot on the iron trivet, he handed Eva the matchbox.

Eddie, Minna, and Eva stood there for a moment, each staring at the Cooking Pot. Who knew it had held so many wise secrets that would continue to guide them in their lives?

Eva took a breath and struck the match, her intention as clear to her as it had ever been in her life.

Then she sat down in her familiar seat and watched Minna stirring her spoon of Mindfulness and Concentration with a level of attention that Eva now understood better than she had when she'd first arrived.

She also knew from previous evenings that there would be a moment when she could be of use, when all hands were needed to help get dinner on the table. She smelled the delicious aroma of the heating soup. Ah, ready! She looked at Minna with raised eyebrows, and Minna gave the nod.

So Eva made her way to the kitchen, where Sara pointed at a platter of whole wheat rolls that were ready to go on the table. While Eva was there, she set the table with the utensils and cloth napkins. Then she got a tray for bowls and went back to the campfire, where Minna was ready to ladle out the soup.

They ate the meal silently and mindfully, but with a deep sense of ease and companionship. Eva felt such affection and appreciation for this group of people, this beautiful setting, and the pleasure of being quiet in nature, meditating and exploring the Buddha' teachings, the Dharma.

It seemed that no one wanted to leave the table. Some lingered long over the soup, or took an extra roll, or got up and returned with water or tea. Eva sensed that if anyone left, it would be like breaking a magic spell.

But eventually, the spell dissolved in a natural way, and they all rose, took their plates to the clean-up area, scraped out their bowls, and submerged them in the waiting water. As some returned to their tents, Eva stayed on to help clean up.

She and Minna poured the leftover soup into containers, then put the pot into the sink and washed it out. Connor dried it off, and she knew he would fill it with water and return it to the campfire to heat the water for tea.

When there didn't seem to be anything else she could do, she went back to her little room. She hadn't wanted to disturb Lily while she was preparing her Dharma talk. But she was lying on her back with her eyes closed, her reading glasses resting precariously on her nose, an open book on her chest.

What was she reading? Eva wondered, as she tiptoed through the main room and slipped into her own little nest. Trusty hadn't come with her. He had his little nook in the kitchen area and would stay there as long as anyone was still there.

She was acutely aware that this was the last night, and she couldn't help but think about the next day. *How would it be to return home? And, come to think of it, would she know the way down the hill?* The once-familiar landscape had somehow morphed at every turn, over the past few days. She could only think that when she stormed up the hill that first day, she'd wandered much further than…Well, she wasn't going to worry about it now. It was too exhausting to think about. She felt drowsy and closed her eyes.

The evening bell woke her. She rose and stretched. As she passed through the main area of the tent, she could see that Lily was already gone. She could peek at the book now if she wanted. But it wouldn't feel right. It would feel like taking what was not freely given. She was still curious. But then she remembered that she couldn't read anyway. Was this typical on a retreat? You weren't supposed to read. But to not be able to read? That couldn't be normal. Vicente was surprised she couldn't read. So it was just her. *Maybe when I fell and hit my head, some part of my brain was injured? Stop*, she told herself, as she emerged into the moist evening air. The pixie lights glowed softly in the mist, guiding her back to the circle where everyone was settling in. As she sat down, Trusty nestled beside her, the campfire flame glowing in his eyes. She stroked his fur as she closed her eyes to meditate.

When the bell eventually rang, Eva opened her eyes to see Lily setting down the striker. She was particularly radiant as she sat on her cushion.

She looked at each of them with deep affection and respect, as if silently praising them for all their Wise Effort on this retreat. And then she began her talk.

"So here we are, away from the rest of the world and our daily doings. Away from work and all the ways we engage in the marketplace of our daily lives.

"Tomorrow, we will return. So, it seems even more fitting that we explore Wise Livelihood last on this retreat. Earlier, it would have violated the sanctity of our meditative seclusion, making us think about work. But now it is an invitation to re-enter our daily lives with all the insights and skills we have developed here. From this vantage point, we see more clearly where in our lives we may be straying from Wise Livelihood. Which, by the way, is more than just our jobs. It's also the choices we make in the marketplace.

"The human world is much more complex in this regard than it was in the Buddha's day. I imagine it was easy back then to see where products came from and whose labor was involved. Many people grew their own produce, wove their own fabric, and made their own garments. And if there was anything they didn't grow or create, their neighbors did.

"Now it's the biggest international mystery, isn't it? Much is hidden away and difficult to discern. We do know that corporations are legally required to make building their shareholders' investments their absolute top priority. How they do that, what corners they may cut, what suffering they may cause, and what public relations tactics they may use to camouflage their doings, we, as consumers, don't fully know.

"Try as we might to shop responsibly, protecting the environment, the workers, ourselves, and our families, we just don't know. And while I do love the don't know mind, we want to research further as we make our choices in the marketplace. Some of you only buy used clothing, vintage, as you say. And some of you probably have vegetable gardens or shop at the farmers' markets. And that's excellent! Reduce, reuse, recycle. That too is Wise Livelihood.

"Another aspect of Wise Livelihood is our participation in democracy. If we are fortunate enough to live in one, we don't have the luxury of avoiding that responsibility, because as citizens, we each have an essential role to play in avoiding the creeping trend toward oligarchy, dictatorship…you know all this; I don't need to tell you.

"Some are surprised that this would be part of the Path, but it's part of our engagement in the 'marketplace.' While political debates do not belong in the meditation hall, our practice does clarify the nature of our interconnection and our responsibility to be of benefit to our greater community of all beings. The Four Brahma viharas cultivate *Metta, Karuna, Mudita,* and *Uppekha*. Loving kindness. Compassion. Sympathetic Joy. And Equanimity. These are the joyful ways we interact in the world, aren't they? As we cultivate them, we see how, while we may practice alone on our cushion, our interactions with all beings become increasingly filled with loving kindness and compassion. So when we see injustice, we do what is skillful, peaceful, harmonious, and kind. We don't turn our backs. We don't think it's someone else's problem.

"We come to whatever wise action we take without making an enemy of anyone. Those who cause harm are often disconnected, acting without thought, and influenced by the Three Poisons and Mara's temptations. We have compassion. So we don't act out of violence or anger. We stand for all beings.

"There's an image still lingering in my head from my youth of a young protester placing a flower in a rifle stock aimed at her. This was 'flower power'. She did this with such mindfulness, with such a sense of connection, kindness, and compassion. She didn't see the soldier as an enemy. She knew the helmeted man behind the uniform felt he was 'just doing his job.'

"Just doing his job. Stop and think about that. Many people are simply doing their jobs, just doing what they must do to survive. Taking the time to consider whether it is Wise Livelihood may feel like a luxury. They may feel they don't have the time or resources to consider changing their work. If they feel conflicted about what they are doing but are helpless to change it, they may succumb to mindlessness. They may go home and drink themselves into a stupor. Or lash out at others, even the people they love. Unwise Livelihood takes its toll on everyone.

"So our practice of facing Mara, recognizing that we are causing harm, and cultivating skillful ways to transform our interactions, is the basis of Wise Livelihood.

"And while we don't bring politics into the meditation hall, sangha members may want to gather together to do skillful things focused on benefiting the community and the planet. However, even if the sangha doesn't act, the practice itself helps sangha members remain true to their own deep convictions and find peaceful, skillful ways to engage."

She paused and looked down at her papers. Then she smiled at them all and continued.

"I believe everyone here who is employed is engaged in Wise Livelihood. And thank you for that. However, not all of you have settled on your work path, so I'll share a cautionary tale.

"If we are unskillful in our working life and have a feeling of being at odds with our core values, not addressing that disconnect can lead to a breakdown. Which is what happened to me many years ago.

"In my early thirties, I was employed in advertising. I thought I was lucky to be paid to use my creative writing skills. But what was I really doing? I was crafting clever words and images to entice people into thinking they needed whatever my clients were selling.

"They weren't bad companies or bad products -- even then, I had a sense of ethics — but it was my job to use my skills to lure or scare people into buying whatever our client was selling. It was my job to play the role of Mara. It was my role to utilize my creative skills and psychology degree to convince people that they would be happier, safer, or better off with my client's product. And it made me sick. Literally ill. It was a challenging time.

"Eventually, at the advice of my doctors, I quit my job. I stayed in bed for many months with CFIDS, which is what it was called back then.

Chronic Fatigue Immune Dysfunction Syndrome. Quite a mouthful, and too much for me to say. I'd fall asleep before I could finish saying it!

"Before I quit my job, I remember driving home from work, looking longingly at the homes I passed, imagining knocking on a door and asking if I could just take a little nap on their couch. And I only had a fifteen-minute commute!

"I slept a lot, but I also began to meditate again in earnest. And I listened to my own inner wisdom as I healed, not just from my physical illness but from the mental confusion that had me off kilter. That inner wisdom eventually guided me to work that was more authentic and meaningful for me, helping people. I made less money, and sometimes it was a struggle, but I've always had what I needed, and for that I am grateful.

"So, where did that advertising job fit in the Buddha's list of unwise livelihoods? At the time, it didn't feel like trickery, but it was in a way. I was creating a kind of magic that promised to solve problems that a purchase couldn't solve. Or putting something enticing in front of people, distracting them from whatever it was they were doing or thinking, and putting desire into their thoughts.

"I used the word 'disconnect', and I think that's important to acknowledge. What we do is not who we are, but it is a primary expression of our core values. With all the hours we put into a job, if we can't say what our intention is beyond a paycheck, then we're disconnected. Whatever that job involves – whether getting people from point A to point B, providing them with legal services, helping them file their taxes, building or repairing homes, or creating entertainment that inspires and cultivates joy – we want to be in touch with our Wise Intention. We want to acknowledge that what we provide through our work benefits not only our bank account, but also our broader community.

"Our work is the action we do all day for most of the days of our adult lives, so it needs to be Wise Livelihood. If we are causing suffering to anyone through our labor, we are causing suffering to ourselves. It is all of a piece, all interconnected.

"On the surface, Wise Livelihood seems pretty straightforward. The Buddha offered guidance on the kind of jobs that cause suffering.

"Fundamentally, to be wise, how we make a living must be legal, peaceful, without coercion, violence, trickery, or deceit, causing no harm or suffering.

"He listed some specific kinds of livelihoods to avoid: Dealing with weapons, raising animals for slaughter, slavery, prostitution, butchering, dealing in poisons and intoxicants, and engaging in usury, profiting through moneylending.

"Beyond the *kind* of work we do, there's guidance in the *way* we work, using wise effort, action, and speech. Employers should treat workers fairly, merchants should treat their customers fairly, and workers should be honest and dependable.

"This all seems straightforward, but for some people in certain situations, it can be challenging to choose a job that aligns with their deepest values, so they are not constantly battling inner conflicts at work. In our culture, the desire for wealth and admiration, or the fear of not having enough, can be motivators that lead us astray. A poll revealed that many people dislike billionaires, but an equally large number aspire to become billionaires! I'm not sure what that says about us. I suppose it just says we're human, afraid, and confused.

"But whatever we are doing, however we are paying the bills, we can pause and ask ourselves, '*What am I cultivating in my life? Am I cultivating wellbeing for myself and others? Or am I just going through the motions in a job that makes no beneficial contribution? Am I creating suffering for myself? For others? For the planet?*

"We might ask, '*When I'm in the workplace, am I authentic, or am I trying to be who I think my employer wants me to be?* Conversely, *am I promoting a separate self through my style so I will be seen?*' Either way, there's a shoring-up that is at odds with our true nature. It can wear us down to the point where we make ourselves ill.

"The practice of meditation over time dissolves the misguided goal to be seen as 'a success', however we define it. Instead, our work is a collaborative contribution to the world, a valued and necessary activity that stems from our abilities and interests. Our understanding of the fleeting nature of life, of impermanence, lets us release the unskillful desire for fame. Remember the Eight Worldly Winds! Remember that poor Tube Man tossed about by pleasure and pain, gain and loss, praise and blame, and fame and disrepute! Our practice lets us see them and respond skillfully rather than react unskillfully.

"With our practice, we mindfully take responsibility for how our actions impact all life. If we belittle ourselves, we feel our actions don't matter. But they do. If we get caught up in guilt, we become paralyzed.

"While the list of professions that are not considered Wise Livelihood is short, there's more to it than that, isn't there? Because it's not just *what* we're doing, but *how* we're doing it, and *why* we're doing it that matters.

"Our work environment eventually affects our wellbeing. If we work for a company, we need to ensure that it adheres to these precepts as well. There are now Public Benefit Corporations which are legally required to balance the interests of stakeholders, including employees, customers, the environment, and the advancement of public benefit goals. I hope more businesses will set themselves up that way, but I'm not holding my breath.

"But let's say you've chosen a profession that is Wise Livelihood, your company is highly ethical. Wonderful! Now, examine how you perform your job. Bringing all aspects of the Eightfold Path and the Five Precepts to bear on interactions with coworkers, clients, patients, customers, suppliers, and others means cultivating loving kindness in every interaction.

"As always, we start with loving kindness for ourselves, so we are not beating ourselves up all day, every day. Then we send Metta to each person we meet, each email we send, and each voice we hear on the phone. This is not the syrupy 'kill them with kindness' voice we may be told to use. No matter how challenging a person might be, they still deserve our kindness, our awareness that they are suffering, just as we suffer. They may be unskillful; they may get on our last nerve. But we don't have to succumb to the toxicity. And if we do, and if we're way beyond being able to send Metta, then it's time to look for other kinds of employment.

"But there are few jobs that don't have us interacting with others. So, let's make Metta part of our daily practice. Let's let others be the catalysts for our own ability to cultivate compassion.

"When we act as a conduit for infinite radiant Metta, we transform our own experience and the experience of those around us. This is powerful stuff. In fact, power, as usually perceived in the workplace – who gets to boss whom, who gets the fanciest title, the corner office, the most money, and best perks – that kind of power, pales in comparison to the empowerment of Metta. Think about it: All that power and perks is supposed to make us happy. Because it doesn't, we think it's because we don't have enough. So we do more and potentially cause more suffering for ourselves and others. But being a conduit of Metta brings immediate, expansive, and true happiness. The other is just fool's gold. Some perk!

"As I mentioned earlier, Wise Livelihood isn't only about how we make our living but how we, by our behavior in the marketplace, set other people up to make their livings! When we discussed Wise Action and the Precepts, we were focused on our own behavior. However, if our choices put others in a position where they must violate the Precepts, causing them to engage in unwise livelihoods, that's unskillful, isn't it?

"If we don't make our living by killing animals but we benefit by others doing so, i.e. we eat meat, poultry, or fish, then we are contributing to the harm, both to the beings who are killed and to the person we are encouraging to do the killing – i.e. letting other people do our dirty work for us.

"If we raise crops using chemicals that poison the environment, that is clearly not Wise Livelihood. However, if we knowingly purchase those crops, we are also culpable, because we are helping to create a market where it is not commercially viable for farmers to stop using those chemicals. And those chemicals aren't just bad for the environment; they are poisoning the people who work in the fields, day after day, picking the poisoned produce.

"As an employer, if we pay people wages that leave them and their families hungry and at risk, then obviously that isn't Wise Livelihood. But if we purchase the products produced by manufacturers who treat their workers poorly, then we are also culpable. Our mindset might be that we're getting a good deal, but we need to think beyond that. Price isn't everything. Own less stuff and obtain the things we have with loving kindness for all involved in their creation.

"Once we make a purchase, we are responsible for it. If we dispose of it in a manner that harms the earth, that is not Wise Livelihood either.

"So Wise Livelihood considers not just how we earn a paycheck but how we interact in the marketplace. It considers every person whose life is touched by our interaction, and the very earth as well.

"Now this is a lot of responsibility! By this time, you might be ready to join a monastery to avoid all these complicated pitfalls! Pause and notice if you are feeling any sense of burden or exhaustion. Perhaps you think that Wise Livelihood is impossible, given that, as consumers, we are not always given enough information to make wise choices, and the thought of having to conduct the level of research required to do so is daunting.

"So what do we do?" Lily asked, looking around at their faces.

Everyone was silent. So she answered her own question. "We do the best we can. That's going to be different for each of us at different times in our lives. But if we pay attention, we can sense when our actions and our values are not aligned. It is uncomfortable. I know this from experience.

"The process is ongoing. It begins with noticing not just our actions but the excuses we make for them. In the process of observing with great compassion, we may shift into a sense of interconnection and loving kindness. But it doesn't happen overnight. If we beat ourselves up about it, we slow the process and squelch the possibility of truly coming into alignment.

"Once we come into some sense of alignment, it's important to continue to be mindful, noticing our thoughts and actions. We may become unskillful in a different way, developing a sense of purity around this, vowing that from this day forth we will live in perfect Right Livelihood, and make it our mission that others do the same. All we can expect from such action is misery in our ambition, our striving and our failures; as well as misery for those around us who will tire mighty quickly of any proselytizing we do in our new conversion.

"As the Buddha did, we discover the Middle Way. This is not the half-hearted way, mind you, and certainly not the half-assed way! This is a way filled with mindfulness and compassion for us and others. When we allow this awareness to unfold gently and with Wise Effort, we create joy and ease, and, to the best of our abilities, Wise Livelihood.

"Now I want to switch gears a bit, because we've been talking on this retreat about our perception of self. Who we believe ourselves to be. All those labels that we plaster on the separate fortress of 'I' and 'me'.

"Of course, how we make our living is often tightly woven into that idea of who we are. One of the first things people ask when they meet us is, "What do you do?" And often, we reply with a noun: "I'm a lawyer, a bricklayer, a contractor, a personal assistant to the VP of thingamabobs at such and such a company.""

They laughed.

"Whatever we say, once people know our job or position, they think they know who we are. If they like that profession, they'll say 'Oh, really!' and want to know more. If they don't like it, they'll nod and wander off. In either case, they think they can file us away.

"And that's sad, because while there was the possibility of meeting each other where we were, now there's this field between us filled with all their attitudes, experiences, and opinions about lawyers or whatever.

"And we have the same, depending on what position they hold. Whether these opinions are positive or negative, a barrier remains. Whether they say 'thank you for your service' or 'a car salesperson, huh? I got such a bad deal last time I was at the dealer...' the potential for real connection has been lost in that field of opinion.

"All this to say that our livelihood is so intrinsic to our lives that we tend to be defined by it. Even if we don't get paychecks or run businesses, we are still defined by that. "Retired. Unemployed. Student. All these words define us in one way or another in other people's minds.

"So it's something to be aware of. We don't have to rail against it when we feel others judging us. We have no power over their opinions and preferences. But we can be aware of the tendency in ourselves and make a wise effort to at least try not to judge others by their jobs. Can we see the person behind the uniform? Behind the bank account? Behind the desk? This is a worthy challenge!

"And when people ask who we are, can we switch from nouns to verbs? Can we articulate in our own words the value we believe we bring to the world? Can we restate our Wise Intention? Hopefully without coming off as strange." She smiled. "But try it! Imagine a lawyer saying, 'I defend people in court' or 'I prosecute those who harm people.' Or 'I help people with their legal papers that are so confusing and leave their heirs in turmoil at a time when they are grieving.'

"Doesn't that wording make a difference? It's not defensive! It's just more accurate. And it removes the roadblocks to connect with other people."

Lily paused and looked around.

"So those are some of my thoughts on Wise Livelihood. Most of you have the reference material and can explore further if you are so inclined. But for now we will take a break. When the bell rings, we'll come back for some discussion.

Eva rose and stretched. She thought some tea might be just what she needed. Connor had set up a low table near the campfire and placed a tray of mugs, tea bags, and honey. So she went to see which kind of tea she wanted. But before she chose, she noticed something else on the table: stacks of marshmallows, graham crackers, and chocolate bars, just waiting to become s'mores. And leaning against the table were slender branches, stripped of leaves and twigs, ready to be loaded with marshmallows. Oh my! What a sweet last-night treat. Others had noticed it too and began picking up the sticks and marshmallows. She chose her tea bag - chamomile - and ladled hot water into her cup before everyone gathered around the fire to roast their marshmallows. She sat back down and enjoyed the entertainment.

Normally she would have joined in. But the thought of s'mores took her on too steep a mental dive into her childhood, and the sound of her mother's laughter over her child's excitement and delight.

Still, it was fun to watch the different styles of roasting marshmallows people had. Connor carefully brought his marshmallows to a perfect golden brown. Eddie held up his blazing mass and waved it around, creating flame trails. Minna, like Eva, just watched, laughing and sipping her tea. Lily nibbled on a piece of chocolate that looked suspiciously unlike the milk chocolate bar and very much like the dark chocolate square, her regular evening treat.

Allie taught Sara how to load the marshmallows on the stick and hold the slender branch over the flame enough to char and melt the chocolate into the graham crackers. Sara was delighted and they laughed together as they crunched down on the gooey, stacked mess, as if they were at a Girl Scout camp instead of a meditation retreat.

Eva hadn't noticed Minna leaving the circle, but now she returned with a tray and presented it to Vicente. Was that *churros y chocolate*? How was that even possible? But Vicente laughed with delight, his childhood memories now a part of the circle.

Trusty was standing around looking expectantly from person to person. Clearly this was not a dog treat. But Connor slipped him something that caused him to wag his tail in gratitude, so he was happy too.

After the fun subsided and the area was cleaned up, Lily rang the bell and they all sat back down, and settled in.

Lily looked around at them all and began, "So, having looked at Wise Livelihood, can you look at your own choices? Your choice of career and the many choices you make all the time about where to buy the things you need, and if you have extra funds, where to save or invest it?"

The circle was quiet. Eva stared at the embers in the fire and thought about her own career. Fortunately, it didn't fit in the Buddha's bad job list. Phew! But there were ways she could make it wiser and kinder. She would think about that later, but now, for the first time since she'd been on this amazing retreat, she felt exhausted. Drained. Emptied.

Allie spoke up. "I'm still in school, and it's a big decision which direction to go, but I will really try to bring an awareness of Wise Livelihood into my decision-making. I so appreciate your sharing about your early career, Lily. I'd like to use my creativity. But I don't want to use the Three Poisons to get people to do anything unskillful. And it's everywhere, isn't it? First, we must not fall for it ourselves. Then identify why it is so harmful. Then see that we don't fall into the trap of being part of that system, creating the very lures we've avoided for ourselves."

Lily nodded appreciatively. "Thank you, Allie."

Eddie held up his hand, and Lily nodded. "I work for a solar company. We install solar panels on homes, stores, and office buildings all over our area. And I feel really good about that. It's not perfect, but it is helping to solve a big problem, and it saves people so much money on their monthly energy bills and ultimately overall.

"But when I first joined the sangha, I was in bad shape and depressed about my work. As some of you might remember, I was working as a salesman for a company that manufactured locks, all kinds of locks and other security devices. And the sales pitch I was told to give was to tell scary stories to people, so they couldn't sleep until they got our locks on the doors and safety cameras, etc. It just felt horrible. Statistically, they were in no great danger, but our pitch made it sound like their quiet street was filled with burglars and rapists. The product itself was okay. I have no problem with people locking their doors. But that fear tactic felt so invasive, as if they would never get a good night's sleep again, never trust their neighbors, and never feel safe. So I was miserable, and, just like you said, Lily, I started drinking more beer when I got home and watching more television. The kids started avoiding me. I was a grouch.

"I didn't know what to do and I wasn't helping myself to think clearly. So, I started coming to the sangha, and my habits gradually began to change. And then, I overheard something at work. The company owner was considering branching out and working together with a company that sold guns for domestic protection, thinking it would be a perfect pairing, a package deal. And that's when I freaked!"

"I called my wife from work when I heard about it, and I told her I just couldn't take it anymore. And she said, 'so quit!' Just like that. She said she was sure I'd find another job, a better job, one that was more aligned with my values. Meanwhile, she would get temporary jobs, and maybe it was time she started looking for work herself, since the kids were in school most of the day.

"So I quit! It was scary as hell, but it felt like the right thing to do.

"And then, after a couple of months of job searching -- and soul-searching with the help of the sangha -- I realized I wanted to be part of the solution. And once I was clear on that, I received a call from a solar company. And it's been great."

The circle was quiet; no one else raised their hand, and everyone looked weary. And the fire was just a few embers.

Lily said, "Well, then. Let's set a wise intention to examine our interactions in the marketplace, our investments, our treatment of the planet, and the work we do. Thank you for your kind attention."

She put her hands together and bowed to them, and they did the same.

"I will leave you now, but feel free to stay for chanting." And with that she rose and made her way up the fairy-light path.

As a few others got up to leave, Trusty looked up at her expectantly, but she just pet him, and whispered, "Let's just stay for a little while longer." He sighed, and put his head back down on his paws, staring mournfully at the fire.

Vicente spoke to those who remained in the circle. "Our last evening of chanting together on this retreat. Some of you have been chanting every night, but for those who are unfamiliar with the chant, let me summarize it. These phrases we chant are very simple. They are about taking refuge. The first line, repeated three times, is simply a blessing to the Buddha.

It expresses our gratitude for his wisdom and dedication to sharing his teachings so that all may end their suffering and awaken.

Then we chant three lines about taking refuge:

Buddham saraṇam gacchāmi
Dhammam saraṇam gacchāmi
Saṅgham saraṇam gacchāmi

"First, we take refuge in the Buddha, not as a god, because he made it very clear he was not a god. He was awake! So we take refuge in the Buddha as a reminder that we too can awaken.

"Then we take refuge in the Dhamma, though you're probably more familiar with the Sanskrit word 'Dharma'. It is the Buddha's teachings that have been carefully passed down through generations of monks and Theravada teachers over 2600 years.

"And, finally, we take refuge in the Sangha, the community of meditators who share the wholesome intention to awaken. We support each other and strengthen our resolve to meditate.

"We repeat these same three lines, adding the word *Dutiyampi* at the beginning to clarify that this is the second time. And then we repeat the phrase *Tatiyampi* a third time to really let it sink in.

"I share this because, for me, it's very important to know the meaning of what I'm chanting. But chanting them in this ancient language allows the beauty of the language to shift me gently to a more relaxed but focused state of concentration.

"I see our fire of Wise Effort is winding down, and I think we'll just sit and meditate and chant until the fire's out. Or we are. And if the last person would make sure to douse any remaining embers, that would be appreciated. Thank you all for your dedicated practice."

Then he closed his eyes and began to chant. Some others joined in, and she noticed a few just sat in silence, enveloped in the words that, while foreign to her ears, were now imbued with meaning.

Through Eva's partially closed eyes, what remained of the fire light danced through the screen of her lashes.

Her mind had quieted down completely when an image rose up: a circle of trees. Not these trees, but a grove of eight redwood trees in a perfect circle. She remembered reading about how the redwoods have very shallow roots that are woven together to support each other.

Just like this sangha, she realized. All together here, taking refuge in the Buddha, the Dharma, and the Sangha.

And maybe that was true of the Noble Eightfold Path itself, the eight aspects supporting each other.

When she felt truly at peace, she, like a couple of others before her, bowed to the center of the circle with sincere gratitude, and rose quietly, and made her way up the fairy light path to bed.

'Taking Refuge' Chant in Pali

Namo tassa bhagavato arahato sammāsambuddhassa
Namo tassa bhagavato arahato sammāsambuddhassa
Namo tassa bhagavato arahato sammāsambuddhassa

Buddhaṃ saraṇaṃ gacchāmi
Dhammaṃ saraṇaṃ gacchāmi
Saṅghaṃ saraṇaṃ gacchāmi

Dutiyampi buddhaṃ saraṇaṃ gacchāmi
Dutiyampi dhammaṃ saraṇaṃ gacchāmi
Dutiyampi saṅghaṃ saraṇaṃ gacchāmi

Tatiyampi buddhaṃ saraṇaṃ gacchāmi
Tatiyampi dhammaṃ saraṇaṃ gacchāmi
Tatiyampi saṅghaṃ saraṇaṃ gacchāmi

23 The Last Morning

When Eva woke to the sound of the bell, she could hear raindrops on the canvas of the tent. There was a note from Lily on the tent flap saying to bring any of her stuff with her to the yurt. She put on the warmest clothes and the rain jacket, grabbed her daypack, and looked around to see if there was anything she was leaving behind. Since she hadn't brought much with her, the answer was no. But she realized this must be her last look at this sweet little space, and the thought made her chest ache a little. How she hated endings!

As she walked up the path, she was surprised to see that all the little tents were gone. Everyone had been very busy while she was sleeping. Now she could see just the forest. Not even the strings of fairy lights.

On the covered yurt porch, she set down her pack with all the others stacked there. Then she toweled off Trusty, with special attention to his paws. As she entered the yurt, she noticed a buffet set against the wall, offering a selection of fruit, nuts, and oatmeal bars. The only thing hot was the tea water, so she poured herself a cup. Then she sat on a cushion and closed her eyes.

The heat of the cup in her hands, the sound of the rain on the roof, the sense of togetherness of this sweet sangha--all of it felt so precious. How could she hold it without clinging to it? How could she savor it without mourning its inevitable passing? That was her challenge. Here in this moment on this retreat, and maybe in the rest of her life as well.

When the bell rang, she felt a sense of settled acceptance of the way things are. She didn't feel weighed down by the realization, but strangely uplifted. Yes, this is the way things are. This is what it is to be alive in this moment, in this life.

She felt as if she was in a big balloon, and had been walking on the inside surface, trudging here and there, never getting anywhere, having a very myopic view of things. But now, she was floating in the center of the balloon, able to engage and appreciate it all. One day, the balloon would burst. Her life would be over. But being in the center, she would continue to dance, freed from the burst balloon-skin that would entangle her had she stayed mindlessly trudging on the inner surface.

*   *   *

The bell rang. With the moisture in the air, the sound waves rippled. Beyond the beyond. She opened her eyes and looked around with deep appreciation. Everyone else was doing the same. What an amazing sharing they had had together. How fortunate they were to have this gift of practice. It wasn't the fancy camp or the fantastic food. It was this community, this sangha. It was the Buddha's teachings, the Dharma. And it was this practice of meditation, the Buddha, which simply means an awakened one. So, there is the potential for awakening within each of us. She bowed with deep gratitude and the intention to continue the practice when she returned home.

Over breakfast, Vicente said, "Lily and I want to thank Minna, Connor, and Eddie for arranging this amazing retreat. We would never have thought of making a nature retreat. But it was, I think, quite wonderful. And we appreciate all the accommodations you provide so we elders wouldn't 'suffer' the elements. And thank you to our fabulous kitchen chefs, Sara, Allie, Connor, and Minna, for creating meals beyond anything we could have imagined out in the wild. Thanks to Eva for keeping the bathroom spotless and well stocked, and to Eddie for creating and maintaining the physical camp. Really beyond our wildest dreams."

Minna spoke then, "I think I speak for the rest of us, Vicente, thanking you and Lily for your guidance always. And for being good sports about going on this retreat into the hills."

Vicente and Lily nodded, bowing their gratitude for the praise. Then Lily said, "It was truly a communal effort in all ways. We're both so impressed with the way you each took on the aspects of the Eightfold Path and created opportunities for the rest of us to explore. Well done!"

Vicente nodded in agreement. "On to practical matters. I think we're well packed up, thanks to the rain hurrying us along. And we'll have our closing ceremony here. But first, we will meet with you one-on-one. I'll be holding court here in the yurt, and Lily apparently has a sheltered spot she's been sitting in over the past few days, and she wants to share it with those of you who will meet with her.

"So, Minna, Connor, and Eddie, in that order, will be with me here. And Sara, Allie, and Eva, you'll meet with Lily in her special hideaway. All of you who are not in your one-on-one meeting can either wait on the yurt's covered porch or venture forth — not too far. Feel free to take an umbrella. Or go without one if you want to enjoy the full experience of the rain."

Eva and Trusty took a little walk while she waited for her turn. The trees glistened with gratitude for the rain. Overnight, emerald moss appeared, and delicate mushrooms of all kinds sprouted. Unbelievable! This place was truly incredible! As if it were on a totally different timetable than the rest of nature. She couldn't wait to bring Heather and Chelsea here!

She pulled herself back into the present moment. Aware that these were the last precious hours of her life-changing retreat, she wanted to savor everything. She also wanted to review what she had learned. Each of the aspects of the Eightfold Path seemed so full of gifts that would be of great benefit to her life. But only if she could remember them!

It helped to picture the Cooking Pot Analogy Lily had offered that first night. The matchstick flame of Wise Intention. The well-laid logs and kindling of Wise Effort. The spoon of Wise Mindfulness and Wise Concentration stirring to clarify the contents of consciousness held by the pot of Wise View. And the three plumes of steam wafting into the world: Wise Speech, Wise Action, and Wise Livelihood. She vowed never to forget them, to study them when she returned home, and to cultivate them in every moment. She knew this was her path. It felt so good to find her way. She had been so lost.

After a bit, she saw Allie waving to her from the wooded path to the right of the camp. As Eva approached her, Allie pointed toward a rock ledge. When Eva and Trusty reached it, they came upon Lily sitting inside a shallow cave, protected from the rain; her eyes were closed in meditation, making her look noble and peaceful.

Eva couldn't help thinking of the stereotype seeker who climbs the mountain and sits in a cave to awaken. But Lily wasn't a guru. She was a very kind and wise woman with years of meditation practice and insights, who had been on the Eightfold Path long enough to lead the way. Eva felt so lucky to have found her. But knowing she lived a distance away, she also felt sad that this might be the last time she would see her. Or maybe not? Couldn't they meet on Zoom? What a concept! She would ask for Lily's business card.

Heartened, she sat down on the cushion next to Lily. She looked out at the view of a vast valley. This gave her pause. The terrain below was even steeper and rockier than it was yesterday. The valley was a narrow gorge. It all looked completely impassable. How would she find her way home?

When she felt her heart racing, she took a deep breath to calm herself. This whole time on retreat, she kept seeing things she'd never seen, as if she had a new set of eyes. So why was she surprised at this majestic scene before her? She'd been unable to see a lot of things that should have been obvious.

Lily smiled and said, "You can see why I've been disappearing when all of you go on your hikes. I am so grateful to have found this spot. And you, dear Eva. I'm so glad we found *you*. I hope your time on this retreat has been meaningful. It's common to have all kinds of challenges and difficulties within the intensive meditation and the silence of a retreat --

though this was certainly less silent than most! So this is your opportunity to ask questions, share your experience, and clear up any misunderstandings."

"Oh, Lily, this has been so meaningful for me, and I'm so grateful. I hope we can stay in touch. Can I get your card? I know you're not near here, but maybe…"

"Ah, yes, well, I'm afraid that won't be possible."

Eva was disappointed but not surprised.

Lily brightened and said, "You're quite fortunate to live here in this beautiful place."

"Well, that's the strange thing, Lily. The more I look around, the more I feel like I'm also hundreds of miles from home. But, of course, that makes no sense. I guess I just didn't have the eyes to see?"

Lily looked at her thoughtfully. "That could be. We're often blind to what's right in front of us. It all becomes so familiar that we stop paying attention, using our senses. But to keep those senses fully present and attuned, we do need our daily meditation practice and our sangha. So I encourage you to find a group near you."

Eva's heart sank. She realized she probably wouldn't see any of them again. Her voice became small, like a little girl, almost pouting. "But I feel so at home with all of you."

Lily smiled, "Oh, that's not unique to our group. All who follow the Buddha's Eightfold Path with Wise Intention and Wise Effort become wonderful companions on the path, supporting each other. It's just the nature of sangha.
"But we have so enjoyed having you and Trusty on this retreat."

Trusty wagged his tail at the sound of his name.

Lily continued, "And it's always interesting how things work out. If Isaac had followed through on his intention to join us, we wouldn't have had a spot for you. We would have just made sure you were okay after your little fall and wished you well."

Eva's eyes filled with tears at the very thought that she might have missed this experience. Now she dreaded saying goodbye to them all. But as she was about to say this to Lily, she took a breath and thought about the nature of impermanence. Everything changes. And everything is interconnected.

Lily asked, "Is there anything that's come up for you that you want to talk about now?"

Eva, realizing this would be her only chance, told Lily about how she'd fallen for Chad. She was over him, but she was having a hard time understanding how it had happened and how to keep it from happening again with someone else. She worried about being a victim of her own desires and about her complete inability to judge character.

Lily nodded, clearly having heard this kind of story before, which made Eva feel both more normal and more ridiculous.

Then Lily said, "But it's not really about this man, is it?"

"What do you mean?"

"What emotions were you running from when you ran into his arms?"

Eva was stunned. Because that was exactly how it was! She was looking for a place to hide from her grief about her mother and her own upcoming surgery. She burst into tears.

"That's right, let them flow, let the well of grief rise and fall as it will. Grief is unruly, and there's no right way to do it. In fact, there's nothing to 'do' at all. Just be with it, be with your emotions. And don't apologize for having them or feel you must hide them or put them off for a more appropriate time. That just leads to…well, this fellow you fell for."

Eva nodded, still tearful.

Lily smiled. "Would you like to tell me about your mother? She must have been a wonderful woman to have raised such a daughter."

Eva smiled but shook her head. Somehow, just recognizing that she needed to make room for her grief instead of filling it up with distractions was enough.

"Well, then," Lily went on, "Would you like me to tell you another metaphor that I came up with long ago that's helped me with my losses over the years?"

"Yes, please."

"Alright. See that mountain lake over there, beautiful and pristine?" Lily pointed to a little lake in the distance that Eva hadn't noticed before, and how was that even possible?

"Now imagine that a large rock, maybe even a boulder or a meteor, falls into the middle of the lake." Eva pictured it.

"The death of a loved one can feel like that. When the boulder falls, it churns the water into huge splashes, bubbles, and waves, throwing everything out of balance."

Eva could see the boulder splashing!

"Everything feels upside down and out of control. If we have developed the practice of being aware, what we notice is this sense of being overwhelmed by huge emotions. We may be too overwhelmed to notice. We may rage against the very practices that have supported us because they are insufficient to protect us from feeling overwhelmed. In that moment of incredible pain and turmoil, it feels as if there is nothing to hold onto. We may flail about in the waves and feel like we're drowning.

"So what do we do? We let go. We experience the pain of it. We do the best we can, trying not to make an enemy of it because that only causes more turmoil. We may get lost, but we return to the present moment, come back to our practice, and regain access to a sense of spacious oneness.

"Meditation is not a place to hide. It's a way to be present whatever is arising, even pain and turmoil. No matter how unskillful we may feel we've become, we can still come home to the breath."

"In the following days, weeks, months, and years after the event, we may have periods where life goes on relatively normally, and then moments where we feel thrust 'back' into the churning emotions. We might see this as 'losing ground,' that we should be 'over this by now.' That comes from imagining life is linear and thinking that we should make linear progress away from being affected by this event.

"But then we can remember the lake. When the boulder fell, that tumultuous, chaotic experience wasn't the end of it, was it? Long after the boulder has settled on the bottom of the lake, the water radiates from the point of impact in widening circles. So, too, with a traumatic event. Over time, the calm spaces between the ripples grow wider and the ripples grow smaller, but they still exist.

"So, it is natural for us to wake up one day and feel the emotional ramifications of that event, however long ago it was. Yesterday we were fine, and today our heart aches, as if that boulder is sitting on our chest. At these times, it is most skillful to acknowledge that this is normal, regardless of what anyone says, and to give ourselves whatever kindness we can, not to suppress our feelings, but to create enough spacious awareness to experience them and allow them to be.

"This is an important lesson for all of us, whether the loss is our own or someone else's. Because at these times, a true friend doesn't say 'It's been x amount of time. Get over it already!' or words that sound like that to us, even when put more nicely. Loss is universal, but we each experience it in our own way. No one can tell us how we should feel.

"So you have been coping with the loss of your mother in your own way. See if you can soften your judgments and hold yourself with tenderness. You don't need to hide from the pain. That just makes it worse, doesn't it?"

Eva nodded, really understanding for the first time how she'd been hiding from her grief instead of acknowledging it and making room for it to simply be a presence.

"Shall we just sit together for a few minutes?" Lily asked.

Eva nodded but kept her eyes open so she could gaze at the mysterious mountain lake.

But soon her eyes drifted shut, and she found she was thinking about the cooking pot. Why? Then it came to her. She whispered, "Lily?"

Lily opened her eyes and smiled. "Did something come to you?"

"Yes!" Eva exclaimed, "The cooking pot!"

"Oh, that cooking pot! It really does take hold of the imagination, doesn't it?"

"Yes, it's so helpful! And I realized something: If a rock fell into the cooking pot, there would be ripples. But when the ripples touch the pot of Wise View…"

"Ah! I see. Yes! Being held in Wise View, the ripples touch and maybe even amplify the wisdom."

"Yes! Like the loss of my mother created these painful ripples, but when held in the pot of Wise View, I see an example of the nature of impermanence. And, while it doesn't feel like a gift, because it's painful and difficult, it is still part of awakening. Isn't it? That awareness? If I allow it to inform me? Right?"

"Exactly so."

"And then when I'm aware of impermanence, I'm also aware of the other aspect of Wise View, interconnection, right?"

Lily nodded.

"And how in some ways I'll never lose my mother because she lives on in me, in my DNA and in my memories. She's an intrinsic part of me. I miss her terribly — oh how I wish I could hug her and laugh with her. All my senses crave her! I want to hug her, hold her hand, smell her skin, stroke her hair, hear her voice and her laugh!"

Eva paused and took a breath, sighing. "But I still feel her essence. I can still talk to her, and I know exactly what she would say, what advice she would give in any situation."

And, Eva thought to herself, *she'll still listen to my confessions and offer forgiveness.* "It's not the same. Of course not! But it is a gift I've been ignoring because it's so painful to think of her."

"A beautiful realization," said Lily. She smiled at Eva fondly. That smile reminded Eva of her mother's smile, and she hadn't noticed that before. Perhaps she'd been blinded by her fear of remembering, of grieving, of losing herself in the process.

They both looked into the distance. A fog that had settled on the valley floor rose up and she could no longer see the magical lake.

Overhead the sky darkened and thunder rumbled with foreboding. Suddenly, Eva felt she had had enough awakening for now. She wanted to be home in her cozy house with her two besties. She realized how worried about her they must be. She couldn't remember if she'd texted them or not, but even so… She felt like the worst friend ever!

Eva felt Lily's hand on her back, supporting her, calming her. She took a breath and rested in silence. She sent Metta to Heather and Chelsea. *May they be well.*

Just then, a flock of geese, traveling south. They're attuned to the impermanence of all things, she thought. They're not clinging but following the natural rhythms of life.

Watching the geese disappear in the clouds, she sighed and asked Lily, "Do you ever wish you could fly?"

Lily smiled, "Oh, wings would be lovely. But my bones are brittle enough without being hollow. Do you wish you could fly?"

Eva nodded wistfully.

"Well, what's stopping you?"

"What do you mean?"

"I mean, this is your dream, dear, you can fly if you want to!"

"*Dream?* What? A dream? Wait, Lily, this…"

And then, as if responding to the thunder, the earth beneath her started to rumble. The hillside began to crumble. As she clung to whatever she could grab, she called out to Lily, who had a beatific expression on her face. "Wait! What? Where?"

Lily's whole being emanated love in ripples, as radiant as the sun. She put her hands together, smiled and closed her eyes. Then she dissolved into the mist that lifted up and up.

No!!! Eva felt as if she was losing her mother all over again. "Lily! Please! Wait! Where can I find you? What should I do?"

She could barely hear Lily's voice across the mist. "Just let go, dear! Take refuge in the Buddha, the Dharma, and the Sangha."

The last word, *Sangha*, echoed and etched itself in the mist, then dissolved and reappeared in a rainbow of colors. And then it was gone.

Let go? Eva couldn't let go! She looked down and the valley floor was growing increasingly distant. Thousands of feet! *Let go?* No! Every instinct told her to cling for dear life and to scramble to seek safety in the cave. But with each move, the rock surface crumbled beneath her.

The sky grew even darker. And now, instead of the wild geese, thick masses of crows cawed as they flew above her, and the freezing rain lashed down on her. It felt like she was being punished, that she wasn't worthy. All her self-doubt rose up like bile. She could barely hear Trusty barking madly above the roar of the storm and the raging river far below. She reached out to pull him close. If they were going to fall, at least let them fall together. But she couldn't find him in the storm. Where was he? Where was he?

"Trusty?" she screamed. "*Trusty!!!*"

Then, just as her feet began to slip down the cliff, she woke up.

PART THREE

There's No Place Like Home

24 It Takes a Village

Trusty was barking madly, but Eva could barely hear him over the deafening thumping of helicopter blades. What was going on?

She felt like she weighed a ton, as if she'd landed on earth like a meteor. Every inch of her body ached, her forehead especially. She touched it and could feel there was something, a gash? But now she noticed her ankle was very painful. How long had she been lying there? The helicopter hovered as a rescue basket was lowered. She felt woozy and drifted off again.

When she woke up this time, she was in a hospital bed. In a room much like the one she'd spent at her mother's bedside before she died. She hadn't been there since that sad and lengthy vigil. She felt woozy with the memory of their last conversation, the touch of her hand, and the look in her eyes, acknowledging the end of a bond like no other. Eva felt the tears flow.

A nurse entered and said, "Ah, good, you're awake. Hurts that bad, does it?"

"No, it's just..." Then she had a flash of memory, a thought that maybe she knew this woman. "Minna?"

"No, hon, I'm Sandy. You're here in the hospital and you're safe. I'll let the doctor know you're awake."

"Where's Trusty? My dog?"

"He's outside with your friend. Don't worry. Everything is fine. Just rest."

Sandy checked the monitor and the drip, then left the room.

Eva ached all over. She hoped the drip would take the pain away. But it could just be something to rehydrate her. How long had she been out? It felt like forever!

As she lay there in bed, aching all over, she closed her eyes and started to remember a dream she'd had. A dream about…hiking further up into the hills, further than she'd ever gone in her whole life…and she was on a retreat, a meditation retreat, with all these lovely people who…she was trying to remember, because suddenly it felt so important. It was a Buddhist retreat, yes. And it was about the Buddha's Noble Eightfold Path. She'd read something about that somewhere, or maybe it was Heather that told her about it. Anyway, that didn't matter. What mattered was that these people were all exploring their lives through a lens that was so much clearer, so much truer and more honest than all the ways she had been hiding, struggling, avoiding, and just making a mess of things the past few months. She'd been chasing after distractions. She'd been foolish. She hadn't wanted to be with the difficult…impossible…sense of loss without her mother to turn to. Everyone had always envied their close relationship. And it was true. Even after Eva went off to college and only came home for holidays, she and her mother had stayed close. And now…

Tears streamed down her cheeks and when she raised her hand to wipe them away, she jiggled the bag of whatever fluid they were dripping into her. It was like the fluid was coming into her arm and pouring out her eyes. *A river flows through me. I am a part of the river of life.*

Exhausted, she dozed off again. She didn't know how much time had passed when she woke up to see a doctor checking her chart. Seeing she was awake, he said, "Well, you certainly made for an eventful Sunday afternoon for the rescue crew, didn't you?"

But before she could answer, he looked at his chart again.

"Fortunately, your ankle is only twisted. You'll need to take it easy for a few days, stay off it as much as possible. But you really shouldn't have been hiking up in the hills alone."

"I wasn't alone. I had my dog with me."

"Well, until your dog knows how to dial 911, I suggest you have a human companion. It's pretty much a miracle that you were found. And you were very dehydrated. And so was your dog, by the way."

Eva felt properly chastised. "You're right, of course. I was very foolish."

"But both of you will be fine, and that's the important thing. I'll write you a note for your employer. You're a teacher, right?"

"Yes."

"I think my daughter was in your class a while back. Liza Evans?"

"Oh yes! How is she? She must be in high school by now!"

"A senior! She's been accepted at her first-choice college."

"That's wonderful. Please tell Liza I'm proud of her."

"I will."

Just then, Heather peeked in the door. The doctor said, "Sandy will be back with some papers and a wheelchair to get you out of here." With that, he left, nodding to Heather.

Heather came to her bedside and said, "Oh my God, Eva, you had me *so* worried."

"I'm sorry, I screwed up. I was just so…"

"Oh, hush, just rest. You look like crap, but you're alive and no permanent damage. That's all that matters now."

"How's Trusty?"

"He's okay. At first, they told me to take him home or to the vets, but he refused to leave you here. So they relented and just gave him a basin full of water, and he drank almost the whole thing. Then he settled under the bench by the front door and snoozed. But every time the door opened, he got up or at least peeked. He's desperate to see you."

"Poor Trusty. How could I have done this to him?"

"Well, he's okay. And so are you. Let's sort the rest out later."

"What about Zippy? It's been parked on Chad's street for days."

"Days? No, just a few hours. Matthew gave me a ride over to pick it up, talking all the way about how this was all his fault, something about a dare and a celebrity crush? I assured him, but I think he needs to hear it from you."

"Give me my phone. I'll text him."

"Not now! Don't worry. Just rest."

"Okay, but Heather, I had the wildest dream. It keeps coming back in little bits and pieces, but I was way up in the hills on a Buddhist retreat, and it was amazing. I know you've been…"

"Wow, that's so cool! I thought you weren't listening when I've gone on and on about the group…"

"The sangha…"

"Yes! Yes! The sangha…OMG, you have been listening. Anyway, as I've told you several times, you're welcome to come with me. I think you'd really get a lot out of it."

"I'm sure I will. And I will come with you. Don't let me forget. I'm so afraid I'll forget what I learned in that dream." Then she drifted off to sleep again.

* * *

She woke up when Sandy came in with a release form to sign. Eva panicked. What if she couldn't read the form?

Seeing the look on Eva's face, Sandy said, "Oh, I know it looks like a lot of legalese, but it's standard. Don't worry about it, your insurance will cover it."

When Eva took the form and saw all the letters grouped in familiar patterns, she felt an inexplicable sense of relief. Why on earth was she worried about that? Had she thought the knock on her head had made her illiterate? Weird!

"Let's get out of here," she said to Heather.

"I'll go pull the car upfront."

Sandy appeared again with a wheelchair. Eva hobbled into it and held her daypack in her lap as Sandy pushed her out the main entrance.

Trusty greeted her with great excitement, jumping up on her in a way he had been trained never to do. But she was so glad to see him, she couldn't scold him. Instead, she bent over and held him close and whispered to him. "Oh, Trusty. Do you remember the dream, too?"

She hoped he did because he had a great time. She couldn't stand to think he had just been awake, barking madly over her unconscious body.

At home, Eva saw the overnight bag she'd left at Chad's.

Chelsea hugged her gently, afraid to hurt her. Then, seeing Eva looking at the bag, she said, "Oh yeah, that happened. So, get this: The next-door neighbors were out raking leaves, and their kids were just getting ready to jump in the pile by the curb, when your Prince Charming pulled up in his ridiculous Lamborghini and scattered leaves everywhere. Then he tossed the bag on the lawn, revved the engine a few more times for good measure, and took off at breakneck speed, leaving the poor kids in the dust."

Eva was horrified but also relieved. "I'm so sorry, you guys. I promise to listen to you next time you try to warn me off someone. But it's going to be a while, so don't worry. I'm just so grateful to be home."

She went into her room, dumping both the bag and her daypack on her bed, then sat down gingerly on her quilt. Whatever painkiller they had given her was wearing off.

Her roommates hovered at the door. She raised her hand and waved them in. She looked around the room, feeling like she'd been away forever. All of it was very familiar, but it was like returning from a long journey, and everything seemed different, as if she had fresh eyes. She looked at the photo from her college graduation day with the tassel of her mortarboard awry, her ear-to-ear smile, and her mother holding her, looking so proud.

She sighed. Then she turned back to Chelsea and Heather and said, "It's so good to be home. But I'm still confused how they found me."

Chelsea said, "Heather found you!"

"Huh?"

Heather looked sheepish. "Well, remember we set up those location tracking apps on our phones a while back? I confess, I've been worried about you, and I never trusted that guy. Soo…"

"So you tracked me?"

"Well, yeah. I got a very creepy feeling this afternoon. I just peeked to make sure you were at his house or, hopefully, on your way home. But I could see you were up in the hills, so maybe you were just walking Trusty on a hike or a picnic. But then I checked again much later, and you were still in that spot. I was so worried, but I didn't know what to do. I would have gone up after you, but you were so far up there, and if I found you and you were…"

Eva could see Heather's body trembling and her eyes welling up with tears. "Oh, Heather, I'm…"

But Heather put her hand up. She wanted to finish explaining, "Then I got a text from Elliot that totally freaked me out. He said that Chad dropped the house keys off at his office and told him to put the house on the market, as he no longer needed it. He would be sending a van in a few days to pick up his belongings.

"Elliot said Chad seemed distracted and in a rush. And I, oh Eva, I couldn't help thinking that he'd killed you and dumped you up in the woods."

Now Eva reached out and drew Heather into her arms. They cried together, and then both reached out their arms and drew Chelsea in. This made Trusty bark excitedly, and they all laughed, tears streaming down their faces.

"But the helicopter?" asked Eva.

"That was Elliot's doing," Chelsea said, picking up the thread of the story. "He felt so terrible that he'd ever invited Chad to the party, and if anything happened to you, he would blame himself. So he was running around like a madman trying to help. Fortunately, he knows everyone in town, and he called someone who knew someone in the sheriff's department. They said they'd get right on it, and they did. Thank goodness!

"You were so dehydrated, and with that ankle, you wouldn't have made it down on your own."

Eva shook her head, amazed at all that had happened. "I'm so sorry I caused everyone so much trouble and distress." She bent down and hugged Trusty. "I'm so sorry, T. I should have trusted your judgment more. You know a bad guy when you see one, don't you?"

Trusty wagged his tail and gave one definite *yes* bark. They all laughed.

"I'm just so grateful to be home now. And so glad Chad's moved away! I won't ever have to deal with him again. I feel like a load has been lifted. I'm too tired to celebrate now, but let's plan something fun."

Her roommates agreed and grinned at each other, relieved that finally Eva had come to her senses!

*   *   *

That evening, they sat Eva on the sofa with her foot propped up. They ordered a very decadent pizza, and usually, they would be laughing and gabbing. But the stressful events of the day had caught up with them, and, exhausted, they said goodnight and returned to their rooms, leaving their doors open in case Eva needed anything.

Eva was about to hang her daypack on the hook on the back of her door when she thought she had better be sure there wasn't any food rotting in there. She had the feeling she'd left half a sandwich, but she didn't know where she would get that.

But no, there was nothing but a few dog treats, her empty water bottle, and her journal, which she took out to put by her bed.

She had never been much for journaling, but she had been jotting down notes to herself lately to maintain her sanity with all of Chad's gaslighting and confusing behavior. How could she possibly have put up with it? But she was too exhausted for her usual ruminations.

*   *   *

As she settled in for the night, she decided to write herself a stern reminder to never fall for anyone like Chad again.

Heather peeked in. "Everything okay?"

Eva nodded. "I'm still just so confused, but at the same time I feel like I found something. That dream, I tell you, was unlike anything. It lasted for days. It was so real. And I…"

"Well, do you remember what you said in the hospital? That you wanted to come to my sangha with me?"

"Sangha? That's the meditation group? Yes. That would be good. Maybe I can learn to take a breath before diving into a bad relationship."

"Great! I can't promise it will solve all your problems. Some of it is very similar to what I share with my yoga class. But it's wonderful for me to have a place where I can be just me, not a teacher, and express my very human feelings."

Then she smiled deviously. "Lately, you'll be interested to know, I've shared how sad I feel that my dearest friend has abandoned me."

"You didn't!"

Heather laughed, "No, but I could have! I'd much rather bring you to the next meeting. The leader is wise but not a know-it-all, and the sangha members are just down-to-earth, good people. And no, it's not a cult. Buddhism's been around for millennia!"

"2600 years," said Eva.

"Yes! You and your trivia. We really need to start attending some Trivia nights. Anyway, this is the most secular branch of it. Some think it is too secular, but that's another story. It works for me. Maybe it would work for you."

"I look forward to it."

"That's great!"

Heather gave Eva a big hug, and Eva cried out in pain.

"Oh, shoot, I'm sorry, SOOO sorry!"

Then they looked at each other and laughed until tears streamed down both their faces.

"We look like hell."

"And we don't care."

Hilarity ensued, and Trusty started barking to join in the party. Then Chelsea peeked in to see what was up. She laughed at the sight of them all. "May I join you?"

"Of course!" said Eva, and Heather made room on the bed for the three to sit, steering clear of Eva's elevated ankle.

Heather quieted down and gave Chelsea a concerned look that Eva didn't understand. Chelsea smiled and nodded. "I'm fine, really."

"Wait, what am I missing? What happened?"

Chelsea said, "Daddy died. I'm heading home in the morning to help plan the arrangements."

"Oh, Chelsea, no!" Eva cried, reaching for her and rocking her in her arms. Chelsea sank into the embrace gratefully and let her tears flow.

Heather said, "We didn't want to tell you when you were in the hospital, and then when we got home, Chelsea said she'd rather just eat pizza and not talk about it anymore today."

"Oh, no," said Eva. "If I've learned anything from the mess I made with Chad, it's not to stuff down emotions around losing Mom. So, Chelsea, please don't hold back."

Chelsea sobbed. "Daddy worried about all of us all the time. But now I feel his presence, telling me to not to worry, just trust in the Lord. It makes me feel like even from heaven, he's finding any way he can to take care of us. I do trust in the Lord, but I trust Daddy more, and that's the truth."

Both Heather and Eva stroked Chelsea's back as she let her tears flow freely.

"Thank you both. It means so much to have friends for housemates. I'm so lucky."

"We're all so lucky." Heather agreed. "Will you let us know when the funeral is?"

"Yes, let us know. We'll be there," said Eva.

Chelsea wiped her eyes and looked at them both, amused. "Have you ever been to a Black Baptist funeral?"

When they both shook their heads, she smiled and said, "Well, let me prepare you: First, the church will be standing room only — everybody loved Daddy so much. He was a deacon at the church, and he was always ready to help others. And more than one of those fine ladies had a crush on him, for sure. Much as they love Momma.

"And there will be an open casket, and you'll be expected to pay your respects, and the body…" Chelsea took a breath, clearly hating the thought of her father lying in a coffin. "Well, it probably won't look like the man you remember.

"Now the choir is worth driving thirty miles for. I won't be part of it this time, but all that singing and swaying really helps the congregation, and it really does feel like we're helping raise the one who's passed up to heaven. Daddy clearly doesn't need any help," she added, looking again at the precious message from beyond. "But some need all the help they can get!

"Which reminds me, I have to warn you. At some point, there's a good chance the preacher will be pounding the lectern with a warning to the unsaved, that'd be you two… among others I could name but won't.

"Then there's bound to be someone, usually an old lady, falling out, fainting. And maybe people will be weeping and begging Jesus for a blessing. Are you sure that you're up for that?"

Their eyes were wide open, telling one story, while their heads nodded. Yes, they wanted to be there for her and her family.

"Okay then. Well, you are in for a real treat. And the repast in the church basement will fill you up for a week."

Her brightness faded fast. Seeing her wilting, Eva opened her arms. "Oh, honey."

Both she and Heather held Chelsea as she wept again. After a moment, she raised her head and looked at Eva. "It's so good to have you back home. I mean, you're really home now, aren't you? No more of that nonsense?"

"No more nonsense, I promise."

"Well then, welcome home, Eva. Welcome home."

25 Insight

Early Monday morning, Eva's housemates headed out, Heather to the studio and Chelsea to help her mother with funeral arrangements and other sad chores that Eva knew only too well from her own recent loss.

But before leaving, they set Eva up on the couch with her ankle elevated on pillows, a carafe of hot tea, snacks, and an assortment of carefully curated reading material to entertain and inspire her stacked on the coffee table. They also assembled Trusty's favorite plushy and other toys by his bed.

They had moved the couch so she would have a view of the back garden through the French doors. "Here's a sketchbook, in case you get inspired to draw out some ideas for planting. It's never too early to start planning!" said Chelsea. Eva recognized how her friend was thinking ahead to the spring to avoid the painful present. She nodded and gave her hand a squeeze.

Heather made one final adjustment of the pillows. "Okay, I'll be back to bring lunch and walk Trusty. Any preferences for takeout?"

Eva shook her head. "You decide. And if it doesn't work out, don't worry. I'll survive on leftovers, no problem. Trusty can make do with the backyard if need be. But thanks for all you've done. Best friends ever."

It was true. Eva so appreciated their fussing over her. But she was also relieved when they left and she could, for the first time since the accident, be truly alone to process all she'd been through.

She knew that her escape from Chad's, her long hike, the painful fall, eventual helicopter rescue, and hospital visit all happened over a few hours, but it felt like days had passed. She kept thinking it was Thursday. Her roomies kept setting her straight, but she couldn't take it in. How was that possible?

It felt like she'd been on a long journey with a lot of people, even though except for Trusty, she'd been all alone in the hills. She shivered at the thought of what would have happened if they hadn't rescued her. How would she have gotten back down the hill? Would Chad have…?

Then she purposely let that train of thought go and opened to the possibility of remembering more of the dream she'd had when she fell. There was something in it for her, some message, she felt sure. She closed her eyes and rested her attention on her breath, as if she were in Heather's yoga class. Then she let random images float through without judgment.

Her muscles relaxed and she felt a warm, easy sense of calm…and a feeling of being supported by community…awe and wonder…a campfire and faces around it, eyes closed, glowing, together in an intimate exploration of some kind…under a circle of trees, surrounded by mountains, lakes, creeks, waterfalls, boulders, and grasses rich with life on a tiny scale that, somehow, she could see up close and personal.

Her typical dreams were often populated with students in her class or friends. (She wished her mother would come to her in a dream, but she hadn't. At least not yet. Anyway, this dream was different. She didn't know anyone, yet she felt like she knew them, knew some of their stories…

Just as she was beginning to drift deeper into the dream, her phone chimed with a text message. It was Matthew, hoping she was okay. She assured him she was and thanked him for retrieving her car. It was a relief to know Zippy was sitting in the driveway and not stuck over in that cul-de-sac. He texted:

—Let me know if you need anything else. (*hug emoji*)

—I'm good but thanks a bunch. (*heart emoji*)

—Cad was all my fault. (*sad face emoji*)

She laughed at the typo of Chad's name, and texted:

—Not!! But you never told me your celebrity crush.

—I've moved on anyway.

—Me too. So let's just forget about it.

— (*hug hearts emojis*)

— (*single heart emoji*)

The conversation was over, but now all thoughts of her dream had vanished and instead her mind was filled with memories of Chad and how foolish she'd been. Ugh! She looked at the text thread again and Matthew's typing 'Cad' instead of Chad.

Was that what they'd all come to call him? 'Eva's cad of a boyfriend?' *Oh, God. They were right. I was blind.*

She took a breath and tried to cultivate some compassion for herself. But it came out as more of a string of pathetic excuses in a whinny little girl's voice: *I lost my mother! I was worried about my childless future, worried that no man would want me. So I tried to escape into what I thought was a harmless fantasy. But I was just blinded by fear.*

She doubted anyone blamed her for falling for Chad, hunk that he was. But then, when his character, or lack thereof, became apparent, and with her best friends warning her… *Yes, I should have listened, but again, I was running on empty, afraid of what the future held, and still upset about that last conversation I overheard between Mom and Aunt Evelyn at the hospital. I can't believe Mom had been in communication with my father, and she hadn't told me! Anyone would be upset, confused, overwhelmed. Right?*

Right, she agreed with herself. *How is that so easy for me to see now when it had been so difficult to see before?*

It wasn't Mom's fault. It wasn't Aunt Evelyn's fault. It wasn't my father's fault, who hadn't even known he was a father. And it wasn't my fault.

She decided no one was at fault! It was just life in all its strange configurations, some unskillful, unwise, but no one was being intentionally unkind.
And even if they had been, it was probably out of fear.

Like Chad. He was afraid of so many things, so he made bad choices.

And so did I. Just a bad choice at a challenging time.

She thought about how even Rusty Dean, that awful schoolyard bully had that horrid Gregory Allen Dean for a father. *Poor him! And maybe even —can I be that compassionate?—Gregory Allen Dean himself.* She knew he must have suffered some emotional abuse or neglect to turn into someone who purposely promotes fear, who deals in greed and aversion. *He has to be truly miserable and misguided. I wouldn't want to spend even a minute with him. Even seeing his face would make me puke! But maybe I can be compassionate from a distance? Is that a thing?*

As a teacher, she knew that bullies were abused, neglected, and rejected by the people they most longed to love them. She knew all this. She'd always known this really. In theory anyway. *Why now is it suddenly all becoming so clear to me?*

She sighed and took a sip of tea. Trusty picked up his head and looked at her, then settled back down. She regretted what she'd put him through and was just grateful he was okay.

She was also relieved that the dysfunctional relationship with Chad was over. *What in the world had I been thinking? I must have been...*

To distract herself from going any further down that rabbit hole, she looked over at the stacks of books and magazines. From Chelsea there was a Smithsonian book of space photography, thick and too heavy to pick up at this point. As a stark counterpoint, there was a bodice ripper paperback, which made Eva laugh. She'd had enough of that drama in her own life for now, thank you very much.

Atop Heather's offerings were a couple of magazines. As Eva paged through them, looking for distraction, all she saw were ads to purposely activate greed and fear, and provocative articles to activate envy. For some reason, instead of entertainment and information, it all felt like catering to preexisting emotions just to get her eyes to travel from one advertisement to the next. She dropped the magazines onto the floor, startling Trusty.

"Sorry, T. Here, how about this." She picked up a toy from the pile and tossed it toward the kitchen door. He stood up and ambled after it dutifully, as if he was doing her a favor. After their outing yesterday, he was feeling as physically exhausted as she was. Poor guy.

Next up on Heather's reading pile was the most boring-looking slim brown paperback. It seemed familiar, and as she picked it up, she realized she had looked through it a few weeks ago. It was by a Buddhist monk named Bhikku Bodhi, and it was titled *The Noble Eightfold Path, Way to the End of Suffering*. She opened the first chapter and was intrigued at the way it felt like a homecoming for her soul.

*　　　*　　　*

Eva was surprised to hear the front door open. She had been so deeply engrossed in the book, she hadn't realized that hours had passed. She noticed she'd taken the sketchbook and scribbled notes and drawings. A pot on a campfire with a spoon and three plumes of steam rising. Huh, that wasn't in the book she was reading. *Where did it come from?*

"How are you doing," Heather asked as she carried bags into the kitchen.

Trusty shook off his sleepiness and looked refreshed and ready for an outing. Eva and Heather laughed.

"Poor guy is bored stiff. But this book!" Eva said, holding up Bhikku Bodhi's book. Deceptively dull looking, but…wow!"

Heather came back into the living room and noticed Eva with the slim volume in her hand. "I think I told you that we've been studying the Eightfold Path in the Insight group and the leader recommended that book. I haven't had a chance to get into it, but the Dharma talks and discussions in the sangha have been great. Very inspiring."

Eva nodded. "I feel strangely as if I'd been…this sounds crazy, I know …but it's as if I've been on a retreat about the Eightfold Path. I…"

"Yes, you mentioned that in the hospital."

"I did?"

"Yes, and I want to hear more. Maybe we can talk this evening? Right now I've got fifteen minutes before I need to head back to the studio. But if your ankle is better by next Tuesday, you should come with me to the Sangha."

"I think I will."

"Great! Now, I've got some veggies and hummus or a turkey sandwich. You choose."

"How about we share?" Sharing had been their tradition for decades.

"Perfect." She turned and went back into the kitchen. Trusty followed, ever hopeful.

Eva stretched and smiled, relieved to see him returning to his normal self. *And what about me?* she wondered.

She looked around the room, out into the garden, and at the book still in her hand. A calm contentment came over her, as she pondered how running away into the hills, foolish though it may have been, had somehow led her to a deeper sense of homecoming.

Epilogue

Since this story came to me in a dream and ended when Eva was reunited with her housemates, I don't know the rest of her story. Just as I don't know the rest of my story, and you don't know the rest of yours.

And it's really *your story* that matters. This novel is not a story to read and forget. It's an invitation to an inner exploration in developing beneficial skills that make a difference in our lives. I hope that you downloaded the .pdf workbook and found it helpful in exploring the Noble Eightfold Path for yourself. If not, try it now!

Although the Noble Eightfold Path, the Buddha's prescription for the end of suffering, is over 2600 years old, it can be as fresh as this moment, because of its inherent truth and generosity.

But it can, at first glance, appear to be just another of the Buddha's many valuable lists that can become overwhelming to remember. So the challenge is how to share these essential core teachings in a way they can be remembered and incorporated into our daily lives in a way that benefits us, those around us, and radiates out to all beings.

The Buddha used many metaphors to help students understand his teachings. So when I came up with the Cooking Pot Analogy decades ago -- and it was whole-heartedly approved by my teacher, Spirit Rock co-founder, Anna Douglas -- I made it central to my sharing.

Although the initial metaphor came to me full-blown, over the following years, each time I taught the Cooking Pot Analogy, more was revealed either through my own insights or insights of my students. For example:

Speech, Action, and Livelihood are the first things we notice because they have an odor that wafts throughout, and if they are unwise, they give off quite a nasty stench.

The wafting plumes also remind us that words and actions, once said and done, can't be taken back. They are out there in the air.

The trivet under the pot, a relatively recent addition, represents the Triple Gem of the Buddha, Dharma, and Sangha that is always central to the Buddha's teachings. Together they support our practice and the teachings, just as the trivet keeps the pot and its contents (our consciousness) stable.

In general, humans remember stories and characters more easily than lists. So, here I offer the teachings in this novel form, with each character sharing one aspect of the Eightfold Path.

Did you happen to notice the mnemonic device to further help you remember each aspect? No?
Okay, think of the characters on the retreat. They taught the aspect of the Eightfold Path that began with their initial:

> **Vi**cente taught Wise **Vi**ew.
> **I**saac intended to teach Wise **I**ntention. Eva filled in for him.
> **E**ddie taught Wise **E**ffort.
> **Mi**nna taught Wise **Mi**ndfulness.
> **C**onnor taught **W**ise Concentration.
> **S**ara taught Wise **S**peech.
> **A**llie taught Wise **A**ction.
> **L**ily taught Wise **L**ivelihood.

The local politician **Gregory Allen Dean**'s initials, not surprisingly add up to: Greed, Aversion, and Delusion -- the Three Poisons.

And **Eva**? She was on a dream adventure exploring the Eightfold Path.

Whether Eva makes sense of the sketch she made of the Cooking Pot Analogy or not, *we* have it! May it be of benefit to our exploration and our lives, helping us remember the aspects and understand how they work together.

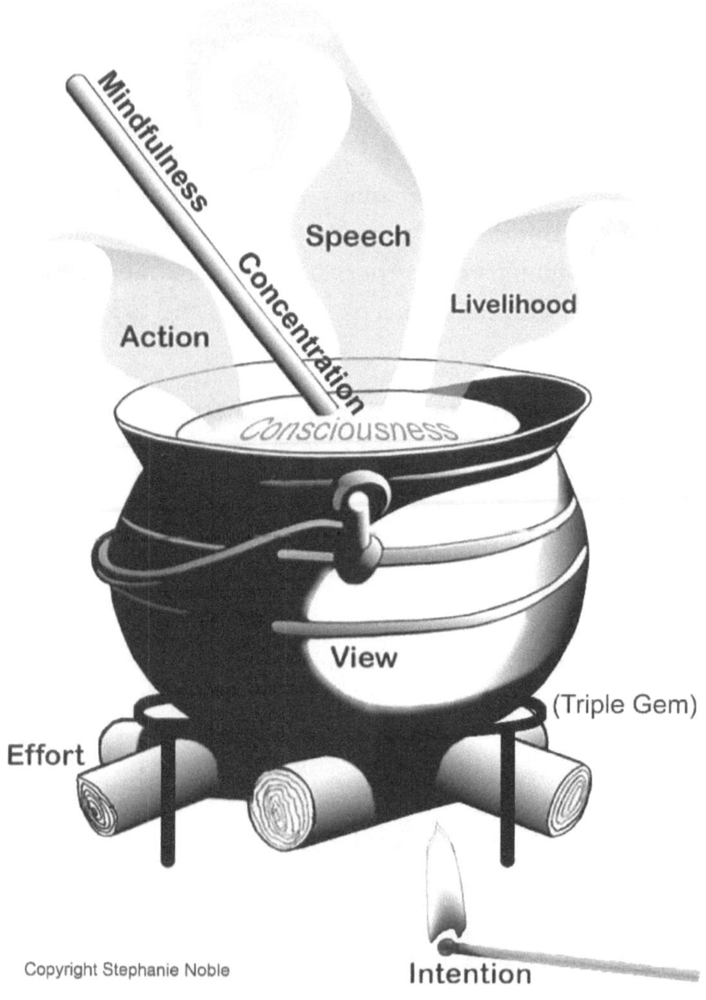

The Cooking Pot Analogy copyright © Stephanie Noble 2010

If you are interested in further study, it's valuable to know the traditional way to explore the Path:

Three Pillars and Eight Factors of the Buddha's Noble Eightfold Path

Wisdom *(Pañña)*

Right View/Understanding *(samma-diṭṭhi)*
Understand the Four Noble Truths, impermanence, and karma.

Right Intention/Resolve *(samma-saṅkappa)*
Cultivate thoughts of renunciation, goodwill, and harmlessness.

Ethical Conduct *(Sīla)*

Right Speech *(samma-vācā)* Abstain from lying, gossip, harsh and divisive talk.

Right Action *(samma-kammanta)* Ethical behavior: not killing or taking what is not freely given, including sexual activity.

Right Livelihood *(samma-ājīva)* Ethical work and engagement in the marketplace, such as avoiding trades in weapons or poisons.

Mental Discipline *(Samādhi)*

Right Effort *(samma-vāyāma)* Prevent unwholesome and cultivate wholesome mind states.

Right Mindfulness *(samma-sati)* Developing awareness of body, feelings, mind, and phenomena.

Right Concentration *(samma-samādhi)* Developing deep mental focus and calm through meditation.

Downloadable Companion Workbook

Because the Noble Eightfold Path is something to incorporate into our lives, I created the **Companion Workbook** to turn Eva's exploration into something more personal and vital for each of us. I hope you have been using it all along, but if not, you can download it now.

Scan this QR Code to access the page on my website, and put in the password: noble

May we live our lives aligned with the Noble Eightfold Path, both deepening our understanding and decreasing suffering for ourselves and all beings.

Although we don't know what tomorrow will bring, we can trust that if we live wisely in each moment, fully present and radiating loving kindness, that we will weave a loving future for ourselves and all those whose lives we touch, radiating out in all directions.

And that's what I wish for you, dear reader. May you be well. May you be at ease. May you be peaceful. And may you know the joy of being fully present in this moment, just as it is.

Stephanie Noble
May 2026

*If you don't have a QR code scanning app, you can easily download one on your phone. If you don't have a phone, contact me through my website, stephanienoble.com, and I'll send you the link.

References, Resources & Inspiration

Books & Audio

The Noble Eightfold Path, The Way to the End of Suffering
Book and audiobook by Bhikku Bodhi

The Noble Eightfold Path of the Buddha
The original lecture series, given by Urgyen Sangharashita. Dharma
Audiobooks Talks and Lectures

Satipatthana, The Direct Path to Realization
by Bhikku Analayo

Mindfulness, A Practical Guide to Awakening
by Joseph Goldstein (book and audio)

Breath by Breath, The Liberating Practice of Insight Meditation by Larry
Rosenberg, Shambhala Classics, 2004

Websites

Stephanienoble.com
Blog posts, classes, and info/links to other books

BuddhistInsightNetwork.org
Find a Buddhist Insight sangha or retreat center near you

Spiritrock.org/about/bookstore
Insight meditation books, including those by Stephanie Noble

Dharma.org/resources/glossary/ Pali terms

Related Courses

Living Dharma Program, Spirit Rock Dharma Institute
An eight-month program on the Buddha's Noble Eightfold Path.
Monthly interactive meetings, optional study groups. Stephanie took
the 2024-25 course led by Mark Coleman and Dawn Mauricio.

Walking the Eightfold Path with Jack Kornfield – An online recorded course
for independent study. Stephanie took it in 2025. Thirty-five short,
recorded talks by Jack, two Zoom Q&As at the beginning.

Acknowledgements

While writing is a solo task, it takes a village to usher a book into publication. So let me introduce you to my project village:

My Sangha: My Marin Women's Insight sangha sisters who asked me to transform my Dharma talks on the Eightfold Path into a book; Bonnie Peterson, my initial reader; Susan Weir, founding teacher of Insight Meditation Ann Arbor, my second reader; Scott Jordan who offered his publishing expertise and extensive guidance in appreciation for my years in a leadership role of the Buddhist Insight Network.

My fellow members of the BIN Board, Steve, Mark, Susan, Rick, Nina, and Caleb, for freeing me up a bit to focus on this book.

My Living Dharma Program study group: Angelique, Paula, Molly, Debra, and Gretchen, for our exploration of the Eightfold Path.

My family: My husband Will for helping to organize my Dharma posts, polish the visuals, and proofread the book. Our son Josh for proofing and formatting advice. Our daughter Katie for encouragement and offering a book launch venue. My co-grandma Casey for proofreading with an exacting eye from a career of being the final set of eyes on important legal documents. My niece Lisa for offering to spread the word in the Northwest. My sister Rose, who has my paintings on her walls and my poetry book on her bedside table. In memory of our sister Stella, who shared my first book, *Tapping the Wisdom Within*, with everyone she knew. And she knew everyone!

My friends: For cheering me on, with special shoutouts to Ellen, Laurie, Nancy, Anna, Jane, Marleen, Debra, Kathleen, Alice, Judi, Phil, Indi, Carol, Linda, Riva, Gwen, Diane, and Prartho.

There's not enough room to express my gratitude to everyone whose kindness and generosity has touched me but thank you all! As a reader you are part of my village, and I hope you will let your village know about this book!

May everyone have a village filled with so much loving kindness!

About the Author

Stephanie Noble has practiced and taught insight meditation for decades. She is the founder of Marin Insight Women's Sangha and teaches by invitation at other sanghas, including Marin Sangha, Napa Valley Insight, Boulder Insight, and Rick Hanson's Wednesday class.

Her first book, *Tapping the Wisdom Within, A Guide to Joyous Living,* was the result of a nine-month-long 'horizontal retreat' due to illness. With the success of that book, she was asked to lead a meditation group. When they went on a field trip to Spirit Rock Meditation Center, she knew she'd come home. She told the group, "I can't teach anymore. I need to be a student now."

She has completed many retreats and in-depth training courses at SRMC and elsewhere. After a decade, Anna Douglas, PhD, cofounder of Spirit Rock, encouraged her to teach and mentored her.

Her guided meditations are on the Insight Timer meditation app.

Her poetry has been widely published and twice nominated for the Pushcart Prize. *In Celebration of the Winter Solstice* is read around the world in December. An animated version can be seen on YouTube.

Stephanie has served on the board of the Buddhist Insight Network since 2019. BIN serves to connect Insight teachers and sanghas around the world for mutual support.

She lives in Marin County CA with her husband, the artist Will Noble. They have four children and five grandchildren.

She shares her Dharma talks on her website, Stephanienoble.com.

Scan the QR code to visit her site: